KEZZIE
AT WAR

THERESA BRESLIN

CORGI BOOKS

KEZZIE AT WAR
A CORGI BOOK 978 0 552 56524 0

KEZZIE
First published in Great Britain by Methuen Children's Books
Text copyright © Theresa Breslin, 1993

A HOMECOMING FOR KEZZIE
First published in Great Britain by Methuen Children's Books
Text copyright © Theresa Breslin, 1995

This collection first published in Great Britain as
KEZZIE AT WAR by Corgi, an imprint of Random House Children's Books
A Random House Group Company

This edition published 2012

1 3 5 7 9 10 8 6 4 2

Copyright © Theresa Breslin, 2012
Cover artwork copyright © Gordon Crabb, 2012

Set in Bembo MT

Corgi Books are published by Random House Children's Books,
61–63 Uxbridge Road, London W5 5SA

www.**kids**at**randomhouse**.co.uk
www.**totallyrandombooks**.co.uk
www.**randomhouse**.co.uk

Addresses for companies within The Random House Group Limited can be found at:
www.**randomhouse**.co.uk/offices.htm

THE RANDOM HOUSE GROUP Limited Reg. No. 954009

A CIP catalogue record for this book is available from the British Library.

Printed and bound in Great Britain by CPI Group (UK), Croydon, CR0 4YY

CONTENTS

CONTENTS

Book I:
KEZZIE

For Agnes McCall
'Aunt Agnes'
with much love

BOOK I:
KEZZIE

PART ONE
Scotland

CHAPTER 1

Canal trip

'Run, Kezzie, run!'

Kezzie could hear her little sister's shrill voice as she rounded the last curve on the field and saw ahead of her the rope, held at either end by the minister and the Sunday school teacher. Her bare feet thudded on the grass, dry after many sunny summer weeks.

Peg McKinnon, on her right, was still in front and running fast, her long plaits dancing at her back. Could she catch her? This would be her last year to run in the annual race. When the school returned after the holidays she would be a senior and much too dignified for this. Kezzie's long brown hair flew out behind her. She was aware her ribbon was loose, her yellow ribbon which her father had tied in her hair that morning. Oh! How she would love to win, and beat the long-legged Peg just this once!

John Munro, a tall good-looking man of about forty, stood with a group of fellow miners fifty yards short of the finishing line. They were holding back the rest of the younger children who would otherwise have crowded on to the track.

'My money's on the tall one with the print frock,' said the colliery foreman.

John Munro shook his head.

'The lassie with the yellow ribbon,' he said.

And, as his daughter drew level with him, he shouted, 'Now, lass, now!'

Kezzie heard her father's voice beside her and she thrust herself forwards. Head back, power surging in her body, she flung herself at the finishing line.

'Yeeees!' Lucy was there, grabbing her legs, the end of her skirt, anywhere, with her little fists. 'I knew you'd win, Kissy. I just knew you'd win. I said so. I told everybody. Didn't I, Daddy?' She held her hands outstretched as her father approached and he gathered her up and swung her across his back.

John Munro looked at his eldest daughter.

'We all knew,' he said quietly. He put his hands on Kezzie's shoulders. 'Hold still, now, while I fix your ribbon.' And he retied the bright yellow silk among the long brown curls.

They came home with all the rest down the canal in the coal scows, which had been scrubbed out by the carters and decorated for the occasion. The ponderous Clydesdale horses, beribboned and tasselled, made their way along the towpath. There would be a prize for the best decorated! Aunt Bella's husband always won. He spent long hours pleating and combing the horse's mane, intertwining lace, coloured wool and ribbon among the heavy glossy hair. One year he had even got Bella to knit the horse ear muffs! A purple plume nodded on its forehead. Bells and brasses, polished and shining, hesitated, then swung on, as they opened the bridge at Auchinmarloch. In the gathering dusk the scows glided through towards Stonevale and home.

'This has been the best ever,' said Lucy as she snuggled into her father's jacket. 'Hasn't it?'

John Munro glanced at Kezzie.

'What do you say?' he asked.

Kezzie smiled back. She loved the annual treat. The trip along the water away from the village and the grim grey houses of the next town of Shawcross, then out to the country. Tinnie round their necks, the children lined up for their lemonade, their bun, biscuit and rock cake. And then the competitions! Well, she had her prize, her pencil and book *and* her dad's team had won the tug-of-war, and Grandad . . . She glanced behind her. Old John Munro was having a great day too. Sitting in the back, a big slab of a man still, despite his white hair and moustache, red kerchief knotted at the neck of his collarless shirt, cap pushed to the back of his head, he was arguing, as always, with his friends.

'Nationalisation,' she heard him say. 'It's the only thing if mines are going to be modernised. The owners will never put money in for new machinery. We're years behind Europe. We're relying on the same wooden props that my father made; they've got conveyor belts and we're still using the ponies.'

'Well,' said another old miner sarcastically. 'If ye keep yer safety levels low it saves ye payin' off if there's a slump. We're in 1937 and there's thirty miners injured an hour. Nae compensation, a tied hoose and some still paid by piece rates. Ye canna win.'

'Amn't I the one who knows about no compensation?' said Kezzie's grandad indicating his crippled leg. Her grandad had been retired early from his job as a skilled engineer after an accident. 'That's why the pits should be nationalised,' he insisted, 'and, we will win. They tried to break our backs in 1926 in the General Strike.'

'Aye and did it too,' said one of the other men bitterly.

There was a silence.

'It's the Jarrow men I feel sorry for. There's nothing there for them.'

'Now there was a piece of chicanery, if ever there was,' said Kezzie's grandad. 'That's a classic case of owners looking after themselves. Palmer's Yard in Jarrow was bought out by a group of other shipbuilders and then to keep their monopoly they deliberately closed that yard down. An' I'll tell you what the President of the Board of Trade said to one group of marchers after the march to London, "Go back to Jarrow and work out your own salvation." And that's where they are yet. On the dole.'

Kezzie knew her grandad had been on one of the hunger marches to London and still got upset when he spoke about it. The marches hadn't seemed to affect the thinking of those in power, though she had been told that all the way down the long road south people from villages and towns, some of them very poor themselves, had come out to give the men food and shelter. Already on Tyneside this decade was beginning to be known as the 'Hungry Thirties'.

'Trade's picking up slowly,' said another miner, 'if the appeasement policy wins through and there's no war with Germany and Italy we can progress internationally.'

'Appeasement,' snorted Kezzie's grandad. 'You don't appease bullies like Adolf Hitler and Mussolini.'

'Come on, Dad,' said Kezzie's father.

The boat was tying up and already some of the windows were lit in the miners' rows.

Kezzie's father took Grandad by his sleeve. 'Time to go home now.'

CHAPTER 2

Aunt Bella

'How do you spell "Kissy"?' Lucy asked on their way home from school one day a few weeks later.

'"*Kezzie.*" How many times do I have to tell you?' laughed Kezzie. 'You're nearly six now, you should be able to say my name properly. K–E–Z–Z–I–E. Why do you want to know?'

'It's a surprise,' said Lucy. 'You've not to know about the cake.'

'What cake?'

Lucy put her hand to her mouth. 'You weren't to know,' she wailed.

'Know what?' asked Kezzie.

'Well, it's a secret,' said Lucy, 'but if you promise not to tell . . .'

'But it's me that's not to know,' Kezzie giggled. She regarded her little sister gravely. 'Can't you keep a secret?'

'I don't want to,' said Lucy, 'not from you. Grandad and I are making a cake for your birthday. It's going to have icing and your name on it. We're going to make it when you go to see the headmaster with Daddy, and then we'll hide it and it'll be a surprise for your birthday tomorrow.'

Kezzie shook her head and laughed as Lucy skipped on ahead past the washhouses to play with her friends. Kezzie went on to their house at the end of the row. Her grandad was sitting at the door in the sun peeling potatoes.

'Aye, lass,' he acknowledged as she went indoors.

Kezzie had always thought of herself as lucky. Being at the end of the row their house had three rooms compared to the others with only two or even one. They had space to live with each other, some plain but serviceable furniture and pretty net curtains at the window. She placed her books on the dresser and put on the cross-over flowery pinny, which had belonged to her mother. Then she set the big kettle of water to boil on the fire. She dragged the tin bath out from under the recess bed and put a towel and soap on the little stool, ready for her dad coming off his shift at two. She took his shifting clothes from the cupboard and hung them on the clothes horse to air, catching sight of the photograph of her mother on the mantelpiece. She was said to resemble her mother, tall, with brown eyes and hair. Kezzie couldn't properly recall her, just remembered a special loving smell and someone singing when she was little.

Yes, they were luckier than most. Her father had never dropped a shift and with the money her grandad made doing odd jobs on a nearby farm they managed quite well. Well enough for her father to be able to let her stay on at school. Not so Peg, her great running rival, who had not returned after the summer holidays. Her parents didn't think it was worthwhile for girls to be educated. Peggie was now working as a maid in one of the big houses along the main road and Kezzie saw her on her day off each month. She said she liked it fine and she got to keep a few pennies of her 'own money' and she acted so grown up, but Kezzie knew Peg had longed to stay on and go to college. Their teacher had called her a mathematical genius. She would have studied book-keeping and accounts. It didn't seem a lot to want.

Kezzie scraped the remains of the morning's porridge into a dish and sat it on the dresser. With some warm milk it would do for supper for Lucy. She went out to collect the potatoes from her grandad. Aunt Bella was approaching, two of her children at her side and a cup in her hand.

'Uhuh,' Grandad grunted and got up. 'Here's Bella Borrow. She must have seen ye coming by.' He went to stand at the gable-end of the house to smoke his pipe.

'Eh, hello, hen,' said Aunt Bella glancing nervously towards the old man. 'I don't suppose you could spare a wee drop of . . .'

'Of course,' said Kezzie kindly. She knew that Aunt Bella's husband didn't earn as much as her dad and much of what he did never reached his wife, but instead found its way into the pockets of the innkeeper at the canal bridge. She went inside and took two sticks of liquorice from a little jar on the dresser and gave them to the children. Kezzie noticed the porridge.

'Would this be of any use to you?' she asked. 'I was going to put it out anyway.'

The older woman took the dish gratefully.

'You're a good girl, Kezzie, kindly, just like your mother was. She never turned anyone away. She would have been proud of you. The way you keep this house and look after the wee one. You're going to stay on at the school, I hear. That's a great thing for the likes of us. Aye, she would have been that proud.'

When Bella left Kezzie put the potatoes on to boil, and then sat down at the table and opened her school books. She chewed the end of her pencil and frowned in concentration. She was going to pass the exams. She wasn't going to let her father down and besides she had to get good grades if she was going to achieve her ambition. As yet she had told no one about that.

CHAPTER 3

The silver locket

'Blow out your candles!' cried Lucy. 'And make a wish!'

Kezzie closed her eyes and wished.

'What did you wish for?' asked Lucy.

'You're not supposed to tell,' said Kezzie.

'But you can whisper it to me,' said Lucy. 'I won't let ANYONE know.'

Everyone around the kitchen table laughed as Kezzie cut her birthday cake.

'Did you see what Aunt Bella gave me?' Kezzie showed her father the leather-bound notebook. 'Isn't it beautiful?' She stroked the black binding.

Lucy opened it up.

'This book has no story,' she complained.

'I'll tell you a story before you go to sleep tonight,' said her father.

'Aunt Bella bought me the notebook for my school work. I'd better do some fine work in a book like this.'

Kezzie's grandad snorted.

'She'd be better off putting food in her bairns' mouths

than running up her book at the Co-op on fancy presents.'

'Grandad,' said Kezzie gently. 'It's her way of saying thank you.'

'And here's mine,' said Kezzie's father, interrupting. He handed her a little red box.

Kezzie opened it up. A dainty silver locket with a fine chain lay inside.

Kezzie had never seen, far less owned, anything like it. She felt her eyes fill with tears. She let the chain run through her fingers.

Her father took it from her and fastened it around her throat. He kissed the top of her head.

'You're a woman now. Happy fourteenth birthday.'

There was a soft knock on the door. Lucy jumped down from her chair and ran to open it.

A woman stood there with a baby across her shoulder, happed up in a plaid. By her side was a barefoot boy of about twelve. Their clothes were threadbare and they had a weary look.

'Your da at home?' the woman asked.

John Munro got to his feet at once.

'Come in, now, come in. There's some stew here, and milk for the baby.'

The travellers came regularly round the village but were not welcome at every door. The two of them sat down at the table, the boy on the very edge of the chair. The woman filled a bottle with milk from the jug on the table and began to feed her baby.

'Where's your man tonight?' John Munro asked.

'In jail, in Perth. Quadded for poaching.'

'Bad fortune,' said Kezzie's grandad as he ladled stew into two bowls.

'Shaness,' repeated the woman in Cant, 'that allows one man to own the birds of the air and shoot them for sport, and another to be put in prison for trying to feed his family.'

She wrapped up her baby, lifted a spoon and began to eat her food slowly.

Lucy was staring at the boy.

'What's your name? Mine's Lucy, and this is Kezzie. She's my big sister and it's her birthday,' she said.

'Matt McPhee, miss,' the boy said, touching his forehead with his fingers.

'Would you like a piece of cake?' Kezzie offered him the plate.

His face flushed and he took the cake and carefully put it in his mouth.

The boy's mother took Lucy's hand.

'Let me see now, what good luck is coming your way.' She studied Lucy's palm. 'A journey,' she intoned, 'a long journey, across the water.'

Lucy's eyes opened wide. 'Where?' she asked.

'That I can't rightly say, lamb. Only that it's a faraway country, and ye'll be going soon.'

Kezzie held her hand out. 'What about me?'

'Now, you're the same. A journey, in a great boat.'

'Oh, Kezzie,' cried Lucy. 'We're going in a boat together!'

'I didn't say ye'd be together,' said the woman. She frowned at Kezzie's palm. 'You're with someone on this boat, but it looks like a young man.'

It was Kezzie's turn to blush.

'Is he handsome?' asked Lucy.

'Is he rich?' asked Kezzie's father.

'Aye, he's both,' said the woman. She took hold of Grandad's hand despite his protest. 'Now, here's an interesting hand, a long lifeline, and ye're going to meet a queen.'

Everyone laughed.

'Well, if the King and Queen ever visit Stonevale,' said Kezzie's grandad, 'I'll certainly be havin' a word with them.'

'I tell ye now. It's true,' the woman protested. 'There's a royal connection in your life.' She looked at her son. 'Am I ever wrong, Matt?'

The boy shook his head.

Kezzie's father stretched his hand across.

'Now, tell me I'm to meet a princess,' he laughed.

There was the briefest hesitation, then the woman slid her own hand under John Munro's and turned his palm face down on to the deal table.

'You have two beautiful princesses sitting right beside you at this very minute,' she said brightly. She exchanged a glance with her son.

He scraped his chair back quickly and stood up. 'Any work need doin', mister?'

'Yes, indeed,' said John Munro, pointing to a cupboard in the small hall at the front door. 'That press in the lobby needs filling with coal from the cellar, and my boots need a good dubbing. And there's a half-crown in it for you if I can see my face in the polish.'

Kezzie guessed that her father was saving the boy's pride by giving him the work.

She cleared the table as Lucy got ready for bed. She could hear her dad and grandad talking outside with other miners as she washed the dishes at the window sink. As their house was at the end of the row it seemed the natural place for people to gather in the lighter nights. Kezzie knew it was also because her father and grandad's opinions were respected in the village. The men played quoits and smoked their pipes, soft curls of pungent blue smoke in the evening air.

'I don't know if I fancy these mechanical cutters,' one man said. 'I was talking to a man who worked with them down south and he said you're eating dust all the time, an' you have to shout to be heard. If you can't hear down a pit, you're in mortal peril.'

There was a murmur of agreement.

Kezzie remembered her grandad telling her about how clear his hearing became in the dark in the pit. How he could hear men who were working a seam a quarter of a mile away, talking and laughing. How he learned to listen for any movement, every small dark sigh of the earth, each little creak or groan, or dribble of shale; the miner's ear tuned for danger.

'Nothin' wrang wi' yer ain pick an' shovel,' said another voice.

'Aye, ye'll be carrying yer graith tae yer grave, Andra,' Kezzie's father joked.

Everybody laughed.

'The mines need to be owned by the miners,' said Kezzie's grandad. 'That's the only way we'll get decent conditions. Changing facilities at the pit head and the like.'

'We'll hae spray baths wi' hot water laid on for us, ye reckon,' said another.

The men all laughed again.

'Aye, ye can laugh. They'll be lookin' tae please us soon enough when they need the coal. Re-armament's started. There's a war coming.'

There was a silence.

'Well, war or no',' Kezzie heard her father say. 'I'm away in to put my bairn to bed.'

Kezzie made up her father's sandwiches for the next morning and packed them firmly into his rat-proof metal tin. She then made a treacle sandwich for Lucy's supper and set a little enamel mug of milk to warm at the fire. She combed the tugs out of her sister's blonde curls, and, winding some strands of hair round her fingers, she pinned a little cockscomb on the top of her head. Her father and grandad came in. Her father sat down in the big chair and pulled Lucy on to his lap to read her a story. Grandad set out the chess board on the kitchen table.

'Are you for a game tonight, lass?' he asked.

Kezzie sat down. The chess pieces were very old, hand carved from wood and Grandad was the best player in five villages. He took his knight and bishop from the board.

'Right, now, let's see what you can do.'

CHAPTER 4

Disaster

'Wait for me, Kissy, wait for me!'

Kezzie looked back down the hill where her sister and her friends were trailing a long way behind. She put the pail, half-full of bramble berries, on the grass and sat down to wait for them to catch up. Below her the little village trailed plumes of smoke, black and grey into the sky. The evenings were cooler, the sky a sharper, darker blue at night. Over to the left she could see the colliery, the wheel still, waiting for the shift changeover. In a few hours her father would be home, time enough to fill the pail for jam, if Lucy left any. Most times she had eaten half what they had gathered before they arrived home, her mouth stained with berry juice.

Kezzie lay down on the grass and squinted at the clouds. She liked to imagine places from their shapes. That one looked like India. She would travel there one day. Her dream, her birthday wish. She was going to be a doctor, and then a missionary. After she had cured all the people in Scotland she would go to faraway countries. She'd read about David Livingstone and Mary Slessor. She wondered what it was like to be an explorer and visit foreign lands. The only foreigner she had ever seen was the Indian who came round from time to time, selling goods from a large brown suitcase. He looked strange in his business suit with a heavy turban on his head. Stockings and ribbons and packets of pins, and little jars of cold cream to take wrinkles from your face. Bella always bought a jar of this, at the same time declaring, 'It's a bliddy big bucket of the stuff Ah need, with what Ah've to put up wi'.'

Kezzie looked again at the clouds. She put her hands behind her head and stretched herself out. She loved the berry time, hot days and soft warm evenings. It was very quiet. There was a terrible stillness between the earth and the sky. Then . . . the world seemed to stagger, and she felt rather than heard a great muffled thump from beneath her. A dull thud which echoed inside her.

Kezzie sat up and instinctively looked towards the pit. Before her horrified eyes the huge whorl wheel started to creak slowly forward. She leapt to her feet knocking over the pail. Berries spilled out across the grass. She was halfway down the hill and running fast when she heard the siren sounding.

It was still wailing as she joined the group of villagers streaming towards the pit head. People had run out of their homes and washhouses, women with sleeves rolled up, men half-dressed. Old women with shawls flung about their shoulders, little children snatched from play and gathered up on the way. Kezzie jostled herself forward until she was at the head of the crowd and could see into the lamp cabin where the miners' lamps were kept in rows upon the shelves. She was hoping that her dad's lamp would be in its place. Perhaps he had taken sick and not gone down this morning? Maybe someone had asked him for a change, or there had been a flood or some other reason for a stoppage, and his shift wasn't in.

His lamp space on the shelf lay empty.

There was someone beside her in the crowd. It was her grandfather.

'His lamp's away,' said Kezzie, her chin unsteady.

Grandad put his arm around her shoulder and gripped her tightly. And they stood there with the rest and did what women and children and old folk had done for generations before. They waited.

And the waiting itself took its toll. Their wearied faces, in anxious lines, huddled into their shawls and coats. While the minister and the priest came and went among them, and the Salvation Army arrived with hot soup and kind words. Through the night and into a grey morning they waited with an occasional rumour scurrying through them like an agitated wasp.

At one point the crowd scattered as the rescue team from Shawcross roared up with extra breathing equipment. Two ambulances arrived and stood by.

Kezzie was slumped, exhausted against Grandad, when they heard the three bells sound. The steel cable vibrated and then the cage began to rise.

There was a cry from someone at the front of the crowd.

'There's men coming up. They've got some out!'

The ambulances were loaded and pulled away quickly.

'A bad fall. A right bad fall. And then another,' Kezzie heard. 'No warning, just an almighty crack.'

'It's those props,' she heard another voice. 'Rotten timber props, should have been renewed years ago.'

There was confusion everywhere. Men being brought into sudden daylight, women crying tears of joy. Suddenly the crowd fell silent, then parted. Kezzie saw the section deputy coming towards them.

A voice in the crowd. 'That's the worst job in the world he has to do now.'

The official ushered Kezzie and her grandfather into the pit office.

'You've got bad news for me,' said Grandad.

'The worst,' said the deputy. 'Sit down.'

'I'll take this standing up,' Grandad replied.

'It's been restless all week, spitting and crackling,' said the deputy, 'but today, quiet . . . Aye, too quiet. We should hae kent. The whole length of the face took a seat. Caught Alec McKinnon and his son, and a lad from Shawcross. No hope for them. A lot of bad injuries with the rest trapped. John was at the heading with another group eating his piece. Him and Michael Duthie went back up. We said to wait, wait for the rescue equipment. He said they didn't have the time. He was right. Those others wouldn't be out alive if it wasn't for him. He had the last one in his arms, only a boy. He had just passed him back to me . . .' The deputy's voice cracked. 'The whole lot came down on him . . .

He would know nothing about it, mind, if that's any consolation.'

He turned to Kezzie. 'Your father is a hero. There's men owe their lives to him,' he was saying. 'His section was clear yet he went back along the seam.'

Kezzie didn't understand. She gazed at him. If her father was a hero then where was he?

She turned to her grandfather.

'Where is he?' she asked desperately. 'Where is my daddy?'

'Your dad is dead,' Grandad said stolidly. 'My son is dead.'

A vast void opened up in front of Kezzie. She tried hard to concentrate. She opened her mouth but no sound came out.

'Lucy?' She looked around her. Voices and faces were not matching properly.

'Bella's got her.' Her grandad took her arm gently. As if in answer to a prayer Bella appeared at the office door. She crossed quickly and gathered Kezzie into her arms.

'I'll take her away home with me.'

Kezzie's grandad nodded. He addressed the deputy.

'I'll go down and collect my son's body.'

The deputy wiped his mouth wearily with the back of his hand.

'I don't think you appreciate what it's like down there. There's flooding and a trace of fire damp.'

The old man smiled.

'I know exactly what it's like,' he said. He pointed to his twisted leg. 'I got that in a fall the same as this one.

Somebody pulled me out or I'd be there yet. My boy's not biding there.'

Old John Munro leaned over the desk and picked up the deputy's own safety lamp.

'I'm going now to bring my son home.'

CHAPTER 5

Eviction

They buried the four miners a week later in the cemetery at Shawcross two miles away.

Peg McKinnon's mother was too distraught to attend and the two girls, arms supporting each other, led the cortege through the town. Shopkeepers pulled the blinds and closed their doors as they passed. The streets were lined with silent crowds. Men took off their caps and women bowed their heads in respect. The weather itself appeared to take notice of the great grief that swelled through the whole countryside. A grey dreich sky hung over the mourners as they laid their loved ones to rest: John Munro beside his wife and the baby boy she had died bearing.

Kezzie was totally numb as she watched her grandad lower her father's coffin. The retiring hymn 'Abide With Me' still sounded in her ears, the soaring notes of the organ and the voices from the church, filled to over-flowing, would remain with her a long time. Now she knew what her father had meant when he had talked about the price miners' families paid for coal. Far from getting it cheaper than others they paid for it in blood. Grandad had warned her against being bitter, and she knew her father would not have approved of the terrible rage she felt inside her. Her hatred of the whole world engulfed her from time to time. Bella had tried to help, despite being busy with her own children, watching her in sorrow unable to ease her suffering. The older woman had seen all this many times before. She tidied the house and cared for Lucy.

And Lucy, poor little Lucy, who had not fully understood what had happened.

'But I do not want him to die,' she had said stubbornly on the night of the accident. She had looked at Kezzie uncomprehendingly. 'Doesn't God know that I do not want Dadda to die?'

And Kezzie saw then that she could not explain it away to the little girl. She would not accept trite phrases and meaningless words.

'Nor did I,' she had said finally, realising that indeed there were no words which would ease that pain, that great lonely grief. And the two of them had cried together and held each other close, against the dark and the fear and the cold that was both outside and inside their little house that night.

Peg came to her among the crowd as she left the graveside.

'I'll say goodbye just now, Kezzie,' she said. Her face was blotched and she had her hankie screwed up in her hands. 'We're moving to Glasgow to try to get work. My ma won't let my other brother go back down the pit, so we'll have to get out.'

25

'Will you write to me?'

'What address?' asked Peg.

Kezzie looked at her friend, not understanding. Peg knew where she lived. They were separated in the crowd before Kezzie could ask her what she meant.

It wasn't more than a few days before Kezzie found out the meaning of Peg's words.

It was early morning when a sharp knock sounded on their door. There was a smartly dressed older man standing there with a rough-looking man and woman and some raggedy children.

She didn't have time to speak when the man in the suit said, 'Right now, girl, I want no trouble here. I'll give you twenty minutes and then these folk have to get in.'

'What?' said Kezzie.

The rough-looking man was carrying some heavy sacks. He pushed past Kezzie and dumped them in the hall.

'What are you doing?' asked Kezzie, her voice rising in alarm.

'Give them time now, give them time,' said the older man, but he kept his foot in the door and the group of people tried to come into the house.

Kezzie stepped back and gripped the coat she had put on over her nightdress more tightly around her.

'What is going on?' she demanded.

'These are mine owners' houses, there's no one lives here employed by the mine now. You have to get out.'

'Get out? This is my home!' shouted Kezzie.

Bella came running out of her house at the commotion, curlers in her hair.

'You ought to be ashamed of yourself,' she said to the older man. 'The man o' this house is dead bare a fortnight and yer flingin' his weans on the street.' She set herself beside Kezzie and lifted her arm. 'Get away outa here.'

'Aye and that's two weeks' rent that's due,' the man replied angrily, 'and it's me that'll have to make it up. They got a letter sent. They should have been out already.'

Bella cast about for a weapon and spied the poker by the fire. She picked it up and advanced on the group.

'If ye don't move yourself from this door in ten seconds flat it's no letter ye'll be getting fae me,' she yelled.

The man hurriedly moved out and down the road a bit.

'You're only making it worse for yourself,' he said to Kezzie. 'I'll need to get the police.'

'If we have to go, then we shall,' said Kezzie with dignity. 'I must have missed your letter. I haven't yet opened all the cards and letters of condolence which came for us, and it may have been among them. I will pay you the rent due and we'll be out as fast as we can.'

She closed the door and leaned her back against it. Then she caught sight of Bella, her face bright red, curlers falling out of her hair, with the poker in her hand and her nightie half open.

'Aunt Bella, you're not decent,' she gasped.

Her aunt looked down at herself and after a moment started hooting with laughter.

'Well,' said Kezzie wiping the tears from her eyes, 'I never thought I'd laugh again for as long as I lived. Did you see his face when you shook that poker under his nose?'

'I'd have laid it on him as well, and fine he knew it,' said Bella angrily. 'Ah kent him when he had nae backside in his breeks. Now he's a jumped-up factor tellin' decent folk what to do.'

The two of them worked quickly, laying out blankets and piling all the household goods in the middle, dragging clothes from the pulley, then gathering the corners and securing the bundle in a big knot. They waited until everything was done before waking Grandad and Lucy.

'See here, your Auntie Bella's got a surprise for you in her house,' said Bella rousing the child gently from her little box bed.

Lucy followed Bella next door while Kezzie went to wake Grandad.

He looked so old and thin, Kezzie thought, as she watched him hurriedly pull on his trousers and jacket. He seemed to have shrunk over the last days and looked to her to make decisions.

They managed to half-drag and carry their bundles to Bella's house. Her children ran to help them lift the table and chairs. Those and the dresser they put against the back wall of her house, with all their bedding piled on top. Grandad refused even a cup of tea.

'We'll not get lodgings with no wage coming in, and Bella has no room. I'll go away to the farm and ask about and see if I can find something.'

Kezzie tried to put out of her mind what might happen if they did not find anything. There were hostels in Glasgow for destitute men. She had heard they were dreary places and people had to roam the streets by day. She would perhaps find somewhere as a maid with her keep as part pay. But what about Lucy? She would be farmed out to different ones who would take her for a short time and then . . . ? Kezzie set her chin. No one was going to put Lucy in a home, she was determined they would all stay together.

She went next door and collected their last few items. The fire, unattended, had gone out. It seemed appropriate. She took the clock and her mother's picture from the mantelpiece. Her father's pit boots lay on the hearth. She bent to pick them up.

'I'll gae ye somethin' for them,' said a voice from the door. It was the new tenant returned. 'I could do wi' a new pair.' He came in and surveyed them critically. 'Half a crown.'

Kezzie gasped at the effrontery. She snatched up the boots.

'They are not for sale,' she said angrily and marched out of the house.

CHAPTER 6

The bothy

It was early afternoon before Grandad returned wearily to the village.

'The farmer's got a place he'll let us stay until we find something better,' he told Kezzie. 'I've tried everywhere else but things are bad all over. Everyone wants to help but they're all in the same boat.'

They put some essentials into bags and Bella promised to get their chairs and table brought to them.

'The farmer said it wasn't up to much,' warned Grandad as they made their way on to the country road, 'just an old bothy, but I reckoned we ought to take it. If we don't, and the authorities see the bairn homeless . . .' He nodded at Lucy.

Kezzie realised Grandad had been thinking the same thoughts as she had. At this moment she didn't particularly care where they went. She wanted away from the rows before the early shift came home. It was more than her heart could bear to see the men trudging up the street and know her father was not among them. She pictured him so well, the muffler wound round his neck, cap pulled down, his face black with coal dust. For the last week or so Lucy and she had sat in the house at shift changeover, and as the tramp of feet went past the window the little girl would look up, and then come silently to stand beside Kezzie.

At the present time she was skipping along the road ahead of them picking flowers from the hedgerows and thinking this was a great adventure. Kezzie buttoned up her coat. The weather was getting colder. Well, at least they would be in shelter for the night.

'I think this must be it,' said Grandad eventually.

They stared across the field at a ramshackle little hut with a sagging roof. Kezzie felt her spirits sinking.

'Right then,' she said cheerfully. 'Over the gate,' and she lifted Lucy up.

They squelched through a rutted track to the bothy. There were holes in the roof, one wall was sloping gently, and the door, when she pushed it, gave way altogether and fell to the ground in front of them. Inside was an earthen floor with animal dung and broken pieces of machinery scattered around. The pane of glass in the one window had a long crack. Kezzie backed out of the doorway and laid her bags on the grass.

We can't stay here, she thought.

She turned to her grandfather. The old man was sitting on a large stone holding his head hung down in his hands.

It was Lucy who saved the day. She ran up to him with a bunch of wild flowers she had picked.

'Come on, Grandad,' she said, and threw her arms

around his neck. 'You can pick a place for your bed. I've picked mine already. It's going to be under the window. Come on,' and she tugged him to his feet and led him into the bothy.

Just as they crossed the threshold she said, 'See, Grandad, you mustn't let them grind you down.' Then Lucy added a curse word.

Kezzie's hand went over her mouth and she stepped smartly after her sister to give her a good telling off for saying such a word. Inside the bothy Grandad was leaning against the wall helpless with laughter.

He wiped his eyes with the back of his hand. 'Did you hear that one?'

'I did indeed,' said Kezzie tartly, 'and she knows better than to use language like that.'

'Let her be,' he said, 'it's the smartest thing anyone's said all day. Look at her now. We'd best follow her example.'

Lucy was collecting the pieces of junk and throwing them outside. It took them until dark. Grandad fetched his tool box and repaired the roof and fixed the door. Friends came down from the village with their other bits of furniture and stayed to help them. Kezzie told Bella to keep the dresser. By nightfall, a fire was going, the lamp was lit and the place was cosy. Grandad lit his pipe and looked about him.

'Well, it's not much, but it's home,' he said. He set the board out for a game of chess. Kezzie finished tucking Lucy up in bed.

'And we're together,' she added.

* * *

There was no question of her going back to school. Kezzie knew this quite well. The subject was never discussed. Who would she have talked to about it? Her grandad deferred to her when decisions had to be made. She was now the leader of her little family. He was up at dawn every day, tramping for miles, looking for any type of work. The farmer still gave him bits and pieces to do, but he had always earned small sums, just enough for some tobacco and a bottle of beer. He came home with this little amount and put all of it in their money tin on the table. Occasionally there would be a ten-shilling note or a few pounds in it. It was some time before Kezzie realised what he was doing. Small objects disappeared, then their best linen sheets and one day, his good suit. She discovered he was walking to Glasgow and back to the pawnbrokers. One night he came in and sat down. He didn't look at her as he spoke.

'They're taking on for the tattie-howkin',' he said, eating his dinner and gazing stolidly at his plate.

Every autumn many children were excused school to help lift the potato crop. John Munro had never let his daughters go, he didn't want them to miss any days' study. Next morning Kezzie rose early and went to the farm.

The farmer scratched his head. 'Let me see,' he said, handing her a basket, 'where's the best place for ye?' He pondered a moment and repeated what she had said. 'You're fourteen years and this is yer first time liftin' tatties?' He shook his head in disbelief.

'I learn awful quick,' said Kezzie anxiously.

'Oh, aye, aye, aye. I ken fine who you are. John Munro's yer grandad. It's just that a lot o' the squads are made up lang syne . . . tell ye what, try yer hand wi' the Irish. A bundle o' them came off the boat fae Donegal last night, and they seemed short-handed to me.'

The Irish were singing in the field. And as Kezzie approached, her basket in her hand, she was aware of curious glances in her direction. The tractor was at the opposite end with a posse of gulls in attendance and Kezzie stood by the hedge not sure what to do, reluctant to interrupt. Their song rose to the sky in the clear autumn air, a lilting tune in Gaelic, which kept them in the rhythm of their work and a smile on their faces. And they worked hard. Kezzie saw this as she watched them move down the shaws, digging, lifting, swinging and emptying the heavy baskets.

'You're looking for someone?'

A woman had stopped beside her and addressed her in a soft accent.

'I've to work here,' said Kezzie. 'The farmer said . . .'

'Sure that's grand. Just you slide yourself in alongside Michael there,' the woman instructed her. 'And don't you be annoyin' that girl, now, Michael Donohoe,' the woman added as she noticed the wink the young man had given Kezzie as she took her place beside him.

She was utterly hopeless. Like a thoroughbred untrained for labour trying to pull a milk cart. The more she strained and tried to keep up, the worse she became. Clumsy, fumbling and inept, the other workers stepped politely out of her way and soon left her far behind. By lunchtime she was exhausted, and worse, she hadn't thought to bring any sandwiches. She had also dressed in completely the wrong clothes for such work. She sat down in the shade of a tree and thought what she might do. She would have to stay. Her pride told her that. That, and the empty money tin on the kitchen table.

'Is this space taken?' a voice asked. Kezzie looked up and the young Irishman, whom she had been placed alongside, was standing above her.

Kezzie shrugged and looked away. He was laughing at her. She was sure of it. His dark blue eyes in his brown face were full of devilment. She had often wondered why Aunt Bella stayed with her husband, or indeed had married him in the first place. Now and then, usually after 'a wee refreshment' Aunt Bella would tell Kezzie her life story. How, when walking out with various young men, her man had seen off all other competition. And it was due to his dark eyes, Aunt Bella would declare, full of mischief and life. Kezzie was sure that the eyes of Michael Donohoe showed that he was full of mischief.

'I wonder if you would do me a favour here?' he asked. He hesitated. 'You see, I've far too much food with me to eat today, and if I throw it away . . . well, beside being a waste, it encourages the birds, and then the tractor man will be in a dreadful rage with me.'

Kezzie turned and stared at him. He was all wide-eyed innocence. Did he suspect? she wondered. She would die of embarrassment if she thought that he had guessed that she had been so stupid as not to bring food with her.

'You don't mind? Do you?' he enquired. And before she could answer he had put some sandwiches and an apple on the grass beside her. He saluted her and went away.

They resumed work after twenty minutes. 'I am going to collapse,' Kezzie said to herself. She had never realised that potato picking was such hard work. She was absolutely determined to try to keep up but very soon thought, I'm going to fall over, and when I do, I will never get up again.

She was aware of someone humming quietly beside her. She glanced to her side, and through the rivers of sweat streaking down her hot face she spied Michael Donohoe.

'Good afternoon,' he said pleasantly.

She grunted in reply.

'Now we haven't been formally introduced,' he went on pleasantly, 'but I'm sure that you will not mind me mentioning this . . . After all I'm a stranger in a foreign land and you Scots are noted for your hospitable ways.' He paused.

Kezzie stopped and eased her aching back. If he was making fun of her, she would hit him over the head with the basket, she decided.

He placed his hand between her shoulder blades and rubbed gently.

'Begging your pardon,' he said courteously. He bent down and placed her basket at a different angle. 'Like this,' he said, 'you stoop like this,' and he showed her how. 'Now I'll dig this row, and you follow after.' Then he moved on ahead of her using the graip, and she gathered in the potatoes behind him. She was aware that he was making slower time, but, as she could not move past him, she had no choice but to work at the slower pace he set.

They worked that way for the remainder of the day.

He sang with the others, sometimes quietly as the work was hard, sometimes their voices rivalling the birds' evensong for harmony and beauty.

He carried her basket to the farm buildings for her, and then saluted and bade her good night.

Kezzie could scarcely walk the mile and a half home.

CHAPTER 7

Potato harvest

Kezzie was at the field first the next morning and every morning after that, determined to show that she was as able as anyone else. And by some strange chance, no matter where she started off she always found herself working beside Michael Donohoe. And he always had a great story to tell her.

'Did I ever tell you about the time I was working at the fair in Ballyshannon, and the fellow with the dancing bear said to me, "Michael, hold this chain for one moment while I step inside this public house to wet my throat". And didn't the very next minute an old man with a barrel organ appear and start to wind the handle. And right away the bear put his arms around me, and there we were the two of us doing a jig down the main street.'

Michael stopped and wiped the back of his neck with his hankie.

Kezzie always pretended that his stories didn't interest her much.

'Mmmm?' she said, head down, working hard.

'I never made as much money that day as I did any other. And the fellow comes out of the pub after an hour and gives me a shilling for minding his bear. But the sorrowful part of it was . . .'

'What?' Kezzie asked before she could stop herself.

'After that the bear wouldn't dance at all. Now at first we thought it was because it was all worn out with the dancing it had done that afternoon, because besides a jig, we had also danced a waltz and a polka. It was a very educated bear, you see. But we soon discovered it was a different reason altogether. And it wasn't until I ran into them a few weeks later at Limerick Fair and the poor man was pulling his hair out as he told me his story of how his bear would not dance a step . . . when suddenly the bear caught sight of me and leapt up and gave me a great hug. And then it was clear what had happened. The bear was pining away. And do you know the reason why?' Michael gave Kezzie a wicked look.

'No,' said Kezzie, feigning indifference.

'Why that bear had fallen right in love with me.' Michael clasped his hands across his chest dramatically. 'Its heart was broken, don't you know?'

Kezzie grabbed a large potato and flung it at his head.

'I never heard such nonsense in all my life,' she said.

'You think it's nonsense that someone would fall in love with me?' he asked her slyly, his eyes bright and shining in his face.

'Perhaps not a poor dumb animal.' Kezzie pretended to ponder the question for a moment. 'No,' she said finally, 'even a poor dumb animal would have more sense than to fall for the likes of you.'

He began to walk her a bit of the road home at night and although she enjoyed his company she didn't want him to see the shack where they stayed. She always managed to put him off after a mile or so but he was a person who was not easily put off, and so she was not really surprised one evening just before sunset to see him coming across the field.

She sighed and went to meet him.

'I just happened to be passing,' he said innocently, 'and I thought I'd pay a call.'

'Come in,' said Kezzie, 'and meet Grandad and Lucy and I'll make you a cup of tea.'

Lucy took to him at once of course, and he told her three stories before she went to bed. About how he was a runaway son of the King of Ireland and lived in a castle with a drawbridge, and how he'd gone with gypsies and travelled all over Europe.

'Stop filling that child's head with nonsense,' said Kezzie eventually. She went with him to the gate.

'Where *do* you live, Michael?' she asked him. She imagined a whitewashed thatched cottage by the shores of a quiet beach. It was obvious to her the way the Irish workers spoke that they loved their country and thought it very beautiful. It must be disturbing to have to leave home every year for weeks in order to make some money to survive the winter. She had heard them use a saying which must be common at home. 'Donegal will never starve as long as there are potatoes in Scotland.' There was something wrong with the world, thought

Kezzie, that most people seemed to have to break their backs for bread yet, day by day, in the newspapers and on the wireless all the talk of troubles in Europe meant that vast sums of money were being spent on building warships and making guns to prepare for a war against Hitler's Germany.

'Where do I live?' Michael repeated. 'I'm afraid that I don't live anywhere at the moment.'

She knew by his voice that this was not one of his stories.

'You and I are similar, Kezzie,' he said, 'in that we are orphans. I don't recall a mother or father. I just woke up one day in a children's home in Belfast. Except that no child should ever have been made to stay there and it certainly wasn't a home. And about four or five years ago, when I was about thirteen, it was Australia's turn for free child labour and I was one of the ones picked to go. I didn't know anything about Australia and I decided I didn't want to know either, so I ran away.'

'What do you mean "free child labour for Australia"?' asked Kezzie.

'There's not many people know or even care, but the British children's homes send children to their colonies. Now, lots of people leave their own country to go abroad where they hope they will live in plenty. The Irish are famous for it. We are as the wild geese. But this is different. It is more of a compulsory emigration.'

'I suppose,' said Kezzie slowly, 'if you have no kin, and you're destitute it might be a better life.'

'But it's not only orphans that go,' said Michael, 'and they separate brothers and sisters, and they don't always

41

enquire if there's family. These places have great power. They can take children from parents if they feel they are not being cared for properly, and then they think they own them.'

Kezzie shivered, thinking again about her own fears for Lucy on the day of their eviction.

'See, now in my case I did have some kin, only they hadn't bothered to tell me. It was just by chance that I found out an old aunt of my mother's lived in Donegal. I stay there in the winter, though there's not much room.'

It was now quite dark. The stars were out and the harvest moon hung yellow and transparent in the sky.

'We have a sing-song in the barn the night before we sail,' said Michael. 'Will you come, with Lucy and your grandfather?'

'I'd love to,' said Kezzie. She hadn't realised the season had passed so quickly. She would have to think about work for the winter. They had saved a little but it wouldn't see them through. Besides Lucy had grown in the summer. Her coat and boots were far too small for her now.

She said good night to Michael. He hesitated for a second, then patted her on the head, vaulted over the gate and went off up the road whistling cheerfully.

CHAPTER 8

Michael's farewell

They could hear the sound of music from the big barn as they came across the fields. Fiddle and accordion carried on the clear night air. Kezzie breathed in.

'Isn't it beautiful?' she said.

The moon was riding high in the sky and all the trees and bushes had an incandescent light upon them.

They had brought brown baps and scones, and little pancakes which Lucy had helped make. Her grandad had some beer, and everything was wrapped in a clean cloth in their basket.

Michael saw them and came over at once. He looked very handsome with his white shirt and black waistcoat and his dark hair smoothed down.

'Come and sit with me,' he offered. He took Lucy by the hand. 'What have you in that basket, Careen?' he asked her. 'Anything for a starving man?'

'Pancakes, which I made myself.'

Michael clutched his stomach.

'Pancakes!' he exclaimed. 'How did you know that is

my very favourite thing to eat?' He made smacking noises with his lips. 'Let me at them.'

'We have to put them on the table,' said Lucy primly. 'You will have to wait like everyone else.'

They laid their food out with all the rest on a trestle table which had been set up at the far end of the barn. There were plates heaped with potatoes, which had been baked in the open fire, bread and butter, cheese, hard boiled eggs, soda scones and a barrel of beer from the farmer.

'Now, isn't he the generous one,' Kezzie heard someone say.

And it was true. Some farmers did not like the Irish, saw them only as a source of cheap labour, to be used and got rid of as quickly as possible. Like the travellers, thought Kezzie. These two groups of people had similar ways, migrating across many miles seeking work. Most of the year they followed the harvests, from Ayrshire to the Lothians, down to the Borders and up past Perthshire. Even though many farms now used the new digging and haymaking machines, workers were needed for lifting the potato crop, and for turnip singling and mangel pulling. She wondered if she would enjoy it herself, this nomadic life, moving on at intervals, meeting different people. And what of those others, the emigrants of whom Michael had spoken? Those who left their homeland to become immigrants in a foreign country. What would it be like to be one of them? She supposed it would be interesting to learn about new and strange customs and have a chance of more prosperity. She would miss her own native land though, she knew that, the hills heather-purple and the village and its folk.

'Right, now,' said Michael. 'I'm going to teach you how to dance the "Walls of Limerick".' He grasped Kezzie firmly and swung her on to the floor.

And so the night passed. The Scots and the Irish with a common Celtic heritage in singing and dancing, sang and danced, mournful and happy by turn.

Lucy and Kezzie were flushed and exhausted after an eightsome reel.

'Wait now and I will get you a lemonade,' said Michael, and he went to fill up their enamel cups. Kezzie looked at where her grandad was arguing fiercely about something with a group of men. He hadn't enjoyed himself so much in weeks.

'Sing us a song, Michael,' someone called. 'Come on, now.'

Lucy leaned forward and tugged his sleeve.

'Make it a jolly one,' she said.

Michael winked at her. He stood in the middle of the floor, and bowed low. 'This is a song of special significance for a special person, not forgetting her sister.'

He hooked his thumbs into his braces;

> *Goodbye to all the boys at home, I'm sailing far*
> *across the foam*
> *To try and make me fortune in far Amerikay.*
> *There's gold and money plenty, for the poor and for*
> *the gentry*
> *And when I come back again, I never more will*
> *stray . . .*

Soon everyone was clapping and joining in.

So goodbye Muirsheen Durkin,
I'm sick and tired of workin'
No more I'll dig the praties,
No longer I'll be fooled.
As sure's me name is Carney,
I'll go off to Californay,
Where instead of digging praties
I'll be diggin' lumps of gold.

Lucy hugged him when he sat down.

'I liked that one, that was a nice song,' she said. 'Except your name's not Carney.'

'What did you mean, "it was of special significance"?' asked Kezzie.

'I'll tell you later,' said Michael. 'Come on.'

He pulled Kezzie to her feet and waltzed away with her to the 'Pride of Erin'.

'This babby is nearly sleeping,' said Michael softly as they reached the bothy.

It was after midnight and he had carried Lucy home with Kezzie walking beside him. From time to time they had stopped to look at the stars which seemed close enough to touch.

'I'm not a babby,' said a small voice.

'Deed you're not,' said Michael stoutly, and he set Lucy down gently. 'And if the big sister wasn't watching me, sure I'd be stealing a kiss from a pretty girl like you after walking her home on a beautiful moonlight night like this.'

He stole a sidelong glance at Kezzie.

'Be darned,' he said. 'I'm going to steal one anyway.' And he kissed Lucy on the top of her curly head. 'Now away to bed at once, before you drive a man wild.'

Lucy skipped inside laughing.

'I'll be there in a minute to tuck you up,' Kezzie called after her.

Michael turned to Kezzie.

'I'm not going home tomorrow with the rest,' he said.

Kezzie's eyes opened wide.

'Where are you going?'

'London.'

'But you hate the cities. You told me that!' she cried.

'Just for a few months. There's a cousin of my mother's there. He can fix me up. See, I'm planning to go to America and it's the only way I'll get enough money. Working the way I am now you only make enough to live on through the winter, and then it starts all over again. I've got to break the cycle and get out.'

'I know what you mean,' said Kezzie slowly. 'I've been thinking the same myself. We cannot live like this for ever. Lucy needs something better. I shall have to get some kind of steady work.'

Michael fiddled with his shirt collar.

'You wouldn't think of America, yourself, would you?'

'America!' said Kezzie in amazement. 'America! What would we do in America? I don't know anyone in America.'

'Well, you might know me,' said Michael carefully.

'Oh.'

Kezzie looked into his dark blue eyes. He was not joking with her. His face was serious.

She didn't know what to say.

He put his hand on her shoulder.

'You might think on it,' said Michael. 'I'll come back and see you before I sail.' He grinned. 'Now, I'll have a kiss from the big sister,' and he brushed the side of her cheek with his lips.

Kezzie felt something catch at her heart.

She lay in bed with Lucy cuddled in beside her and gazed out at the moon through the little window. She heard her grandad coming home and going heavily to his bed. It was a long time before she fell asleep.

CHAPTER 9

The rag doll

The weather became colder. The track to their home was now rutted mud and Kezzie felt the hard ground under her boots each day she walked out. Boots, which were now so small they cramped her feet badly and with soles so thin as to scarcely keep the damp out.

Each day she left Lucy at school and looked for work. Just before Christmas she was lucky and got some time at the pit head at the picking tables taking the rocks and the slats from the coal. She hated working there, hated the sound of the whistle, the noise of the bell and wheel turning, but it was all she could get. Grandad was having worse luck, Christmas was approaching and their summer savings and sacks of potatoes were running low. But with this job she could also bring home coal and it kept the hut cheery and warm.

'Do you think Santa Claus will know where we are?' Lucy asked anxiously one night.

'Santa knows where all good children are,' said Kezzie, not looking up from the sock she was darning.

Lucy climbed on her grandad's knee.

'Tell me a story,' she said.

Grandad reached for one of the books in the box beside the fire.

'No,' said Lucy, 'tell me the pony story.'

'Oh, that old story. You don't want to hear that again?' said Grandad.

This was just a routine they went through now and then, because Grandad knew that it was their favourite story. He let Lucy plead for a moment or two, and then, knocking the ash from his pipe against the chimney, he began.

'I was a pit lad at twelve. Did you know that?'

'Yes,' said Lucy snuggling in against his chest.

'Well, I was up at five in the morning and down the pit by half-past six, and it was a long long walk there and back, and hard hard work when you got there. But I looked forward to it every day of my youth, and do you know why? Because the best friend I had in all the world lived down that pit.'

Kezzie stopped her darning to listen.

'This friend's name was Meg and she was a beauty. She had brown hair and soft brown eyes, and as soon as she heard my voice in the morning calling her she would come to meet me. Now you might ask yourself what was a nice young lady doing living down a mine. Or perhaps you've guessed the secret already?' He bent his head and looked at Lucy.

'Meg was a pony!' Lucy cried.

'Yes, Meg was a pony,' agreed Grandad. 'And she wasn't just pretty, she had brains as well. And I'm going to tell you how I found that out.' He settled himself more comfortably in his chair.

'The ponies pulled the trains of coal hutches backwards and forwards, the full ones from the face, the empty ones back, on separate lines. One day Meg and I were bringing the empties back along their rails when she stopped dead, and then crossed over on to the full track. Her ears were back and she was trembling. I was very surprised. Meg had never done anything like that before. And then I heard the sound of a runaway train!

'I thought quickly. I couldn't tell which track they were one, but if it was the full one we would both be killed with the weight of the coal in the hutches. On the empty track we might get off lighter. I grabbed her harness and pulled her back over. The crashing noise of the wagons were almost on top of us when she tossed her head and, with me still hanging on her halter, landed us both on the full side. I screamed. I thought my end had come. Then the runaway wagons, five unloaded hutches, roared past us on the empty line.'

'And that,' said Lucy, finishing the story for him, 'is how a pit pony saved the life of a pit lad.'

After Lucy had fallen asleep Kezzie took out the rag doll she was making her for Christmas. She surveyed it critically. She had cut up a good cotton pillowcase for this doll and she was very proud of it. It was stuffed to a nice plumpness and had brown woollen hair, two blue button eyes and a stitched red smile on her face. Kezzie was now sewing her a dress and cape from an old tartan scarf.

'That's awful bonny,' said Grandad, handing her a cup of tea.

She was knitting him a new muffler and had to snatch moments to work on it when he was out looking for odd jobs. He was even thinner. He hadn't managed more than a few shillings over the last weeks. It must be so frustrating, Kezzie thought, to have trained skills and only be able to mend bits of farm machinery from time to time. They were all less healthy than they had been. They couldn't afford to keep the fire burning all night, and Lucy had developed a wheeze and cough.

Kezzie worried about her extravagances, but when Christmas came she couldn't resist using most of their savings to make it special. They had a small chicken and cake to eat. She had filled their stockings with little things, tangerines, sweeties, some ribbons. She bought Grandad a bottle of beer and some tobacco, and Lucy gloves and a bonnet. Lucy had made them both hankies in school with their initials embroidered on. Grandad, too, had squandered his money and proudly brought out two books, a flower fairy story for Lucy, and *Catriona* for Kezzie. Grandad put his muffler on at once and insisted on wearing it while eating his dinner. Kezzie watched anxiously as Lucy pulled the doll out of her stocking.

'Look what Santa gave me!' she cried. She kissed it again and again. 'This is the most beautiful doll in all the world,' she said.

'Have you given her a name yet?' asked Grandad at night when she was in bed with her doll tucked up snugly beside her.

'Her name's Kissy,' said Lucy.

Later Kezzie was glad she had spent the money. In the grim days ahead she could look back often and remember that Christmas day and the warm glow it gave her helped her struggle on.

CHAPTER 10

The pit boots

Coming back from the outside privy in the half-dark one morning Kezzie saw a large brown rat sitting on their table cleaning its whiskers. She shrieked and it ran away, scuttling across the floor towards the fireplace. She shivered and got back into bed beside Lucy. She could not fall asleep again. Hunger was gnawing at her. She had rationed out supper in a very miserly way last night and her small piece of bread hadn't filled her stomach at all. The child beside her whimpered softly in her sleep. She had been doing that a lot recently.

Kezzie lay and tried to think of the most economical way of using the few shillings they had left. She and Grandad had found no work at all that week. After Christmas no one had anything to spare and the little errands she had run for coppers were now not needed. They cut logs from the nearby wood to save coal, but it took up so much time and the wood burned quickly and gave off little heat. Grandad had taken the clock from the mantelpiece the week before and now she knew there was only one other thing they might get money for.

In the early afternoon she knocked on the door of the house that had once been hers. It was a sorry sight that she saw when the woman opened the door to her. The floor was littered and the range that she had black-leaded so lovingly was tarnished and dirty. The man pushed his wife out of the way.

'Oh, it's you,' he said. 'Ye've come back. I thought ye might.'

Kezzie held out her father's pit boots.

'I'll give ye a shilling for them,' he said.

Kezzie was dumbstruck. A shilling! She had thought that he would offer less when she went back. But a shilling!

'D'ye want me tae make it sixpence?' he enquired rudely.

She put the boots down on the ground, took his shilling and turned away, walking blindly down the road.

'Lassie,' she heard someone call before she had gone very far, 'lassie.'

She turned and the woman of the house was coming towards her. She looked around her furtively and, taking a paper bag from under her shawl, she gave it to Kezzie, then hurried away. In the parcel was the heel end of a loaf and a piece of cheese.

The next day Kezzie went to see Bella. She knew her husband had been laid up for some time and he had no pay, but Bella was a picker at the pit head and at least she had something. It was in Kezzie's mind to ask her to take Lucy in for a time.

'Amn't I glad to see you,' declared Bella, putting the kettle on at once. 'That one next door is always in here borrowing and her hoose! Well . . .' She stopped, sensing that Kezzie was upset. 'What's the matter, pet? Are things not so good with you?'

'Not very good,' said Kezzie. In the past she had never let the older woman guess quite how bad things were with them.

'You can sell stuff at the pawn, ye know. Ye mustn't be too proud. That good suit of ma man's has been up an' down that road so often, it kens the way to go itself.'

Kezzie laughed.

'Aunt Bella, we've pawned everything we can. I sold my father's pit boots to him next door yesterday.'

'My God, lassie, I didn't know it was as bad as that with you.' She twirled her cup in her hands for a minute or two, and then said, 'Have ye been tae the minister?'

Kezzie looked at her.

'Go on the Parish Relief? I couldn't.'

The older woman studied the floor for a moment. Then she sighed.

'I have,' she said.

The minister was setting his dinner on the table when Kezzie knocked at the back door. Two small potatoes, a drop of stew and a bit of bread were on his plate. He's not doing much better than us, Kezzie thought, as he made her welcome and sat her down.

'I can give you a three-shilling allowance each time,' he said. 'I know it's not very much, but I have to keep to the rate. I must be fair. There are so many, and I must make sure every person gets something.' He looked at her kindly. 'I had no idea things were so bad with you. You should have come sooner.'

He insisted that she ate the food on the table, saying he had more in the pot. She didn't really believe him, but she was so tired and hungry that she did as she was told. She hadn't tasted meat for some time and she chewed it slowly. He brought through a ledger and entered the family details.

He closed his book and said gently, 'You know ... your grandfather would get a place in a hostel in Glasgow, and some of the children's homes can be quite nice. I'm sure Lucy would adapt very quickly ... and then I could probably find you a place as a stay-in scullery maid in one of the big houses. You would win through, I'm sure. I remember your mother and father. You Munros have all got such a strong spirit.'

'No,' said Kezzie firmly. 'No.'

His mentioning her father gave her strength. 'Lucy wouldn't adapt. She would break her heart, and it would crush Grandad completely, and me ... why, I would lie down and die. The reason we have such a great spirit is because we're together. We are a family.'

The minister nodded his head and smiled.

'I thought that would be your answer. You're a brave girl. Have you been to the mission in Shawcross?' he asked her.

She shook her head.

'They give out necessities, like tea and margarine. I'll write you a letter.'

She read it as she walked home.

'This is to certify that the bearer of this letter, one Keziah Munro of this parish, is destitute. She has two others in need of support and requires any such goods as you may give her.'

Kezzie folded the letter very carefully and put it in her pocket.

It was true then. It was written down. She was destitute.

CHAPTER 11

Starvation

Kezzie left Lucy at school the next morning and walked to the mission at Shawcross. There was a queue of people waiting to be served at a counter at the far end of the hall. There were some very dirty people jostling along in the group, folk with threadbare and greasy clothes. She tried to keep her distance as they pressed up against her. She waited in line for nearly an hour. When it came to her turn a very severe-looking woman behind the table put out her hand.

'Book,' she snapped.

'Book?' Kezzie repeated. She hadn't noticed that the others had a book which they handed over. 'I don't have a book.'

'No book. No goods.' The woman looked beyond Kezzie. 'Next.'

'I have a letter,' protested Kezzie. 'My minister said if he wrote a letter . . .'

'You need a book,' said the woman, already dealing with the next person. 'We need to mark in the date and what goods you receive. You only get a certain amount each month. Otherwise people like you would be in here every day getting stuff for nothing.'

'I'm sorry,' said Kezzie politely. 'Where do I get a book?'

The woman ignored her while she served three other people and then said, 'Go to the office.'

'Where is the office?'

Again she made Kezzie wait for a few minutes, then said, 'In the corridor. You must have noticed it on your way in.'

Kezzie returned to the corridor and found the office. It was closed. The notice on the door read OPEN MONDAYS AND WEDNESDAYS. Today was Thursday. In order to get a book for rations she would have to wait four more days. Kezzie went back into the hall. The queue was now double the length. Kezzie marched to the front.

'Excuse me,' she said, placing herself directly in front of the woman. 'The office is closed.'

'Is it?' was the reply. 'Then you'll have to wait until it opens.' She snapped her fingers for the next person to come forward.

Kezzie side-stepped smartly and blocked them off.

'I can't wait four days,' she said. 'The reason I have the letter is because I am desperate.'

'You should have thought of that sooner, miss,' said the woman, 'before you let yourself get into such a state.'

Kezzie gasped.

'Do you think I want to be like this?' she said. 'To come here and have to beg from someone like you?'

'You be careful, madam. Talk that way to me and you'll get nothing. Now stand aside and let me deal with these people.'

The people who were waiting had become very quiet as they listened to this exchange of words.

'I will not stand aside. I was told to come here for food and I'm not leaving until I get some.'

The crowd murmured its approval.

The woman hesitated for a second. 'If you are really so desperate you can wait until the end. If there is anything left you might get something.'

Kezzie swallowed and tried to keep her temper. She thought of Lucy, with her outgrown boots and coat, and her thin peaked face. She thought of her grandad, away from early morning until nightfall each day and coming home with pennies. Her hand closed around the minister's letter.

'Blast you!' she shouted. 'Blast you for ever more! Keep your food. Keep your stupid book. I'll do without it!' And she crushed up the letter in her fist and threw it into the woman's face.

She ran outside. She could still hear the cheering and clapping from inside the hall, as she stamped down the street, an angry fire inside her. She knew that she had done something really stupid and would regret it later, but at that moment she didn't care. No human being should have to crawl to another, especially not for food.

'Miss, excuse me.'

Kezzie stopped. Someone was calling after her. It was an older woman, carrying a baby.

'Miss,' the woman hesitated, and, as she came nearer,

Kezzie saw that in fact the girl could have been scarcely twenty.

'Miss, I heard what happened inside there. The Salvation Army give out soup and bread every day at their place, and they have clothes . . . if you need them.' She touched Kezzie on the arm lightly, and was gone.

This incident, instead of cheering Kezzie, made her feel even lower. The thought of queuing at a soup kitchen was too much to contemplate. People should be allowed to keep their dignity and not be humiliated, she thought, as she turned the corner into the main street. With this in her head it was just the wrong moment for her to catch sight of her grandfather.

At first she didn't realise it was him. What she saw ahead of her in the street was an old man standing with his head down and his cap outstretched in his hand. A woman dropped a copper in, others walked past ignoring him, then one man pushed him roughly aside. Kezzie retreated a few steps and then turned and fled. She got round the corner and hurried away as quickly as she could through lanes and back alleys praying that he had not seen her.

The next day was bitterly cold, and Lucy protested strongly as Kezzie tried to force her feet into her little boots. They were far too small for her. Kezzie had at last to admit to this. She found a pair of her own from last year that she had outgrown and by putting a pair of Grandad's socks on Lucy's feet and stuffing the toes with paper she fitted them on her sister. They set off for school. Kezzie was in an ill humour. The events of the previous days and her sister's complaints had brought her down completely. The very sight of the child wrapped up with a huge wool scarf against the cold, with her skinny arms sticking out of her outgrown coat sleeves, stumbling along in the big boots, enraged her. Lucy was walking far too slowly and would be late for school. Kezzie wrenched cruelly at her arm.

'Hurry up,' she snapped.

Lucy pulled her arm away. 'I can walk to school myself,' she shouted, and with as much dignity as she could muster clumped determinedly off up the road.

Kezzie walked six miles into another town that day. She couldn't risk seeing her grandfather begging in Shawcross. She got nothing at all until almost closing time when a greengrocer said to wait behind and help shut up the shop. She dragged sacks of potatoes and boxes of apples and vegetables in from the street, then swept the floor. The man was kindly enough and gave her a bag of bruised fruit and vegetables as well as her money to take home. As she left the shop she saw her reflection in the lowered blinds. She looked unkempt, her hair was matted, her coat stained and missing a button.

It was a long six miles home in the dark carrying some boxes the shopkeeper had given her for firewood. When she arrived at the bothy the fire was barely burning and Grandad and Lucy were sitting at the table waiting for her.

'Have you not eaten?' she asked sharply.

'We were waiting for you,' said her grandfather. 'You are late, we were worried something was amiss.'

'And would you just sit there all night,' she cried, 'and

let the fire go out and never think to make yourselves something to eat?'

Lucy opened her mouth.

'You be quiet,' said Kezzie. 'I've had enough of your moaning for one day. No one does much here except me, and I'm sick and fed up with it all. Look at this place. The roof is leaking and the wind is blowing in through the walls.' She glared at her grandfather. 'It's time you did some repairs around here instead of traipsing all over the town each day for no good whatsoever.'

He lowered his gaze and looked away. Kezzie began to set out cups and plates noisily on the table. She caught sight of her hands, chapped and red, her fingernails dirty and broken. She realised with a sudden shock that she was just like the other people she had waited with in the queue the other day. The people she had moved away from and tried to keep at a distance. She pulled open the drawer of the kitchen table to take out the breadboard and knife. The handle came away and dropped painfully on to her foot.

'This is exactly what is wrong!' she shrieked. 'Someone should have fixed this handle. It has been loose for weeks and neither of you would think of doing something about it.' She drew in a deep breath. 'You,' she pointed at her grandfather, 'get your toolbox and fix this and anything else that needs fixing. You,' she addressed Lucy who had gone to stand beside her grandad, 'get that grate cleaned out and this table top scrubbed and then bring out your sum book. You haven't done any school work for weeks and it's time you started.' She pulled a piece of bread for herself from the loaf and snatching up her coat she opened the door. 'I'm going for a walk and this must all be done when I come back. That is if I decide to come back at all.'

Kezzie walked in the woods for nearly two hours. It was a clear and beautiful winter's night, with frost sparkling on trees and grass, but she did not see it at all. Her thoughts were confused and desperate. She knew that they were at the end of their road. Her outburst tonight had shown that. They had had arguments and fall-outs before like any normal family, but tonight had been different. She waited until Lucy and Grandad would have gone to bed and then returned home.

They were waiting for her when she softly opened the door. The fire was burning brightly, the grate swept and the table clean. Grandad was leaning over Lucy and her school books. They regarded her silently as she stood at the door.

'I'm sorry,' said Kezzie, and burst into tears.

She didn't know quite how it happened but next she was settled on Grandad's knee in the big chair by the fire with his arms around her, and Lucy brought her her doll to cuddle.

'Here,' said her sister generously, 'you can keep Kissy tonight if you want.'

Later with the doll cuddled between the two of them Kezzie prayed: 'Dear God help us. If you don't do it soon then we surely will starve.'

And starve they would have if it had not been for the timely arrival of Matt McPhee.

CHAPTER 12

Matt McPhee

A few days later Kezzie awoke suddenly in the early morning. She reached blindly for the small stone she kept on the floor beside her bed in case she ever saw a rat again. Nothing moved inside the bothy.

She got up quietly. Something or someone was creeping around outside, she was sure of it. She cautiously opened the door. In the half-light she saw, lying at her feet, a dead rabbit.

'Something wrong?'

Her grandad was beside her.

'Look.' She pointed at the ground.

Grandad stepped outside and glanced about him. There was no one in sight. Then a low whistle sounded from beyond the trees. Kezzie's grandfather raised his arm in a salute, and picking up the rabbit, he came back inside.

'It's the travellers,' he said.

They had rabbit stew at seven o'clock that morning, and all of them ate fit to burst.

'My tummy's sore,' said Lucy happily.

'Don't you DARE be sick,' said Kezzie, laughing. She stirred the pot on the fire. 'There's enough here for tonight, as well.'

'I'll get some potatoes from the farmer today,' said Grandad, 'and we'll manage rabbit soup with them tomorrow.'

Kezzie persuaded her grandfather to go back to the farm and ask for employment. He repaired the tools and machinery. Kezzie was sure that the farmer was only making work for her grandad out of friendship and pity, but she didn't care. It was better than letting Grandad go back into town to beg. Even if he couldn't pay, the farmer always gave them milk each day, and some potatoes or turnips to get by on.

Kezzie had also set Lucy little tasks to do in order to keep her occupied. No matter how tired or hungry she was, Lucy had to keep a jam jar on the table filled with fresh evergreens and berries. Her school work, which had been neglected, was now done every night, and Grandad was teaching her to play chess.

On the third day, when they had finished the soup, Kezzie opened the door in the morning to find a small chicken there. And so it went on. Every few days something was left, two plump pigeons, fish, eggs, then a fine buck hare which lasted them nearly a week.

The wind shifted round and there was a tingling in the air, as Kezzie got Lucy dressed for school one morning. She had gone previously to the Salvation Army clothing store and managed to find a pair of boots to fit her sister. She wrapped her up well and they were about to go outside when the door opened and in stepped Matt McPhee.

He touched his forehead, but did not speak.

Kezzie realised that it was a sign of respect. He was waiting for her to greet him first.

'Come in, please,' she said. 'Would you take some tea?'

He nodded and sat at the table.

'Matt,' said Kezzie as she poured his tea and cut him some bread. 'We want to thank you for your gifts.'

His face reddened and he concentrated on his cup.

'No, truly,' said Kezzie. 'These last days, you have stood between us and starvation.'

'As you did with us in the past.'

'How did you know that we needed help?' asked Kezzie.

'We had finished the berries at Blairgowrie and were on our way north. We met up with cousins at a camp in Brechin and they said they had been past this way. They had called at your house and had abuse and a shoe thrown at them. We knew that your da would never do that. He was a gentleman, your da. It's not a big house or money that makes you gentry. My mother sent me back down the road to see what was amiss.'

Kezzie suddenly remembered the travellers' last visit and Matt's mother telling their fortune.

'She knew, didn't she? Your mother knew?'

Matt looked away and then back towards them. He shook his head.

'Not exactly, no, or she would have warned you. She just told me that your da's hand was cold, very cold.'

There was a silence. Matt finished his tea and wiped his mouth.

'I came to speak with you as I'll need to be going back up the road soon. We always winter in Skye and I've got to get my two hundred days' schooling or the Cruelty fine us.'

Kezzie felt as though she had been struck.

'Go away?' she said.

'Aye, but before I do we will have to sort you out a bit better.' He stood up and glanced around him critically. 'This is a hole you're in and the snow's coming. I can smell it in the wind. I've sent word to other kin of ours in the Borders and we should get you fixed up with something else soon. Also, after you leave the bairn off to school I'm going to give you some real education. The kind that you don't learn from books, but it'll keep you 'til springtime.'

And that is what he did. Over the following days Matt showed Kezzie how to live as well as nature would allow, how to rob a nest and set a snare, which berries were edible and which were not and how to follow animal tracks.

One afternoon just after Lucy had returned from school he appeared with a great smile on his face.

'Come quickly,' he said, 'and see what I have got for you.'

He led them to the other side of the wood, near where a clear stream ran.

'This is a better place for a camp,' he said, 'less damp, fresh water, and look . . .'

Parked beside the burn was an old-fashioned gypsy caravan.

'The man who had this has a modern trailer now,

pulled by a car, would you believe?' Matt laughed. 'Not for the likes of me, I'll tell you. I'll have a yoke and a tent any day. Anyroad, it's yours and it has a stove and a sink and all, it's watertight and it's up off the ground.'

'It's wonderful,' said Kezzie. The thought of leaving the bothy overjoyed her. She would get their things together at once and settle there tonight.

Matt seemed restless and she turned to speak to him.

'The people who brought this are waiting for me at the end of the lane,' he said. He held his hand out awkwardly. 'I must say goodbye.'

Impulsively Kezzie went forward and hugged him, not caring that he was rigid with embarrassment.

'Thank you, Matt McPhee,' she said, 'and tell your mother thanks. And may we have better fortune when we see you again,' she called after him as he ran off down the road.

CHAPTER 13

Kezzie plays a trick

They settled themselves in the caravan and, as Matt had predicted, the snow came. They awoke one morning to that particular brightness and strange quietness that tells of a heavy fall of snow during the night. Lucy was delighted.

'No school!' she squealed and, pulling her coat on over her night clothes, she ran out to play.

And with not much persuading, Grandad and Kezzie joined her. For a few days while the first fall lay white and clean, Grandad and Kezzie gave up their search for work. When Kezzie thought about it later, she felt that their temporary return to childhood had been good medicine for both of them. They made snowmen and had snow fights, tried skating on a nearby frozen pond and even attempted to build an igloo.

At last a thaw came and with it the very first frail snowdrops scattered under trees and hedgerows. Kezzie felt better. The indication that the year was on the turn gave her hope, and as if to prove her right, Bella arrived breathless one day with what she hoped was good news.

'The new knitwear factory in Shawcross,' she gasped, out of breath with hurrying, 'they're hiring tomorrow at ten o'clock.'

Kezzie rose early and set out for the town, aiming to be there by eight o'clock, in plenty of time as she thought. She was aware of the noise as she approached the site but was totally unprepared for the crowds of people already gathered and waiting. She cursed her own foolishness for not thinking ahead. Some, obviously really desperate, must have been waiting since before dawn. Was she not really desperate? She asked herself this in anger. She estimated the crowd to be around three or four hundred. They were taking on, how many? Fifty? One hundred? No more certainly. She leaned against the wall and tried to think, hardly aware that she was fingering her silver locket. Your brain is in charge of your body, not the other way about, her father used to say. Use your brain.

She detached herself from the wall and hurried back the road she had come. She reached the Manse just as the minister was entering. He had been sitting all night with a dying old man whose family had all gone out to Australia. He heaved a sigh as he hung his coat and scarf on the hallstand. 'One of the sad things about emigration,' he said, 'is that it can break family bonds. When the young ones go off there's no one left at home to care for the old.'

'I'll not keep you one minute,' said Kezzie, and explained what she wanted.

He wrote the letter of reference as she asked and handed it to her. She hesitated.

'Would you put it in an envelope please? And,' she added as he did so, 'will you address it "BY HAND, THE MANAGER"?'

He smiled.

'I can do even better,' he said, and sealed it with red wax.

Kezzie next went to Bella's house.

'Have you anything I can borrow?' she enquired. 'Something to wear to make me appear older?'

A wistful look came over her aunt's face.

'I may have the very thing,' she said.

She pulled an old kist from under the recess bed and took out a dark blue two-piece suit. It had a fitted jacket with a peplum waist and a long accordion-pleated skirt.

'This was the costume I was married in,' said Bella.

'I can't take that,' Kezzie protested.

'Why not?' asked Bella. She indicated her ample figure. 'It's never going to fit me again.'

She found a pair of black shoes with heels and little bows at the front. They were slightly large but stuffing the toes made them stay on Kezzie's smaller feet.

'Mmmm,' said Bella, walking round Kezzie, examining her, 'a bag and, I think, some make-up.'

They found a purse-style handbag and Bella combed Kezzie's chestnut hair and pinned it up into a French roll. She then applied make-up and some lipstick and rouge.

'Right,' she instructed, 'you go in there and kill them dead.' She threw a shawl about her shoulders and postured about the kitchen giving a display of how she imagined famous film stars acted. She puckered her lips together and minced up and down. 'Now, just you bat

73

yer eyelids, pet, and if it's a man give him one of yer big smiles. Oh, and don't forget, wiggle yer bum a wee bit as ye walk across the room. Men like that.'

Kezzie ran all the way back to Shawcross. She knew that she had to get there before the factory opened at ten. It was just a few minutes to the hour when she reached the site again. She took a couple of deep breaths and walked purposefully to the head of the queue.

'Excuse me,' she said to the people at the front, 'I have a letter to deliver.'

She rapped on the door set in the wooden gate. No one came. She tried again for longer and louder. After a pause a shutter slid back and a face appeared.

'We're not opening until ten,' a man said brusquely.

'I know,' said Kezzie pleasantly. 'It's just that I was sent with this letter.'

'Give it to me then.'

'I was told to deliver it personally,' said Kezzie firmly, pointing to the writing on the envelope. 'There's something I have to explain.' She gave the man her brightest smile and tried to appear calm.

He hesitated, then opened the door a crack. She was in!

Kezzie hurried to the office buildings. Out in the yard she heard them getting ready to open the gate. There was a door marked SECRETARY. For a second she faltered, then went past it to the one marked MANAGER. She knocked briskly and walked straight in.

There was a small bald-headed man sitting behind a desk. He was dictating to a lady who was writing in a note pad. They both looked up in surprise.

'Oh! I do beg your pardon!' said Kezzie as politely as

possible. 'I thought this would be the office for the interviews. Did I make a mistake?'

The man consulted his pocket watch.

'Goodness, it's ten o'clock already. I didn't realise.' He stood up. 'We'll continue later, Miss Dunlop. I'd better see these people right away.' He glanced out of the window to where the queue was assembling in the yard. 'Some of them have been waiting since before dawn.'

He indicated for Kezzie to sit down.

'Now what experience have you had with knitwear machines?' he asked her.

Something about his manner gave Kezzie a clue to how to react. She looked him straight in the eye.

'Absolutely none,' she stated truthfully. 'However, I do learn extremely quickly. I was intending to go to university but my father's death prevented that. I have my leaving certificate and a very good reference from my minister.' She handed him the letter.

He examined the seal closely before opening and reading it.

'Very impressive,' he said. 'It says here that you are diligent, truthful, hardworking, intelligent, punctual and of a neat and tidy appearance.' He smiled. 'Do you agree with all of this?'

'Yes,' said Kezzie.

The manager laughed out loud.

'How could I not employ you?' he asked. He took a card and wrote her details down. 'You start on Monday. The shift is eight o'clock until five-thirty, with an hour for lunch. Tea is for sale but not food, so bring sandwiches.'

Kezzie stood up.

'Thank you very much,' she said.

'Don't you want to know what the wage is?' the manager asked her.

She blushed and sat down again quickly.

'You will start on the coarse knitting at fifteen shillings each week, and if you show promise you might progress to fine knitting.' He consulted a sheet. 'Fine knitting pays seventeen and sixpence.'

Kezzie's eyes brimmed. Seventeen and sixpence! What she could do with seventeen and sixpence! She was going to show the most promise of any person on the whole factory floor.

'Thank you again,' she said. She paused. Something had just occurred to her. It was worth a try. Boldness had got her this far already, and she sensed that he was sympathetic.

'Is it possible,' she enquired, 'for me to have an advance against my first pay?'

He stopped with his pen in mid-air and regarded the girl in front of him. He had noted the cheap suit and the make-up, and her feet sliding out of the too large shoes. He was sure that she had tricked herself in first this morning in some way. She was very thin and had a barely concealed desperation about her. But she was also striking-looking and determined and he could see the spirit shining out of her. He might probably never see her or the money again, he thought ruefully.

'I can advance you five shillings,' he said, and marked it on her card. 'Give this to Miss Dunlop and she will give you the money and file your card. Congratulations, Miss

Munro, you are our very first employee.'

Kezzie stood up. She had to control a sudden urge to run round the other side of the desk and kiss the factory manager on the top of his shiny balding head.

Instead she took her card demurely and went to see the secretary.

She completely forgot to wiggle her bum.

CHAPTER 14

A trip to the seaside

Kezzie skipped home like a child out of school. She went to Bella's to tell her the news and give her back her clothes.

'No, no, you hang on to them,' Bella insisted. 'You've set a standard, now you'll have to keep it up.'

Kezzie stopped at the village shop to get sweets for Lucy, dolly mixtures, aniseed balls and liquorice. She bought tobacco for her grandfather, and for herself a bar of scented soap. As her goods piled up on the counter she sobered up a little and asked for corned beef, condensed milk and some other basics to see them through the week.

Almost immediately there was an incredible change of atmosphere in their caravan. The prospect of a weekly income removed the spectre of starvation which had hovered in their company now for many weeks. Lucy sang as she set the table or washed the dishes. Grandad smiled more often. Kezzie couldn't believe it was all her imagination because she, too, felt as if a burden she had not known she was carrying had been lifted from her shoulders.

Spring came very slowly. The weather was wild for days on end as Kezzie walked to Shawcross and back each day. She didn't mind at all. Wrapped in a huge mackintosh, which had belonged to Bella's husband, Kezzie would willingly have trudged double the distance. She liked the factory. The girls were pleasant and it was good to have company of her own age each day. She was quick and deft at her work and concentrated more than the others, and she soon progressed to the fine knitting, which was easier as you could sit rather than stand. She enjoyed the noise and the bustle even though she was tired with working long hours. She had bought Lucy an almost-new coat and had actually started putting some money away in a savings account.

At the farm the lambing had started and Grandad was getting some work again from the farmer. They were eating better, mince and stews rather than the daily soup and potatoes. Kezzie started to teach Lucy to bake and they had great fun with scones so badly burnt that even the birds would not eat them.

One Thursday night as Kezzie was about to leave work, the manager stopped her.

'Miss Munro,' he said, 'Miss Dunlop's assistant is off ill and we have the wages to make up. Would it be possible for you to wait on?'

Kezzie thought quickly. It would probably mean extra pay, and she could treat herself to a bus ride from Shawcross to the village and not be home any later.

She nodded and took her coat off.

'The floor supervisor says that you are an intelligent girl,' said the manager. 'Have you ever done work like this before?'

'No,' said Kezzie sitting herself down at the table, 'but I –'

'– learn very quickly,' the manager finished for her.

They all laughed.

'One day,' he went on, 'you must tell me how you bluffed your way in here first on the interview day.'

Kezzie's face went red and she bent her head and busied herself sealing the wage packets as fast as she could. They finished within an hour or so and he gave her five shillings for overtime. On the way out Miss Dunlop walked with her to the bus stop.

'My assistant is thinking of leaving in the near future. She is to be married in a few months. I wondered if you would be interested in the position? You would require training, but there are classes for shorthand and typing and books you can study. It would be a wonderful opportunity for you.'

A wonderful opportunity, thought Kezzie, on the way home. Yes, it was, and she knew it, but there was a faint feeling of disappointment as well. If she trained as a secretary then she was saying farewell to any chance of becoming a doctor. It was ridiculous to hold that dream still. She was being greedy. Not so long ago she had no job and barely enough food, now she was being offered something many would trade places with her for.

She was still unsettled on the day for the works' outing. The firm had hired a bus so that all workers and their families could go. Kezzie was glad to have a day out. It would serve Lucy instead of the annual Sunday school outing. She just could not bear to imagine Lucy, Grandad and herself going on that trip without her father. She had decided that they would be busy with something else that day.

Lucy hardly slept the night before, asking questions every two minutes. How far away is the sea? Will we be on the bus for a long time? Can I make a sandcastle? Eventually Kezzie threatened to leave her behind if she opened her mouth again.

The next day everyone made a pet of her. Even the usually austere Miss Dunlop took Lucy on her knee and pointed things out to her through the window as they passed by.

'Your sister is a beautiful child,' she told Kezzie as they climbed off the bus.

Kezzie looked to where Lucy was running ahead, pulling Grandad along in her excitement. She *was* very pretty, Kezzie thought, with her blonde curls and blue, blue eyes, but she was still quite thin from the winter, her little body almost frail. And she was so trusting, she would go with anyone, a child unaware of any badness in the world. She must stay that way as long as possible. Time enough for her to come to Kezzie's realisation of the grimness of ordinary existence.

They went on to the sands with their picnics.

'What is it?' asked Lucy in amazement. 'What is it?'

'It's the sea,' said Kezzie, laughing at the wonderment on Lucy's face. 'It's the sea.'

'Come on,' said Grandad. He had taken off his socks

and shoes and rolled up his trousers. 'We'll go for a paddle.'

'It keeps moving, Kezzie,' Lucy informed her sister when she came back after about half an hour. 'It moves all the time.'

They had a glorious day. It was warm and sunny and they ate ice-cream and rode on the donkeys, and made sand pies and jumped the waves until they were exhausted. While Grandad and Lucy packed up their things in a bag, Kezzie walked along the beach by herself. Her bare feet sank into the cool sand. The sun was beginning to go down and the sky was green and cream and gold. She breathed in and faced seawards. What was out there, far away where she could not see? Ireland, Michael's home, America, then far far away India and Africa. That was where she was going some day. She would do the secretarial work just now, but she would not give up her dream. She touched her silver locket without knowing it.

On the bus going home they ate chips and the men drank beer. The driver had the headlights on as darkness came down and as they roared along the country roads, someone started a sing-song. Lucy fell asleep on Grandad's knee.

The bus dropped them at the end of the lane and they carried Lucy home in the gloaming and put her to bed. There was sand in her shoes and in her hair and ears. Kezzie decided she could wait until the morning for a wash.

Grandad made some tea and they sat by the fire drinking it and talking softly.

'I think I've spent all our savings,' lamented Kezzie.

'It was worth it,' said her grandfather. 'Did you see the wean's face when I sat her on that donkey and took her for a wee trot around?'

'She must have had about nine rides up and down,' said Kezzie. 'The man was letting her on for nothing at the end. And the ice-cream we ate! Oysters and nougat wavers. No wonder I don't have any money left.'

'Don't you worry too much about the money,' said her grandfather. 'I've got good news for you. I was talking to your manager fellow and he says he might be able to fix me up with a job with a friend of his in Glasgow.'

CHAPTER 15

The royal connection

Absolutely nothing, thought Kezzie, could have made her more happy than the expression on her grandfather's face some weeks later when he came back from Glasgow and said: 'I've got a job.'

She had watched him walking down the lane and knew even before he spoke that his news was good. His back seemed straighter and he was swinging his arms.

She brewed some tea as he sat down. Lucy climbed on to his knee and he tucked her into the crook of his arm and began to fill his pipe.

'Come on, tell us,' begged Kezzie.

'It's a proper job,' he said, drawing slowly and making the tobacco glow, 'but I'm not telling you too much about it because I'm planning a wee surprise.'

No matter how much both of them coaxed him in the days which followed he revealed very little. Kezzie knew that he must be at his trade again because he spoke of tools and engineering equipment. She marvelled at the change in him now he felt he had a purpose in life again.

His shoulders and arms filled out and there was colour in his face. He was more cheerful both with them and with his cronies whom he had avoided in their bad times. It was so unfair, thought Kezzie, when he needed friends the most he had been ashamed to be seen with thread-bare trousers and no money for tobacco or beer.

Finally one weekend, he told them to get ready as they were going to Glasgow.

'Put on your best clothes,' he said. 'I'm taking you to meet royalty.'

Royalty? thought Kezzie as she dressed Lucy with white ankle socks and buckled her new sandals. She remembered Matt McPhee and his mother telling their fortunes.

'There's a royal connection in your life,' she had told her grandfather.

Lucy bounced up and down on the bus seat as they travelled the six or so miles to Glasgow. As the bus entered the city it passed through some very dirty streets with tenement buildings blocking the sun, and ragged children playing in the gutters. Kezzie looked away. She hated to see the children so ill-kempt. It made her uneasy. It must be so much worse, she thought, to be poor in a great city. At least in the country they had fresh air and sunlight.

They went on a tram. For Kezzie and Lucy it was the first time. It made a tremendous noise and seemed to travel at a great speed, although as she watched the houses sliding by she realised they were not going so fast as it appeared. Lucy was scared. She hung on to Grandad as the conductor punched their tickets, rang the bell and called the stops. They passed Queen's Dock and Yorkhill Quay, where the Anchor Line ships came and went across the Atlantic. Through Yoker to Clydebank, past Rothesay Dock and then they stopped at John Brown's shipyard.

'The Clyde,' declared Grandad. He pointed to the great grey mass of water which breathed life and hope into workers and their families, a prospect of employment, of pay and food, but more than that, of a pride in something. A job well done, a mission completed, a statement made.

'There she lies,' said Grandad, 'my queen.'

He had taken them through the shipyard gate and they stood a little way off gazing at the huge hull of an ocean-going liner. She was immense. The vastness of her loomed over the little family. The gantries and scaffolding were petty fripperies to be cast aside before her launch. She had a power and a presence that belonged to her alone, a queen indeed.

'I'm on the engineering side of it,' Grandad explained. 'When they got this contract, due to the recession they were actually short of skilled workers. I've got a squad of lads under me. She's due to be launched in the autumn, but even then I'll still be involved in the fitting out.'

He was so proud, Kezzie thought. Proud of his work. Proud of the ship, and of the workers and the skill it took to build something such as this. Only four years before the *Queen Mary*, the first ship over 75,000 tons, had been launched in 1934 from Clydebank. When this one was completed it would be the largest liner in the world. And he was proud of them too, Kezzie realised, as he introduced them to various people he knew on the site.

'My son's bairns,' he said. 'The wee one's awful bonny, and the older one, she's bonny too, and has brains as well. Got herself a good job, good prospects, fine thing for a woman today.'

In the second part of the day they visited the Empire Exhibition at Bellahouston Park in Glasgow. Kezzie had heard about it on the radio in the factory. She'd listened with the rest of the girls to the recording of King George VI's speech from Ibrox Park, and the commentary on the royal couple's progress through the Pavilions. According to the reporter, Queen Elizabeth had purchased two Shirley Temple dolls for the little princesses, Elizabeth and Margaret Rose.

Kezzie and Lucy and Grandad got off the tram at Mosspark Boulevard and went through the turnstile. The exhibition was quite spectacular. They went to the Palace of Engineering first, as this was what Grandad wanted to see. There were models of dams, bridges and ships, as well as domestic appliances.

'Look at that, Kezzie,' said Grandad, 'a machine that can do the washing for you, while you read a magazine.'

'That'll be the day,' Kezzie laughed.

They wandered round the park. They saw Canadian Mounties and a copy of the Victoria Falls in Africa with a model train travelling beneath the water. Lucy was fascinated with the fountains, she kept running to trail her fingers in the water. They stopped at the bandstand and sat on the green folding chairs where they could listen to the music while eating lunch. Grandad made Lucy a paper boat and she went to sail it in the lake. Kezzie looked around her. The music was playing a lively march and there seemed to her to be a lot of smartly dressed people about, chatting and smiling.

'Do you think things are getting better?' she asked her grandfather. 'Maybe folk have more work now, with all this building.'

'I don't know,' he said. 'Rearmament's a false salvation, whether you agree with the war or not. The world's changing and Scotland's not keeping up. Engineering skills and tools will have to progress or we'll slump again. I suppose that conditions will improve as the government places defence contracts, but what a price to pay for employment. War will come, unless someone sorts that bully Hitler out in his own back yard, and then . . .'

Kezzie shivered in the sun. She didn't like to think about war. It was only twenty years since the last one had ended. Her grandad rarely spoke of it. A carnage, she had heard him say once. War didn't belong here, with mothers pushing prams and couples strolling hand in hand, and the sound of children's excited screams from the amusement park. Earlier they had visited the Peace Pavilion. Perhaps it was significant that it was a small wooden building tucked away from the main exhibition.

They collected Lucy from the lake and spent the rest of the afternoon in the Amusement Park. They saw Indian dancers and a magician and persuaded Grandad to have a ride on the mountain switchback railway. When they came out it was dark. The fountains were still playing but were floodlit in changing colours of red, blue, green and yellow. They could see the coloured cascades running down either side of the hill. Above it all, like a beacon of hope, rose Tait's Tower, the Tower of Empire. The silverised steel shaft glittered in the brilliant floodlights and its three observation balconies were edged with red, green and yellow light.

It was an unforgettable sight and they gazed at it for many minutes before turning for home.

CHAPTER 16

The accident

Kezzie adapted to working in the factory office very well and Miss Dunlop was pleased with her. She had a good memory and more and more she was being left to work on her own. The firm had an insurance scheme for non-manual workers and as the money was taken from her wages each week before she received them, Kezzie hardly noticed the loss. Because of this, and Grandad's steady employment, Kezzie had peace of mind and for the first time in a long while she felt safe.

As their fortunes improved and the summer faded she and Grandad began to discuss leaving the caravan and finding better accommodation for the winter.

'We could try for one of these new houses the council are building just outside Shawcross,' said Grandad. 'Now that we're on regular wages we would manage the rent.'

Grandad was obviously well thought of in the ship-yard – respected by men and managers alike. The foreman had called him aside one day and enquired if he would be willing to travel to Edinburgh with a group of other workers for a special job the following week.

'We'll wait until you come back before looking for a house,' said Kezzie as she saw him off at the bus station in Shawcross. She would be sorry to leave the caravan with its cosy familiarity but the thought of living in a house again with proper washing facilities and space to move about in appealed to her.

It was Friday and as she finished work with her pay in her pocket she felt light-hearted at the prospect of a weekend with just her and Lucy in the caravan. She would take the bus tonight, she decided. It would be quicker, then they would have time to do some baking. They would go for a walk and pick flowers and maybe stay up late and make toast by the fire. Sunday, they would visit Bella who was laid up with 'flu.

There was light drizzle falling as she boarded the bus, not enough to dampen Kezzie's spirits, but just enough, she realised later, to make the roads slippery and dangerous. It was a single-decker. She sat at the front and wrote a shopping list for tomorrow.

She looked up as the bus approached the crossroads at the edge of town. Kezzie heard the driver curse. Crossing slowly, and directly in front of them, was a dray pulled by a Clydesdale. Kezzie gasped and gripped her seat as the driver braked hard. On the wet road the bus skidded and the last thing Kezzie could recall was the red brick wall rushing towards her.

Lucy had walked to the end of the lane and back hundreds of times, she thought. She was hungry and it was getting cooler and still Kezzie did not come. It was going to be special tonight, Kezzie had promised her, with Grandad away. Lucy had changed into her old clothes, greased the griddle and set the table and washed her hands twice, and still Kezzie was not home.

She looked up and down the road and then very cautiously stepped out into the middle. She was forbidden to go any further than the end of the lane on her own, but would it do any harm to walk just a little way along and see if she could spot Kezzie coming? She made up her mind to go. After all, when she met Kezzie she could help carry the shopping. She ran back to put on her coat and taking her doll for company she set off down the road.

'Is it right or left?' Lucy asked her doll as they reached the road junction. She gazed up at the signpost. The black letters were all worn away with the wind and rain and anyway one of the arms pointed into a field. 'That's silly, isn't it?' said Lucy. She lifted her doll so its mouth was at her ear and pretended to listen to what it was saying. Then with great determination she started down the road on the left. Behind her the signpost pointed the way to Glasgow.

She HAD to meet Kezzie on the road, she told the doll, after she had walked a few miles. There was no other way to go. She held the doll up in her arms so that she would be able to see Kezzie first. After another twenty minutes or so her arms got tired and she tucked the doll inside her coat and buttoned it up. A breakdown van towing a bus with a smashed windscreen passed her slowly. The driver called to her: 'Are you all right, little girl?'

'Yes,' said Lucy. 'I'm going to meet my sister.'

The man waved and drove on.

Eventually Lucy saw a scattering of houses on the road. She had no sense of how far she had come or indeed where she was, only a fixed idea in her mind that if she kept on walking she would meet Kezzie. Perhaps she could ask at one of the houses if anyone had seen her sister. As she approached a big black and tan dog ran at her and started barking. She hurried off, further into the city. Very soon she was completely lost and although she had decided to walk back to the caravan she did not know which road to take. It was getting dark and the streets where she wandered became mean and dingy. She sat down on the edge of a pavement and tried hard not to cry.

'Are you lost, hen?' a wheezing voice asked.

Lucy looked up. An old woman with a black shawl was bending over her. She was very smelly, Lucy thought, and didn't appear to have any teeth at all. Lucy would normally have found this quite funny but at the moment she was too concerned with her sore legs and empty stomach.

She hesitated. She shouldn't speak to someone she did not know, but there was no one else about.

'A little bit,' she admitted.

'Aw, ma poor wee lamb.' The old woman sat down beside her and began to finger Lucy's coat. 'That's a lovely coat you've got on,' she said, 'but I can see it's a wee bittie too small for you. Would you like a new one?'

Lucy looked at the sleeves on her coat. It *was* getting

too small for her now, but she hadn't dared mention it to Kezzie because she had already had a new cardigan and skirt for going back to school. Was it greedy to want so much?

'And yer boots,' the woman was untying the laces, 'are yer wee toes pinched in them boots?'

Lucy nodded.

'I thought as much,' said the woman gently,' you just slip them off and hand them to me. There's a shop at the end of the road where they change things for ye.'

Lucy hesitated.

'Here's a barley sugar for ye tae suck while yer waiting,' the woman wheedled.

That decided it. By this time Lucy was very hungry. She grasped the barley-sugar stick in one hand and with her doll in the other, sat down to wait for the old lady's return from this magic shop where you could get new clothes for old ones.

An hour passed and it became very dark and Lucy began to realize that the old woman was not coming back. There were people passing by staring at her, rough people who shouted and swore. She got up and stumbled on.

It was very late and the pubs were emptying their last regulars into the streets. She paused outside one as the door swung open and jammed. She could see lights and warmth and she wanted more than anything to be back in her own home. A man came towards her with a bottle in his hand.

'Hallo, pet,' he asked kindly. 'Are ye waitin' for yer da?'

'My daddy's dead,' said Lucy.

'That's a shame, yer ma then?'

'She's dead too,' said Lucy sadly.

The man burst into tears. Lucy stared at him. She had never seen a man crying before.

'That's a terrible shame,' he sobbed. He took a drink from his bottle and then handed it to her. 'Here,' he offered generously, 'this'll cheer ye up.'

Lucy drank some of the tea-coloured liquid. It burned her throat, but quite soon she did feel better.

'Would you help me find my way home?' she asked him.

'Certainly.' He waved his arms about. 'Just point me in the right direction. I can always find my way home.'

'I don't know the direction,' said Lucy, her voice wavering.

The man put his arm around her shoulder. 'Come over here and sit down and tell me how you got here, and then we'll work out how to get back.'

The two of them sat down with their backs to the pub wall. Lucy sipped some more of the cold tea, and told the man her story. When she had finished she turned to ask him to take her home. He was fast asleep!

She stood up, uncertain what to do next. Maybe he wasn't well and she should ask someone for help. She herself was beginning to feel very unwell. She staggered down the road, trailing her doll by one arm.

CHAPTER 17

Where is Lucy?

Kezzie was walking in fog. It drifted and swirled about her and she couldn't see in front of her at all. She must sit down and rest. She was very tired. Her head ached so badly and she knew that there was something important which she must remember. There were reports to file, and order forms to make up. Miss Dunlop would be cross with her if she didn't finish them.

Miss Dunlop was cross with Kezzie, very cross indeed.

'This is the third day she has not turned up for work,' she snapped at the manager. 'These young people have no sense of responsibility. I trained up that other girl then she decides to get married, and now this . . .'

The manager tapped his pen slowly on the edge of the desk.

'It's not like her, you know, not Miss Munro. Even if she was ill I would have thought she would have sent a note.' He paused. 'I think I'll give the shipyard where her grandfather works a ring and enquire.'

Fifteen minutes later he came through to Miss Dunlop's desk.

'They say he's gone to the east coast for a week's work, and as far as they know the girls were fine when he left. They say he's always talking about them so they're sure he would have mentioned if they'd been ill.'

They both looked at each other.

'We'll take a run out to where she lives in your car after work tonight,' said Miss Dunlop briskly, 'and find out what's what.'

Far from finding out what was what, their visit to the caravan only worried them further. The door was ajar, the table set for tea but the fire was out and the place was cold.

'The police station, I think,' said Miss Dunlop, pulling on her gloves. Her hands shook a little. She would never have admitted it but she had developed a real fondness for Kezzie, and was now very concerned that something quite awful had happened to her and the child.

An hour later they were in the cottage hospital.

'We had no means of identifying her,' the doctor told them, 'and no one came forward to report her missing. Any bag which she may have been carrying was not recovered from the wreck. She's actually lucky to be alive.'

'Is she very bad?' asked Miss Dunlop, gripping her bag tightly.

'It's hard to say. She's severely concussed. She could be that way for months, or wake up tomorrow.'

Miss Dunlop came out of the hospital with the factory

manager. She stopped with her hand on the handle of the car door.

'Where,' she said, 'I wonder, is Lucy?'

'LUCY,' repeated the lady in the white starched apron. She wrote it in the orphanage register. She smiled at the small waif with the stained clothes and tangled hair in front of her. 'And you can't remember your second name?'

Lucy shook her head. She couldn't remember anything at this moment. It had taken an hour of coaxing to get her to say her first name. She couldn't remember how she got here or where her coat and shoes were. The policeman, who had found her wandering drunk beside the river at three o'clock in the morning, had never seen such a terrified child before.

Her mother and father were both dead, at least they had established that, and she had obviously been deliberately abandoned by whoever was supposed to be looking after her. It was a disgrace, thought the nurse. Children always suffered the most in a depression. She would have to give her a second name. She recalled where they had found the child. 'Clyde,' she added in the book.

'Come on now, Lucy Clyde,' she said gently, 'and we'll give you a nice bath and some warm soup.'

'You've got room for her then,' said the policeman, glad that the problem was now someone else's.

'Actually, we haven't,' said the matron. 'We're full to bursting. But there's a group of orphans being emigrated to Canada at the end of the week, and if she's not claimed by then we might manage to squeeze her in.'

'Where in Canada do they go?' asked the policeman.

'All over,' said the matron. 'They are sent to Receiving Houses in various places and then placed in good homes. I've had letters from there, and Australia and New Zealand. Lots of children now have whole new families, and are enjoying open spaces and sunshine.'

'Wish it was me,' said the policeman, snapping shut his notebook.

Miss Dunlop visited Kezzie in the hospital the next day. Kezzie's grandfather arrived as she sat by the bedside. She spoke to him of her concern for Lucy.

'Don't worry,' he said, 'Aunt Bella will have her.' He placed his hand on Kezzie's forehead. 'Come on now, Kezzie,' he said, 'you've slept long enough.'

Kezzie could feel the mist clearing slowly from around her. She felt warmer. The sun must be shining and, better still, her headache was less severe. She opened her eyes. It was very bright, and she was not outside as she had imagined but in a room lying down in bed. Her grandad was there, and Miss Dunlop. She wanted to laugh, they looked so serious. She smiled at them.

'I'm all right,' she said. Then she remembered her dream and the thing she had been trying so hard to recall. 'Is Lucy with you, Grandad?'

Kezzie became like a person demented. She discharged herself from the hospital immediately, despite the doctor's dire warnings. When she eventually realised that Lucy had not been seen for days her distress was profound. They went from house to house in the village and then started a search of Shawcross.

'A child that age, wandering off,' said the sergeant at the police station, 'anything could happen to her. She could fall in a burn or go away across the peats. We might never find her.'

Kezzie clenched her fists and tried not to scream. It was all she could do to control herself. She felt like running up and down the streets shouting wildly.

'Or the tinkers,' the sergeant went on, 'taking a child's the sort of thing they would do.'

'They would NEVER do something like that,' said Kezzie angrily. She was just about to say something very rude when her grandfather came running in.

'One of the bus drivers at the garage saw a little girl walking on the road to Glasgow last Friday. She told him she was going to meet her sister.'

'Glasgow!' cried Kezzie. 'Glasgow!'

'She must have taken the wrong turn at the road end,' said Grandad. He turned to the sergeant. 'Can you check with the Glasgow police, if any child has turned up there?'

By evening they were speaking to the matron of the children's home.

'I don't understand how you can do something like that.' Kezzie was in tears. 'She's halfway to Canada with a different name and her own family don't know.'

'To us she was an abandoned child,' said the matron defensively. 'Lots of children have been sent out over the years. Very few go now, but it gave many a good start in life. We have letters from them telling us how well their new families treat them. We were doing it for the best.'

'If I get a passage right away,' said Kezzie as she and Grandad walked down the High street, 'I'll only be days behind her when she lands and I should catch up with her easily enough over there.'

'It's a big country,' said her grandad doubtfully. 'You can't go alone.'

Kezzie turned to face him among the crowds of people which, as always in cities, seemed to be hurrying by.

'Grandad, you know that I have to go. There is no other way to be absolutely sure of bringing her back. She will be terrified and she needs me with her as quickly as possible.' Kezzie stopped, her eyes brimming with tears. 'You also know,' she went on, 'that it's best you stay here and keep on your job, for us to have something to come back to.' They walked on in silence.

Kezzie pawned everything she had, and gave the tickets to Bella. It didn't come to much, she thought, as she counted the money into her purse. She would need every penny, not just for her passage, but also for whatever travelling she might have to do in Canada. So, she only hesitated for a second when the pawnbroker, eying her carefully, said, 'I'll give you two and six for that silver locket you're wearing.'

'Three shillings,' said Kezzie, unfastening it and placing it on the counter.

The factory had a collection which the manager and Miss Dunlop made up to fifty pounds. Kezzie was speechless.

'I can't guarantee you the same position when you return,' said the manager, 'but you'll get the first vacancy on the floor.'

At the dockside her grandad kept wiping his face with his handkerchief as they said goodbye.

Eventually Kezzie said, 'Grandad, I'm going aboard now, and I'm going below deck so don't stay to wave me off.'

They kissed and hugged each other and as they separated Kezzie saw, striding towards her, the tall dark-haired figure of Michael Donohoe.

He wrapped his arms around her.

'I went to visit you all, and I met Bella who told me of your misfortune. Kezzie, I wish I was going with you.'

'Why don't you?' asked Kezzie. 'You said you wanted to emigrate.'

He avoided her gaze for a moment.

'Things did not go as well as I had hoped in London . . . and, well, I've joined up.'

'The army?' Kezzie was aghast.

He shrugged. 'There's a war coming, and it's regular pay with meals.'

The ship's hooter sounded. Kezzie lifted her case.

'I've something for you,' said Michael quickly. 'Some sandwiches.' He pushed a brown paper parcel into her bag. 'And . . . I got one of your Colleen Bawn tickets from Bella.' He opened his fist and in it lay Kezzie's locket.

Kezzie drew her breath in.

'Michael,' she said softly.

He shifted his feet uncomfortably. 'Now, you be sure and find her,' he said.

'Oh, I shall find her,' said Kezzie. 'I shall cross the sea and travel the land until I do. I shall search all Canada for her. In every town and village I shall look for her. And I *will* find her,' she stopped and then went on, 'and when I have, then I will bring her home.'

PART TWO
Canada

CHAPTER 18

A game of chess

Lucy thought she had died and gone to a bad place. She had not been good enough for the angels to take her to Mummy and Daddy in Heaven. She was in a little wooden coffin with a lid which she could reach up above her head and touch, and it kept heaving up and down, up and down. She gripped her dolly desperately. She was going to be sick.

Kezzie waited until they had left the Tail o' the Bank before she opened Michael's brown paper parcel. She should have known, she thought, as she gazed at the money. Ten and five pound notes spilled on to her lap. There was a note laboriously scribed by someone not accustomed to writing letters.

'My Dear Kezzie please take this money to find Lucy and do not be so proud as not to use it. Who knows what might happen on the other side of the water. Money opens doors. I know this and I also know I love you. Your friend Michael.'

Kezzie saw the horizon through a blur of tears. She stayed on deck a long time and watched Scotland growing smaller and the sun setting before going to her cabin.

The next day was calm and beautiful and people strolled about on deck. Kezzie spoke to no one. She had cried herself to sleep last night, with the thought of Lucy, travelling steerage, frightened and alone. She could not cope with company just now, and was not inclined to make idle chat. She waited until the dining-room was almost empty before taking her meals, and always sought the most isolated part of the ship to sit with her book and read. She was not the only person doing this, she noticed after several days. A young man with sandy hair and the beginnings of a moustache often came last to eat, usually accompanied by an older woman. It wasn't difficult to also notice that he walked with a limp – an iron calliper clamped his left leg just below the knee of his plus-fours and reached to his ankle. He took to nodding across to Kezzie each day and finally she conceded his presence with a small wave.

The sea was rougher and the waves higher as the days passed and autumn came with cold rain which lashed the deck and sent most people below. Eventually even Kezzie gave up and entered the small non-smoking lounge with her rain-soaked book in her hand. Her friend from the dining-room was sitting at a table playing himself at chess. The lady was doing some crochet. Kezzie studied his game from her seat a little way off. As he reached to move the white bishop she drew in her breath. He looked up quickly.

'Do you play?' he asked in surprise.

'Why not?' asked Kezzie at once.

'Why not indeed?' he laughed. 'Would you play me?'

The woman looked over with a slight frown on her face.

'Sorry, I should have introduced us. This is my mother, Mrs Fitzwilliam, and I am William James Fitzwilliam.'

Kezzie held out her hand.

'I am Kezzie Munro, from Stonevale,' she said.

The older woman hesitated for the smallest second before taking her hand.

'My husband is Sir Gerald Fitzwilliam,' she said distinctly, 'from Close Manor near Derby.'

Lady Fitzwilliam then detached her hand from Kezzie's and took up her crochet.

'What kind of name is Kezzie, my dear?' she enquired very politely, after a moment.

Kezzie felt slightly crushed, as this woman had no doubt intended, she thought. She could feel her face redden and her temper rise.

'It is a Biblical name,' she replied, equally courteously. 'Keziah was one of the daughters of Job, if you are familiar with that story.'

'Oh, well played, Kezzie!' cried William enthusiastically. 'I knew when I first spotted you that you had a fine spirit. Just ignore Ma,' he went on, 'she is a dreadful old snob. I am trying to educate her out of it.' He patted his mother affectionately on the head and took his place again at the table.

Kezzie was appalled at such cheek and looked anxiously at Lady Fitzwilliam. To her surprise she was smiling.

'You are an impertinent young man,' she said fondly to her son. She turned to Kezzie. 'One has to be very careful these days, especially on Atlantic crossings. All sorts of people travel abroad now.'

William laughed again.

'See what I mean?' he said. 'She probably suspects you of being a "New Woman". You don't smoke or drink or drive a car or anything?'

'No,' said Kezzie.

'Drat!' said William, snapping his fingers. 'I've been waiting all my life to meet a fast woman.'

'William James!' cried his mother. 'Don't use such language.'

'OK, OK,' he replied. 'Now,' he said to Kezzie, 'shall I take a handicap?'

'Whatever for?' said Kezzie, as she arranged the pieces on the board.

Three hours later they agreed on a draw. Thank you, Grandad, Kezzie said silently as they went into dinner.

William was cheerful and kind and as the weather worsened and his mother stayed more in her cabin, the two of them walked the decks together, or played chess in the lounge. She told him of her mission and he explained that they were travelling to America via Canada to seek treatment for his leg which was wasting below the knee.

Kezzie viewed the heavy iron brace with distaste.

'Do you need that thing on all the time?' she asked him one day. 'It must weigh you down and surely prevent development. Perhaps if you removed it from time to time and exercised your muscles, it would help.'

'You are a very clever girl,' he replied, 'and if you promise not to tell Ma I'll let you into a secret.' He showed her the top of the calliper. 'I got the village blacksmith to fit this like so,' and with a little tap the brace fell apart. 'Now, I have been doing exercises to build up my strength, but Ma would have a fit. She thinks I would collapse completely if this contraption was removed.'

It was the sort of thing that would have intrigued Grandad, thought Kezzie, as William put the parts together again. Anything requiring skill in metalwork interested him. Grandad . . . he seemed so far away, Scotland and Stonevale, and Bella and the rest.

A week passed and Kezzie was grateful for William's company. He seemed to sense when she needed time by herself to think, and when she was low his bright conversations cheered her immensely.

One morning she was awakened early by the sound of the ship's foghorn. She dressed warmly and went on deck. A dense white fog surrounded the ship. The foghorn sounded again mournfully, as the ship moved forward.

'We're nearing Newfoundland,' said William appearing beside her, rubbing his hands together.

The fog swirled eerily obscuring sea and sky and deadening sound.

'Look!' said Kezzie.

A massive shape half-hidden in the mist loomed beside the ship.

'An iceberg!' said William.

They heard the sailors call immediately, and the

foghorn sounded once more. They continued their slow progress as the iceberg made its stately departure off the starboard bow. It was a magnificent sight and the sense of danger seemed to thrill William. Kezzie fretted all day, aware of the time she was losing.

At last they entered the Gulf of St Lawrence and she calmed herself. Now she could actually see Canada. They would sail up the St Lawrence River tomorrow, and then her search would really begin.

CHAPTER 19

Lucy arrives in Canada

The ship Lucy was in had fared much worse in the crossing. It had pitched and rolled and Lucy had retched so much that she didn't care any more about being made to go to sleep in a coffin. On the few occasions she had been taken on deck she had been very frightened. Why was there water all around? Where was the beach, with sand and the donkeys? Far out at sea the movement of the boat on the surface of the ocean was unlike anything Lucy had ever experienced before. These were not the gentle waters that had lapped around her ankles when she had splashed on the shoreline on the summer outing. The water was grey and roaring and angry. It slid past the rails and heaved the deck about so that she could scarcely keep her balance as the ship tilted and dipped.

The lady who was in charge of them was seasick for most of the journey, and the older children, who were supposed to look after Lucy, teased and made fun of her. One boy, in particular, pushed into her at mealtimes and stole her food.

She was frightened of the sailors who tried to be kind to her. They spoke with words she did not know and they had strange red and blue drawings on their arms.

As they neared the coast the ship was trapped in pack ice for several days, moving forward slowly by degrees as the crew tried to keep the propellors free. The bitter cold was something she was not used to. Her clothes were thin and inadequate and she shivered hopelessly. It was a distressed sick little girl who disembarked from the ship in Canada.

As they filed into the Immigration shed Lucy was aware of only one thing. Although she had no idea where in the world she was, she knew she was very far away from her grandad, Kezzie and their snug caravan.

Alexander Dalgleish had been processing immigrants for many years now. As he surveyed the long shambling queue of people it seemed to him that on some days every nation on earth filed past him. He rubbed the back of his neck and eased his aching muscles. It would soon be the weekend. He would get away out of the crowded city to his cabin deep in the pine woods. A little fishing and a trek in the forest under the stars and he would feel better. It must be in the blood, he thought. His grandfather had been one of the original Nor'Westers, who had opened up the vast track of the Canadian Shield. Forced to quit Scotland, he had arrived in the unknown continent and become one of the fur traders that had paddled and portaged their way up rivers and across lakes to map out the Canadian interior. Explorers, whose adventuring spirit had chartered waterfalls and mountains and left as their legacy their names on maps for ever. He felt that this inheritance was what had made Canada the way it was. A vibrant nation, a people more at ease outdoors, dynamic and friendly.

And now? The Old World and the New World merged before him. New hopefuls arriving on every ship, with talent to offer and a prospect of a chance to use it.

He frowned as he caught sight of the group of children. The Great Depression had lessened the welcoming attitude to immigrants as people were afraid there would not be so much for native-born Canadians. Also, Canadian law had been tightened up over the last few years, with different regulations being passed in order to protect the welfare of child immigrants. Still, it might be a better life here for some of the poor waifs he had seen. Some sun and good farm feeding would give them a new start in life.

When the children cleared Immigration they joined up with another group who had come in on a Liverpool ship. There was a quick conference between the two women who were escorting the children.

'They have to be regrouped and sent to different places,' said the Liverpool escort.

'I must spend the night here and then go to Carrville at the Lakes,' said the woman who had been with Lucy's group. 'And I am heartily glad, I can tell you. I was ill, absolutely ill, on that dreadful boat.'

The other woman consulted her papers. 'I don't believe it! All the way to British Columbia, and the train's due to leave.' She looked around her crossly. 'Where are they?

Right, gather up your belongings,' she snapped at the children.

The women sorted out the certificates and papers.

'Hurry UP,' commanded the woman who was now Lucy's escort, 'or we'll miss the train.'

A train? Lucy thought she would only get more lost if she went on a train. She knew that she was being taken further and further away from where she belonged. Crowds of people moved all about her and made her dizzy and more confused. If only she could think for a minute and decide what to do. She sat down on her little cardboard suitcase and put her doll beside her. She would stay here and wait. That was it! If she stayed still in one place for a while she would stop being lost. It might take a little time, but Kezzie and Grandad would find her.

'Get up,' said an angry voice.

Lucy shook her head. Kezzie MUST be looking for her, she had been lost a long time. If she could remain in one place then it would make it easy for Kezzie to come and collect her.

The next moment Lucy was slapped on the side of the head so hard that she was knocked across her suitcase and onto the ground. Never in her life before had she been treated like this. Even when she had been very naughty she had only been smacked on the hand.

'When I tell you to do something, you do it.'

Lucy got slowly to her feet, utterly stunned. She put her hands to her ringing head. The woman grabbed her arm and shook her.

'Is there something the matter with you?'

Lucy stared at her, unseeing.

'Is this child dumb or what?' the woman asked of no one in particular.

'Yeh,' said the boy who had taken Lucy's food on the ship, 'she's real dumb.'

'Why do I always get the worst ones?' moaned the woman. She picked up Lucy's case and as she did so, the rag doll fell unnoticed to the ground. She took Lucy roughly by the hand. 'Follow me, all of you,' she ordered, 'and stay together.'

Alexander Dalgleish stared after them. He had seen many sights in his years in the Immigration sheds but for callous cruelty that one took some beating. He shook his head and, as he moved forward to deal with the next person in line, he noticed something lying on the stone floor. He gazed for a moment at the small crumpled object with its tangled woollen hair which lay with one arm outstretched. He turned away. Then he glanced back again.

He hesitated for a second, then he vaulted the bench, scooped up Lucy's doll and ran after the forlorn little group.

CHAPTER 20

William's accident

Kezzie could see the Canadian Red Ensign fluttering beside the Union Jack on the top of the biggest building in the harbour. She and William were right forward on the ship watching the sailors unloading from the hold. Her first impressions of the country were the huge scale of everything, and the amount of people moving about the dockside. There seemed to be a vast amount of ships of every nationality loading and unloading.

'Hold on,' said William, 'I'm going to take your picture.' He ducked under the barrier and walked backwards with his Box Brownie camera in his hand.

'Don't go too far up there, William,' called his mother who was standing a little way behind Kezzie.

'Don't fuss, Ma,' he called back. 'I'm miles away from the hold.'

He indicated the open hatch several feet away from him, and bent his head to look in the viewfinder.

What happened next took only seconds but to Kezzie it was like a drama played out before her eyes in slow motion. The load from the hold swung across high above them and, as the black shadow of it passed between her and William, something detached itself from the netting and fell.

'Smile please,' cried William. Then he was struck on the back of the neck, spun round and toppled over the side.

Kezzie reached out automatically with her hands, as she heard William's mother scream. She looked round for help. Lady Fitzwilliam had fainted. No one else had seen what had happened. Kezzie ran to the side and stared at the water. It was black and oily. There was no sign of him, only his cloth cap floating on the surface. He might be unconscious. And then she thought of something else. With that calliper on his leg he would sink like a stone.

She dragged off her jacket and skirt and, aiming at the spot where she guessed he had gone down, she dived from the rail.

Kezzie had learned to swim, as all the village children had, in the local river and canal. This water was different. It was much colder, deeper and darker. She reckoned she had one chance. If she didn't locate him the first time it would be too late. William, manacled in iron, would sink quickly. So she dived as deeply as she could, groping blindly with her hands at anything.

Her lungs were bursting and her heart was thudding. She would have to go up. She struck out wildly around her and, grabbing to the side, found the rough cloth of a tweed jacket. She had him!

He was a dead weight. She couldn't pull him up at all. In fact he was pulling her down. She manoeuvred herself under his body, and felt for the calliper. With the ends of her breath releasing into the icy water she battered the clip. It fell away and at once he started to rise.

There were coloured lights in her head, and though by now she had a firm grip on his belt, she felt herself weaken. Water trickled into the side of her mouth. She looked up, no light above. She was failing and she knew it. It had been too late – for both of them. Time drifted . . . It would have been like this in the pit, she thought . . . black . . . nothing. She closed her eyes and in the double darkness she could hear her father . . . softly . . .

'*Kezzie.*'

With the little strength she had left she kicked for the surface.

Two sailors were in the water beside them and Kezzie felt herself being lifted and William taken from her. Then she was violently sick in the bottom of a rowing boat.

On Lady Fitzwilliam's instructions they were taken to a private clinic and despite Kezzie's protests she was put to bed and made to rest. Lady Fitzwilliam entered her room a few hours later.

The older woman came and at once placed her hands over Kezzie's.

'My dear child,' she said, 'you are intelligent enough to know what William means to me. He is dearer to me than life itself. If I can ever be of assistance to you, you must tell me.'

'I need help now,' replied Kezzie. 'I must leave here at once, I have lost time already and I am so worried about my sister.'

'I know,' said Lady Fitzwilliam. 'I have already made enquires on your behalf. I went to the Receiving Home here and have discovered that a party of children stayed there and then were sent on to Carrville, near the American border.'

'Can we be sure it is the right group?' asked Kezzie.

Lady Fitzwilliam smiled triumphantly.

'I'm afraid I may have bullied them just a little,' she said.

Kezzie could imagine that only too well.

'At any rate I persuaded them to allow me to see their records. One of the children was called Lucy Clyde!'

'Lucy!' said Kezzie. She was close to Lucy.

'How do I get to Carrville?' she asked.

Lady Fitzwilliam opened her bag and took out some documents. 'I have that in hand for you. This is an aeroplane ticket which I booked on your behalf. I thought it would be much quicker than travelling by train. Also, here is a letter of recommendation,' she went on. 'It may ease your way with officials. My husband is slightly acquainted with John Buchan, the governor general. He is a Scot, you know.'

'Yes,' said Kezzie.

She packed her suitcase. William's mother had sensed that to give her money would have been insulting but had insisted on buying Kezzie some new clothes to replace those ruined in the river.

William was to stay at the clinic for a few days until the cut on his head healed. Kezzie's goodbye to William saddened her. He had become a cheerful friend which she had badly needed.

'I want you to have this.' He took a fountain pen from his pocket. 'I would like you to have something which belonged to me to remember me by.'

They looked at each other.

'I will write to you,' said Kezzie reassuringly. 'And you have my aunt's address. And your leg *will* get better.'

'If you say it will, then I believe it.' He gripped her by the shoulders. 'Good luck, Kezzie,' he said. 'Dear Kezzie, the bravest and the best.'

CHAPTER 21

Niagara Falls

When Kezzie arrived at the airfield she stared hard at the aeroplane which was to take her down to Carrville. She knew that it was thirty-odd years since two American brothers had managed to get a power-driven machine into the sky and that many advances had been made since then. But the appearance of the plane itself, when viewed up close, did not inspire confidence. One could see the joins quite clearly on the pieces of metal and the wings seemed too fragile to hold together once the engine started, and yet at the same time too heavy to allow the plane to stay airborne.

As she climbed the stair trolley to board the aircraft Kezzie remembered how daunted she had been when boarding ship in Glasgow to sail across the Atlantic. Now that seemed a minor adventure compared with actually allowing yourself to be lifted up into the air to a great height, and remain there with nothing at all above, around or below you.

She settled herself in her seat and pulled back the little

curtain to look out of the porthole. She swallowed nervously. The ground seemed far enough away already and they weren't even airborne!

The engines were switched on, and a tremendous roar filled the cabin. The plane began to shudder. Kezzie closed her eyes and gripped the arms of her seat.

'You all right, honey?' said a voice beside her.

Kezzie opened her eyes. A little old lady had taken the seat on her left.

Kezzie gave a brief smile, and then her eyes opened wider as the plane began to move forward rather bumpily towards the runway.

'First time flying, isn't it? I thought so,' said the lady who introduced herself as Janine le Pointe. 'Going down to see my folks at the Lakes. Flown dozens of times myself.' She rummaged in her handbag and brought out a bag of barley sugar sweets. 'Here, suck on one of these,' she advised.

Kezzie did as she was told and as the plane rolled faster and faster along the grass she managed one more quick peek out of the window. She gasped at what she saw. They had taken off! She, Kezzie Munro from Stonevale in Scotland, was flying in the skies above the continent of the Americas.

The plane twitched and dipped, pulled by the air currents, and then the pilot set its nose up and they climbed higher. Suddenly they were above the clouds. Despite her fear Kezzie could not stop gazing out of the window. A rumpled white carpet of cloud lay below them, and the sun shone in a sky of the clearest blue she had ever seen.

'It's unbelievable,' said Kezzie, speaking louder above the noise of the engines.

Her companion nodded.

'I always get the same thrill, every time I go up,' said Janine. 'Look now.' She pointed down where the mass of white clouds were drifting apart and they could see below them a thick forest of spruce trees with many little mirrors of lakes reflecting back at them.

They flew over checker-board fields with small farms and churches picked out in white clapboard. The city of Ottawa lay to their right as the plane headed south following the line of the St Lawrence River. The clear water flashed many feet below them. Kezzie could see the river busy with boats on this main trade artery of both Canada and America.

Kezzie explained the reason for her journey and Janine chatted to her, telling her about her family. She was a French Canadian who'd lived in Montreal all her life. Her son had married and gone to live near the shores of Lake Erie to grow grapes and produce wine.

'His wine is the best in all Canada. It has the taste of summer and the sun. We are still very French,' she said proudly.

As the plan reached the outskirts of Toronto the pilot swung away to the left, out over Lake Ontario.

'Ah,' said Janine. 'I'd hoped he would do this. Not all of the pilots do. Now,' she instructed Kezzie, 'do not take your eyes from the window for a single second.'

Kezzie sat up and did as she was told and several moments later saw a view which was to remain with her to the end of her days.

The great tumbling falls of Niagara were suddenly in her sight. A tremendous natural waterfall, cascading, never-ending, glittering water. Far below she could see the *Maid of the Mists* boats cruising as close as they dared, with the tourists' upturned faces. What could man create which could equal this? A shroud of mist hung over the waterfall with a wraith of a rainbow suspended between earth and heaven.

Kezzie gasped.

' "Ontario" is a word from the Iroquois,' said Janine in her ear. 'It means, "beautiful water".'

Kezzie could well understand why the native people had named this place with such words. The tiny plane swept over the abrupt drop and Kezzie could see the emerald waters foaming below her.

'The water is green because of the mineral deposits,' Janine went on. 'Many lakes in Canada are this beautiful colour. In the wintertime the Falls are quite spectacular. The spray remains frozen on the surrounding trees, and the whole area has a magical look about it.'

When they landed Janine led Kezzie quickly and efficiently through the terminal building. For all her small size she was a woman who commanded attention. They shared a cab into the town, passing fruit and vegetable sellers with their goods in baskets by the roadside.

'You'll find lots of the people hereabouts are French or Scots,' said Janine. 'The type of work available in Canada seems to suit Scottish people in particular, farming and fishing. The big new addition to the power house at the Falls was dug out of the cliff face by men from the Isle of

Lewis. It was very hard and dangerous work. Of course a lot go over to the States because the money is better and there's work in the car factories in Detroit.'

Kezzie remembered Janine on the plane pointing out the United States of America, just a few moments away from them. She thought suddenly of Michael, who had given up his chance of emigrating by giving her all his savings. A sudden pang of homesickness took hold of her.

'I'm sorry I can't be of more help,' the older woman said when they reached the station, 'but I've a train to make.' She patted Kezzie on the cheek. 'Don't look so worried, honey. I was a school teacher for forty years, and I reckon I'm a good judge of character. You are a young lady with a very strong sense of purpose. I just *know* you'll find your little sister.'

An hour or so later when Kezzie was sitting in the supervisor's office in the Rescue Home at Carrville she tried to make herself have the same conviction.

Seeing the stunned expression on the girl's face before him the supervisor repeated what he had said slowly and clearly.

'Although we did have papers for the child Lucy Clyde, we did not have the child. She definitely did not come with that party. There must have been an error. When we realised this we sent the papers on.'

'She is not here?' Kezzie asked dully.

'If it will make you more easy I will take you to meet all of the children. None of them are at all close in age to your sister.'

Kezzie nodded. She must think. She must not panic. She had to think.

'It is too late for you to travel anywhere now,' he said. 'You are welcome to spend the night here, and then in the morning you can decide what to do.'

Kezzie gripped her bag tightly. She had already decided. There was only one thing she could do. Return to Montreal and start again.

CHAPTER 22

On the train

By the time Kezzie returned to Montreal the Fitzwilliams had left for America. She went straight to the Receiving Home.

The officer in charge was sympathetic but regretful.

'This is just a clearing home,' he said. 'Sometimes they don't even come through here. They go directly to a real home.' He checked the ledgers and found the record relating to Lucy Clyde. 'It was a mistake,' he said. 'The children from Liverpool and Scotland were regrouped to make a more even balance, and her papers were sent to Carrville in error. She must have gone with the other party, to a home in Dalton in British Columbia.'

Kezzie went back to Immigration. Yes, children had come through. A week or so ago. They had been in two groups, one going south, to Niagara, the other west, all the way to British Columbia.

Had Lucy definitely been with the other group, or was she somewhere else altogether? The confusion with the papers upset Kezzie deeply. How could she be sure where her sister was? Was she even in search of the right person? Surely someone would recall seeing a child as pretty as Lucy?

It was a very distraught Kezzie who went through the Immigration sheds trying to find someone who could help her. Did anyone remember a little girl? Blonde, age about seven, blue eyes. She showed them the cracked and blurred photograph, taken at the seaside many months ago. The happy face smiling from behind the sandcastle didn't seem to be connected to her little sister at all. She couldn't even tell them what Lucy was wearing now.

Eventually she came across a tall bearded man with a faint Scottish burr in his voice. A little girl? He checked the files. There was a Lucy Clyde listed. Did he remember anything about her – anything at all? He thought carefully. There was one child he recalled, smaller than the rest, very pretty but poorly, clutching a rag doll. Kezzie's heart jumped. Lucy's doll! The one she had made her for her Christmas present. It had been missing from the caravan! He checked the records again. It must be her. The next older child was ten. Which way? Which way? Dalton, he was almost sure, B.C.

'You take the Canadian Pacific Railway. It goes all the way,' he said proudly, 'from sea to sea.'

Kezzie turned away. 'Poorly.' He had said Lucy was poorly. She had a great unease in her mind. Lucy was ill.

At the exit there was a huge map of Canada pinned to the wall, and as Kezzie stared at it she felt quite faint. British Columbia was hundreds and hundreds of miles away. She traced the line of the railway, she could barely make out Dalton. It was on the other side of the

130

Rocky Mountains! A wave of dizziness swept over her.

'You all right, ma'am?'

She shook her head, trying to clear it.

Someone took her firmly by the elbow and led her away from the crowds to sit on one of the wooden benches which ran along the wall. A glass of water was put in her hand. Her fingers shook as she drank. She looked up. It was the tall immigration official.

'Thank you,' she said. 'I'm quite all right now.'

She made to stand up. He pushed her gently back down.

'With respect, ma'am, no you ain't,' he said. 'You're going to have to take it easy for a little while.'

'I cannot wait,' Kezzie said wildly. 'I have lost too much time already. You said yourself my sister was unwell. I must press on and find her. She may be in great danger.'

He consulted his pocket watch. 'The train for B.C. doesn't leave for some hours yet. Why don't we book you a ticket, then go and have something to eat? My guess is that you haven't breakfasted at all today.'

Kezzie hesitated. It was true. She couldn't remember when she had last eaten.

'I thought as much.' He smiled at her easily. 'Now you ain't going to do your sister or yourself much good if you collapse on the street and end up in hospital.'

Kezzie followed his broad figure as he shouldered through the throngs of people. He organised her ticket and baggage and then led her to a small restaurant close to Windsor railway station. It was comforting to have someone take command, and as she started to eat she found herself telling Alexander Dalgleish all about her life.

'You are an amazing girl, Kezzie Munro,' he said. 'To come all this way on your own.'

'But your country is so vast,' said Kezzie wearily. 'I have already travelled hundreds of miles and I feel I am as far away as ever from her. And,' she pointed out of the window, 'there are so many people. I have never seen so many people in my life. I could search for ever and not find her.' She felt her eyes fill up with tears.

Impulsively he reached forward and gripped her hand.

'I'm sure you'll find her,' he said. 'I have dealt with the people involved in the juvenile immigration scheme. Dr Barnardo's, Sheltering Homes and various church organisations have brought many children to a better life in Canada. It has been going on for a long time and they are very well organised. The foster homes are carefully selected and they have an efficient after-care system of inspection. I'm sure Lucy is being well looked after.'

Later Alexander Dalgleish watched Kezzie make her way towards the train. Her long dark curls and elegant clothes made her stand out in the crowds. He sincerely hoped they would meet again. She was a fine-looking girl, with the type of spirit a developing country needed, and so concerned for her sister. He had not liked to tell her too much about the state of the child or the cuff on the side of the head which he had witnessed Lucy receiving.

Although her nerves were fraught with worry, being on the train, as with being on the boat meant that Kezzie had time to sit and observe. In an attempt to distract her thoughts she leafed through the collection of newspapers and magazines in the restaurant car. Ontario's crop harvest was up on 1937's despite extensive damage by army worms. There were pictures of farmers taking in their harvest. They would be doing that at home, thought Kezzie, in the fields around her village.

Most of the rest was news of bombings and killing. In Germany, Jews had been ordered to carry special identity cards. The British government had commissioned a thousand new Spitfire fighters. As more and more outrageous acts of hatred and aggression occurred, the whole world seemed to be racing towards war. Then an item in *The Globe and Mail* for Saturday, 6 August caught her eye. 'QUEEN'S READY' ran the headline.

Kezzie smiled as she read the article. So her grandad's 'royal connection' was about to be launched from John Brown's yard on the Clyde. She felt better at once. It had given her a brief link with home which cheered her and she knew that her friends and family would be thinking of her. She was still on edge at every stop but it eased her mind to know that at least she was making progress. Dalton was the end of Lucy's travels, surely she would catch her there?

Canada was beautiful, Kezzie had to acknowledge the fact. She gazed from her window as the train took her across the face of the continent.

It was autumn, the Canadians called it the Fall. The country was coloured in crimson and gold. They passed Lake Superior at Heron Bay. On the Prairies the flat farmlands stretched to the horizon, with a farmhouse and little lakes dotted here and there. The train stopped at small towns with their tall grain elevators. Kezzie became accustomed to the bell sounding and the cheery call of the railwaymen. She consulted her map. The names intrigued her; Medicine Hat, Swift Current, Moose Jaw. Eating up the miles the train travelled across the country. She sometimes went to the observation car. She preferred to be there at night, or the early morning, with only the sound of the engine pulling and the wheels rattling for company. She would pray as she watched the sun rise on another day, but her prayers had no words, only a thought, a deep intent.

'Let Lucy be safe. Let Lucy be safe,' she whispered in time with the rhythm of the rain.

CHAPTER 23

Jane Smith

Lucy felt far from safe. The motion of the train for days had been only marginally better than that of the ship. When she had looked out of the window it seemed to her like another sea, a great expanse of grass and grain with waves which never stopped in the wind. She sat slumped, stupefied in her seat.

On arrival at the home their escort discovered that some of the children's papers were missing.

'Must have gone with the other group,' she fumed. 'I don't know, the organisation gets worse. I'm due to go back to Montreal. I'll have to leave you to sort something out.'

The matron shrugged. It was not the first time she would have to assign new names and ages to unknown children. She was understaffed and the Canadian government now frowned on child immigration. She would try to place these ones as quickly as possible. With the homes being run down perhaps she would be able to retire soon. Each batch of children appeared to her

135

to have more problems and be more undisciplined than the last.

The rougher ones gave her the greatest headache. One boy called Jack, who'd arrived last year, had been sent back three times by the different people she'd put him with. A swarthy little creature, who constantly stole anything and everything left unattended, she despaired of ever placing him. He had obviously been badly abused at some time and trusted no one.

She had given the new group a quick assessment on arrival. The older boys were very rude, but seemed quite strong. Perhaps some of the logging camps would take on a few lads. It was a good job. Hard work, but fairly paid and out in the open air. These children were so pale and undernourished. She thought they must come from some of the worst slums in Europe. She had heard that Glasgow had a bad record of child mortality. Houses built too close together blocking the sun, and lack of milk and proper food meant that many children suffered from rickets. Well, at least here they had a chance to thrive in the clear air.

The children were playing outside. She glanced out of the window. The child with the doll who shrank in the corner of the yard, staring around her vacantly, was going to be difficult to get rid of, though she recalled an outback couple who had been looking for a girl to train as a servant. They certainly weren't the type you would want one of your own to go to, but an idiot child like that would have to take what she could get. She'd contact them tomorrow.

Lucy stood as far away from everyone as she could possibly get. Only one other child, a boy of about nine, did not join in with the rest either. He was sallow and skinny, with black hair and furtive eyes. He played with a ball at the edge of the yard, talking all the while to himself.

'Atsit,' Jack would say, as he bounced the ball against the wall. 'Gerronyer.'

If anyone came near him or tried to take his ball he would snarl in a most ferocious manner. Jack had been in the home the longest and had established certain territorial rights.

'Goal!' he cried as the ball soared up and over the fence.

Lucy watched him vaguely as he climbed over to retrieve it. On the way back he slipped and crashed heavily to the ground. The ball fell from his grasp and bounced towards her. Instinctively she put up her hands and caught it. She waited but he did not get up. She stood still, not sure what to do, and then walked slowly towards him. He rolled over, his face screwed up in pain. There was a deep gash on his leg. She looked round for help.

'Don't tell. Don't tell,' he said quickly. 'I'll sort it myself.' He took a grubby hanky from his pocket and spat on it. 'I'll catch it for climbing the fence if they find out. Then I'll get locked in the cupboard.' He mopped up the blood. 'Don't like bein' in the cupboard, 's dark an' all. You won't tell, will ye?'

Lucy shook her head.

At dinner that night Lucy was by chance beside him.

He ate his food noisily and greedily. She picked up her spoon, meanwhile gazing about her, trying to make sense of where she was. She looked down at her plate. She didn't recognise this kind of food. It wasn't like anything Kezzie had given her to eat. A lump of brown meat lay half submerged in gravy. She looked around her hopelessly. Grandad always cut up her meat for her.

There was a piece of bread beside her plate. She reached to pick it up and as she did so the boy from the ship stretched across the table and grabbed it from her.

'Ha! Ha!' he crowed.

As he went to put it into his mouth, Jack with a quick movement punched him on the face, took the bread back and gave it to Lucy.

'Quick,' he said, 'eat it fast.'

Lucy gobbled her bread.

The other boy got up and came round the table towards Jack. He was much bigger and heavier, Jack did not move until the boy was beside him. Then he swung round and kicked him viciously with his hobnailed tackety boots, and, leaping to his feet, shouted, 'Matron, that boy's out of his seat!'

The matron hurried over. She regarded Jack suspiciously. He continued eating his dinner with an air of innocence. The other boy gave him a look of hatred.

Jack grinned at Lucy.

'Has yer doll got a name?' he asked, nodding to Lucy's constant companion.

Lucy looked at her doll sadly. She was stained and smelly. Her clothes were torn. She had lost one eye and her hair was falling out.

'Kissy,' she whispered.

Just before bedtime Jack was ambushed in the washrooms. Lucy could only stare mutely as Matron pulled him out of the middle of the fight. The boy from the ship had a bloody nose and there was a bruise rising on her protector's eye.

'He started it, didn't he?' the bigger boy asked the rest menacingly. They nodded.

'It's the punishment room for you, my lad,' said the matron, dragging Jack down the corridor, 'and you can stay in there for two days this time.'

Lucy watched from a distance.

As Kezzie's train entered the high passes of the Rocky Mountains the matron of the home in Dalton made arrangements for Lucy's adoption.

'Jane Smith is the child's name,' she told the couple before her. 'Though you can change it if you will.' She looked at them. They were mean and shabby but the child was lucky to get even that. She rang her bell. 'I'll get someone to bring her down.'

When she was sent for Lucy came from the top of the house where she had been scrubbing the floors. She passed the cupboard at the bottom of the stairs in which Jack was locked. She thought of him in the dark, all alone for such a long time. She remembered herself in the coffin ship with only her dolly beside her. There was a little snib on the door. She gazed at it, a small figure in black button boots and a white pinafore covering her brown orphan's dress. She looked up and down the corridor and then opened the door. Jack was crouched in the corner with his hands over his head. His face was streaked and blotched. Without a word Lucy handed him her doll and then went away.

CHAPTER 24

The rag doll

Kezzie folded down her couchette bed for the last time. Tomorrow she would be in Dalton, she had travelled over two thousand miles in the last few days. She felt a great peace inside, brought about by the fact that she knew she was close to the end of her travels but also by this great country itself.

Each person she had spoken to in Canada was so very proud of their nation, from Janine and Alexander Dalgleish to her fellow travellers on the train.

'Sure we have still got those tin-and-tarpaper shanty towns on the outskirts of the big cities,' a construction worker she'd met in the dining-car had told her, 'but our fish canning and tannery works are expanding. This year the Bank of Canada has been fully nationalised. They'll control the credit rates so we're going to make progress out of the Great Depression.'

The train conductor had talked of the opening up of the country. A trans-Canada Air Line had recently been established, and now with the Canadian Broadcasting

Corporation being publicly owned it beamed a great variety of programmes and news right into the remotest areas. He'd been with the railways all his life and had watched as the ranchers followed each new track laid. Central Canada was now a vast chessboard of growing crops, warmed in spring by the strong gusty wind known as the Snow Eater, which blew down from the Rockies, and which the native people called the Chinook.

He told her to look out for Calgary, its Gaelic name meaning 'preserved pasture at the harbour'.

It was still very much a frontier town and had been originally a fort for the North West Mounted Police. They'd had to control the wild wolf hunters from Montana, and the American whisky traders who created unrest among the native tribes, the Blackfoot, Salish and Sarcee. Soon after that she would see the most beautiful part of Canada as the train would swing in a great loop north and enter the eastern foothills of the Rocky Mountains.

The territories through which the train had passed seemed to show nature's every part. Vermilion foliage, golden plains stretching out to the limits of the earth, rivers, forests, lakes and the jagged peaks of the Canadian Rocky Mountains. The sky was a blue canopy without horizons above her when she wandered down the track to stretch her legs at the various stops. At night the air was clear and cold and the stars seemed bright and close.

The train had reached Banff, climbed past Lake Louise to the highest point at the Great Divide of the Atlantic and Pacific watersheds. The conductor had pointed out to her the stream, parted, one to flow east to the Hudson Bay, one to flow west to the Pacific. Descending from the steep Kicking Horse Pass via the spiral tunnels, over many mountain ravines and then back up through the Selkirks to the Connaught Tunnel under Mount Macdonald. Kezzie had gazed back at the carriages snaking behind the engines across the vast gorge at Stoney Creek Bridge. What engineering skills and fortitude it had taken to conquer these mountains!

She hardly slept at all that night and was dressed and fully packed as the train drew in to Dalton early the next morning. It was a strange thing, thought Kezzie, as she made her enquiries firstly at the station office and then the town hall, how one's clothes mattered. Lady Fitzwilliam had bought her the most expensive costume she could find, with matching shoes, gloves, hat and handbag. And it seemed to Kezzie that people *were* more respectful and attentive to her. It was unfair, she thought.

She arrived at the Distribution Home, a grey forbidding house with iron railings all around. Kezzie gazed up at the windows. Was Lucy behind one of those faded net curtains?

'You've come all the way from Scotland?' the matron said in disbelief. 'Well, I'm sorry to disappoint you but I can't give just anybody access to my records or to the children in my care.'

Kezzie nodded calmly and handed her the letter from Lady Fitzwilliam.

'You know this person?' The matron hesitated.

Kezzie looked her straight in the face. 'A relative, actually,' she lied.

The matron flicked through her books.

'No one of that name has been here at all,' she said finally.

'There must be some mistake,' said Kezzie, now quite frightened. 'The Immigration in Montreal told me, and Lady Fitzwilliam,' she added quickly, 'that she had come here.'

The matron hesitated.

'Papers sometimes go astray,' she said. 'The records are not always . . . quite accurate. Names and personal details may change. There have been two or three children of about that age. One is still here.' She rang her bell.

Kezzie examined the forlorn child with the red pigtails who stood in front of her.

'That is not Lucy,' she said.

'There was one other child of a similar age who passed through my hands recently,' said the matron. She coughed. 'She'd been given the name Jane.'

'Can you describe her?' asked Kezzie.

The matron thought for a minute. 'She was quite small . . .'

'Blue eyes?' Kezzie asked anxiously.

'I think so . . . Yes.'

'Her hair,' continued Kezzie excitedly, 'little blonde curls all over her head. She is a beautiful child.'

The matron sighed. The child she was thinking about had not been beautiful at all.

'I don't think so,' she said. 'In fact I'm sure this child's hair was brown, it was certainly quite lank, and she was not attractive at all.' She paused for a second. 'Was there anything wrong with your sister?'

'Pardon?' said Kezzie.

The matron cleared her throat.

'It's just that this child was . . . well, not quite right.'

'What do you mean?'

'The child was mentally retarded, and had no speech.'

'No!' cried Kezzie.

'Well, that's it then.' The matron closed her book with finality.

Kezzie stood up from the chair stiffly. Her body and brain were numb. To come so far . . .

'Would you like some tea?' the matron asked more kindly.

Kezzie shook her head. She had to find somewhere quiet. She had to sit and think. What would she write to Grandad and Bella after her first hopeful telegram? Had they made a mistake in Montreal? Was Lucy in Carrville? Was she even in Canada?

She waited in the hallway while the maid brought her coat and suitcase from the back. Kezzie looked round at the scrubbed lino floors and the polished wooden banisters. Very clean, too clean for children to play in. Not a happy place for someone like Lucy. Was she in another similar place on the other side of Canada? Kezzie had fought through their months of starvation to save Lucy from a fate such as this. A spartan orphanage, a sham of a 'home'. She had failed her. Had she made a bad mistake? Was Lucy still in Scotland? Where was her sister?

The maid helped her on with her coat. Kezzie's arms were leaden. As she picked up her suitcase she heard a snuffling noise from the small cupboard under the stairwell.

Kezzie looked at the maid questioningly. The maid dropped her eyes. Kezzie glanced towards the front door where the matron was waiting to see her out.

There it was again, a strange whimpering sound. Kezzie reached forward and opened the cupboard door.

There was a small boy crouched in the corner. He covered his face with his hands as the light shone on him.

'There's a boy in this cupboard,' said Kezzie.

The matron hurried forward, tutting.

'Yes, yes. That is the punishment cupboard. And that is a particularly bad boy. He is often in there.'

Kezzie was horrified. 'You lock children in a cupboard because they are naughty?'

'He is more than naughty. He is bad. Don't criticise what you don't have to deal with.'

Kezzie stepped back reluctantly. It was none of her business, but the boy seemed so frightened and pathetic. As she turned away he reached out his hand towards the light, and the thing he was holding fell to the floor.

Kezzie picked it up and leaned forward to return it to him. And then she stopped . . . She looked more closely at the object in her hand. A raggedy doll with torn dirty clothes . . . and one blue button eye which gazed at her unblinking.

'Where did you get this?' she asked the boy hoarsely.

He shrank from her into the furthest corner of the cupboard. Kezzie knelt down and, reaching in, tucked the doll firmly back into his arms.

'I'm not going to keep it,' she spoke quietly. 'It's yours.'

She waited for a moment.

'I knew a little girl who had a doll just like yours,' she said gently. 'Perhaps you met her?'

He only stared back at her.

'I know that she would have liked you for a friend,' Kezzie went on. 'And that she would have given her doll to someone to watch for her, or . . .' Kezzie glanced around the cupboard. 'Or keep them company in a dark place.'

Something in his eyes changed.

'I just wondered,' Kezzie said carefully, 'does this doll have a name?'

There was a long silence. Then the answer came softly.

'Her name's Kissy.'

CHAPTER 25

The farmstead

'That's the place you're lookin' for.'

Kezzie surveyed the farmstead to which the hired waggon driver from Dalton was pointing with his buggy whip. It was a very run-down-looking homestead, she thought. The paint on the wooden slats, which made up the walls, was bleached and flaking. The curtains in the windows were torn and dirty. There was no garden to speak of, just weeds and broken bits of crockery and tools lying about the yard.

'You are sure this is the place?'

'Yup. That's the Tchekov's section. Beats me why someone like you is visiting with folks like them.' He spat a long squirt of tobacco juice on to the side of the road. 'Ain't none o' my business though.'

Kezzie climbed down from the waggon.

'Will you wait here for me please? I won't be long.'

She picked her way towards the front door. There was a faint trace of smoke coming from the chimney, but apart from that she could see no sign of life. Kezzie rapped on the door. Nothing happened. She knocked louder, and glanced back at the waggon driver. He was staring at the horizon. She rattled the catch and the door fell open. Kezzie's first reaction was to turn and leave, such was the scene of squalor which met her eyes. The room was filthy, the floor unswept for many months, the chair covers and linen unwashed. Food, clothing, pots and pans lay about everywhere. She stepped inside.

'Here, what do you think you're doing?'

There was a woman stirring a pot on the fire in the corner.

'I'm sorry,' said Kezzie. 'I knocked on the door. No one answered so I came in . . .' She trailed off and looked around her. Could Lucy possibly be in a place like this?

The woman's eyes narrowed as she looked at Kezzie.

'What do you want here?' She advanced on Kezzie with the ladle still in her hand. 'What call has the likes of you got to come around here?'

Kezzie stood her ground.

'I've come from the children's home in Dalton,' she said. Well, it wasn't quite a lie. 'I've come to see the little girl you took.'

The woman relaxed her grip on the ladle.

'The home child,' she said. 'That was a bad deal we got there, not much work in her, always poorly, needin' feed.' She tapped her forehead. 'Ain't able to talk, not right in the head neither.'

'Where is she?' asked Kezzie as calmly as she could. Her heart was pounding.

'Out in the lean-to.' The woman stared at Kezzie.

'What do you want to see her for? What business is it of yours?'

Kezzie smoothed her gloves into her fingers and held her head up and stared back at the woman.

'I told you,' she said firmly, 'I am from the home. Now take me to her at once.'

The woman led the way through the yard to a lean-to at the back of the house. Here, scraggy chickens pecked in the dirt and an old cat with matted fur slunk away under the house.

The woman pushed the door of the shed open.

'She ain't been well the last few days,' she whined. 'I've been having to nurse her. That was soup I was making her, extra work for me on top of everything else I have to do.'

Kezzie barely heard her. She had stepped past her into the darkness. By the light from the door she could see a straw mattress on which a small figure lay huddled, half-sitting against the wall. The air was foetid, it was a place one would not have kept animals in. The stench of urine and vomit made Kezzie gag. She went forward slowly and looked at the child in the bed. She was smaller and thinner than Lucy had been. Her hair was coarse and tufted and moving with lice. Her face was sallow and sunken, her skin was lacerated and covered with scabs. But worse, much worse, were the child's eyes. They stared blankly out at nothing. The woman was right. This child was indeed an idiot.

Kezzie felt anger. Anger at the woman who had treated a child so badly, and anger at the authorities which had allowed a child to be placed with people such as these. She would go straight back to Dalton, but not to the home. She would go to the police and report this. She turned towards the door. And then the fact of the matter hit her.

If this child was not her sister, then where in the wide world was Lucy? She had followed the trail very carefully and had not found her. Where could she be? Not in Scotland, not in Canada. Where? There was nowhere else left for Kezzie to search. Lucy was lost to her for ever.

Kezzie paused with her hand on the door. A feeling of the greatest despair came over her. The woman was watching her. Kezzie put her forehead against her hand and bowed her head in defeat.

There was a silence in the room. Nothing. Kezzie felt a breath against her cheek. She sensed something . . . an echo. She raised her head. The woman had not moved. She glanced in the corner of the shed. Neither had the child. Then what? Kezzie looked at the woman.

'Did the child say something?' she asked her.

'I told you,' said the woman. 'She be dumb . . .'

Kezzie held up her hand to silence her and walked towards the bed.

'Did you speak, little girl?'

The child gazed at her vacantly.

Kezzie knelt down beside the child's bed. She took one thin hand in both hers.

'Little girl,' she said gently. 'Did you say something?'

There was a terrible empty silence in the room. Kezzie felt as though the world had stopped turning. She moved her head slightly to try to catch the child's gaze. Was there something there? Was her imagination playing tricks? A gleam of light in the eyes. Was it a reflection of something? Kezzie felt at her throat for her little silver locket. She held it up before the child's eyes.

'See,' she said.

Nothing.

Kezzie sat back on her heels. She closed her eyes. She could feel the warm tears beginning to trickle through her lids.

'Oh, Lucy, where are you?' she whispered.

Then she heard, no more than a breath on the air, a sigh. One word.

'Kezzie.'

CHAPTER 26

Papers

Kezzie opened her eyes very slowly. The child was staring at her fixedly. Kezzie reached out her arm and the child seemed to shrink away from her. Kezzie longed to hold her sister and hug her, and cry and shout with joy, but something told her that it would be the wrong thing to do.

'Lucy, Lucy,' she said softly. 'I've come for you. I've come to take you home.' And very gently she stroked her sister's cheek with the back of her hand.

Lucy looked around her with wide frightened eyes. She struggled to speak again.

'Home?' she said. She closed her eyes.

Kezzie stood up and brushed her skirt down.

'I want to take this child away now,' she said to the woman.

'You can't,' the woman said. 'You need papers, or something.' She had a sly look on her face.

Kezzie thought quickly.

'I have them,' she said. 'In my bag.'

By the Lord God, she decided, I am taking Lucy away from here if I have to knock this person down.

'Show me,' said the woman.

Kezzie looked at Lucy lying on the mattress. Her eyes were half-closed. She appeared to have lost consciousness.

'We will discuss it in the house,' said Kezzie and walked out of the lean-to.

They went round the side of the shack.

'I'm going to speak to the driver for one minute,' said Kezzie. She went to the buggy. 'I have some business to discuss with that woman,' she said to the driver. 'While I am doing that I want you to take the travelling rug, go to the lean-to at the back and wrap up the child who is there and put her in the buggy.'

The driver looked at her for a long minute.

'It is quite legal,' said Kezzie, 'she is my sister.'

The driver hesitated.

'I'll double your fare,' Kezzie pleaded. Then she said, 'She is my sister. She was put up for adoption by mistake. I have come from Scotland to find her.'

'All right,' he said.

Kezzie went back to the house.

'Show me your papers,' said the woman.

Kezzie took out the letter written by Lady Fitzwilliam. The woman glanced at it, and something in the way she did caught Kezzie's attention.

'I don't know,' said the woman, 'doesn't seem right to me.'

Kezzie saw her ship's boarding pass lying at the bottom of her bag. She placed it in front of the woman.

'This is the official form from the home which we both sign, and you may keep it as proof that you handed the child over to me.'

Kezzie held her breath. The woman stared at it for a second or two.

'That's official then?' she asked.

Kezzie let her breath out slowly. She had guessed correctly. The woman could not read. She took the fountain pen which William had given her and signed the boarding pass with a flourish.

'You sign the bottom or make your mark,' she said. Then with a flash of inspiration, she added, 'And of course you are due payment. I am authorised to give you twenty dollars.'

Kezzie counted the money out on the table. Any reservations which the woman might have had vanished completely. She picked up the money quickly.

Kezzie stood up.

'My driver has taken the little girl out to the buggy. I will take my leave of you.'

It required all of Kezzie's willpower not to run down the path. She climbed in the back where the driver had laid Lucy and stroked her hair and talked to her all the way back to town.

'Dearest child, beautiful child,' Kezzie murmured, stroking Lucy's hair.

'Which room you in?' asked the driver as they stopped outside the hotel.

Kezzie told him and he carried Lucy straight up.

'I'd say that child needs a doctor,' he said.

'I intend to find her one right away,' Kezzie answered

him. She opened her purse. 'I have another three dollars to give you.'

He shook his head. He looked at Kezzie.

'You come all the way from Scotland to get her?'

Kezzie nodded.

'Ain't no more'n a child yourself,' he said and went out closing the door behind him.

Kezzie bathed Lucy gently with a cloth as she waited for the doctor's arrival. At first she had thought to get on the first train and put as much distance between herself and this town as she could, but Lucy's condition seemed to worsen. Her breathing was shallow and she could never have travelled in the condition she was in.

There was a rap on the door.

'Dr McMath. There is a sick child here?' The man was about sixty with silver hair.

'My sister,' said Kezzie.

The doctor put on a pair of glasses and examined Lucy. He gave Kezzie a severe look.

'What exactly is going on here?'

'She was put in an orphanage in Scotland by mistake when I was involved in an accident. They sent her to Canada, and some terrible people adopted her, and I got her back today.' Kezzie could hear her own voice begin to shake. 'I . . . I . . . is she very sick?'

'She will need to go to hospital,' said Dr McMath. 'There is more than physical sickness here. What you tell me explains it a little. She is deeply traumatised, shock, you know.'

He took off his glasses and put them in his top pocket.

'No hospital,' said Kezzie at once. 'I will nurse her here.

She is not going to hospital. She is not going anywhere away from me.'

'Young lady . . .' began the doctor. He was interrupted by a loud knocking on the door.

Before either of them could move the door was opened abruptly and a man in blue soiled work overalls stood there.

'You,' he shouted, pointing at Kezzie. 'You were at my place today and took my girl. Well, I've come to take her back. This ain't legal.'

And to Kezzie's horror she saw that he was holding in his hand her ship's boarding pass.

CHAPTER 27

The doctor's house

Kezzie stepped between the man and the bed where her sister lay. She felt herself go rigid with fright. She looked down at Lucy lying so still, barely making any indent on the bed. Kezzie felt as though Lucy was almost unreal, a frail little spirit caught into its body only by her, Kezzie's will . . . and now, she felt herself faltering.

Dr McMath's voice when he spoke surprised her. It was polite and gentle, very gentle.

'What's the matter, John?' He went towards the farmer. 'Something wrong?'

'I got that girl, fair and square from the home. You know the trouble we've had, we've got no help on our place. Now, she ain't been much use, but she's ours. I don't know if this is legal.' He waved the boarding pass again in the doctor's face.

Dr McMath took Kezzie's boarding pass from John Tchekov's hand.

'What is this?' he asked.

Kezzie held her breath.

'It's her authority, she says.' The farmer pointed at Kezzie. 'She come and took the child and this gave her leave to do it, she says.'

The doctor looked at the card.

'I . . .' he started.

'Fifteen dollars ain't enough,' said the farmer.

'Fifteen dollars?' said Dr McMath.

'Twenty,' said Kezzie immediately. 'I paid twenty.'

'Twenty?' asked the farmer. 'She only said fifteen.'

'Twenty,' said Kezzie. 'That's what the children's home told me,' she added quickly.

'The home told you?' Dr McMath raised an eyebrow.

'Twenty?' said the farmer once again. 'She said fifteen.'

'I paid your wife twenty dollars,' said Kezzie, thinking to herself, you are not going past me.

Dr McMath groped in his pockets for a minute or two.

'I don't seem to have my reading glasses with me,' he said. He held up the pass to the light and squinted at it. 'It's certainly an official document of some sort, John,' he said. 'What I'll do is this. I'll hold on to it just now and investigate this properly for you. In the meantime, you couldn't take this child back with you anyroad. She is quite ill. I will have to take charge of her.' With that the doctor put the boarding pass in his bag and led the farmer to the door.

'She was poorly when she came to us,' said the farmer. 'It's not our fault.'

'I'm sure it's not,' said the doctor soothingly. 'You never ill-treated a living thing in your life, John.' He saw the farmer out. 'I'll call by later in the week and see you.'

Dr McMath came back into the room. He took his

glasses from his pocket and studied Kezzie's boarding pass. Then he said, 'Now, young lady, I'd like you to tell me exactly how you and your sister got here.'

Twenty minutes later Kezzie and Lucy, wrapped in a travelling rug and several blankets, were on their way in the doctor's car to his house in the nearby village of Waterfoot.

His wife, Sarah, a plump grey-haired woman, came to meet them. Kezzie liked her at once. She asked no questions but only took Lucy from her sister's arms, carried her upstairs and put her to bed. Dr McMath followed. He gave Lucy some clear medicine and then they all went downstairs to the kitchen.

'I don't know how people can behave like that to a child,' said Kezzie, pacing up and down.

'Ignorance,' sighed the doctor. 'True ignorance, and of course the Depression.'

'That's no excuse,' fumed Kezzie. 'The place was not clean. We were as poor but we did not let ourselves get into such a state.'

The doctor's wife said nothing as she set out a meal of potatoes and pie.

The doctor regarded Kezzie gravely.

'Perhaps you do not appreciate exactly what it is like to live through hard times. Farming in Canada has suffered from real drought. Plagues of grasshoppers and a lessened demand for wheat. At one stage the Prairies were in total financial collapse. The amount of small farms lost to mortgage companies was colossal. All over Canada men were riding the rails. Travelling on the roofs of the freight trains in freezing cold looking for jobs that did not exist.'

Kezzie was silent. She remembered the bothy they had stayed in, and how she had felt the start of their slow slide into misery. Only having a sliver of soap and no hot water. Being utterly tired, day after day. The amount of energy needed to wash and dress oneself, when lack of food and lack of purpose was ever present. What would have happened to them if their fortunes had not changed? She recalled the people in some of the areas in Glasgow, the hopeless and helpless slouch of the men on the street corners.

'Britain is rearming,' continued Dr McMath, 'and whatever you may think of that, it does provide employment.' He paused. 'Besides which . . .' He got up and went to look out of the window. 'I helped John Tchekov bury eight children in the field behind his farm, not one of them lived more than a year. I reckon his wife was looking for something to love and just couldn't cope when it went wrong on her.'

Kezzie put her head in her hands. She felt ashamed, instead of triumphant at having found Lucy. She was overcome with weariness and worry.

Mrs McMath brought a cot bed for Kezzie and placed it beside the bed in which Lucy lay. Kezzie drifted into a troubled sleep gazing at her sister and woke in the morning still tired. Lucy was no better.

Kezzie wrote to Grandad via Bella telling him where they were but not giving much detail of what had happened. She said that Lucy was improving. She could not bear to write the truth.

Another day passed the same way. Dr McMath was

161

worried. Kezzie could see that. He had dosed Lucy regularly and at least her breathing seemed easier. Kezzie, who scarcely left Lucy's side, mentioned this to him.

He frowned. 'It's not her bodily health which concerns me the most,' he said. 'It is the child's spirit. She has put a barrier between herself and reality because life became too painful for her. We have to work at removing it. If we can,' he added.

It was true, though Kezzie. Even though Lucy spoke now, it was only a 'yes' or a 'no' and that very reluctantly. Mostly she lay propped up in bed in a half-dream. Kezzie could have wept when she thought of the little girl who had screamed with delight on the roller coaster or gone with her jam jar to search for tadpoles in the burn.

'I am going in to Dalton,' the doctor told her a few days later. 'I'm going to speak to a few people and see if I can do something about having that rescue home closed. I thought most of these places had gone, apart from the farm school on Vancouver Island. They're obviously not screening staff applicants properly and I doubt if they are sending out inspectors to check on the children they have placed.'

CHAPTER 28

Jack

Later that same evening the telephone rang. Kezzie heard Sarah McMath call her from the hall.

'It's the doctor. He wants to speak to you.'

Kezzie took the handpiece from her. The doctor was calling from Dalton. The home was being closed. All the children were placed and accounted for. Except one. Did Kezzie remember seeing a boy called Jack?

'It seems as though the child has run away,' said Dr McMath. 'They're very concerned, what with winter coming on.'

Kezzie tried to remember. She couldn't really recall any of the children's names at the home. The only little boy she remembered distinctly was the boy in the cupboard . . . and he was locked in . . . She suddenly realised that he would be exactly the type of child who would run away.

'Can you describe him?' she asked.

It was Jack, of course. Kezzie spoke to the matron who sounded dreadfully worried. Kezzie felt sorry for her.

The woman was trying to justify her treatment of the boy.

'I had to lock him up,' she said. 'He was violent towards other children. What could I do?'

What else, indeed? thought Kezzie as she replaced the telephone on its stand. Perhaps spoken to him, cuddled him? Maybe he was rough and aggressive. All Kezzie had seen in the cupboard was a very scared and lonely small boy.

She went slowly into the front parlour where Mrs McMath was sewing.

'The doctor is going to stay on for a while in Dalton to see if they turn up any trace of the boy,' she said.

The lamp was on in the room. Kezzie went to draw the curtains. She looked out of the window. It was dark and cold with a heavy sky threatening rain. Was Jack outside in this weather, with little protection in his thin orphanage clothes?

Sarah McMath got up and came and stood behind her. She put her arms round Kezzie.

'He'll be all right,' she said. 'If anyone can find him, my Andrew will.'

Three days passed before Dr McMath returned home.

Kezzie was sitting at the side of Lucy's bed reading to her. She was not sure if her sister was listening as Lucy's eyes were almost closed. She hesitated as she turned the page. Then she heard voices outside the bedroom door.

'Go on in,' she heard Dr McMath say.

The door opened and a scruffy boy entered cautiously. Kezzie saw her sister's eyes open, and then widen in surprise.

Jack advanced into the room in a cocky manner.

'So this is where ye went,' he said, looking around, 'not bad for some, eh?' He strolled about the room picking things up and examining them. He went to the window and looked out at the yard and the garden. 'Not bad, not bad,' he said. Then he sat down on the end of Lucy's bed. 'Here! This is real soft. Bet ye wish ye were back in Dalton, an' I don't think.' He leaned forward. 'Look you,' he said, 'if they don't treat you right, tell *me*. I'll sort 'em out. I can fight anyone. That big one there,' he pointed at Kezzie, 'or even the old codger with the white hair.'

To Kezzie's amazement Lucy smiled.

'I got somethin' for ye.' Jack reached inside his pullover and brought out the rag doll. 'She's a bit mussed up,' he apologised, 'but that was on account of me having to hide her from the dragon lady.'

Lucy gave a piteous little cry and took the doll from him. The three of them watched her as she stroked its hair and cuddled it to her and mumbled nonsense words in its ear in a sing-song voice.

'I think,' said Dr McMath, 'that we may just have found the key to unlock this child's mind.'

They left Jack sitting beside Lucy's bed drinking milk and munching home-made cookies. He was full of himself, chattering away to her. He didn't take note of any strangeness in her manner and was so brimming over with life and mischief that she was forced to pay attention to him. He was starting to tell her of his adventures. Of how he had climbed down a forty-foot wall to run away and met up with hungry bears and wolves in the woods around Dalton.

Mrs McMath set out some food on the kitchen table.

'However did you find him?' she asked her husband.

'Well,' the doctor replied with a certain smugness, 'I reckoned with the whole of the Royal Mounties out looking for him they would cover all the obvious places, the logging camps and the railway stations. So there wasn't any use me following them around. Then I sat down and thought to myself: "What would *I* do if I was that boy and I decided to run away?" After that it was easy.'

'Tell us,' said Kezzie, pouring out the coffee.

'I reckoned he would head this way, of course,' said Dr McMath. 'He's a smart boy. Most troublesome children like that are. They've a lot of energy that needs good direction, that's all. After Kezzie told me what she knew on the telephone, I just worked out that he would try to follow the only two people who had ever shown him any kindness.'

He took a long drink of his coffee.

Mrs McMath walked briskly round the table and took the cup from his hand.

'Andrew McMath. Kezzie and me, we have been worried sick these last days. If you don't leave off drinking that coffee and tell us the rest of this story at once, you will get absolutely no dinner this night.'

The doctor laughed.

'Well, I only drove very slowly up and down the road from Dalton to Waterfoot several times, stopping here and there to have a picnic, and making sure that the food was on plain view. It must have been the sight of those blueberry muffins you made, Sarah, because sure enough, on the second day a small figure appears as cheeky as you like and asks if I'd be passing through Waterfoot, because he might just do me the honour of accepting a lift from me.'

CHAPTER 29

Christmas

The first trails of snow saw Lucy up and walking about. Jack was a tonic to everybody. To begin with he drove Dr and Mrs McMath to distraction. Nothing was safe from him. Ornaments fell from tables and broke as he passed, windows cracked of their own accord when he played football in the yard.

One day Kezzie was helping Mrs McMath put the winter quilts on the beds. They were in the small attic room where Jack slept, when on turning the mattress they discovered a vast quantity of food crushed under the bed. Most of it was rotten or had mould growing on it.

Mrs McMath sat down in a small chair.

'Lord, Lord,' she said. 'What does that tell you, Kezzie?' she asked.

'That he is a thief,' said Kezzie reluctantly.

The older woman shook her head.

'It tells me that at some time he has starved.'

Jack came into the room at this moment and immediately turned for flight.

'Jack!' Mrs McMath called sternly.

He crept back, with such a look of fear on his face that Kezzie had to turn her head away.

'Come with me,' Mrs McMath commanded him. She led him downstairs through the kitchen to the pantry. 'Do you see this door?' she asked him. 'It is never locked. That means that anyone who lives here may go inside and eat as much as they please – whenever they choose. Do you understand me?'

He nodded warily.

'Eat as much as you want, Jack. Eat until your belly's sore and you cannot swallow another crumb.' She laughed and patted him on the head. 'And then go in and eat some more,' she said.

They went sleigh riding just before Christmas. Dressed Eskimo-style in hooded parkas they whizzed down the lanes and roads with the bells jingling. The runners hissed on the hard-packed snow and in the background the mountain ice caps shone diamond blue. They were on an expedition to the forest to cut down their own Christmas tree. Jack and Dr McMath spent some time studying various trees and discussing the merits of each, until eventually his wife called from the sleigh that the girls were getting cold, and if they didn't take the axe to a tree right this minute she was driving home without them. They selected a fine Douglas fir and brought it home.

The streets and buildings were decorated and brightly lit, and as they came back through the town their breaths frosted on the air with 'oohs' and 'aahs' as they saw the different coloured baubles and lights in the shop windows.

On Christmas Eve they exchanged small gifts. Kezzie had knitted the doctor a pair of fingerless mittens and embroidered a book mark for his wife. Against her better judgement she bought Jack a penknife. His face when he opened up the parcel made up for any doubts she may have had.

Lucy had crept on to Sarah McMath's knee and was opening her presents. Kezzie felt a tremendous pang of jealousy as she watched them. The little girl was looking up into the face of the older woman, who was stroking her hair and reading her the Christmas story from a book they'd given her. She was aware of Dr McMath's hand on her shoulder.

'Are you not opening your present, Kezzie?' he asked gently.

Kezzie fumbled with the bulky parcel and pulled the wrapping away. It was a chess set. The pieces had been carved in soapstone by Eskimo craftsmen, the original Canadians, the doctor had said.

'Perhaps with this set I might win a few games,' said the doctor.

Kezzie looked at him. They understood each other very well, she thought. He seemed to know when she was troubled or upset or homesick, and would suggest a walk or a game of chess to lift her mind.

After Christmas Kezzie counted her savings. Buying herself and Lucy winter clothes had used up most of her money.

'I must look for work,' she announced at breakfast. 'You have been more than generous with us, but I cannot allow this to go on.'

The doctor and his wife exchanged glances.

'We thought you might say this one day,' said Sarah McMath. 'We were going to make a proposition to you.' She glanced at her husband.

'I need help with my surgery, Kezzie. Sarah says she is getting too old and her eyesight is not as good as it was for dispensing. So, if you are agreeable to work with me, I could pay you a small wage.'

'Only if you deduct money for our keep,' said Kezzie firmly. Her heart was beating very fast. To work with a doctor and learn about medicine!

'And Jack,' said Mrs McMath. 'We must do something about him, also.'

They found Jack work at the local grocery store owned by Miss Hannah Chiltern, a lady who spoke to him severely but petted him in quite a ridiculous manner. He lodged in a room above the store and now considered himself an independent gentleman. He wore a long calico apron and would rush forward to serve them when Kezzie and Lucy did the shopping. Kezzie had to try not to laugh, but Lucy absolutely adored him. She took him very seriously and would insist on buying whatever Jack recommended, or what he said was a good deal that day. He was immensely proud of the bicycle which he used to deliver orders, and no matter what his destination always managed to ride past the doctor's house at least once a day.

Lucy spent more and more time with Mrs McMath in the kitchen, helping her bake or mainly getting under her feet, Kezzie thought. She was growing stronger as each day passed, fed on the good natural produce of the country, milk and eggs and the fruit stored for winter, pears and plums and apples.

Dr McMath had started to train Kezzie to help in the dispensary. She was now quite deft at using the little brass scales with their tiny weights and measured out the powders accurately. She was absorbing the names of drugs, complicated Latin terms and Greek symbols. She felt excited and thrilled at being surrounded by such vast quantities of knowledge. She could learn so much here.

One day Miss Chiltern came to see the doctor. She had Jack firmly by the collar. Kezzie felt her heart drop. What trouble had he been up to now?

'Do you know,' declared Miss Chiltern, 'that this here boy can't read or write?'

'Doesn't surprise me,' said Dr McMath, polishing his spectacles. 'Shouldn't surprise you neither, Hannah. You know what some of those homes were like.'

'Doesn't surprise me at all,' she answered tartly, 'but what I cannot cope with is the boy just refusing to go to school to learn.'

She shook Jack slightly and then released him. Lucy had gone to stand beside him.

'You won't go to school?' Mrs McMath asked Jack.

He shook his head, his face red with embarrassment. Lucy put her hand in his.

'You have to go to school,' said Miss Chiltern, 'or you can't work with me.'

Jack hung his head.

'Kezzie,' said Lucy. 'Please, Kezzie. Don't make him go. They'll put him in a baby class and then everyone will laugh at him. Kezzie, you could teach him. Couldn't you? Please?'

CHAPTER 30

A letter from home

Jack was a quick learner and with Lucy's help soon made good progress. Kezzie came through from the kitchen one night leaving them both bent over their books at the table.

Dr McMath folded his newspaper and smiled.

'School over?' he asked.

'Yes,' said Kezzie, sitting down with a sigh. 'He is an intelligent boy. For his education to be neglected for so long is a scandal. These so-called philanthropists, who sent children out here, should be put in jail.'

Mrs McMath put her knitting down.

'Kezzie,' she said gently. 'It was not a bad thing in all cases. For some orphans who were destitute or in a workhouse, it was a unique opportunity.'

'Well,' said Kezzie, 'I can hardly believe it. I would like to meet such a child.'

'You have,' said Sarah McMath, 'two in fact. Andrew and I were Home Children.'

Kezzie sat up in her chair.

Dr McMath looked at his wife with a fond smile. 'We were sent over by Quarrier's Homes in Scotland at the turn of the century.'

Kezzie was astounded. 'You!' She looked from one to the other. 'What happened to you?'

'We were orphans,' said Mrs McMath, 'and I suppose that the home thought that they would give us a fresh start in a new country away from the slums in Glasgow.'

'Do you remember the journey, Sarah?' asked Dr McMath. 'It took eighteen days to get to Halifax, and then the train, a gigantic monster pouring out steam.'

'I remember rats running around in the steerage,' said his wife, 'and seeing whales in the ocean spouting water. It was the most exciting thing that had ever happened to me.'

'I was put on a farm back east,' said the doctor. 'It is much colder there in the winter. The first snowfall was measured in feet, not inches. My mattress was a straw tick made from flour bags with a sheet and a blanket. I rose at dawn and worked all day, milking cows, hoeing corn, lifting potatoes, splitting wood, harnessing the horses for ploughing. It was hard work, but the folk were kindly enough.'

'I was sent into domestic service,' said Mrs McMath, 'but the old lady treated me as her own. I was very fortunate. She left me her home when she died, and even though it was mortgaged I started up a boarding house and made more than enough to live on.'

'And then one day,' continued her husband, 'a handsome young fellow came to lodge with you because he was going to college in the town.'

'And he took me out for a buggy ride and went into a field and picked me a bunch of brown-eyed Susans . . .'

They smiled at each other.

'"He is the God that giveth the desolate a home to dwell in,"' murmured Dr McMath.

Kezzie took down the chess set from the shelf by the fire.

The world is a strange place, she thought as she set out the pieces, full of contradictions and conflicting ideas.

A few weeks later a letter arrived for her from her grandfather.

My dear Kezzie

I have received your letters and I am glad that all is well with Lucy and yourself, although I sense that you may have been through difficulties but have not gone into detail. Thank the doctor and his wife on my behalf and tell them I will pass their kindness on to someone else as this is the only way I can repay them. Kezzie, I must tell you that I have had a great promotion and that I have a tenement flat to rent in Clydebank. It is very well appointed with extra space and a toilet inside, which I myself do not consider to be hygienic, but it is a welcome facility in the winter-time. There is room for yourself and Lucy, a school close by and also a college. There is an Italian café not far away and I have spoken to the owner and he can let you work there at night and you could take courses in the college in daytime. Now, Kezzie, these are my thoughts. However, you sound as though you are very happy in Canada, and Lucy is thriving, and if you decide to make a new life there I will understand. It is a new land and there must be many opportunities, and you will have many friends.

So, I will understand if you decide to stay, but if you decide
to come back I am here for you.
Your ever-loving grandfather.

Kezzie kept the letter in her pocket all day as she worked
in the surgery. Her mind was in turmoil. The time had
passed quickly since they had arrived in Waterfoot, and
Lucy was now so well that Mrs McMath had been talking of enrolling her in school. Kezzie knew Lucy had
taken a very special place in the older woman's heart.

After dinner when they were drinking coffee in the
sitting-room Kezzie handed them the letter. The doctor
read it carefully and then gave it to his wife. She read it
twice and then took her hanky out and blew her nose.

'Kezzie,' said Dr McMath, 'you must decide what you
think best. All I would say is, that I too had thought of
you studying here and perhaps winning a place at
university.' He sighed. 'What will you do?'

'I don't know,' wailed Kezzie. 'I feel I am being torn in
two. I cannot take this responsibility.'

'No one else can,' said Sarah McMath.

Kezzie folded her hands in her lap. It was true, she
thought. There was no one else to make this decision.
Not Dr and Mrs McMath, or her Aunt Bella or
Grandfather, a thousand and more miles away. Lucy was
too young and vulnerable. She, Kezzie, had to make the
decision of a lifetime for both of them.

In the kitchen warming some milk for Lucy before
bed, Mrs McMath spoke to Kezzie. 'No matter what you
decide there is always a home for both of you here,' she
said.

Impulsively Kezzie hugged her.

Kezzie lay in bed that night unable to sleep. Forsythia would be coming out just now in Scotland, bright yellow on brown bush. There would be a great golden carpet of daffodils beneath the trees, and the tops of the hills still covered with snow. The missing of the place and the people was suddenly a physical pain. She placed her hands on her stomach and then across her heart. Until now she'd been so occupied with merely keeping Lucy alive she had no time to dwell on her own feelings. Now they came back in a rush, the sound of friends' voices, the calling of children in the dusty village street.

The sight of Bella, always cheerful in spite of troubles, with her little ones clutching at her skirt. And Grandad, she had an image of him in her head, his tall figure with his muffler and cap, and the smell of pipe tobacco. It must have taken courage for him to have written such a letter, releasing her as best he could from any obligation to return.

Except . . . there were bonds that you could not break, for instance the one that linked her and Michael Donohoe. The one that had made Matt McPhee turn back on the road to Skye. Kin calling to kin. With a terrible realisation Kezzie knew that if she remained here in Canada then she might never see these people again.

What should she do? Always before, when Kezzie faced trouble, the road had been a hard one to travel but in one way the path was already chosen for her. Now she must decide. This beautiful country with its great open heart was waiting to welcome Lucy and her. And they would prosper here. She knew that as a certainty, as surely as the day followed night. She fell asleep at last, her mind troubled.

Kezzie was awoken the next morning by the sound of honking. She went to her little window and pulled aside the curtain. Across the fields on the marshland she could see a flock of geese, unmistakably Canadian geese with the black neck and head, and a broad white band across throat and cheeks.

She looked at them for a moment or two as they shifted restlessly about, cackling and bickering with each other.

She opened the window to see them better. It was a deep instinctive urge that commanded them. Centuries of inbuilt pattern dictated their direction, as each year, winter over, they returned to their breeding grounds. They are going home, Kezzie thought suddenly, as I should. She wrapped her arms around herself and leaned out on the windowsill. She *would* go back to Scotland, she decided. When Lucy was well enough to travel they would cross the Atlantic and be reunited with Grandad. At the moment, although she had found Lucy, it was as though her journey had not yet finished. She would go home. It would be a completion.

But she would come back. That she knew also. More than a spoken commitment or a resolute thought, it was an urge within her that she would answer. She had an instinctive feeling that she would return to Canada.

From the marshes there came a great disturbance and

flapping of wings as the geese, answering an unseen signal, scrambled to be airborne.

Kezzie looked above her and watched them finding their direction. The birds formed a long distinctive V shape and turned north. They honked loudly, and it seemed to her, happily, as they headed towards home.

BOOK II:
A HOMECOMING
FOR KEZZIE

This story is for Dora Cuollo

BOOK II:
A HOMECOMING FOR KEZZIE

PART ONE
Scotland

CHAPTER 1

Atlantic crossing

'Look!' said Lucy. 'There it is again.'

And she pointed up to where the lone Luftwaffe spotter plane droned above the ocean liner. The ragged sound was an irritant in the hot summer sky, a waspish buzz in a pleasant day.

Some of the American ladies at the side of the boat shaded their eyes to watch. One took her hat off and waved, red and blue ribbons trailing from the brim of her white straw boater.

Kezzie, who was sheltering from the brisk Atlantic breeze in the lee of one of the lifeboats, could now see the pilot quite clearly. Goggled and grim-faced, he gave no signal as he made his second wide arc across their bows.

'He's coming back! He's coming back!' Lucy jumped up and down in excitement beside her. Kezzie frowned and took her little sister's hand.

What made her suddenly afraid? The abrupt blocking of the sun between sea and sky as the pilot completed his turn and passed above them? The sudden darkness, and the chilling of the air?

What instinct made her grab the child and yank her arm so hard that Lucy cried out, 'Kezzie, don't!'

Kezzie turned to face the sea, her eyes following the grey outline of the machine as it banked and tilted purposefully, lining itself up with the ship. Its altitude dropped dramatically and then suddenly the shadow of the plane was sweeping back across the Atlantic waves and racing towards them.

'Kezzie, let go!' cried Lucy.

But Kezzie was running now. Frantically seeking cover on the bleached white deck of the Atlantic liner, with the quoits scattered at random and the deckchairs set in a long line to catch the sun.

An open door . . . It was a hatch to the crew's quarters, nevertheless, a place of safety . . . And she was inside, dragging Lucy with her as the plane came roaring down the length of the boat.

The noise filled the whole ocean. The scream of the engines, the sudden chattering of the twin guns on its forward snout, the frantic cries of the passengers on deck, the shouts of the ship's officers. Kezzie put her hands quickly over Lucy's ears and gathered her little sister towards her. It lasted for seconds only. Then silence, as if a blind had been drawn, a lamp abruptly turned down. The happy conversations and jolly waves on the promenade deck, the playful teasing between young men and girls, the laughter of the children, all shuttered in a moment of time.

And it seemed to Kezzie, when she thought about it afterwards, that although it wasn't until the beginning of September, nearly two months later, that the Second World War started officially, it had been on the cruise liner travelling home from Canada to Scotland that the war began for her.

'Scare tactics,' the captain's voice boomed out from the ship's speakers almost immediately. 'Be assured, there was no serious threat at any time. We were keeping a close watch on him. He had his guns aimed high, and had overshot the deck before he fired. An irresponsible act to try and alarm us. But are we upset?' His laughter echoed in the air. 'I should think not. Now, I want to see all of you at our celebrations tonight. Paper hats must be worn. No exceptions. Everyone to be there, from two to ninety-two. A prize for the best hat.'

Notices were quickly posted all over the ship. There was to be an informal party after dinner, their last night at sea before they docked tomorrow in Glasgow. It was a way of restoring morale after the shock of the incident earlier. Although no one had been injured, the atmosphere aboard changed completely. Few passengers had stayed on deck despite the continuing daylight of the long summer evening. People crowded in the lounges or chatted in groups on the stairs and companionways.

'This is an American ship,' one man with a southern drawl declared angrily. 'How dare they frighten our women and children? They'd better not try to tangle with Uncle Sam. We'd lick them faster than it'd take to whistle "Dixie".'

There were murmurs of approval from his audience. And in every part of the boat the talk was the same.

'Let them come,' Kezzie heard a very elderly Englishwoman proclaim in a tremulous voice. 'We beat them once, we'll do it again.'

The speaker must be at least eighty years old, Kezzie thought. As she led Lucy along to their cabin, she smiled, imagining the old lady dressed like Queen Boudicca and driving a chariot into battle.

'What's happening?' Lucy asked as Kezzie washed and then dressed her in a pretty frock.

'We're going to a party,' said Kezzie, as she combed her little sister's blonde curls.

Kezzie had told Lucy that the pilot of the plane had made a mistake. She certainly was not going to worry the child by mentioning the threat of war in Europe. Her sister had recovered well from her traumas and illness of the last year. At seven years old her understanding was limited but she was still very sensitive to atmosphere.

Kezzie patted her on the head. 'Play with your doll, pet, while I get ready.'

She picked up Lucy's old rag doll and gave it to her. We've travelled far together, the three of us, Kezzie thought as she smoothed down the doll's skirt and adjusted its hat. She remembered the terrible winter of 1937, just after their father had been killed in a pit accident in Scotland. Herself, Lucy and their grandfather had been turned out of their tied house in the miners' rows. The only shelter they could find had been a bothy on a neighbouring farm. With Christmas approaching, and in dire poverty, Kezzie had been determined to make

Lucy a special gift. The nights she'd worked late, cutting up precious linen, stuffing those arms and legs and plaiting the woollen hair! It had been worth the effort and sacrifice. The doll, whom Lucy had promptly named Kissy, not only gave her little sister great joy, but, Kezzie believed, had actually saved the child's life.

While Lucy played with her doll Kezzie changed into smarter clothes. She put on a dark blue suit with a full skirt. The jacket was edged in black piping with corded frogging on the front and fitted closely under her bust. Underneath she wore a white high necked blouse. As she pinned up some of her brown curls on the top of her head, she looked in the long mirror which was fastened with brass studs to the door of their cabin. A tall dark-eyed girl gazed back at her. Kezzie hardly recognised herself from the gawky skinny person with tumbled hair who had left Scotland barely ten months before.

The crew had organised music, games and some ice-cream and jelly to try to dispel the anxiety which now pervaded the ship. There were tables set out with cardboard, paper, scissors, raffia and ribbons. Kezzie helped Lucy make herself a red top hat which promptly slid over her nose as soon as she placed it on her head. Kezzie laughed out loud.

They found a quiet place to sit away from the crowd where Lucy could eat her ice-cream. Before the music and dancing began the captain made a speech of welcome and then spoke of the earlier harassment.

'They'll find that we're not so easily intimidated,' he declared. 'If it comes to a scrap then they'll find we're ready. Ready and willing.'

Rousing cheers came from the floor of the room. Kezzie glanced around her. Men and women were nodding in agreement. Some of the smaller children were waving little flags made from coloured paper. Everyone seemed happy and enthusiastic at the thought of war. Why then was she uneasy? Her grandfather had fought in the First World War. When he talked about it he lamented the terrible loss of life. 'Nothing glorious about it at all,' he had said.

Kezzie thought again of the plane. She recalled Lucy's excitement, she who had never seen an aeroplane before. What had the pilot's thoughts been, surveying their upturned faces as he circled above them? Had he misunderstood the intentions of the lady waving her hat? Perhaps taken it as an angry gesture of defiance, the sight of the colours, red, white, and blue enraging him? Why was it, that a recent invention like an aeroplane was immediately adapted and used by man for the purpose of war and killing? Kezzie's one vivid memory of today was the American lady's hat floating away on the grey Atlantic waves, the bright ribbons bedraggled and sad.

Kezzie shook her head and firmly pushed all these thoughts away. She and Lucy were going home to Grandad. Returning, after an absence of almost a year, to stay with him in his tenement house in Clydebank. She would be cheerful and try not to think about war. The music had begun. Already children and adults were taking the floor. The tunes were mainly popular and light, a combination of British traditional and modern American.

Kezzie felt a touch on her shoulder. She looked up. A tall young man with very black hair was standing just behind her chair.

'May I dance with you?' he asked.

CHAPTER 2

Dinner party

Kezzie glanced at the dance floor, crowded with couples laughing and talking together, and dancing. Then she looked up at the boy who had spoken to her. He wore an elegant dinner suit with a white shirt and bow tie, and had the dark good looks of an Italian. He gave Kezzie the impression that he would dance very well.

Reluctantly she shook her head, and indicated Lucy who was eating her way through her bowlful of ice-cream. 'I don't wish to leave my sister on her own,' she said.

The young man smiled down at her. The effect of his smile, bright white teeth in his tanned face was startling.

'Of course,' he said politely. 'May I sit with you for a little while then?' he asked.

Kezzie hesitated. She was almost sixteen years old, it was 1939, and she had spent some time in North America where the social customs were much more relaxed. However, she wasn't sure if it would be the done thing in Europe. Most people on the ship were travelling

194

in family groups or with male escorts. She should really say no, but it would be so pleasant to have someone of approximately her own age to chat to, and . . . he was very handsome. She glanced around her uncertainly.

The young man smiled again. 'One moment, please,' he said. 'I will return.'

Kezzie watched him as he crossed to another table where an older man and woman were sitting. He spoke to them and then all three stood up and came towards Kezzie.

'I would like to present my family to you.' The boy gave a slight bow. 'My mother, Signora Biagi, my father, Signor Biagi, and myself, Ricardo Biagi.'

Kezzie introduced herself and Lucy, and shook hands with Ricardo and his parents. She invited them to sit down.

'Now we are chaperoned.' Ricardo smiled at her in triumph. 'So everything is swell, no?'

Kezzie laughed at the Americanism which sounded strange to her ears.

'Everything is swell,' she agreed.

Signora Biagi spoke to her. 'You must excuse us,' she said. 'Our English is not very correct, but Ricardo,' she gazed at her son with pride, 'is fluent in both Italian and English. He is a college student,' she added, and stretched across to pat her son's hand.

'Mama,' protested Ricardo. 'You are boasting again.' He turned to Kezzie. 'Do you find that your parents do this all the time?'

Kezzie looked at him. 'I wish they could,' she said softly.

As she grasped the meaning of Kezzie's words Ricardo's mother covered her mouth with her hand. '*Zita!*' she exclaimed. 'You have lost your mama and papa, no? Ricardo. Apologise at once. So clumsy,' she scolded him, 'so clumsy and unthinking.'

'I am so sorry, so very sorry,' said Ricardo. He looked so comically sad and forlorn that Kezzie almost laughed.

'Please don't upset yourselves,' she said quickly. 'Lucy and I have some very happy memories and we talk about them often. Our grandfather has looked after us since our father died. He lives in Clydebank, and we're going back now to live with him again.'

'He works in the shipyards?' asked Signor Biagi.

'Do you know him?' Kezzie asked in amazement.

Signora Biagi laughed. 'My sister tells me, in Clydebank, *everyone* works in the shipyards.'

Kezzie found Ricardo's parents very easy to talk to. They told her they were going to spend a few months in Scotland to help Signora Biagi's recently widowed sister who owned a delicatessen shop.

'Ricardo will help her manage for a little while before he returns to America when his college starts in autumn,' said Signora Biagi. 'Then I may stay on a bit longer. It depends how she is.' She spread her hands out and shrugged. 'Her son is in the army and stationed in England, so she is very lonely.'

After a few minutes Ricardo stood up. He looked at Kezzie. 'Now that etiquette has been honoured,' he said formally, 'perhaps I will be able to have a dance?'

'I can dance,' said Lucy quickly. She placed her spoon on the table and wiped her mouth with her hand.

'Lucy!' exclaimed Kezzie.

Ricardo laughed.

'It *is* a party, isn't it?' said Lucy. 'And I want to dance.'

'Such a pretty little girl,' Signora Biagi leaned over and stroked Lucy's hair, 'should certainly have someone to dance with her.' She offered her hand to Lucy. 'Dance with me, *piccola*,' she said.

Lucy took Signora Biagi's two hands in her own and they both skipped off across the room.

Kezzie stood up slowly as Ricardo drew her chair out. A sudden feeling of shyness came over her as he led her out on to the dance floor. The band was playing a slow number, and he put his arm around her waist and began to steer her around the floor. Although she was quite tall, her head scarcely reached his shoulder. She had guessed correctly, Ricardo was an expert dancer, and they were soon twirling about among the rest of the crowd. Kezzie relaxed and began to enjoy the feeling. It was fun to glide along with the music. She couldn't remember the last time she had danced with a boy.

And then suddenly she did. And the recollection struck her with such force that she stumbled slightly.

'You all right?' Ricardo bent his head to look at her anxiously.

'Yes,' she whispered.

But it wasn't his face that was in front of Kezzie now. Nor his brown Italian eyes that she saw. She was with the potato pickers at the close of harvest nearly two years ago, on Stonevale farm in the west of Scotland. The noise in the barn, the sweet smell of the charred potato skins, the taste of the scones and the buttered bannocks. And the music . . . the fiddle, the thudding beat of the bodhrán . . . and she was being swung around the floor by the young Irishman, Michael Donohoe, and his dark blue eyes were full of mischief as he made up some wild tale, with himself as the bold hero slaying a dozen giants, and rescuing a thousand swooning maidens . . .

Kezzie stood motionless in the middle of the ballroom.

'You are tired,' said Ricardo.

'A little,' said Kezzie.

For no reason at all she felt her eyes fill with tears.

'Then we must stop.'

He took her back to the table. Lucy was sitting on Signora Biagi's knee. She was almost asleep. Kezzie gathered her up quickly.

'Thank you for such kind company,' she said. 'I must say goodnight.' She turned to Ricardo. 'Thank you for dancing with me.'

'My pleasure.' He made a small bow.

Kezzie tucked Lucy up in her bunk and then undressed slowly for bed. As she laid her suit across a chair ready for the morning, she fingered the soft woollen material. Dr McMath and his wife Sarah had bought this costume for her, the day before she and Lucy had left Waterfoot, the little village on the far side of the Canadian Rocky Mountains.

'It's far too expensive,' Kezzie had protested.

'When you wear it, think of us,' they'd replied.

She had thought about them practically every day over the last fortnight. They had become as parents to her and Lucy during their year in Canada. Taking them into their home, caring for Lucy when she was ill, employing Kezzie in their surgery. And more than that, Kezzie thought, much more. They had given out freely of their love, spontaneously and without hesitation, easing from her own shoulders the terrible strain she'd suffered during the weeks she had searched for her sister, when Lucy had been lost in Scotland and ended up in an orphanage in Canada.

They would have liked her and Lucy to stay on with them, Kezzie knew that. They had in fact offered to help Kezzie go to university and realise her own dream of being a doctor, but Kezzie had decided to take Lucy back to Scotland. Her grandfather was old and had been deeply affected by the death of his son, their father, nearly two years ago. He needed her and Lucy now.

Besides . . . she herself had a strong urge to come home, felt that it would be good for Lucy to find her childhood again. They might, in time, return to Canada, a country where ambitions could be fulfilled, dreams were born and came to life. But at the moment, Scotland, despite the impending trouble with Germans, was the place they had to be.

As she lay down that night Kezzie hoped she had made the right decision.

Towards midnight Kezzie awoke. Lucy was standing beside her bed. She had her doll clutched in her hands.

'Kissy's frightened,' she said.

Kezzie stretched out her arms. 'Do you think a cuddle would help?' she asked.

Lucy nodded. Kezzie took the doll and gave it a

long hug. Without letting go she regarded her little sister gravely, then she pulled back the bedclothes.

'You'd better come in and help me watch over her,' she said.

They lay together with the doll tucked between them. In a few moments Lucy fell asleep again. Kezzie was awake for a long time. She felt the heavy seas of the Atlantic give way to quieter waters. As the ship edged its way round the Mull of Kintyre it seemed to her that its movement had altered, the heaving dip and roll of the ocean changing to the quiet flow of the Firth of Clyde. And as she closed her eyes she sensed the slow deep current which was pulling her and Lucy back to Scotland.

CHAPTER 3

Arrival in Clydebank

Lucy and Kezzie were the first passengers on deck the next morning as their ship made its stately journey up the Clyde to the dock at Glasgow.

'Will Grandad be there?' asked Lucy, pulling on Kezzie's hand as they stood at the deck rail. 'Will he? Will he?'

'Hush. Hush,' said Kezzie irritably. 'How do I know? Perhaps he will be working at the shipyard. He's very busy.' She looked down at her little sister, and felt her annoyance flow away from her as she saw the upturned anxious face. 'I've got his address in Clydebank. Don't worry, we'll see him soon.'

He'll be there, Kezzie thought, as she saw the summer sky lighten from the east. The docks and wharfs and water reflected the glow of the rising sun and she watched the buildings slip past. The long warehouses and offices, shops and factories, and tumble of cottages along the riverbank guarded behind by tall tenements.

He'll be there, she thought.

She knew that Grandad *was* busy. He had told her in his letters to Canada. Rearmament work was flooding into the shipyards and factories, revitalising the industrial heartland of Scotland. Firms were receiving government orders as the country prepared itself for war. People were working again. Even the small knitwear factory in Shawcross, where she herself had been employed for some months, had increased production. Miss Dunlop, the secretary, had written to Kezzie in Canada telling her that they were now making hundreds of socks and gloves for soldiers and sailors. The wind whipped up the estuary and Kezzie shivered. She took her shawl from her own shoulders and wound it around Lucy.

'There,' she pointed. 'Now put your hands in your cony muff.' She pointed to the little tube of soft white rabbit's fur which Sarah McMath had stitched herself.

Lucy stuck one hand away, but with the other she kept a firm grip of Kezzie's fingers. Kezzie didn't say anything, despite the fact that she knew the child must be cold. She only pulled her close to her and tucked the little girl in against her skirt. Lucy had blossomed in the last few months in Canada. The good food, the loving care of the McMaths, living in that clean wide country had all helped restore her health. But she was still insecure, afraid of the dark, the unknown, anything new. And now she clung to Kezzie, and without fuss Kezzie stroked her head and talked to her quietly.

'Do you see the birds in the water?' she asked her, pointing to where some ducks bobbed and dived by the edge of the river. 'Don't they look funny with their bottoms in the air? Look at that one. He's stolen a piece of food from his brother. Isn't he naughty?'

So Kezzie passed the time calling out the names of everything she could see as the boat moved further towards the heart of the city. On either side they saw houses and bowling greens, grey streets, lanes and wynds, with soft hills beyond, rolling green and golden with a ripening harvest. And above them the aching cries of the seagulls welcomed them home.

There were more people on deck now. The rails were becoming crowded with the other passengers, all of them craning to see some part of this great city.

Kezzie herself could feel excitement rising within her; her thoughts, like the river, becoming more congested the further upstream they moved. The memories of her journey out to Canada. How unhappy she had been! How anxious and sick with worry! She hardly recalled looking at the sights at all. Her head was so filled with impatience at any delay, willing the boat to go faster to catch up with the immigration ship which Lucy was on.

The crew were getting ready to dock, moving around the foredeck, the officers calling out instructions. Kezzie pressed close against the rail, determined to be in the best position to catch the first glimpse of her beloved grandad. There were groups of people on the quayside. Clusters of families, old folk and young children, some businessmen, horse-drawn traps, a few motor cars waiting.

He would be there. She knew he would. She scanned the faces. Looking for a tall man, white haired. A sudden recollection of how he had looked one night arguing politics with his cronies clicked in her head, like a snapshot from a photograph album. His cap to one side, his pipe gripped in his fist as he made his point. Maybe he wouldn't wear his cap today, just hold it in his hand perhaps? She searched among the waiting friends and relatives. Perhaps he was there and she hadn't recognised him. Was her memory faulty? It was almost twelve months since she had seen him last. He might have changed. She certainly had. Her face was less peaked, her skin browner, and she was taller and stronger.

He would set himself apart, she suddenly realised, not mingle among the crowd. She looked around the dockside. He would pick somewhere separate, a place where he would stand out, knowing that she would be searching for him, desperate for a sight of his face. She and Lucy both.

Her eyes flicked along the length of the quay, past the officials and welcome groups. There were the luggage trolleys . . . a loading bay with tackle and hoist . . . the cargo shed . . . and . . . then, a raised platform for a crane-fixing.

A tall broad figure stood there, red kerchief knotted at his neck, bareheaded, arms waving high above his head.

Kezzie gasped and shrieked. 'He's there! Look, Lucy, he's there!'

'Of course he's there,' said Lucy calmly, although she was far too small to see properly. 'I *knew* he'd be there.'

'Your grandpa?' enquired a voice beside her.

Kezzie turned. It was Ricardo, standing just behind her.

'I think so.' Kezzie felt her voice tremble.

'You follow me, please,' said Ricardo in his precise

English and, picking up her Gladstone bag, he pushed his way through the crowd, making a passage for her and Lucy.

There was a surging mass of people at the exit rail. The crew slung the ropes out, the thick plaits uncoiling across the oily water and onto the quay. The shoremen expertly tied them up.

'This way,' said Ricardo and he took her arm, and guided her to the spot where the gangway was being run out from the side of the boat. He manoeuvred her into a position where she would be among the first to go ashore. Then he handed her back her bag. 'I must go and see to my mother,' he said. 'I will say "*ciao*" but I will call on you some time, if I may?'

Kezzie nodded, and he touched her hair. Then he smiled at her and was gone. She turned back just as the deckhand unhooked the barrier chain.

'Come on, Kezzie.' Lucy's nails dug into her hand. 'Hurry up. I can see Grandad.' She pulled on Kezzie's arm. 'Come on,' she said again. 'We're going home.'

CHAPTER 4

Homecoming

And home they came.

Lucy raced down the gangplank and, worming her way through the mass of people, she ran at once, with no strangeness or hesitation, into the arms of her grandad. He gave a great shout and swung her high up into the air. Then, holding her on his hip, he stretched out his free hand to Kezzie.

And it was she who hung back, feeling more grown up and less able to be so free with her emotions than Lucy, her strangeness making it more awkward for her to come forward. Her grandad was looking at her, his head to one side. She was now almost eye to eye with him.

He smiled at her, the lines of his weathered face creasing up in an expression of absolute happiness.

'Aye, lass,' he said.

And he came towards her, and kissed her, and then she was just as wild as Lucy had been, hugging him and holding on, never to let go.

On the tram out to Dalmuir it was the same. Sitting

close together, the three of them talking all at the same time. It was only as they walked along the street beside the long line of tenements that Lucy began to slow down. By the time they had climbed the first set of stairs in the close where Grandad lived she was beginning to grow weary.

'How many more stairs, Grandad?'

Lucy's voice was tired and breathless.

'We've only come up one flight, hen,' her grandad laughed. 'There's lots more to climb.'

Kezzie, several steps behind them, could imagine how her sister must be feeling. She herself was exhausted. Lucy, younger than she and more frail, must be completely worn out.

'Can we stop for a minute?' she called after them, as they reached the second landing.

Her grandfather put the big suitcase down at once. 'I'm sorry, Kezzie,' he said as she caught up with him. He let go Lucy's hand and put both his arms round her. 'I'm just that keen to let ye see the house. I've waited so long for this moment. I'm like a wean, bursting with excitement.'

A door on the landing opened. 'Mr Munro, is it you who is making all the noise?' enquired a very tart voice. 'My husband and son are on nights, and trying to sleep.'

'Oh no,' said Kezzie's grandad quietly. He leaned over and whispered in her ear, 'This one's a real nippy sweetie.'

He took his arm from Kezzie's shoulder. A woman of about fifty stood in the entrance of her house. She had grey hair pulled severely back from her face. A frilled pinny tied at the waist covered her clothes, and she held a duster in her hands.

'Mrs Sweeney,' said Grandad. 'These are my two grandchildren, Kezzie and Lucy.'

The woman glared at them for a moment. 'Aye,' she said. 'I remember ye saying they were due today.' She put her hand in her apron pocket. 'There's a wee bit tablet for the bairn.' She held it out to Lucy. 'I made it myself.'

Lucy hesitated and looked at Kezzie. Kezzie nodded.

'It's all right,' she said. 'It's like the candy you ate back home. Say "thank you".'

'That's very kind of you, Mrs Sweeney,' said Kezzie as Lucy gabbled a hurried thank you and started to pull the wrapping from her sweet. What could Grandad mean by describing their neighbour as sharp and waspish? She seemed very pleasant.

'Don't mention it, dear,' said the older woman. Her inquisitive eyes roved over Kezzie and Lucy, their clothes and luggage. 'The wee one looks as though she needs some fattening up. And,' her eyes flicked up and down Kezzie disapprovingly, 'maybe yersel too.'

Kezzie set her mouth but said nothing. She exchanged a look with her grandad. 'Told you,' his expression was saying.

'Now,' Mrs Sweeney went on, 'we'll have to come to some arrangement about your turn at the wash-house and drying green. I might have to come upstairs and explain it all to you. A young thing like you will have no notion of running a home.'

Kezzie's eyes widened but, with a great effort, she smiled brightly. 'I'll look forward to that,' she replied.

'Meanwhile, please don't let us keep you . . .' she hesitated, and let her eyes rest on the duster in the other woman's hand, '. . . from any work that you might have to do.' Then she picked up her bag and marched up the next flight of the tenement.

To Kezzie's surprise her grandad was quite gleeful as they continued up the stairs.

'Months and months I've suffered that woman,' he said. 'Every time I'd pass her door, out she'd come, chivvying me about this and that. The sound of my boots on the stairs, muddy footprints on her freshly-washed close.' He laughed. 'You put her gas at a peep, Kezzie. That's the first time I've seen her short of an answer.'

He stopped at last on the top landing.

'Here it is,' he said, and opened the front door proudly.

Kezzie and Lucy followed him inside.

'There's lots of one-room houses in the tenements, they're called single ends,' he explained as he led them through the tiny hall. 'We're a bit better off. It's a room and kitchen, and an inside lavatory. Look.' He opened the first door on the left and proudly displayed the flush toilet with its cistern attached to the wall above, and the long dangling chain. 'It'll be very handy in the wintertime, most of the other closes have a shared toilet on each landing. There's a wee glory hole that I'll sleep in. It's really a walk-in cupboard off the kitchen.' He pointed to the door beside the toilet. 'You girls will have this room for yourselves.' He led them inside. There was a bedside cabinet, a wash-stand and a plain single brass bedstead. A little cot stood in the corner. Grandad looked from it to Lucy then back again.

'Oh dear,' he said.

'I'm a big girl now, Grandad,' said Lucy.

'I can see that, hen.' He laughed and scratched his head. 'I spent weeks making that.'

Kezzie put her arm through his. 'Don't worry, Lucy and I will share meantime. It will be more cosy, at any rate.'

They crossed the hall to the main room. The fire was lit in the kitchen grate and the table set for tea. Two easy stairs and a small stool were set around the fire with a big old chest of drawers opposite. Kezzie gazed at it for a moment or two and at the oval mirror above.

'Grandad,' she said, and then found that she couldn't go on. It was seeing the fire more than anything else that brought back the memories of their life in the miners' rows. The hearth as the heart of the house. Not just for welcome and warmth, but for cooking, and boiling up water to wash and clean. Kezzie felt the tears coming from behind her eyelids. 'Grandad,' she said again.

He came over to her and she put her arms around his neck. He sat her down in one of the chairs. 'You have a wee rest,' he said, and he patted her hand. Then he took out his hanky and blew his nose loudly.

Kezzie wiped her eyes and looked around.

'Some of the furniture . . .' She hesitated. 'It's ours, isn't it?'

'Course it's ours,' said Lucy. 'This is my stool, isn't it, Grandad?' She indicated the stool on which she had sat down.

Her grandad nodded as he stirred up the fire and set

the kettle on the grid above the coals. 'I'd kept all the pawn tickets, and I managed to get some of our stuff back. And young Michael Donohoe helped a bit.'

'Michael . . .' Kezzie repeated the name. 'I was thinking of him only last night,' she said. 'Have you seen him recently?'

'He was billeted at Edinburgh Castle for a while, and he used to visit me.' Her grandad paused. 'Your letters, you see . . . I helped him read them. He wasn't very good with the words and he couldn't ask any of his mates. Then the Argylls were posted to Palestine. He went off not so long ago.'

Kezzie felt her heart move within her. She had missed him! She thought of his letters, sent out to her in Canada faithfully each month. The careful elaborate writing. It must have taken him hours to write those few pages. She looked around the kitchen. It was so like Michael to help her grandfather reclaim up the bits and pieces which they had been forced to sell. She must send him a note of thanks at once.

'How is everyone else?' she asked.

'Yer Aunt Bella's man was laid up again. His lungs are packing in. He's got the black spit, but he's back at work now. She's away to a cousin in the Highlands for a wee holiday wi' the weans.'

'Is the pit on full production?' asked Kezzie.

'Aye, it's the one benefit that war brings. Employment for all. Here, have some tea.' Her grandad was putting milk and sugar into the cups. 'And there's bread and jam.'

He picked up a knife and began to cut the loaf.

Kezzie watched him as he worked. He was so much

fitter than when she had last seen him. The regular pay and the very fact that he was working again showed in his whole demeanour.

She glanced around the room. A rag rug would do very nicely in front of the hearth, she thought. She would teach Lucy how to make one. A few cushions would help too, perhaps an embroidered table-cover, and the window curtains . . . They were just what she would have expected her grandad to choose, heavy and dull. Even if they couldn't afford new ones, she would at least make a nice tie-back or fringe the hems.

She looked up. Her grandfather was watching her.

'You're making plans,' he said. 'I can tell. Ye've got that busy look on your face. Your mother was just the same. A few days like that, then the spring cleaning would start or it would be a great round of baking or reorganising the whole house.'

Kezzie smiled. She got up and put her hands around his neck. 'I was only thinking that a few cushions would make the place a bit brighter. You don't mind, Grandad?'

'Mind? Mind?' said the old man. 'I've waited months for this. Each night sitting here on my own. I'd look around me, and well . . . I knew I had a great wee house, but that's all it was, a house. Now you're here, Kezzie, it will be a home.'

CHAPTER 5

Settling in

During the next weeks Kezzie and Lucy settled into their new home. To begin with Kezzie noticed every little difference in their living pattern. Instead of the calling of the blue jays from the tall trees in the woods around Waterfoot rousing them in the morning, they awoke to the sounds of the Clyde. The elegent fretwork of the ever-moving cranes, black lace against blue sky, made a backdrop to the constant noise. The ringing, hammering and clatter from shipyards, the tramp of tackety boots in the streets, and the blare of the hooters which ruled the days and lives of the workers.

Life in the tenement was strange to Kezzie. She had seen tall buildings as she passed through the big Canadian cities such as Montreal. They called them sky-scrapers on the other side of the Atlantic. The tenements here weren't nearly so large but she found it odd to live in such close proximity to others and to have to share your garden and washing line. The people in each close seemed to think of themselves as a kind of extended

213

family. The three small boys on the first floor now called Lucy their cousin and looked on Kezzie almost as an aunt. Houses were rarely locked, and in the ones with younger children, the front door lay ajar for most of the day. There was great rivalry between the closes. Mrs Sweeney was the self-appointed leader in Kezzie's and looked down with scorn on the others in the street. She carried tales of their inferior conditions. Their middens were overflowing, their children less well behaved, the stairs and landing not so well kept.

Kezzie had quickly been informed which day was hers at the wash-house and when she could use the drying greens. She tried very hard to be friendly and polite, although she found Mrs Sweeney a great strain.

'I think ye might have won her round,' her grandad told her one evening. 'She almost smiled at me tonight. Mind you,' he added, 'it nearly cracked her face to do it.'

Lucy giggled.

'I don't know,' Kezzie sighed. 'She tries to find fault with everything I do. Nothing seems to please her. She thinks I'm far too young to be keeping house.'

There was a sharp rattle at their letterbox and an empty cotton reel dropped through onto the mat. Lucy picked it up and brought it into the kitchen.

'Must be the bairns playing about,' said her grandad. He took it from her. 'But seeing as how it's handy I'll just make ye a wee knitting bobbin.'

Lucy watched fascinated as he hammered in the points of four small nails, one in each corner at the top of the wooden spool. Then he wound some woollen yarn round the nail heads, looping it through so that the tail dropped down the centre hole.

'See?' He took her small fingers in his own and showed her how to do it.

'Ye can make a knitted cord as long as you like, any colour you fancy,' he said.

In a few minutes Lucy was following his instructions.

'What can I use it for?' she asked Kezzie.

Kezzie picked up the end of the thin tube of knitting which was beginning to appear through the end of the cotton reel.

'Lots of things,' she said. 'A hair ribbon maybe, or laces. You can lay it flat, wind it round and round and then stitch it together, and make a hat for your doll.'

Lucy frowned, concentrating hard on her bobbin knitting.

It wasn't until some days later that Kezzie discovered exactly why the cotton reel had been posted through their letterbox. As she returned from the shops Mrs Price from the floor below was standing chatting to Mrs Sweeney on the landing.

'This close is needing a good sweep and scrub if you ask me,' the older woman proclaimed loudly. She shook out her duster vigorously. 'I do my share, and I'm sure you do yours, Mrs Price. It's up to others to do theirs.'

Kezzie put her shopping bag down.

'Would you like me to do it this week?' she asked politely.

'*Like* ye to do it,' repeated Mrs Sweeney indignantly. 'I should think so. It is your turn.'

Kezzie flushed. 'I'm sorry,' she said. 'I didn't know.'

'Didn't ye get yer bobbin?' demanded the older woman.

'Bobbin?' repeated Kezzie. 'I'm sorry, I don't understand.'

Mrs Price smiled and laid her hand on Kezzie's arm. 'I put the empty thread spool in your door a couple of nights ago when my week was finished. I thought you'd know what it meant.'

'No,' said Kezzie, looking from one to the other.

'It means it's your turn to do the stairs,' said Mrs Sweeney, 'and when you've done them, you pass the cotton reel on to the next person. Then they know that their turn has come around again.'

'Oh!' said Kezzie. She covered her mouth with her hand. 'We didn't realise . . . Grandad made Lucy a knitting bobbin with it.' She started to laugh.

Mrs Price joined in, and eventually so did Mrs Sweeney.

'I'm so sorry,' said Kezzie. 'I'll do them at once.'

'Don't harass yourself,' said Mrs Price, 'it can wait.' She looked at Mrs Sweeney. 'Why don't you both come down to my house and have some tea?' she said.

Kezzie accepted the offer quickly. Grandad's house was easy to keep clean and tidy, and she found more and more that her days were dragging out. She had resolved that as soon as Lucy began school she would find a job and then see about taking night classes herself. She'd not forgotten her dream of one day being a doctor and found out that the high school ran evening classes to prepare students for university entrance exams. Towards the end of the summer she would go along and enrol.

Mrs Price too was lonely. She was fairly young, not long married, and her husband was in the army. He was still based in Scotland, but for how long?

'Robert says the war is only weeks away,' said Mrs Price as she poured the tea. 'He's expecting orders to leave at any moment.' Her hand trembled as she picked up the milk jug. 'I might never see him again.'

Mrs Sweeney shook her head. 'Ye'd think after the last time folks would have learnt their lesson. I'm glad my two are firemen. They'll not get called up.'

Kezzie could see the anxiety on Mary Price's face. Her own thoughts were with Michael. She tried to change the subject.

'When Lucy starts school, would anyone come along to the pictures with me?' she asked. 'I've never been to a proper cinema before, and I'd love to see what it's like.'

By chance Kezzie had hit upon the one thing that Mrs Sweeney loved doing. When her husband and son were working nights and had to sleep during the day, then it was a way of passing the time, rather than staying at home and disturbing them. She was an authority on every picture house in the area. She knew the best places and all the films worth seeing. Before Kezzie left to go upstairs and prepare the evening meal they had made a date for her first expedition to La Scala, the local cinema.

When school began, as Kezzie was having Lucy enrolled, the teacher spoke to her.

'There's an opportunity to have the little girl evacuated,' she said.

'Where to?' asked Kezzie.

The teacher shrugged. 'We never really know. They are sent on trains into the countryside and it's decided when they get there.'

Kezzie felt Lucy's hand tighten on her own.

'No, thank you,' Kezzie said pleasantly. 'My sister is staying at home.'

Later in the afternoon, when Kezzie collected Lucy from school, the teacher thrust a piece of paper into her hand.

'Here is a list of articles for evacuees to take with them,' she said, 'in case you change your mind.'

That night, after Lucy had gone to bed, Kezzie read the list out to her grandfather.

'"Spare clothing, toothbrush, comb and handkerchief, and a bag of food for the day." And they tie labels around their necks,' Kezzie went on. 'It's as if it's a parcel you are sending away, not a child. I can't believe it's happening.'

'When the war starts you might be safer in the country,' said her grandfather. He looked across the table at her.

Kezzie stared at him. 'What do you mean?' she asked sharply.

He sighed. 'I'm thinking it was very selfish of me to want ye both to come home. It could be that I've put you in danger . . .'

'We had to come back,' Kezzie said. 'It was the right thing to do, not just for you, but for Lucy and myself too.'

'Yes, but,' her grandad persisted, 'it's possible that this area, with the yards and the docks, isn't going to be

218

very safe. Perhaps we should think about getting her out of it.'

'Never,' said Kezzie.

Grandad looked at her carefully. 'If the bombers do come . . .' He didn't finish the sentence.

'Never,' said Kezzie again.

There was a soft rustling noise from the kitchen doorway. They both looked up. Lucy was standing there in her pink fleecy nightie.

'Kissy can't sleep,' she said, holding up her doll.

Grandad held out his arms.

'Bring her over here,' he said. He took Lucy and the doll onto the chair beside him. 'I've got a new story for ye.' He poked up the fire and then settled back in his chair. 'A royal story,' he went on mysteriously. 'D'ye want to hear it?'

Lucy nodded.

'Well, coorie doon beside me,' he said, 'and I'll tell you all about it. Did you know that when the work is finished on the hull of a big ocean liner, they launch the boat into the water and then take her away to be fitted out?'

Lucy shook her head.

'Well, that's how it's done. And the one I was working on last year was a very special one indeed. It was the biggest and the best, and when it was finished they asked Queen Elizabeth, the wife of the King, to come and launch her. On that very special day, which was September the twenty-seventh, there I was, walking around John Brown's shipyard, and did I not come face to face with the Queen of Britain herself?'

' "John Munro?" ' she asks.

' "Aye, that's me," ' I reply.

' "Ye've made a grand job of her," says she, looking the boat up and down. "They tell me she's the largest liner in the world. I'm fair pleased with you." '

'Your tales are becoming as fanciful as Michael Donohoe's,' Kezzie interrupted.

'It's the gospel,' said her grandad, 'as sure as I'm sitting here.'

Kezzie lifted a handful of peas in the pod from the vegetable rack and put them into a small basin. Her grandad winked at her and went on with his story.

' "Yes," said Queen Elizabeth. "She's a magnificent ship, John. And I'm very happy to be here today." '

' "Thank you very much, Your Majesty", I said. "Now if you'll just excuse me, there's things need doing." '

'And I give her a nod and off I go. And do you know she was so busy chatting to me that she nearly forgot to let the bottle go?'

'Blethers!' said Kezzie.

'It's true,' he protested. 'It's absolutely true. Ask anybody. It was in all the papers.'

Kezzie shook her head and started to shell the peas, as her grandad went on with his story.

'There was a great crack and a groan. The ship had started off down the slipway without anyone realising it! What a panic! But Queen Elizabeth stayed completely calm. She leaned over, quick as she could, snipped the ribbon and let the champagne go. Just in time, she was. The bottle struck the ship on the very tip of her bows as she slid towards the river! What a magnificent sight as she entered the water! What a roar went up! Hundreds and hundreds of people cheering and waving, and the flash and pop of the camera light bulbs. And the rust-red dust from the chains rose up in a great cloud as they dragged along. Everyone flung their caps in the air. It took me three weeks to find mine again!

'And then the Queen catches a glimpse of me, and she gives a wee wave of her hand. And I can see her telling the two princesses, "That's John Munro, the best ship-builder on the Clyde."'

When they were sure Lucy was safely asleep, Kezzie and her grandad talked for a little while by the fire. As if by unspoken agreement neither of them mentioned the war.

'I'm going to look for a job now that Lucy's at school,' said Kezzie. 'Remember you wrote to me when I was in Canada saying you might know of somewhere that would fit in with my studying for university?'

'You don't need to go out to work,' he replied. 'With my wage, there's enough coming in for us to manage.'

She smiled at him. 'I know that,' she said. 'But if I do finally get a university place, then I'll need some savings to fall back on.'

He smiled back at her. 'You've still got that inside you?' he asked. 'Ever since you were small, you were determined that you were going to be a doctor.'

She nodded.

'I'll ask tomorrow,' said Grandad. 'It's a wee café, run by Italians.'

'Oh,' said Kezzie. 'I met some Italians on the boat. The Biagi family.'

'This one's called Casella's,' said Grandad, 'though I

wouldn't be surprised if they were related. It's a shop and a café, right next to the yard, just off Glasgow Road. I'm friendly with the owner, and I'm sure she could do with some help about the place.'

A few days later, early in the morning, Kezzie went to keep the appointment her grandfather had made for her. As she crossed the street in front of the café she could see through the large glass window fancy chairs and tables with smart red checked covers. Further back was a delicatessen with shelves of cheeses, jars of pasta, and various types of sausages hanging from the ceiling. Standing behind the counter refilling the biscuit tins stood a dark-haired boy. He turned around as Kezzie entered the shop. It took several seconds before Kezzie recognised who it was. The last time she had seen him he had been wearing a formal suit with an elegant bow tie.

'Kezzie!' he cried, and his smile was like the sun coming out.

CHAPTER 6

Casella's Café

'Kezzie!'

Ricardo Biagi hurriedly wiped his hands on a cloth and came out from behind the counter. He kissed Kezzie on both cheeks.

'My aunt told me to expect a new assistant today, but I had no idea it would be you! When can you start?'

Kezzie laughed. 'At once if you wish,' she said.

'We are so very busy here,' said Ricardo. 'We serve tea and ices in the café. Many people come from the yards and the workshops. At lunchtime the *garzoni*, the apprentice boys, are sent by their bosses for sandwiches and pies. All day we deliver grocery orders in the van.' He took off his apron and presented it to her. 'You may begin immediately.'

Kezzie found that she enjoyed working in the shop. It was very busy, as Ricardo had said, but it was fun to meet and talk with so many different people. The friendly atmosphere on both sides of the counter compensated for the hard work. Signor Biagi ran the deli, as he called it, ordered the stock and made up the boxes for delivery to houses and institutions. Ricardo's mother and his aunt mainly stayed in the kitchen and cooked, which left Kezzie and Ricardo dealing with the front shop.

Kezzie was intrigued by the vast range of goods on sale. She enjoyed looking at the coloured and patterned labels on some of the boxes and tins, and trying to read them in Italian. Ricardo would spell the words out to her and she repeated them, stumbling over the unfamiliar pronunciation.

He would laugh and hold his head in his hands. 'It's that flat Scottish accent,' he complained. 'It is most unsuited to our melodious language.' The only success she had was when there was an 'r' in the Italian word. Then she would exaggerate the sound and roll it around her tongue to make it sound out.

On the back of the shelves were rows and rows of fancy glass jars with a colourful range of sweets inside. Tiered stands stood in front, displaying slices of home-made chocolate cake and fudge set upon fancy lace doilies. There were cartons of ice-cream wafers, bottles of olive oil, hams and salami, and a variety of cheeses. The whole smell of the place, the mingling of cultures, the very signs marked on the goods gave it the exciting feel of an exotic bazaar.

In prime place above the counter was the large framed photograph of Signor Casella, resplendent in his First World War British Army uniform, proudly displaying his medal and decoration.

After her initial difficulty Kezzie found that she loved

the Italian words. The items on sale, cannelloni and mozzarella, and the Italian places such as Umbria and Calabria. Even Ricardo's friends and relatives who called in, usually on a Sunday, had interesting and unusual names; Bruno and Marietta, Serafino and Rosario. There were cousins, uncles, nieces, who came to chat, or have a coffee or a game of cards. Sometimes when the café was full Kezzie's head spun with their language, so rich and vibrant, and their extravagant gestures as they spoke.

'No more!' she would cry eventually, flinging her hands in the air in imitation of Ricardo's mother when she was agitated. 'I give up! I am not serving any more until somebody speaks to me at less than a hundred miles an hour.'

She liked the weekday customers too. She responded to the cheeky banter of the shipyard workers, the teasing and open flirting. They always noticed if she wore a different blouse, bought a new comb or slide, or altered her hairstyle in any way. And within a few days she knew their special likes and sandwich combinations.

Kezzie and Ricardo worked well together. There was an easy friendliness between them. And his casual manner, which she perceived as being particularly American, made it less awkward for her when confronted by the many branches of his family.

It was good to have him to talk to. The women that she knew and spoke to in the tenement were all married. She had been to the pictures several times now with Mrs Sweeney, and had soon discovered that the older woman was very lonely. With her husband and son's shift pattern she was often on her own. Her son had never married so there were no grandchildren. Kezzie realised that Mrs Sweeney looked forward eagerly to their weekly outings, and although Kezzie enjoyed her visits to the cinema with Mrs Sweeney, she still missed company of her own age. She had enrolled for the night classes but found that it was mostly older men who attended. One of the tutors had made enquiries for her as to the appropriate subjects to study, and she was taking maths and Latin classes. These were not popular subjects with younger women.

Also, she discovered that she had a unique bond with Ricardo in the strange unsettled feelings which tormented her from time to time.

Sometimes she felt a longing for Canada that she could not explain even to herself, far less talk it over with Grandad. Lucy seemed to have little difficulty in read-justing to her life in Scotland. She was a favourite with adults and popular with her playmates. She'd adapted to school life very well, although she was teased sometimes about her accent and the names she used for everyday things, referring to motor cars as automobiles and bis-cuits as cookies. But it was good-natured and some of the children in the close now called their toffee bars and sweets 'candy' as a joke.

It wasn't like that for Kezzie. Occasionally she stood at the tenement window and gazed down into the street. She could see the children playing with hoops and balls. The boys with marbles and bogies and the girls skipping, the rhythmic chant of their song keeping time with the slap of the rope on the pavement. It was all so friendly, homely and yet . . . *different*. In many ways childhood games were the same all over the world, but all the little particular things varied. Yet this was what she had been used to most of her life, and what she longed to be back among, when she was away. So why now did this place, this home, seem strange? Why did she sometimes feel alien to the everyday happenings here?

It was comforting to know that Ricardo's thoughts were similar. The lack of space, he told her, was what had scared him most in the beginning. He was used to the wide freeways, the low bungalows set back from the side-walks, acres and acres of parking lots, four- or six-lane highways.

He saw the gritty grey buildings here closing in on him. The width of the streets was so narrow in places that housewives in the upper storeys had strung washing lines across between their windows. The sky and clouds seemed closer, as if you could reach and touch them. In America, and in Canada also, she told him, the space seemed endless, stretching out and up into infinity.

They spoke about it often, and about the whole problem of adjusting.

Kezzie thought it must have been such a shock for Ricardo's grandfather, who had come so long ago to Scotland, and exchanged the clear sunny skies and the heat of Italy for this mild and wet climate.

'Perhaps we are not so dissimilar, though,' Ricardo had said. 'The family is important here, and so it is with Italians. We stay together, we look out for each other.'

They spent much of their spare time together, and it seemed a natural thing for him to hold her hand as they strolled along the road or through the park. One evening, on their way home from the pictures, as they stood chatting under the lamp post at the end of the street, he bent down and kissed her on the mouth. After a moment he raised his head.

'You enjoyed that, no?'

'Yes,' Kezzie replied. 'It was very pleasant.'

He smiled at her, a soft sad smile.

'Pleasant,' he said ruefully, 'is not what I intended it to be.'

He took her arm and continued to walk her home. She felt she had let him down in some way, but didn't quite know how.

The topic of conversation everywhere was the disturbances in Europe. How long could it go on before Britain was drawn in? Kezzie knew that the Italian families in Clydebank were worried about their position should war break out. In the First World War Italy and Britain had been on the same side, but a few months ago Mussolini had allied himself with Hitler and Germany. Each day the newspapers were full of events and political discussions. Ricardo's parents were now not sure whether all three of them would be better off returning to America, or staying on for a while in Britain. There were rumours of German submarines patrolling the Clyde coast.

'We had no idea things had reached such a state here,' Signor Biagi told Kezzie one day. 'Where we lived in the States, we did not hear much foreign news. Most Americans will not be aware of what is happening over here.'

For the time being the Biagis decided that they would stay.

Kezzie had received a reply from Michael. He felt as badly as she did to know that she'd returned to Britain and he had missed her.

I will desert immediately, he wrote, *and will sail all the way back across the sea. Please stand by the pier at Greenock and look out for a small boat and a very seasick soldier.*

She smiled as she read this extravagant declaration. She knew that there was a fine thread of seriousness in it. She also knew that she herself felt inclined to some similar reckless act so that they could be together.

As she walked to the shop each day it seemed to Kezzie that the mood of the town was changing. Shop windows were taped up, a precaution against flying glass in the event of an air raid. People seemed anxious, and every shop or street corner had someone speculating on exactly what would happen. Sitting in the back green one Sunday, near the end of August, she heard a group of men, of whom her grandad was one, talking together.

'I don't think *we* need tae worry aboot air raids,' said Bill Forbes, who lived in the next close. 'These big bombers they've got could only be used short range. They're far too heavy to stay up in the air for long.'

Kezzie heard her grandad laughing.

'Aye, they said something the same about the *Queen Elizabeth* when we were building her. That she'd be far too heavy to stay afloat.' He tapped the hot ashes out of his pipe. 'She hasn't sunk yet,' he said.

'Well,' said another, 'Scotland's too far away for their fuel to last out. London might get it, but anywhere from the north of England up should be all right.'

'You're reckoning that they would always be travellin' fae Germany,' said Mrs Sweeney's husband. 'Supposin' they came in fae Denmark or Norway?'

'Norway!' repeated Mr Forbes. 'Whit the hell would the Germans want wae Norway or Denmark?'

'I think Herr Hitler wants everything he can take,' said Kezzie's grandad quietly.

'I still think their fuel tanks won't be big enough,' Mr Forbes persisted. 'What with the weight of the bombs, and the size of the planes and the number of crew and equipment needed, they wouldnae hae enough fuel tae get here.'

'They'll have enough tae get here,' said Mrs Sweeney's husband. 'Aye, tae get here *and* get back.'

Mr Forbes shook his head. 'Ye'll be sayin' next that folk will be journeying as far away as the moon,' he said.

Everybody laughed at this. Kezzie looked across. She noticed that her grandad wasn't smiling.

She worried again about Lucy. Perhaps it was best to make some arrangements for her? To get her out of this area? If there were aerial bombardments she knew that Grandad believed that the shipyard would be a target. Should she have taken the chance to evacuate Lucy? Kezzie resolved that, as soon as her Aunt Bella returned home, she would go and visit her and discuss the matter with her.

Meanwhile Europe and the world held its breath and waited.

The last few days of August and the hot summer of 1939 dwindled. On the first day of September German forces invaded Poland. Two days later, on a Sunday morning, Britain declared itself at war with Germany.

CHAPTER 7

War!

'Well, that's us now, isn't it?' said Mrs Sweeney grimly as Kezzie passed her on the stairs the next day. 'Anither war. In my lifetime too.' She shook some Brasso onto her cleaning cloth. 'They promised when the last one finished that it widnae happen again.'

Kezzie stopped on the landing and watched her neighbour determinedly polishing the already gleaming letter-box on her front door. It suddenly struck her that Mrs Sweeney was frightened. As anxious as most people were, but trying not to show it.

Kezzie reached out and touched her arm. 'It'll be all right,' she said. 'We'll manage . . . somehow.'

'You dinnae ken what it was like,' said Mrs Sweeney. 'You young ones, you dinnae ken.' She shook her head, and Kezzie could see that there were tears in her eyes.

Kezzie walked more slowly downstairs and along the streets of Clydebank. Every newsagent's had the headlines displayed outside.

As she approached the café she could see that the blinds were still drawn. Inside the shop, Ricardo, his parents and his aunt were sitting at one of the tables. The two women were holding each other and weeping. Kezzie said nothing but went straight to the kitchen and put the big coffee pot on the stove. The thought of war scared her too. Her grandfather had fought in the Great War and considered it to have been a waste of young life. She knew that many of his friends had been killed. They'd marched away, he'd told her once, hundreds and hundreds of them, thinking it would be exciting and glorious, whole villages joining the same regiment. Then when the big battles were fought sometimes not one boy from a village survived. They came home singly, or in twos and threes, often badly mutilated.

Kezzie made some sandwiches, then poured out four cupfuls of strong coffee with plenty of sugar and took it through to them.

'Eat something,' she ordered. 'Things aren't as bad as they seem.'

'For us,' said Signor Biagi gravely, 'it could be serious. The authorities might try to take the café from us, or put us in prison.'

'What!' cried Kezzie. 'Why would they do that?'

The Italians looked at each other. Eventually Ricardo's mother spoke. 'We are not British citizens,' she said. 'None of us have British passports.'

233

'But I don't think the United States will fight against Britain in this war,' said Kezzie. 'You will be quite safe with your American passports.'

Ricardo's mother and his aunt exchanged fearful glances. 'Our passports are Italian. Even Ricardo does not have full citizenship.'

'It shouldn't be such a big problem.' Kezzie tried to make her voice sound reassuring. 'Signora Castella, your son is British. He'll be fighting in the British Army.' She pointed to the picture hanging on the wall of the café. 'Your husband won a medal in the last war.'

Ricardo spoke up. Kezzie realised that he too was trying to calm his parents.

'Kezzie is right,' he said. 'There is nothing to fear. We have done nothing wrong. We will mind our own business and people will leave us alone.'

A few Sundays later Kezzie was to remember his words.

She had asked for some time off and set out early in the morning to visit Aunt Bella. As the ancient single-decker bus wheezed its way through the countryside towards Stonevale, Lucy's excitement was indescribable. She seemed to remember everything: the burn where she had fished for tadpoles, the hills they'd climbed when berrying, the canal bridge where the horses had to wait until the gatekeeper swung back the heavy wooden barrier to let the coal scows through.

They lurched over the bridge and Kezzie, catching sight of the long barges, suddenly recalled the Sunday School trip of two summers ago when their father had still been alive. It had been the last outing which they'd enjoyed together before he was killed in the pit. It was in her mind now. All of it. The smell of the mown grass in the field where they held the races, the taste of the lemonade, the long gloaming as they glided home along the calm water of the canal. Kezzie saw the scene in front of her blur and dissolve, and raised her hands to wipe her eyes. Suddenly, small fingers were intertwined with her own. She looked down at Lucy, who smiled bravely back at her.

Had the child sensed her grief and was trying to give her comfort? Kezzie gripped her sister's hand tightly.

They came closer to their own village and, as they passed each place and Lucy called out in delight and chattered about some incident which had happened in the past, Kezzie was amazed at how early some of her memories were.

'Are you sure you really remember what happened that day?' she quizzed her sister on one occasion.

Lucy was adamant. She could tell Kezzie the colour of the dress she'd been wearing and whether Kezzie had been cross with her for something she'd done wrong. Kezzie watched her in wonderment. She looked at the little face framed with the fine blonde waves. Her sister's hair was longer now, less baby-soft, and tended not to curl so much, but it still settled round the child's face in an angelic cloud. And as her sister became happier and gayer as they came near the little mining village where they had both been born, Kezzie knew with utter conviction that she had done the right thing in bringing her back from Canada.

It was a circle closing. A last link that had to be made

to connect Lucy's life now with that of her previous one, to give her some coherence, make some sense of her childhood which had been so cruelly disrupted. And as they walked up the road together towards the miners' rows it felt to Kezzie that she herself had completed some kind of particular and significant journey. The air itself, full of the sounds and smells of her homeland, was in her mouth and hair, and then, quite distinctly, in her very being. And like the exile returning, she was suddenly, and to her own surprise, in tears.

Lucy had run on, unannounced, straight into her aunt's house, and Bella came rushing out, tying on her apron, and flung herself at Kezzie. And they were both laughing and crying and trying to tell each other everything at once. But they found that it was not all tears of sorrow that they shared as they sat together and reminisced about the last years. They spoke of the fun of the annual day trip in the summer, and Kezzie told Bella about Canada, and Bella in turn brought her up to date with local news. Her children now were almost as tall as she was, and still as cheeky. But Will, the eldest, was determined to get a foundry or ironworks apprenticeship rather than go down the mine. He was working hard at school and the teacher was giving him instruction in technical drawing.

'Most folks are workin' now,' said Bella. 'There's nothin' good about a war at all, except that it brings employment.'

At the mention of the war Kezzie told Bella about her fears for Lucy.

'I don't know whether we would be attacked, living so

236

far north,' said Kezzie. 'Grandad seems to think so. I'm not sure what's the best thing to do. If she was sent away again, it might distress her too much. Aunt Bella, at one stage in Canada, she was so ill that she didn't know where, or even who she was.'

'Leave her here wi' me,' said Bella at once.

Kezzie thought this typical of Bella's generosity. Her house was already overcrowded, and her husband working less and less as his lungs became weaker and weaker.

At that moment, Lucy, in the middle of some game, came running past the side of the house where Bella and Kezzie were sitting. Bella called her over.

'Ye like yer Aunty Bella, don't ye, Lucy?' she said.

Lucy nodded.

'Then would ye bide here wi' me, pet, for a holiday?' asked Bella.

'No,' said Lucy at once.

Bella laughed out loud.

'Well, that's a straight answer anyway,' she said to Kezzie. She turned back to Lucy. 'Aw, c'mon,' she wheedled. 'Just for a wee while, eh?'

'No,' repeated Lucy. She went and stood beside Kezzie. 'We stay together.' She looked directly at Kezzie. 'You said, didn't you, Kezzie?' she asked her sister. 'You told the teacher at school, I was staying at home.'

'So I did,' said Kezzie, 'so I did.' She drew the child to her and wrapped her arms around her. Through her tears she looked at Bella over the top of Lucy's head.

Bella smiled at her.

'What has to be, has to be,' she said.

As she was about to leave, Kezzie suddenly remembered something else she had wanted to ask.

'Do you ever get any news of Peg?' she asked.

'Which Peg?' said Bella.

'Peg McKinnon,' said Kezzie. 'Her dad and one of her brothers were killed at the same time as . . .' Kezzie hesitated. She glanced to where Lucy was playing a few yards away '. . . as Daddy,' she finished softly. How great the pain had been at the time, she thought. The whole small community crushed by that blow. And yet Grandad and Bella, who had counselled her wisely, had been proved right in the end. Remember the good things and resist bitterness, they'd said, and then all your memories will be happy ones. Kezzie heaved a great sigh. It was difficult, and especially difficult now, in the shadow of the pit, right beside their former home.

Bella reached over and gripped her hand tightly.

'We were friends at school,' Kezzie went on. 'I often wonder what happened to her. The family left the village right after the accident. I think they moved to either Glasgow or Clydebank. She said she would write to me but she never did. I'd love to see her again.'

Bella looked away. 'I heard . . .' She stopped.

'What?' said Kezzie. 'What did you hear?'

'That . . . that they were in a bit o' bother. The mother died. An' the brother . . .' Bella's voice tailed off again.

'Aunt Bella,' said Kezzie in exasperation, 'please tell me. I'm not a child any more that you have to keep bad news from me.'

'No, I suppose ye're not,' said Bella slowly. 'Ye had to grow up gey fast, hadn't ye, hen? Well, the brother's married and has a wean. Or maybe has a wean and is no' married. Who kens? Anyway, he's taken to drink. The woman . . . is . . .' Bella spread her hands out in front of her and examined them for a moment or two. 'They say she goes with men, all sorts of men, even brings them tae the hoose.'

'And Peg still lives there?' asked Kezzie in horror.

'I think she's nae option but tae,' said Bella. 'There's naebody else cares aboot the bairn.'

There were geese settling beside the small loch as the bus taking Lucy and Kezzie back to Glasgow turned on to the main road. Breaking formation as they approached the water, the birds flapped and squawked as they made their ungainly landing. They reminded Kezzie of Canada and the great long lines of migrating birds which had filled the skies in spring and autumn. Kezzie smiled as she recalled the sight, a happy relaxed smile. She was more at peace now with herself. She felt altered in some way by her visit to her home village. She knew that, since her travels, her perspective had changed. Like the pit ponies returning to the surface and having their blinkers gradually taken off, she was now looking at everything in a new way. But her unease was wearing off. Instead of being upset and withdrawing into herself, like some nervous tortoise, she decided she would now look forward and welcome new experiences. Perhaps if more people could travel and meet each other, as she had done, then there would be less prejudice, fewer wars. Folk would appreciate what they had, as Ricardo had said, they would see the similarities which united them.

In Glasgow Kezzie and Lucy got off the country bus and boarded a tram. They were going to go directly to the Casellas' café. It was too late now to go and look up Peg's address, which Aunt Bella had given her, and she'd promised that she would spend some time clearing up in the shop this evening, and preparing food for tomorrow, in exchange for her time off today. Dusk was quietly closing in as Kezzie and Lucy dismounted at the tram stop in Glasgow Road. They hurried along quickly. With the new blackout regulations there was little light, apart from that which came from the sun, slowly setting beyond the Mull of Kintyre. As they turned down the street where the café was located, there was the sound of running feet, heavy shoes and boots clattering on the cobbles. And voices calling, rudely yelling and shouting, with screaming and crying in the distance. Kezzie pulled Lucy into the nearest close mouth as a crowd of people rushed past her.

'Wait here,' she instructed Lucy.

The shop was no more than a hundred yards or so away, and it was with a terrible sense of dread that Kezzie ran towards it.

There were staves of wood and pieces of fencing lying in the roadway. A half brick, some stones and pieces of rubble were scattered on the pavement. And everywhere broken glass. Great pieces of the ornate glass door, on which the name Casella had been proudly etched in fine script, lay in the gutter. The large front window was splattered in mud. Beyond that, in the shop itself, the tables and chairs were smashed or overturned. Kezzie came to a halt, her whole being struck with shock. The lace curtain, now in tatters, flapped at her helplessly. She could now see clearly what had happened.

The café was completely wrecked.

CHAPTER 8

The café is wrecked

Kezzie picked Lucy up and carried her over the shattered glass and in through the café door. Signora Casella was sobbing noisily in a corner, her face buried in her apron. She was being comforted by her sister. Signor Biagi had a small cut on the side of his face which his son was cleaning with his handkerchief.

'What has happened?' Kezzie asked.

Ricardo's face was pale under his tan.

'We were attacked by a mob,' he said. 'Kezzie, I am glad you were not here. We have been insulted, dirt smeared on the windows, people calling us filthy names. My mother,' his voice broke, 'my mother was spat on as she walked to church this morning.'

Kezzie gasped.

'Did you not inform the police?' she asked.

He shook his head. 'What can they do? It is happening all over Britain. Since the Aliens Order came into force, requiring all Italian nationals to register with the authorities, we have been a focus of hatred and fear. We are seen as the enemy.'

'The enemy!' Kezzie repeated. 'The enemy! You are almost American.' She pointed to the framed photograph on the wall behind the counter. 'Your uncle won medals in the last war fighting for the British!'

'I know, I know.' Ricardo picked up a chair which had been kicked over and sat down wearily. 'But I couldn't reason with them. It was terrible. They were gathered outside when I came to open at lunchtime. Some had been drinking. It was very ugly.'

'Did you recognise anyone?' asked Kezzie. 'Were there people that you knew?'

Ricardo looked away.

'Perhaps,' he said evasively.

'You must tell the police,' said Kezzie.

'No,' said Signor Biagi.

Ricardo also shook his head.

'No, Kezzie,' he said. 'That would only make it worse, much worse.'

Signor Biagi went to the back shop and returned with a broom. He began sweeping the broken glass.

Lucy crossed over to where Signora Casella sat. She stood, uncertain and afraid, at the sight of adults crying so loudly.

'Would you like some tea?' she asked after a moment.

Signora Biagi looked up. 'What a wonderful idea, Lucy. I'll come and help you.'

'No,' said Lucy. 'I can manage.' And she went through to the kitchen.

Kezzie looked at the destruction about her. At the

once beautiful glass jars, now lying in pieces on the counter and the floor. Stones and bricks had been hurled at them. The toffees and fudge and all the cakes were ruined and would have to be thrown away. One of the pretty little tables was broken beyond repair.

A feeling of panic was growing inside her. If the newspaper reports were true then this was what was happening to the Jews in Germany. The hounding and persecution of people because they were of a particular race. And ordinary folk were being manipulated to do this. Their fears and worries exploited, their raw emotions stirred up and whipped into a frenzy of violence against their fellow humans, and all because they were of different origins. It was obvious to Kezzie by the expression on Ricardo's face that he had known some of the mob. Perhaps there even were customers among them.

She recalled something which had occurred in her early days of working in the café. Two girls of around Ricardo's age had come in, and they had obviously been very taken with his dark good looks and his charming manners. Very soon they were flirting with him and ordered another ice-cream each. When he brought it to their table, with much whispering and giggling they had demanded to know his name.

Kezzie watched as he smiled his wonderful smile. She could not help smiling herself at their teasing, or indeed overhearing the conversation.

'My name is Ricardo Biagi,' he said.

They made him repeat it until they themselves could say it properly, imitating his pronunciation, his way of making the words sound so lilting and musical. Then they protested that it was too tricky, too difficult for them to remember.

'Why don't you change it?' suggested one girl. 'The way it is just now, it sounds too Italian.'

'But I *am* Italian.'

'Yes,' said the other, 'we know you are. But you could easily alter your first name. Why don't you just make it Richard, instead of Ricardo?'

Kezzie stopped what she was doing and lifted her head to watch Ricardo's face. He took a step back from the café table.

'I am Ricardo,' he had replied proudly, 'Ricardo Biagi. *Not* Richard. My parents chose this name especially for me, and I do not intend to change it.'

He smiled at them to show that there was no bad feeling on his part. 'How can I be something I am not?' he asked. 'I am an Italian. An Italian who is called Ricardo.'

Kezzie looked at him now, slumped dejectedly in the chair, and at the two women almost hysterical with fear. It was possible that they would not be able to keep the café going any more.

A sudden anger filled her mind. How dare people do this to them? Ricardo and his family worked so hard. They cooked and prepared food each day, and kept their little café spotlessly clean. Kezzie looked again at the mess and confusion, and her eye fastened on the photograph of Signor Casella, resplendent in his British Army uniform. Kezzie stared at it for a long moment.

Lucy had cleared a table and was very carefully

setting out teacups. Signor Biagi was sweeping the glass into a pile.

Kezzie went over and took the broom from him. 'Leave it,' she said.

'Such a mess,' he replied. 'We have to tidy up.'

'No,' said Kezzie firmly. She raised her voice and spoke to all of them. 'I want you to leave everything exactly as it is.' She turned to Ricardo. 'Ask your aunt if she still has your uncle's medal and ribbon which he won when he was in the army and, if she has, may I borrow it? And see if she has a photograph of your cousin in his uniform.'

Without waiting for a reply Kezzie dragged one of the café tables over to the counter and climbed on top. She lifted down the picture of Signor Casella from its place of honour.

'Now,' she said, 'we will board up the door so that the place is safe from thieves tonight, and tomorrow we will open for business as usual.'

Signora Biagi opened her mouth to speak. Kezzie raised her hand.

'Listen,' she said. 'We are going to humiliate these people. They will expect you to be cowed and frightened, or angry and vengeful. We will be neither.'

She took the ribbon and medal from Signora Casella and draped it over her husband's picture. Then she placed it on a table with the photograph of his son in uniform beside him. She tore the remaining piece of lace curtain from the window and set the table in the centre, facing out into the street.

'There,' she said. 'Now let them all look at that as they go about their business tomorrow, and as they do so let them also see the brave thank you that the family of those who fight for Britain receive.'

The next morning Kezzie asked Mary Price to take Lucy to school and she herself went to the café very early. She worked with Ricardo and his family to clear up only what was required in order to make the sandwiches and the snacks for the usual orders. They left the overturned chairs and tables and the pile of broken glass in the corner. The stones and bricks which had been thrown lay where they had fallen.

And they didn't complain about the situation to anyone. Ricardo and Kezzie kept smiling as they served their customers, and Kezzie found as the morning progressed that more and more people found it difficult to meet her gaze. She knew that anyone who entered the café had to pass by the two photographs on display.

Just before lunch-time a policeman came into the shop. He walked to the front of the line of people waiting to be served. Then he took out his notebook and nodded to the mess by the window.

'Who did this?' he asked Ricardo.

'I saw no one,' said Ricardo in an even tone of voice.

'Ye must have seen somebody, son,' said the policeman reasonably. He turned to Kezzie. 'Explain it to him, Kezzie,' he said. 'If he can give us a name, we can mebbe do somebody for it.'

Kezzie laughed. 'Ricardo understands perfectly,' she said. 'What he is trying to tell you . . .' Kezzie looked at the queue of customers still waiting to be served. She raised her voice. 'What Ricardo is saying is that he truly believes that no person he knows, or has ever met, or who

247

buys food in his café would ever do something so horrible to his family.'

The policeman closed his book. 'Suit yerself,' he said.

There was a silence in the shop as Kezzie and Ricardo dealt with the remaining apprentice boys and the factory orders. Kezzie determinedly kept up a stream of conversation, making jokes, teasing and calling after them as they left. Around half past two, when the shop had gone quiet, Ricardo leaned wearily on the counter.

'I don't know how you managed to keep chatting all the time,' he said.

Kezzie handed him a tiny cup of the black espresso coffee which he so loved.

'I was rather enjoying myself,' she said mischievously. 'Did you notice that there were very few customers who could look me straight in the face? Those who weren't involved probably have a good idea of who was, and most folk will be ashamed and embarrassed at what has happened here.'

As she spoke the café door was suddenly thrown back. Two young men in their working clothes stood just inside. One of them spoke. 'My boss says he wants this door.'

'What for?' said Kezzie.

'Needs fixin', don't it?' said the other. He took a large screwdriver from his pocket and began to unscrew the hinges.

Ricardo made to come out from behind the counter. Kezzie pulled his sleeve.

'Leave them,' she whispered.

Half an hour later, the door was brought back

248

reglazed. In the meantime a few more lads had drifted in. They began to pick up the broken pieces of glass and crockery, and straighten the chairs and tables. A young woman who lived opposite the café brought over a long piece of white netting. She attached it to the window curtain-pole and hung it back in place. All afternoon this went on, neighbours bringing little gifts and staying to help. By early closing time Signora Casella was in tears. She flung her arms around Kezzie.

'*Grazie, grazie.*' She kissed her effusively.

Ricardo put his hands on her shoulders.

'You are so very clever, Kezzie,' he said. 'What you did has not only resulted in many of our broken things being replaced. It has also given us a place in the community.'

'Remember, Kezzie,' said Signor Biagi, 'if we can ever do anything to repay you, we shall do it.'

Kezzie went home that evening with a comforting warm feeling inside her. Her trust in others and human goodness had won through today. She didn't realise how soon it would be that she herself would be asking the Biagi family for help.

CHAPTER 9

Peg McKinnon

The streets where Kezzie now found herself were mean and dirty. She had walked north on Kilbowie Road, away from the river for nearly twenty minutes, and then turned off to the right. She took the slip of paper on which Bella had written Peg McKinnon's address. There was no mistake. Slessor Street, past Drumry.

It was the correct road that she had turned down a few minutes ago. Kezzie looked around her and sighed. She remembered the neat little houses of the village where they had both been raised. The scrubbed and whitewashed steps, the lines of washing strung out to catch the wind. Peg's mother had struggled to keep their two rooms clean. With three working miners in their family it was a constant round of washing and drying clothes, a labour of love, particularly troublesome in the winter time.

There was something more depressing about the poorer parts of cities, thought Kezzie. When Grandad, Lucy and herself were near starvation in the little bothy at least there was clean air about them.

The atmosphere around these particular tenements was grey and damp. There was rubbish lying in the gutters, empty beer bottles and horse dung. The grimy window panes were broken and the curtains grubby. The appearance of these houses suggested that no one cared.

Or perhaps deep, unrelenting poverty did this, thought Kezzie. Constant unemployment, where hope had long since left the hearts of the people caught in this situation, and they found that they turned in circles until their energy was gone.

Kezzie stopped at the entrance where the number she was seeking was written in faded copperplate on the wall. She mounted the inside stairs warily, peering at the doors in the dim light. She smiled to herself. Mrs Sweeney would have a fit if she saw the state of this particular close.

'Middle floor left.' Kezzie read the instructions on her note.

The door in front of her had no name or number on it. It needed repair and a coat of paint, but the handle and surrounds had been washed down and the little mat, although worn, was clean. Kezzie knocked on the wooden panelling. From inside she heard a baby begin to cry. Someone yelled out, 'Shut that wean up, can't you? I'm trying to sleep.'

The door swung open violently. A man stood there. He was swaying on his feet.

'What d'ye want?' he demanded roughly.

'Johnnie?' said Kezzie. She took a step back in order to see him better. 'It is Johnnie McKinnon, isn't it?' She smiled at him, overcome with an unexpected feeling of affection. Despite his aggressive manner and his unshaven face, she recognised him immediately. Where Peg's hair was golden like her dad's, he favoured his mother, with thick carroty red curls. And his voice too placed him at once. He hadn't lost the country lilt, the soft vowel sounds which were at odds with the flatter tones of the city.

'Johnnie,' laughed Kezzie, 'don't tell me you don't know me. After all the times you pushed me off the top of the coal bings!'

He narrowed his eyes and said gruffly, 'Who are you?'

'Kezzie Munro. You used to pull my hair and tease me until I cried.' And without being able to help herself Kezzie reached up and kissed him on the cheek. They had strong links of friendship, the McKinnons and the Munros. Having no brother herself, it had been Peg's two brothers who looked out for Kezzie in childhood scraps. They had all grown up together, Peg and she sharing everything: their secrets, life at school and at home, and eventually death too. Kezzie's father had died beside Peg's in the local mine. Peg's other brother had perished in the same disaster.

'Come away in.' Johnnie McKinnon grabbed Kezzie's arm and shouted out loud, as he pulled her into the house. 'Look who is here after all these months! Peg! Look who has come to visit us!'

Peg McKinnon was sitting by the fireside, holding her brother's baby on her lap. The little boy was gurgling happily as she crooned to him and stroked his back. She turned and placed him in his crib and stood up to greet Kezzie.

Again Kezzie felt this great rush of love and fondness, and she could see that Peg was experiencing the same. The two girls hugged each other for several minutes.

'Gosh, Kezzie,' said Peg at last, 'you are so much taller and browner. Canada must have treated you well. I'd heard of your trouble with Lucy, and I'm sorry I never tried to get in touch.' She shook her head. 'But our circumstances are such that we can hardly get by ourselves, far less help anyone else.'

'Yes,' said Kezzie awkwardly as they sat down. 'I heard things weren't very good for you.'

Peg wiped her hand wearily across her face, tucking some hair back behind her ears. 'I remember reading a newspaper notice at the time Daddy and Sandy were killed,' she said. 'It gave details of the fall at Stonevale pit. "Not a major disaster" were the words they used. Well, it was for us. That one accident killed not only my father and one brother,' Peg sighed. 'It also killed my mother. She just pined away. And it's ruined Johnnie's life.' She glanced at the door of the room where her brother had gone to lie down again. 'He can't stay away from the drink.'

Kezzie looked at her friend. She wasn't many months older than Kezzie herself but her face had an altogether sadder set to it: her big eyes grey and melancholy, her soft mouth turned down.

Kezzie glanced around the kitchen. Despite her friend's best efforts, the room was drab and bare. Kezzie guessed that most of their possessions had gone the same road as her own once had. Pawning household goods and personal belongings became a way of life for many people struggling to live.

'Have you tried to look for work?' she asked Peg. 'It would get you out of here for a bit, and bring in some money.'

'I'm terrified to leave baby Alec for any length of time.' Peg lowered her voice. 'Johnnie's wife . . . she doesn't always come home, and when she does she often brings drinking friends. I don't think she feeds him properly. And . . . I think she hits him sometimes.'

Suddenly Peg started to weep. Kezzie put her hands around her friend's shoulders. She was thinking furiously. 'I may know a place where you can get a few hours' work,' she said. 'And we'll figure out something for the baby. There are these new crèches and day nurseries now for mothers who are working to help the war effort.'

Kezzie decided to go straight back to the café and ask them to employ Peg. She wondered if Mary Price, who sometimes collected Lucy from school, would mind the baby. Mary seemed to enjoy any company, and Peg could give her a few shillings from her wages. Knowing how much Italians loved children, perhaps Peg could even bring the baby with her to the café. Called for his grandfather, baby Alec seemed to be a contented wee soul. She would check with Ricardo. They knew that they could do with some extra help in the café, even another pair of hands to wash the dishes would be of use.

When she returned to the café she found Ricardo in the tiny back garden. He was erecting an Anderson shelter.

He had already dug a large hole and set in the end wall and the side pieces of curved corrugated steel. She watched him as he bolted them together at the top and then began to shovel earth on the roof. They said it could withstand a five-hundred pound bomb going off less than fifty feet away.

Kezzie tried to imagine what it would be like, a whole family crouching down in the small space for hours on end, listening for the all-clear to sound. Would they hear the noise of the dropping bombs, as they sat there with their gas masks on, wondering and waiting, without knowing what was happening above them?

Lucy and Signora Biagi came out of the back door of the café. Ricardo's mother shuddered. 'Please God we never have to use that. I'm too old to stoop down to get in there.'

Kezzie smiled as she thought of Signora Biagi, who was always so perfectly turned out, hurrying to the shelter in the middle of the night.

Lucy was waiting impatiently for Ricardo to complete his work. She already had cushions and an assortment of books and toys ready to furnish the shelter.

'I think it'll be great fun,' she said.

Signora Biagi smiled sadly and murmured, 'Such are the days now that children think of war as fun.'

As she had guessed, Ricardo and his aunt readily agreed to employ 'Kezzie's friend'. What Kezzie had not anticipated was how apprehensive Peg was about the prospect of going out to work again. She brushed and redid her hair several times and complained to Kezzie about the state of her clothes.

'Look,' she wailed, pointing to her elbow. 'I've darned this cardigan twice already, and the wool doesn't even match properly.'

'Nonsense,' said Kezzie. 'Everyone is doing the same now. Mending and patching things. Only the other day I cut down one of Grandad's shirts, worn at the collar and cuffs, to make a perfectly good nightie for Lucy.'

They approached the café from the other side of the road. Kezzie could see Ricardo leaning on the counter reading a newspaper which was spread out in front of him. Beside him his father was packing boxes.

Peg dragged Kezzie to a stop. 'I'm so nervous,' she said. She fiddled with her hair for a moment and adjusted the belt of her coat.

'You look trig,' said Kezzie.

And she was being truthful. Peg had long legs and her coat with its cinched in waist showed off her slim figure. She had pleated her dark golden hair into a single plait which hung over one shoulder, and had pulled her beret down on the other side.

'Very smart,' Kezzie repeated, and propelled her across the street.

Kezzie was right behind her as they entered the shop so she did not see Peg's expression when her friend first caught sight of Ricardo. But she did see Ricardo's face quite clearly. He glanced up as the café door opened. He recognised Kezzie, had been expecting her in fact, but was so engrossed in his newspaper that his eyes flicked away from her again, back to study the article he was interested in. Kezzie saw his head start to bend . . . and then stop.

Ricardo looked back at once to the two girls, but it wasn't Kezzie he was staring at. It was Peg. Peg who had his whole attention.

Signor Biagi also witnessed the scene. He followed his son's gaze to the young woman who stood just inside their café. Then he turned his head and gazed fondly at his son. He clicked his tongue between his teeth, and Kezzie heard him say something in Italian.

'*Colpo di fulmine!*' he murmured.

CHAPTER 10

Love at first sight

Kezzie looked at Peg, then she looked at Ricardo. Her friend's cheeks were flushed pink and Ricardo's usual radiant smile was not in evidence. His face was very solemn.

'We have met before, I think,' he said to Peg.

Peg stared at him without replying. Kezzie nudged her.

'What?' Peg turned to Kezzie.

'It isn't me that's speaking to you, Peg,' said Kezzie. 'Ricardo is asking if you've met him before.'

'I . . .' Peg hesitated. 'I don't think so,' she said.

'No?' said Ricardo. 'I was so sure . . .'

He stared very hard at Peg's face. In return she lowered her head and then glanced at him sideways.

'I don't think we've met,' she murmured.

Kezzie regarded the two of them in amusement. They could hardly drag their gaze away from each other, yet didn't seem able to conduct a coherent conversation.

'I'm going through to the kitchen to make some fresh coffee,' she said loudly.

Neither of them appeared to hear her.

'*Un colpo di fuliuine,*' Ricardo's father said again as he followed Kezzie into the kitchen.

I can say *buona sera* and I know what *ciao* means,' Kezzie laughed, 'but *colpo di* whatever is too much for me.'

Signor Biagi made a gesture with his arm and placed his hand theatrically on his chest. 'It means a thunderbolt. Struck by lightning. Just here,' and he pointed to where his heart would be. 'Love at first sight is the translation you might use. And there is no cure,' he added. He opened the kitchen door a crack and peeked through. Then he turned to Kezzie and winked at her. 'Nor would it seem that those who are thus afflicted wish there to be,' he said.

Peg's nephew was an immediate hit with Ricardo and his family. They had agreed that Peg could bring him along for the few hours she worked each day, and he thrived in their warm loving care. Signora Casella found her own son's high chair from when he was a baby, and Alec would sit, propped up with pillows, watching everything that happened in the kitchen. Lucy adored him and he would turn his head at the sound of her voice when she sometimes dropped in on her way home from school in the afternoons.

Kezzie wondered about his natural mother.

'Doesn't she miss him at all?' she asked Peg one day.

Peg wiped a dribble of food from the baby's chin. 'I don't think she notices that he's not there,' she said. 'Johnnie shows him more affection than she does.'

The café shut earlier now in the winter months. Custom had fallen off in the evening anyway and the streets were much quieter at night. There had been so many road accidents that the blackout regulations had been relaxed slightly. People were allowed a small torch with a dim light when walking home after dark, and the shop van could use lights if they were properly shaded. White lines were painted on kerbs, tree trunks and lampposts.

Everyone had a gas mask, in case the enemy dropped containers of poison gas. Even baby Alec had a Mickey Mouse one. He hated it and used to yell and scream when Peg tried it on him.

'There, there.' Ricardo picked him up and cradled him in his arms. He rested the small golden head on his shoulder and walked up and down for a few minutes, rocking the little boy gently and crooning to him in Italian.

'You have no idea at all how to treat a baby? Do you?' he scolded Peg.

'Of course I have!' she replied indignantly. 'I've taken care of him since he was born.'

Ricardo placed his finger on his lips. 'Shh!' he said severely. 'You mustn't raise your voice. It will alarm the child. This boy and I have a great *simpatico*. We are not well treated by Miss Peg McKinnon. All we require is a small amount of affection, and do we receive this? Do we?' He pretended to ask the now sleeping child, then he shook his own head sadly. 'No, we do not.'

Peg looked at him, her face going pink.

Ricardo's eyes gleamed. 'Just a tiny piece of kindness

occasionally would do,' he went on. 'A fond look, a sweet smile, perhaps, would make us so very happy.'

Kezzie saw Ricardo hand the sleeping tot back to Peg who smiled up at him. His hand brushed Peg's bare arm and she blushed. As she watched them flirting with each other, Kezzie suddenly thought of Michael Donohoe and a terrible loneliness came over her. He had written again and she'd replied at once. But it wasn't the same. Nor anything like it.

She didn't know whether to be glad that Michael's battalion was in the Middle East and not on mainland Europe. The Argyll and Sutherland 51st had now gone off to France. There was talk that they were guarding the Maginot Line, and would be the first to see action, yet the weeks went by and nothing much seemed to be happening. People had relaxed to such an extent that many of the children who had been evacuated all over Britain came home again.

At the end of that year, and the beginning of 1940, it was as if Christmas came twice for Lucy and baby Alec. The Italians celebrated the visit of the three kings on January 6th. So, in addition to having Santa Claus bringing presents to their own homes, the two children also had the Befana, or the good witch, who brought gifts to well behaved children. Little packets of sugared almonds and pieces of marzipan cake were hidden around the café for Lucy to find.

The very same month the Government decided to ration some food items, and, as sugar was one of the first chosen, it wasn't long before the café had to stop selling ice-cream. It only made a small difference to the café's business, but many Italians, who sold mainly ice-cream, were badly affected. Kezzie knew that Ricardo and his family were worried, not only from the commercial side, in that suppliers were becoming difficult to obtain, but also the political aspect of the war frightened them. Mussolini was obviously prepared to collude with Hitler in his territorial ambitions. What position would they be in if Italy openly allied itself to Germany? The war had seeped in to all parts of ordinary existence. Everywhere now people were in uniform, of one kind or another, or rushing to join the volunteer services. Grandad was fire-watching most nights, and Peg and Ricardo went to first aid classes. Everybody wanted to help, 'to do their bit'.

In the early spring Kezzie received a letter postmarked Derby in England. It was from William James Fitzwilliam, the young man she had become friendly with when she'd been on her way out to Canada to search for Lucy. He told her that he'd been accepted by the RAF. He finished his letter with the words, 'If Douglas Bader can do it, then so can I.'

He was referring to his leg which suffered muscle deterioration below the knee. The doctors he'd consulted in America had given him exercises and therapy to try to stop the wasting process. Kezzie wondered about William's mother, and how she felt about him enlisting in the armed forces. He would be sure to see active service against the Luftwaffe, who were a powerful and skilled fighting unit. When Kezzie had met the Fitzwilliams on the boat cross-ing the Atlantic to Canada, Lady Fitzwilliam had barely been able to let William out of her sight. But perhaps she felt it a great honour for him to be in the Air Force.

And then the war news became more grim.

In April German troups invaded Denmark and Norway. A few weeks later they overran Belgium and Holland. The main body of troops, including the Highland Regiment, were sent forward to halt the enemy advance through the forest of Ardennes. The German Army proved unstoppable. By the end of May, the British Expeditionary Force had been driven back to the sea on the northern coast of mainland Europe. They were exhausted, outnumbered, and completely encircled. In and around the small French town of Dunkirk they were fighting for their lives.

Signor Biagi turned the knob on their wireless set. The voice of the broadcaster crackled through from London, sending out the call for the little boats to come and bring the soldiers home. And they responded, streaming out from every port, along the South Coast, and from further north they came, river cruisers, fishing smacks, anything that could float.

'This is crazy,' said one of the apprentice boys standing at the counter. 'These are ordinary sailors they're asking to do this, just civilians. Some of their boats are no bigger than dinghies. You can't expect them to go over there and face shells and bombs just to pick up half a dozen men.'

'They'll have to get them off any road they can,' said Kezzie's grandad, who was in the café. 'That's the most experienced troops we've got. We can't let them be rounded up.'

They looked at each other, each one with their own thoughts. It could be Michael, Robert Price, Signora

Casella's son, and any one of all the rest, brothers, lovers, husbands, fathers, waiting on the shoreline to be rescued. Being pounded by artillery and rifle fire, hoping that help would arrive.

Kezzie's grandad spoke heavily. 'We're taking a beating today. Now their U-boats will control the Channel. We might have to fight an invasion . . . The only thing that stands between us and them now are the boys in the Air Force.'

In the next few weeks Britain waited . . . and prepared itself. The Home Guard was formed and 250,000 men volunteered for this citizen's army. On Kezzie's last visit to Bella the road signs had been removed. No church bells were to be rung. The country knew that when next they heard the peal of bells it would signal that the enemy had arrived.

Just after Dunkirk, on the 11th of June, Mussolini declared war on the Allies. One late afternoon when Kezzie was at home ironing, there came a tremendous pounding on the front door. She ran quickly to open it. Peg stood there. Her hair was wildly uncombed and her face was streaked with tears.

'The police,' she gasped, out of breath with running so quickly upstairs. 'The police and some military men . . . In the café—' Her voice was shaking and she was on the verge of hysteria. She grabbed Kezzie by the front of her dress.

'Kezzie,' she sobbed, 'you have to come at once. They've arrested Ricardo and his father!'

CHAPTER 11

1940: Internment

When the two girls reached the café it was shut and in complete darkness. They knocked on the door and rattled the window but no one answered. Kezzie went through the pen at the side and round to the back entrance. She banged on the service door.

'Signora Casella! Signora Biagi!' she called loudly. 'It's Kezzie and Peg. Let us in!'

Several minutes elapsed and then the door was cautiously pulled open a crack. Such fear on their faces made Kezzie shiver. Alec was squirming in their arms as they clutched him desperately. They had expected men with guns, thought Kezzie, as she followed them upstairs into the house.

The two women were beyond tears.

'The *combattenti*,' Signora Biagi told Kezzie. 'They took my son away.' She kept repeating, more to herself than anyone else, 'We have done nothing wrong. We have done nothing wrong.'

Kezzie and Peg looked at each other helplessly. They

sat down round the big circular table. Signora Casella twisted the hem of the embroidered cloth over and over in her fingers. She turned her large brown eyes on Kezzie. 'My sister and I, we are scared to go out on the street. What can we do? What will happen now?' she asked.

Kezzie shook her head. 'I don't know. First of all we have to find out what is going on.' She stood up. 'I'll go to the police station and see if I can get any information. I'm sure it's all a terrible mistake.'

Half an hour later Kezzie discovered that it was not.

'Sending them away?' She repeated the words the desk sergeant had just said. 'All the Italian men living in Britain? Where are they being sent?'

The sergeant shrugged his shoulders. 'I don't know. They're setting up camps in different places.'

'Camps?' said Kezzie sharply. 'What kind of camps?'

He hesitated before replying. 'Like detention camps, sort of,' he said. 'They'll be all right,' he went on. 'It's just a precaution.'

'You mean camps such as they have in Europe?' demanded Kezzie. 'The same as the Nazis have done. Those people that we are fighting against.' She heard her own voice rising higher and higher. 'One of the reasons we are at war, in fact?'

The policeman fidgeted under her gaze. 'Don't take on so, hen. It's not as bad as you think. They'll get treated quite well.'

Kezzie took a deep breath. 'Where are these places?' she asked quietly. 'And where are the Biagis just now?'

The sergeant consulted some papers. 'I can't give you exact information,' he said. 'They could be on their way to one of the islands. There's also been talk of shipping them out to Canada or Australia for the duration. Come back tomorrow and ask again.'

As Kezzie hurried back to the café her thoughts were swarming in confusion. The policeman had said 'the duration'. Did he mean the whole of the war? How long would that be? And what could she tell Signoras Casella and Biagi? Or for that matter Peg, who was completely distraught about Ricardo?

She felt desperately sorry as she gave them her news.

Peg was stunned. 'I didn't know they could do things like that in Britain,' she said.

'When there is a war, they can do anything they please,' said Signora Casella.

Despite the restrictions on reporting, the newspapers carried the story over the next days. The entire Italian male population of Britain between the ages of seventeen and sixty had been rounded up. There was a large Italian community in the west of Scotland and many of Signora Casella's friends and relatives were involved. Eventually they discovered that Ricardo and his father were part of a group who had been kept at Maryhill Barracks and then sent on to the Isle of Man. Their cases would be reviewed in time, meanwhile the family could apply for permission to visit, though it would not be for many weeks.

'This is awful,' cried Peg. 'How can we afford to travel all that way to see them? How can we take the time away from the shop?'

'The shop,' said Signora Casella. 'How are we going to manage the shop? How are we going to survive?'

Her complaint was echoed in a thousand other households. The internment had struck a blow into the very hearts of the Italian families. Worse was to follow.

One of the ships transporting some of the men to detention in Canada was torpedoed and sunk. Only hours after its departure from Liverpool the *Arandora Star* was attacked by a German U-Boat and over four hundred Italian men were drowned.

A great gloom settled over the shop. No cooking was done or food prepared. Kezzie found that she missed the smells of the frying oil and the baking dough, the constant flow of the Italian conversation. She and Peg stacked the café chairs and tables to one side, and only sold the grocery goods. Custom began to fall off. It was a sad place to be, and even Lucy, coming in from school, swinging her legs from one of the high bar stools commented on it.

'There's no happy noises in this café any more.'

Kezzie realised it was true. The wireless was only switched on for the news bulletins, and Peg and herself hardly spoke as they served behind the counter in the deli. Occasionally Kezzie could hear one or other of the older women breaking out in a heart-rending lamentation. Peg wasn't much better, wandering around listlessly, beginning a task and not completing it. Baby Alec quickly picked up the mood of the place and became grizzly and fractious. Their supplies were running low. Kezzie saw that if they didn't reorder soon the shop would have to close. She called them all together one morning and told them that she had made a decision.

'We are reopening the café tomorrow,' she announced.

Signora Biagi shook her head sadly. 'Not without the men,' she said.

'Yes,' said Kezzie, 'we can. Lots of other women are doing it, working in factories and on the land while their men are away. They can manage, so can we. Also I hear that there are tribunals we can appeal to. There is a very good chance that they might be released early, particularly Ricardo. His citizenship papers were almost cleared.'

'I cannot cope with it any more,' said Signora Casella.

'Do you want your own son to come home from the war to no business?' demanded Kezzie. 'If we don't begin our sandwiches and lunchtime snacks again soon then we will lose all our customers.' She appealed to Peg for help. 'We can run the front, can't we?' she asked.

'Yes, probably,' said Peg. 'I suppose we owe it to them to keep going.'

'We've got to try, at least,' said Kezzie. 'It's not doing us any good moping every day. Look at you,' she spoke to Signora Biagi. 'You were always so neatly dressed, with your hair so beautifully arranged. What a welcome for your husband should he return just at this moment.'

Signora Biagi glanced in the mirror hanging on the wall. She sighed and fixed one or two hair grips in place.

'Kezzie is right,' she said. 'We must at least try.'

'So.' Kezzie rubbed her hands together. 'Tonight you will make some pasta. We will share our ration coupons and make some chocolate cake and pies. And then we will begin again.'

CHAPTER 12

Kezzie learns to drive

To begin with it was really Lucy and the baby who kept them going. Alec was teething and demanded constant attention. With the shortage of teachers Lucy was attending school only in the mornings and spent most of the afternoon in the café helping out, alternately petted or scolded, depending on the prevailing mood in the kitchen. She was becoming an expert in pasta making, mixing and beating the flour and egg and water, rolling it out and cutting and folding the special shapes. Her favourite was ravioli, and Signora Biagi had taken much time to demonstrate exactly how to press and flute the ends together.

Kezzie watched her sister working so seriously, looking up every so often to check with Signora Biagi that what she was doing was correct.

'Is this enough?' Lucy would ask, her hand holding the flour shaker above the pastry board. She would wait until one of the signoras nodded their head before continuing.

And Kezzie noticed that she didn't shirk the unpleasant or difficult tasks. Lucy would wait until the dishes were done or the surfaces scrubbed before untying her apron and saying, 'I think it's time for some tea.' Everyone laughed on the first occasion Lucy came out with this expression. But now, despite her youth, she was rapidly becoming one of the work team in the kitchen.

Ricardo and his father wrote frequently. Their letters were amusing and light-hearted. Kezzie was sure that they guessed how anxious Signora Casella and Signora Biagi would be and deliberately filled the pages with remarks about their seaside vacation and the wonderful bed and breakfasts which they enjoyed. Many passages were blocked out by the censor but they'd been held at a temporary camp in Wales before being sent on to the Isle of Man. There they were put in what had been holiday hotels, and the accommodation, although cramped, was bearable. They'd fared much better than some of the others who were sent to Canada and Australia, and kept in what were no more than prisoner-of-war camps.

At home there was a frightened tenseness in conversations with neighbours and friends which Kezzie had never been aware of before. The bravado and old-style jingoism disappeared. People kissed and embraced each other more obviously when parting even for a short time, and what was more unusual, they did so in public.

The new Home Guard trained and drilled regularly. At first the butt of jokes with their ludicrous and out-of-date equipment, more and more people realised that these men might have to make the last stand before the enemy. Many veterans of the First World War had enlisted, men older than her grandfather.

'If they do land, they'll find it harder to beat us than they expect,' said one old man, sipping his weak tea in the café. 'We'll fight to the bitter end.'

It was a mood which seemed to prevail through the whole country. Listening to a recording of the Prime Minister's speech one evening on the radio gave Kezzie an eerie feeling. The slow drawl, the hesitant slur of the words coming from the squat wooden box set on its shelf in the corner of the counter. Churchill's voice giving hope to millions of people.

'We shall defend our island, whatever the cost may be, we shall fight on the beaches, we shall fight on the landing grounds, we shall fight in the fields and in the streets, we shall fight in the hills: we shall never surrender.'

In the café they kept the business going, and drafted Mary Price in to help wash dishes and mind the children.

'It's giving me something to take my mind off worrying about Robert,' she told Kezzie, 'and I love playing with the wee ones.'

She'd had some news from her husband. In the retreat his battalion had reached Cherbourg, and were finally safely evacuated to England. There was talk of the rescued troops being sent to open up a new front in the East or in Africa. Or were they in fact preparing to fight on British soil?

Mary was an energetic worker and a cheerful soul. She tuned the radio station to *Music While You Work* and sang along with the current hits. She taught Lucy all the words. Their favourites at the moment were the songs from the Disney version of *Snow White*. They sang together, to the amusement of the customers, while Mary danced around the kitchen with the baby on one arm and Lucy holding on to the other.

She's like a child herself, thought Kezzie. And even though Mary was older than her and married, Kezzie felt that in some ways she was more mature. The days of the summer of 1940 slipped away, each one told off like beads on a prayer circlet. Counted out singly, every sunset and sunrise a bonus of peace as the country braced itself for the expected invasion. Special buses and trains took the children away from the south coast of England far inland. Some of them had been evacuated previously from the larger cities. And above their heads in the long hot summer the RAF fought a desperate battle for control of the skies over Britain.

Carefully worded letters from William James made Kezzie realise that he was part of it. His mother now also wrote to Kezzie. Her letters showed how proud she was of him, yet her anxiety and worry lifted off the very page as Kezzie read them. She tried to reply to each one as best she could.

Day by day the invasion seemed imminent. By August over a thousand enemy planes were sent on sorties daily into Britain. How long could the RAF keep them at bay?

Then on the seventh of September the Luftwaffe broke through the defences of Fighter Command and set London ablaze.

Kezzie's grandad scanned the papers. 'They're not telling us the half of it,' he said.

Night after night they kept coming. The Londoners fled to the underground stations, carrying bedding, children, food and water. It was a city under siege from the sky. And in the mornings the Londoners came out of the darkness and looked upon the devastation of their homes.

Lady Fitzwilliam wrote to her.

Kezzie, the bombing continues. They will not stop, neither will they go away. Our boys will fight until they die, each and every one of them, yet the safety of our children concerns me deeply. I sense and know that you would not like to lose sight of Lucy, nor she of you, for even a short time. I suggest that you both come and stay with me. I am far out in the country and it would be as safe here as anywhere else. Please give the matter some thought. I already have some children billeted here, so it would be no trouble to me. Also, I would appreciate your company, as would William, that is if he ever does get any leave.

Kezzie didn't show the letter to anyone. She knew that at the moment she was needed in the café. It was taking her full attention and, as the days passed, the finances became more grave. By not delivering the large orders which they'd done before, they were starting to lose money. One day Kezzie asked Ricardo's aunt for the keys of the delivery van and went out to the wooden lean-to where the van was garaged.

'It can't be *so* difficult,' she said, assuming a great air of confidence. She took the keys quickly from Signora

Casella's hand. 'I've watched Ricardo lots of times when he was driving.'

She sat in the van and turned the key in the ignition. The engine roared and the van leapt forwards and smacked against the wooden wall of the garage.

'Ooops,' said Kezzie.

'There's something about gears,' she told Peg when she returned to the café later. 'I think that bit of it is important. If I could just get someone to explain it to me, I'm sure I could pick it up fairly quickly.'

She tried to coax one of the apprentice boys to give her a lesson.

'Nae chance.' He shook his head. 'Women can't drive. They're not built for it.'

'Nonsense,' said Kezzie. 'I think you're scared,' she said, attempting to goad him.

He grinned at her. 'Aye, ye're right there, hen,' he said. 'I'd rather face the Jerries than get behind a wheel wi' you.'

Kezzie put her hands on her hips. 'There must be some way I can persuade you,' she said. She stared at him boldly. 'Something I could give you, perhaps?'

'Aye . . .' he said slowly. He looked her up and down. 'I'll tell ye what ye could gie me . . .' He broke off.

Kezzie snapped her fingers. 'I know,' she said. 'My sugar ration!'

'Yes,' said Peg from the other end of the counter. 'You can have mine too. And my butter as well.'

'And mine,' volunteered Lucy, who had come through from the kitchen without anyone realising it.

'I . . . I . . .' the boy stuttered. 'I didnae mean that.'

275

'And what did you mean, exactly?' asked Kezzie, hands on her hips again.

'Oh nothin',' he mumbled.

And so his fate was sealed. Kezzie's first lesson was the very next afternoon.

'How do I stop it?' she asked, after a few minutes, turning round in her seat.

'Put yer foot on the brake!' he yelled. He made a grab for the steering wheel. 'And keep yer eyes on the road!'

'You didn't show me the brake to begin with,' said Kezzie later when they returned to the café.

The apprentice boy sat down in the nearest chair, took his cap off and, pulling a hanky from his pocket, he wiped his face.

'How was your driving?' asked Peg.

'It's quite easy actually,' said Kezzie. 'I don't know what all the fuss is about. The Government is thinking of introducing tests and examinations before you can get a certificate. I can't imagine why. A child could do it.'

'Give me a coffee,' said her instructor. 'An' make it black and strong,' he added.

The bombing of London continued. By the end of September over seven thousand civilians had been killed by enemy action.

'They won't stop coming, will they?' Kezzie asked her grandad one night after listening to the latest broadcast. 'And there's not much we can do about it, is there?'

'If our night fighters can't keep holding them off . . . then we're defenceless,' said Grandad.

'You think they'll come north?' she asked him.

He raised his head and Kezzie saw that his eyes were shadowed. She realised that he didn't want to cause her distress, but he thought that she needed to know the truth.

'Aye, lass,' he said. 'They'll come. And soon.'

CHAPTER 13

Lucy runs away

Grandad's words were on Kezzie's mind that night. She knew that if she gave the matter any thought at all, then it was obvious that this part of Britain would be a target. Clydebank was a shipbuilding town, known all over the world. John Brown's yards were famed for boatbuilding, both commercial and naval. Warships and troop transportations were slipping in and out of the Clyde ports all the time. Ships from some of the other navies belonging to their allies, such as Poland and Belgium, were repaired or refitted here.

In addition to the yards, there were many other types of production plants clustered around the Clyde. Light and heavy engineering and armaments supplies, the Rolls-Royce works at Hillington and Beardmore's heavy armour plate. When you looked across the central belt of Scotland then the amount of industry concentrated in this one area was immense: from the huge Singer factory and timber yards to smaller units making parts for engines and automobiles. The works ran on from Glasgow City, down the great river and all along the estuary.

One or two enemy spotter planes had flown over, keeping well out of range of the anti-aircraft guns. Everybody reckoned that they must be taking aerial photographs, surveying weather conditions and gathering information to report to their own intelligence units. Probably recording the position of the docks and the layout of the surrounding works, perhaps noting the big oil terminals at Kilmarnock. And no matter what precautions the Government took, such as removing all directional signs, or even the more complicated manoeuvres of installing street lights among the surrounding hills which were empty of people, they could never obliterate one feature: the Clyde. On the darkest nights it glittered like a thick silver cord, twisting, fat and slow, among the tenements and houses spread all around it. And all these ingenious schemes to divert and fool the enemy could not disguise the location of the sea to the river, and the river to the town.

Even young children knew the names of the aircraft. Spitfires and Hurricanes, Heinkels and Junkers. To them it was exciting and interesting to spot a plane and try to identify it. There were great arguments about the respective fire power and merits of each kind of machine. It was, of course, a huge game that adults were playing and not to be taken too seriously. Lucy would climb on top of the Anderson shelter in the garden at the back of the café and pretend to drop bombs on baby Alec sitting up in his pram, and he would shriek with laughter.

'Play a nice game now, *piccola*,' Signora Casella would

plead with her. 'Come, and I will cut some paper dolls for you to dress.'

Ricardo's mother hated hearing the news bulletins. She would cover her ears with her fingers when the broadcasts began.

Peg had laughed. 'You're an ostrich, Signora,' she said. 'Pretending it isn't happening won't make the war go away.'

Was that what *she* was doing? thought Kezzie, as she lay with Lucy cuddled up beside her. Was she burying her head in the sand?

Lucy turned in the bed, and Kezzie adjusted her position so that there was more room. Her sister slept the sleep of the innocent child. Her body heavy, her breathing regular. What should she do? Kezzie tried to think through her problem logically. She had a complete conviction that if Lucy was sent away again it would have a dreadful impact on her.

And myself, thought Kezzie suddenly. I would hardly be able to bear it. And what of Grandad? The previous separation had torn the little family apart. Perhaps it was selfishness then. She lay considering this for several minutes and while she did so, her sister shifted yet again and, muttering something, stretched out her arm on the pillow. What was she dreaming of? Kezzie wondered. The room was so dark with the blackout blinds on the windows that she could not see Lucy's face. What was she thinking of, her little sister, as she slept on through the night? Lucy's trust in Kezzie was absolute, believing that she knew what was best for her. But now Kezzie was tormented. If she made a wrong decision it could mean the difference of life or death for Lucy.

Kezzie turned once more in the bed, leaning on her elbow as she thought about her own life. Her great inspiration to study medicine seemed almost a self-centred indulgence compared to the war being fought. Yet she knew that it was the right course for her, had known it since she was very young. Her missionary zeal had faded a little, the desire to travel to foreign lands and do good was something she now realised might not be fulfilled. But her determination to qualify as a doctor had not altered. She thought then of Michael. How he'd encouraged her ambitions. Their lives, so far apart at the moment, were joined by a fine link which was unbreak-able. She wondered what he was doing at this very moment. Was he thinking of her? Kezzie slept at last, and smiled as she dreamed.

The Blitzkrieg continued. Almost nightly, bombs were dropping on London, and then other industrial cities and ports. Daily radio news bulletins and newspaper head-lines told of great destruction and death. Docklands and industrial targets were pounded again and again. Then on the 14th of November over four hundred planes attacked the city of Coventry, dropping nearly a thousand incendiary bombs.

In the local shop, Kezzie stared at the pictures of the shell of Coventry Cathedral. Its centre had been annihilated in the space of a few hours. The remaining latticed windows and small elongated spires were etched in monochrome relief against the sky. People photographed in the streets were wandering about dazed and stupefied, clutching a few possessions, children sitting amongst the rubble.

Kezzie bought some newspapers and went back to their house. Her grandad was just in from night-firewatching and eating his breakfast. She spread the newspapers out on the table in front of him.

'I'm taking Lucy to Aunt Bella's today,' she said.

He didn't say anything at all. Only stared straight ahead and nodded. When Kezzie returned in the early afternoon he was still sitting at the table. The fire had gone out and he hadn't rekindled it. The room was cold.

'I had to get her away from here,' said Kezzie as she took her coat off and hung it up on the hook at the back of the door.

Her grandfather looked up at her. 'You did it for the best,' he said.

Kezzie sat down at the table opposite him. She put her head in her hands. 'But is it?' she asked him. 'Is it for the best? I don't know.'

'I'm surprised that she stayed,' he said after a bit.

'I tricked her,' said Kezzie wearily. 'I told her I was going to the shop, and then caught the bus back to Glasgow from the end of the road. I couldn't even say goodbye properly in case she suspected something.' She put her teacup down unsteadily. 'Bella said she'd tell her after a few hours.'

'Poor Bella,' said Grandad.

About half-past four their letterbox rattled loudly and Grandad went to answer the door. Bella came rushing through to the kitchen.

'It's Lucy!' she cried. 'She's run away!'

CHAPTER 14

Ricardo returns

Bella's coat was flapping open, showing that she still had her apron on. Her face was without powder, her hair falling down.

'Kezzie, John, I'm sorry. I'm sorry.' She looked wildly from one to the other. 'Kezzie, she kept askin' where you were, and what was keepin' you. Ah kept puttin' her off like, with wee stories an' givin' her things to dae. An' then another wifie who'd gone down the road after you, came back up, an' I saw Lucy speaking to her. An' then the wean came over the road, an' she said tae me, awful quiet-like, "Aunty Bella, Kezzie's gone home without me, hasn't she?"

'I just nodded. Ah couldnae say the words. An' what a look she gied me, Kezzie.' Bella put her hands to her face. 'I ken now how Judas felt. But she never complained, nor cried. Nothin'. Only asked me if she could play outside for a wee while.' Bella sat down heavily. 'An' me bein' that stupid, an' that glad she was takin' it so well, says, "Aye, on ye go, hen." An' then half an hour later when I went to fetch her in . . .' Bella pulled a handkerchief from her pocket and wiped her eyes.

'Have ye told the police?' asked Kezzie's grandad.

Bella shook her head. 'No,' she said. 'I came straight here.'

'Where d'ye think she'd go, Kezzie?' her grandad asked.

Kezzie couldn't think at all. She realised now that she should never have left her sister like that, in such a cowardly fashion. But it would have been too much for her to cope with if Lucy had cried or become hysterical when she told her that she was returning to Clydebank without her.

'I don't know,' she said dully.

Grandad made some tea, and as they drank it they talked over what to do.

'I'll go to the police station,' he said. 'Then I'll walk the road back to Stonevale.'

Kezzie looked at him. He seemed to have aged tremendously in the last few hours. It was as though his two grandchildren were the life force which sustained him. Now he was drained and barely able to function.

'Yes,' she said. She got up slowly. What should she do now? Her great dread was that Lucy would lapse into the almost catatonic state she'd been in when she had gone missing before. When she and Kezzie were separated previously the shock had been so great for Lucy that she had been unable to tell anyone her name, or where she lived.

Kezzie walked to the window. It was almost dark. Mindful of the blackout regulations, she started to draw the curtains before she lit the gaslight. She stood at the window for a moment and looked out into the night. Where was Lucy? If she was running away where would she go? Kezzie frowned. A memory returned to her, faint yet insistent, of herself standing at a window . . . watching, waiting . . .

Now she recalled what it was. In the McMaths' house in Waterfoot, she'd stood looking out into the Canadian wilderness, anxious for news of Lucy's friend, the boy Jack, who'd absconded from the orphanage where Lucy had been placed. 'Where does a runaway child go?' she had asked.

'To where they would be welcome. To people who show love and kindness.' Doctor McMath's words slipped into Kezzie's mind. She turned from the window.

'I think I'll take a walk along to the café,' she said. 'Bella, will you wait here?'

Kezzie hurried through the blacked-out streets, feeling along the brick walls, stumbling off kerbs and hesitantly seeking her way across the roads. She tried to block her mind from the fact that somewhere Lucy might be doing the same. By the time she arrived the café was closed, but Ricardo's mother and his aunt sat with her, in the dark with the door left open, just in case . . .

They made coffee and drank it, and to pass the time they told Kezzie stories of their childhood in Italy. The little farm in the hills of Umbria where they played with the goats in the summer-time. Of how their father had walked all the way through France and England to Scotland, to find work. He had been helped by a *Padrone*, a man from the adjoining village who'd already established his business in Gourock and sent for young men and women from his community to work in his shops. Their father had worked hard, they told Kezzie, and when his elder daughter was married he was able to help her and her husband buy this café as a wedding gift.

Despite Signora Biagi's protests they listened to the news bulletins. There had been another raid on London in the early evening.

Signora Casella shook her head. 'The Londoners suffer so much,' she murmured. 'I hope we can bear it so well when it is our turn.'

Signora Biagi shuddered. 'The very thought of that Anderson shelter makes my skin crawl,' she said.

'I don't know if it is so awful,' Kezzie said reassuringly. 'Ricardo made it very cosy, with a rug and some cushions and a lamp. It is just like a little house. Lucy loves to play in it . . .'

Her eyes widened and she gripped Signora Biagi's arm.

'The Anderson shelter,' she whispered.

It was Signora Biagi who restrained Kezzie when they opened the door. Lucy had the oil lamp lit, and was quietly reading a book with the rag doll propped beside her.

'Lucy!' Kezzie screamed and stepped forward. Signora Biagi held on to her arm. 'Do you know the trouble and worry you have given everyone? You are a wicked child to do this.' Kezzie found she was shaking with rage and fear.

'No, I'm not,' said Lucy. 'You lied to me. It was you who caused the fuss. We agreed that I was to stay at home. You changed your mind, and you didn't even tell me.'

'What could I say?' Kezzie asked Peg the next day. 'She was speaking the truth, and was also rather proud of herself that she had found her way there without getting lost.'

'Is your mind more settled now about her staying in the town?' Peg asked Kezzie.

Kezzie laughed. 'Well, I suppose it has to be. She has told me that she'll just run away if I try to evacuate her, so I don't really have any choice.'

But still Kezzie couldn't help but worry. At the beginning of December three thousand incendiary bombs were dropped on the city of London in one night. It was the worst raid ever.

The Chief Fire Officer at Surrey Docks called desperately for help. 'The whole bloody world's on fire,' his signal read.

And it seemed as if his words were true. A red flame-coloured cloud two miles high hung over London. The press referred to it as 'Black Saturday'. The fires were out of control and burned for days. The picture of the outline of the dome of St Paul's ascending through the pall of smoke disturbed Kezzie greatly.

Peg took the newspaper gently from her hand.

'When there's nothing you can do about something, then you must try to stop worrying about it,' she said. She put her arm around her friend's shoulder. 'How do you think I cope with Ricardo being away? It's awful. We don't really know if he and his father are keeping well on the Isle of Man, but I force myself to stay cheerful, for his mother and aunt's sake.'

And Bella also tried to cheer Kezzie up.

'Listen tae me, hen,' she'd said on Kezzie's last visit. 'Who kens what's going tae happen? It's all in the hands of the Almighty. I read the paper yesterday. There was a woman living right out in the country, in Fife, I think it was. Ah mean if yer going to be safe anywhere, it's Fife. Nothin' ever happens in Fife. Nothin'. Anyway, she'd just scrubbed her front step an' whit happens? A stray plane goin' home jettisons its bombs. Blew her tae kingdom come.'

Kezzie nodded. 'I heard that story. If they can't find their targets, the pilots have to unload their bombs or they don't have enough fuel to get back. It was a tragedy.'

'You're tellin' me,' said Bella. 'All that work tae get yer front step clean, an' some bliddy wee Jerry comes along and messes it up, just like that.'

An appeal was sent out by the Red Cross for relief ambulance drivers. There were few women who could drive and most of the men who could had been called up or were in essential occupations. Kezzie volunteered at once. At last there was some war work which reflected her interest in medical care. She already had first-aid training but, due to the staff shortages, the drivers were often expected to know and do a bit more. Driving the ambulance was even more difficult than driving the delivery van. It was heavier and more awkward on the corners and Kezzie took a lot of teasing from the men at the depot. She was given a uniform and a cap, of which she was very proud. She had only bumped it three times, she told Peg proudly, and just once with a patient in it.

Just before Christmas the door of the café opened and a tall young man with a sallow complexion and a thin face stepped inside. He closed the door quietly behind him, and standing with his back against the glass he looked around him slowly.

Peg was refilling the biscuit tins with her back to the counter. She was managing mostly with one hand as she had Alec propped up on her shoulder, and was talking nonsense to him as she worked. The baby, facing the street, suddenly let out a crow of delight. Peg turned round, screamed and then burst into tears.

Kezzie came running from the kitchen. 'What is it? What's wrong?'

Ricardo was at the counter with tears running down his face, his arms around both Peg and Alec. The little boy looked from one to the other and then started howling.

'For goodness' sake,' said Kezzie, half-crying herself. 'You're distressing that baby. Here, give him to me.' And she pushed Peg and Ricardo ahead of her into the kitchen. Within minutes everyone was in tears. Kezzie ran through to the front and turned the 'Closed' notice to face out.

Ricardo was disinclined to talk about the camp. His

passport had been cleared by the American Embassy and his father had insisted that Ricardo return to Clydebank without him.

'Father is well and sends his love,' Ricardo told his mother. 'He hopes to get out soon but perhaps he will not be allowed to return here immediately.'

His mother covered her face with her hands.

'You must be brave,' said Ricardo. 'They are releasing those who will help with the war effort, working in some industry or perhaps taking part in bomb-damage clearance. Father does not mind this so much.' Ricardo hesitated. 'From the camp,' he said sadly, 'we could hear Liverpool and Birkenhead being bombed. We heard the noise. We could see the sky. It was red with fire.'

Kezzie thought of the firewatchers like her grandad who would have been on duty. What could they possibly do, confronted with hundreds and hundreds of incendiary bombs setting the trail for the main bombers to follow? What would he do when they started dropping on Clydebank? What could they do?

'They will wait now until the winter is over,' said Ricardo. 'Then when the weather is better they will return.'

He was proved right. At the beginning of spring 1941 the bombing spread to other locations.

'It seems to be the ports that they are targeting,' said her grandad. 'It's up to our nightfighters. The RAF can keep them out of the skies by day but not in the dark.'

Kezzie's work with the Red Cross increased to such an extent that most nights she returned home exhausted. Ricardo had to report each day to the police station and there were still some areas where he was not allowed to travel. So he worked mainly in the shop and Kezzie did the deliveries. Not that he or Peg minded at all. They took joy in each other's company. With baby Alec they seemed to make a complete family and Kezzie was happy for them.

Each night as Grandad was leaving to firewatch Kezzie was usually returning from her duties and, as he was out most nights, she slept in his bed. Lucy was growing bigger. She was now nine years old and took up a great deal more room.

One night in March Kezzie came home around eight o'clock. Lucy was already bathed and in bed.

'I warmed the stone pig and put it in the bed for ye,' said her grandad. He hugged her as he left for his firewatching. Every family was the same. Working all hours to keep the troops supplied and their spare time taken up with voluntary work. Her grandad's post was down by the docks.

'Good job I like ships, isn't it?' he'd commented.

The shipyards would be the first to get hit if Clydebank is attacked, Kezzie thought, and they would almost certainly come off worse.

She was wrong.

That Thursday night, the thirteenth of March, Kezzie gave her grandad his sandwiches and a bottle of cold tea. She smiled as she watched him pack it in with his gas mask and helmet. She'd bought him a vacuum flask, but he rarely used it. It was an old miner's habit. He insisted that cold tea, which would be chilled by the time he drank it, had special reviving powers.

She shut the door behind him and peered into the bedroom. Lucy was asleep. Kezzie took some soup from the pot, then undressed quickly and slipped into the warm bed in the little windowless room off the kitchen.

She was fast asleep with the door closed when the first alarm sounded.

CHAPTER 15

1941: The sirens go off

The noise of the air-raid siren woke Lucy almost at once. She sat up in fright, clutching the rag doll in her hands. What was it? A dreadful screaming noise pierced through her head, the wailing going on and on, like an animal being tortured. She slipped out from under the blankets, shivering as her bare feet touched the cold linoleum, and trotted quickly through to where Kezzie lay asleep.

'Kezzie,' she whispered, 'Kezzie.'

Her sister's eyes were closed fast. Dark smudges of exhaustion showed beneath the sockets. Lucy shook Kezzie gently.

'Kezzie,' she whispered again.

Kezzie didn't stir. Her mouth was partly open and her breathing was regular and deep. Lucy waited a moment or two. She could still hear the awful sound echoing round the streets, coming right into her house, climbing higher and higher. She held her doll more closely to her and whispered in its ear.

'What is it?' she asked. 'What is it, Kissy?'

Then suddenly Lucy knew what it was. It had been weeks, months even since she'd heard that particular noise. It was the warning. The one Grandad had told her about. She had laughed, and thought it was a great game when he'd made her practise what to do. Go into the hall, put on her coat, take her gas mask and run all the way downstairs. Right out the back entrance of the close, and she hadn't to stop until she reached the concrete shelter. They had races to see who was the fastest. She usually won.

Lucy puckered her face. It was definitely the warning noise, the air-raid siren to let you know that the enemy was coming. They would be in the sky now, flying towards them to drop bombs on their head. Yet . . . it didn't seem right. The noise wasn't the same as before. Perhaps it was a trick, a joke, a made up game. Lucy shivered again. She didn't like this game. But now there seemed to be more noise. Other sirens were joining in, one after the other all over the town.

So . . . she should wake Kezzie and go downstairs.

Her grandad's voice was in her ear. 'If a siren sounds you *must* go to the shelter. Promise me you *will* go, Lucy. No matter how tired you are, no matter how cosy and warm in your bed. Don't snuggle under the blankets. Promise me that you will get up at once and hurry outside.'

And she had promised. Standing solemnly in front of her grandad, she had promised.

But now she couldn't wake Kezzie. What should she do?

Lucy took a handful of Kezzie's hair, and tugged

gently. It didn't seem to bother her. She shook her shoulder and called her name. Nothing. She grabbed a great chunk of Kezzie's hair and pulled hard. Kezzie turned and pushed her sister's hand away. She moaned something in her sleep, then settled down again. Lucy closed her own eyes. 'Sorry Kezzie,' she said, and yanked the long brown hair even harder.

'Don't,' said Kezzie sharply. She moved across and drew the bedclothes around her.

Lucy was now completely at a loss. She couldn't wake Kezzie up, and she had tried, really tried. She looked around the little room. It was very dark, with no windows, the only light coming through the kitchen from the tiny oil lamp left burning in the hall. Perhaps if she closed over the door and crept in beside Kezzie then the planes in the sky wouldn't see them, and they would be quite safe. Just the same as being in the shelter, she thought. In fact, better, because here it was warmer and not so smelly and damp.

In fact . . . maybe it was only another false alarm. Lucy raised her head and listened. Faintly in the distance she could hear yet another wail starting, rising and falling like some dreaded banshee.

She touched Kezzie again. She didn't stir. She would have to give up. *Nothing* was going to wake her sister.

Lucy went out of the small room and into the kitchen. She slid quietly between the curtains and the window and edged the blackout board to one side. Far away across the roofs she could see lights in the sky. Long white pencils of white stretching across the darkness, moving, crossing and recrossing. In the distance she saw a strange sight. Big white mushroom shapes floating down, dropping behind the houses and across the river and then suddenly the sky was full of colour. Great sparklers and cartwheels and rockets everywhere.

It was very exciting. Like a party with special fireworks. She could hear noises now, thuds and cracks and loud booms, mostly in the distance but coming nearer to her.

Lucy watched for about a minute longer and then turned and slipped back into the room. She was cold now. Perhaps she should just go back to bed. Kezzie was too tired to get up. She worked long hours, first in the café and then in the ambulance, driving. And if this noise didn't wake her then *nothing* would.

On her way back to bed Lucy passed the kitchen table, where the bowls and spoons and the jug of milk were set out for breakfast in the morning.

Kezzie slumbered on, in a deep untroubled sleep. She was walking in the park. It was sunny and warm, and she was hand in hand with someone, but when she turned her head she couldn't see the person's face. She could hear noises, like children crying, and she knew it should worry her, but she didn't care. She was happy.

Michael Donohoe was in her dream. He couldn't be there, for he was far away, yet she was not surprised to see him. He was standing by the fountain, and he was laughing. Smiling and joking the way he always did. And there was an ache in her heart because she knew he wasn't real. And then he said something to her. But she couldn't hear him. And he called out again and turned to look at the fountain, at the falling water. And the water was falling, falling from the sky. There was rain on her face, soaking her hair, running down her chin, and she was laughing because she was so wet. But the liquid on her face was not pleasant. She wiped it away in annoyance.

'Don't,' she said in her sleep. Her neck and the top of her dress were soaked. She tried to dry herself. Her hands touched the soft fabric of her nightdress. Kezzie opened her eyes.

'*Lucy!* What are you doing?'

Lucy looked at the empty milk jug in her hands. She took a quick step backwards.

'Kezzie,' she gabbled. 'The sirens are making an awful noise. Grandad said we must get up and go to the shelter if the siren went off. I couldn't get you awake so I . . .' she looked again at the jug in her hand.

Kezzie lifted her old Gladstone bag which they kept by the front door. Inside it had the family papers and photographs, birth certificates and ration books.

'Wait,' said Lucy. She ran back and picked up her dolly.

They passed Mrs Sweeney's house. She was locking her front door.

'Bother,' she said and turned back.

'What have you forgotten?' called Mary Price from the next landing.

'The ration books,' said Mrs Sweeney. 'I'll just run back for them.'

'You go on, Kezzie,' Mary said. 'I'll wait for Mrs Sweeney.'

Kezzie went down to the first floor. The three little boys were lined up outside. Their mum was getting the pram out of the lobby.

'Need a hand?' asked Kezzie.

'No,' she smiled. 'My man's at home tonight. Thanks anyway.'

Kezzie went down to the ground floor. The noise increased as she got lower, fire bells mixing with sirens and police horns. This was no false alarm or ARP practice. She went to the close mouth. The baffle wall was directly opposite the exit. It blocked her view of the street and the sky. It really was *very* noisy, she thought. Now that she was almost outside she was more aware of the thumping vibration in the air. Kezzie craned her neck forward and looked at the sky. Huge fingers of light criss-crossed the skies above her. She could hear the ack-ack battery at Duntocher and out in the river a warship was firing away for all it was worth. She saw a plane quite clearly, an enemy raider flying low almost directly above her. Grey metal glinting in the beam of the searchlight. It appeared to be trapped in the blinding glare, another locked on to it, and then another, and then, just as suddenly they lost it, and it was gone.

So they have come, thought Kezzie. Her heart began to thud heavily but she felt quite calm as she thought out what to do. She looked above her head, at the roof which had been reinforced with thick steel tubing. Should she stay here or make a run for the shelter? Perhaps she should wait for the others? She heard Mrs Sweeney's door bang and the sound of her shrill voice. One of the boys started crying. Better not to wait, she thought. They would be coming down the stairs in a moment, carrying the wee one with the pram. It would be too crowded here in the close for all of them. Better to go on ahead and set out the blankets for the children.

Kezzie took a firm grip of Lucy's hand in one of her own and, grasping her Gladstone bag in the other, she took one step outside.

At that precise moment, a high-explosive land-mine scored a direct hit on the tenement opposite and blew the whole street to bits.

CHAPTER 16

Blitzed!

A great blast of air plucked Kezzie and Lucy off their feet and slammed them both violently against the side wall of the close. The rag doll was abruptly snatched from Lucy's grasp and the Gladstone bag from Kezzie's hand. Then the front of the building sheared off and collapsed into the street, and the remainder tumbled in upon itself.

Neither of them made a sound, not a cry nor a whimper. All the air in their lungs was torn out of their bodies as the explosion impacted through the close. With a shattering roar a huge invisible giant cuffed them both to oblivion.

And then the masonry was falling, floor after floor, crashing down and down, crushing life out of everyone, destroying all in its path. Further down the road the gas main fractured. Seconds later a spark ignited, and with a loud bang the gas caught fire at the point where the pipe was broken. At the far end of the building the gable end remained upright. The whole structure shuddered and teetered precariously. From time to time small pieces of brick and plaster broke off and fell into what had been the back green.

Elsewhere in the town the rescue services were working themselves to a standstill. Among the many fires started, the ones at Singer's vast timber yard and Yoker Distillery, which had been set alight almost at once, were the worst. The high quantities of inflammable material in both places meant that it was almost impossible to extinguish them. The main bomber groups which followed used the fires as target guidelines. One of the biggest water mains, which brought water down from the hills to the town, was destroyed early on by a bomb, and three of the Auxiliary Fire Service Stations were also put out of action at the start of the raid. A call went out to neighbouring authorities. Sixty-five extra units rushed to help. It wasn't enough. The inferno raged on.

Then the parachute mines and the high explosive bombs started falling. Whistling down from skies bringing devastation and death.

By the time the all-clear sounded and dawn came, there was hardly a street in Clydebank without a fatality. Hundreds of civilians had been killed, and hundreds more seriously injured.

It was at first light on the Friday morning that a rescue party reached the place where Kezzie's tenement used to be.

'Gas main gone here,' said the patrol officer. He took his notepad and scribbled down some information. Then he tore off the sheet and handed it to the young boy who was the messenger for his team. 'Here, son, see if you can

301

make it back to HQ and get that one marked up.' He watched as the boy mounted his bike and wobbled off in the direction of the town hall. He grinned at his deputy who was standing beside him. 'Jim's been blown off that bike three times already and he's still determined to ride it.'

'With nearly every telegraph line down, it's just as well lads like him volunteered,' said the deputy. 'We couldnae manage without them.'

The two men surveyed the remains of the tenement block. The deputy shook his head. 'Don't think anyone got out of that, do you, George?'

George Murdoch shook his head. He consulted his notebook. 'According to the warden for this area none of them got to the main shelter. So . . .' He chewed his lip for a minute. 'The only chance ye'd have . . . is if ye were directly under the steel beams at the close mouth.'

'Even then . . .' The deputy shook his head.

'Aye, ye're probably right, Willie. But I'll just go and take a wee peek.'

'Watch out for that gable end, George. Ah don't like the look of it at all.'

The patrol officer squinted up at the wall. It was as though the end of the tenement had been sliced off with a giant's carving knife. Each floor lay exposed to the world. By the fireplace on the first floor was a wooden clothes horse with little vests and pants hung to dry. On a mantelpiece in one room sat two wally dugs with a clock in between. The clock was showing the correct time. On the top floor the table was set for breakfast. The remains of the tenement shuddered from top to bottom.

George Murdoch smiled. 'Aye, Willie,' he said. 'Ah'll keep my eyes open. Ah'm none too happy about it myself.'

He clambered over the ruins and among the wreckage to where he judged the safest part of the building had been. He hunted around and called out loudly for several minutes. He waited for a bit, calling again and again, then, squatting down and putting his ear to the ground, he listened. After a while he began to make his way back. Willie came to meet him.

'Nothing?'

'Nothing.'

'We've got a runner from HQ sayin' they need us two streets away.' The deputy handed him the scrawled message.

Behind them the building groaned and shifted slightly. The two men took a last quick look around.

'There's somethin' there, beside that pipe.' George Murdoch had seen a small object which had been flung aside by the explosion.

'It's only a doll, George,' his deputy said, and kept walking.

'Well, if there's a doll, there must just be a child close by.'

George Murdoch clambered over the pile of bricks which had been the baffle wall, erected to protect any bomb blast going through the close. As he bent down to pick up the rag doll he caught sight of a small hand sticking out from under the rubble.

'Hang on a minute!' he called. He knelt down and took the child's hand in his own.

It was quite cold.

'Oh, no.' He barely spoke the words. It was now seven a.m. and he had been working since just after the siren had gone at nine the previous evening. He was weary, his body tired and his mind stunned with the cases he'd dealt with during the night. 'Wee kids,' he'd told his wife on the one occasion he nipped back to his own house to get a cup of tea and collect a spare tin helmet, 'that's the worst to deal with. Some burnt beyond recognition. Whole families have been wiped out. Is this what the world has come to? That we put our children in the front line?'

His big rough hand closed over the frail little one.

'Not another wean,' he said aloud. He rubbed his eyes with his sleeve. 'I don't think I can go much more of this.'

'Come out of there, George,' the deputy shouted again. 'That wall's goin' to collapse, and you'll be under it if ye don't move yerself.'

'Aye, aye.' He got to his knees. As he did so, his years of first aid training made him instinctively check the wrist before he let go. Just before he dropped the child's hand he automatically felt for the pulse.

He had turned his face away. The sight of the small fingers with the rosy pink nails covered in plaster dust had disturbed him. When he thought about it later he reckoned his sense of touch was that bit more alert, his fingertips a fraction more sensitive as they located the point where the child's life blood throbbed through the artery from the heart.

'Bloody hell,' he muttered and started to scrabble frantically at the rubble.

'What are ye doin', George?' called one of the team, glancing back.

'A pulse,' he yelled. 'I've got a pulse. This wean's alive!'

'Ye'll need tae stop.' His deputy was beside him now. 'Look,' he pointed at the end wall of the tenement. High above them a large piece of flooring had worked loose and the joist ends were slipping out of the wall plate. 'We'll get some steel rope and drag it down from the other side. Then we free this child.'

'How long d'ye think that'll take?' asked George.

'Half an hour, maybe.'

George looked down at the little hand he still held in his own. 'This wean canny wait half an hour,' he said.

Willie sighed. 'Ah thought ye were going to say that.' He knelt down beside his mate. 'We'll need to do it brick by brick,' he said. 'Any big movement and you an' me are goin' have right sair heids the morrow.'

George Murdoch put his hand on his friend's shoulder. 'Ye don't need to wait, Willie,' he said.

'Aye, I do,' said Willie. 'But I'll tell the rest of the squad to stand back.'

Twenty minutes later they brushed the thick grey dust from Lucy's hair and face. She opened her eyes.

'My sister,' she said distinctly. 'My sister was beside me. Will you look for her, please?'

Kezzie was easier to find. Slumped in a sitting position, she was tucked right down into the cavity made by the steel piping which had bent under the force of the explosion to form a protective ring around both her and Lucy. She was unconscious.

The two men didn't like to question the younger child

but she was the only person alive and able to speak.

'Anyone else, pet?' they asked her as they carried her and Kezzie towards the stretchers. 'Did any other person come down the stairs? Was there anyone with you at the end of the close?'

Lucy turned her big blue eyes on them both and thought hard. She shook her head. 'They were just about to,' she said, 'Mrs Sweeney and Mary. We heard them talking on the landing above, with my three wee cousins . . .' She stopped. 'But they didn't actually come down. They were still on the stairs. Kezzie said not to wait. That we'd meet them at the shelter. We went to the end of the close to step outside . . .' Her voice faltered. 'I don't remember anything else.'

George Murdoch and his deputy exchanged looks. The tenement staircase had been completely obliterated.

'We'll move on,' said George to his team, 'and send a clearing squad in.'

'Could I have my dolly?' said a small voice.

George Murdoch regarded Lucy gravely. The neck and shoulders of the little girl he had just rescued were badly gashed, and he was sure that her wrist was broken. Yet she had not made a murmur as he had worked to free her.

One of the stretcher-bearers tutted in exasperation. 'We've got more important things to do than look for a doll.'

'Oh, I don't know,' said George. 'That seemed like a very important dolly to me. Just give us a minute here, mate.' He passed Kezzie on to the next person in the line, then moving very slowly he went back across the rubble and reached down into the hole.

He lifted Lucy's doll and held it up high for her to see.

'Got it!' he cried triumphantly.

'George! Watch out! The wall's going!' yelled Willie.

The ARP warden tucked the rag doll swiftly into his belt and then raced for his life across the debris. He jumped clear just as the gable end of the building crashed behind him.

CHAPTER 17

Buried alive

Kezzie felt as if she had toothache in each separate part of her body. There was a throbbing pain at the back of her skull, and there seemed to be a weight pressing on her chest. She opened her eyes very slowly. She could remember going to bed last night . . . but after that . . . nothing. She looked around her. She seemed to be in school. There were benches and desks piled up at one end of the drill hall, and when she raised her head she could see that she was lying on the floor along with a long line of other people. Suddenly she was aware of the noise. Women sobbing, children shouting, babies crying. She gave a moan and lay back down again.

'Kezzie,' said a voice beside her.

She turned her head.

'Lucy,' she whispered. 'What has happened?'

'We've been blitzed,' said Lucy. 'A bomb dropped right in our street. A big one,' she added.

'What time is it?'

'Morning-time. They said they'd give us breakfast soon, if we waited.'

'Waited?' Kezzie repeated the word stupidly.

'Yes,' said Lucy. 'After they fixed my wrist and bandaged me up, the lady said we could be sent on somewhere else, or wait until later. I said we'd wait here.' She looked at Kezzie. 'I made the decision,' she said importantly, 'because you were knocked out. I thought we'd best find out about Grandad before we went anywhere else.'

Kezzie reached over and took Lucy's hand. 'You're a very clever girl,' she said. 'We'll go home now and get some clean clothes and wait for Grandad there.'

'You don't understand, Kezzie,' said Lucy patiently. 'It's all gone. Our house, everybody's house. They've been crunched up in the explosions. All of them.'

'Everything gone?' asked Kezzie. 'Everything?' She suddenly remembered that she'd been carrying the Gladstone bag. 'My bag?'

Lucy nodded.

'We have absolutely nothing left?' Kezzie asked again.

'Just this.' Lucy grinned at her sister. She held up her rag doll.

The next moment Kezzie didn't know whether she was laughing or crying.

The nurse in charge told Kezzie that no-one else from the tenement building had survived. Despite being numb with shock, Kezzie left the first-aid post and set out for Casella's café. She knew that her grandad would be wild with worry and the café seemed the most sensible place to go . . . if it was still standing.

She held Lucy close to her as they made their way through the stricken town. There were great piles of rubble where there had once been rows of tenements. Ruins of homes stood stark in the lightening sky, wedge ends of buildings with their insides ripped out. They came across a trolley bus which had its roof torn off. There were dead bodies still sitting on their seats, while some had been flung into the road. Huge bomb craters made the roads impassable in places, and many streets had been cordoned off as the police and rescue teams discovered more and more delayed action bombs. The tram rails were twisted out of shape and corkscrewed into the air. Pathetic groups of people huddled around mobile canteens set up to distribute cups of tea. Kezzie pulled Lucy in against her coat and tucked her head under her arm. They stumbled on.

The little café, jammed in between the tall tenement blocks, had survived. They'd just turned the corner into the street when they saw their grandad. He ran and gathered both of them in his arms.

'I've been back and forwards to Dalmuir a dozen times,' he said 'checking every church hall and first-aid post in between.'

'How are you?' Kezzie asked him.

'One bomb,' he said bitterly. 'One bomb dropped inside the perimeter of the yard. All the rest . . .' He stopped speaking, and looked at Kezzie. 'It's very bad,' he said. 'The town's almost completely gone.'

'We know,' said a small voice beside them. They looked down at Lucy. 'We saw it, Grandad,' she said.

He took them quickly into the café and sat them down. All the windows had been blown out, but the Biagis had swept up the mess, and hung out a sign saying 'Free Tea and Sandwiches.'

They had spent the night in their Anderson shelter.

'A beautiful shelter,' proclaimed Signora Biagi. 'A wonderful shelter. There is none other like it in all of Clydebank.'

'Well, perhaps just one,' laughed Ricardo. 'I built another for Peg and the baby in her back garden, and dug it twice as deep.' He looked anxiously at the café clock. 'I thought she would have arrived by now. I think I'll go and see if all is well with them.'

'I'll come with you,' said Kezzie, 'and then afterwards I'll go to the first aid post. There must be something I can do to help. You wait here until one of us comes back,' she told Lucy.

'I can look after myself,' said Lucy primly. 'After all,' she reminded Kezzie, 'it was *me* who got you rescued.'

The area where Peg lived was badly damaged. Each and every street had been hit. Second Avenue, Radnor Street, Granville Street, all were destroyed. Schools and churches were burned out, the fire station and the pub completely gutted. There was hardly a wall intact anywhere. As they progressed further and further, Ricardo became more and more silent. Instinctively both of them began to hurry. By the time they reached the end of Peg's road they were running. They scrambled around the deep crater which marked the beginning of her street and climbed over a mountain of debris.

Ricardo clutched Kezzie's arm. '*Jesu Maria!*' he whispered.

He took a few paces forward and then stepped back. He looked around hopelessly. 'What do we do? What do we do?' he cried.

Kezzie herself was trying to come to terms with what was in front of her. There was no part of the building left standing, and the ruins were charred and black. It must have taken a direct hit.

Kezzie thought Ricardo was about to start running in circles. He bent over, doubling up, holding his stomach, as though someone had given him a violent blow. He stayed almost on his knees for a moment and then he straightened and began walking up and down, running his fingers through his hair, moaning and crying.

'Peg, Peg.' He turned beseeching eyes on Kezzie. 'Do you think she is alive? Could they still live, under that?'

Kezzie didn't know what to say to him.

'Where was the Anderson shelter exactly?' she asked.

But Ricardo was not listening to her. He was striking his head with his hands and sobbing.

'Ricardo!' she shouted at him. 'Tell me where the Anderson shelter should be.'

Suddenly a fierce yelling voice sounded behind them. 'What are you doing here? This area has been cleared.' An ARP warden was running towards them.

'We knew . . . know,' Kezzie corrected herself, 'some-one in that building. A young woman and a baby.'

'The building took a direct hit. No one came out of it, nor are they likely to now,' said the warden. 'We searched that area thoroughly.' He looked at the boy in front of him. 'Sorry,' he added. 'Now I'm going to have to ask you to leave. There's an unexploded bomb in the street.'

'No,' wailed Ricardo. He fell to his knees. 'No, no. I beg you.'

The warden spread his hands. 'Look, son, I'm sorry. Truly I am. At the moment there's nothing else anybody can do.'

'Well, there might just be,' said a voice behind them.

Kezzie turned. It was her grandfather.

'I guessed you might need help here,' he said. He turned and surveyed the remains of the tenement. 'This is not good,' he said slowly, 'not good at all.' He went over to Ricardo and shook the boy roughly by the shoulder. 'There's work to be done here,' he said. 'If you can pinpoint the exact location of the shelter then we'll try tunnelling in.'

The ARP warden touched his sleeve. 'I can't ask anyone to help you do that. That's above and beyond. You'll need to get volunteers.'

'I only need the one,' said Kezzie's grandad. He nodded at Ricardo. 'An' I think I've got him here already.'

Ricardo dragged his jacket off and handed it to Kezzie. He rolled up his sleeves. 'Now,' he said, 'we dig now.'

'No,' said John Munro. 'We prepare properly first.' He took his pipe from his pocket and sucked on the dry stem for a minute or two as he surveyed the job. 'I need a pick and shovel and some stout props.' He spoke to Kezzie. 'This will take hours. You'd be better helpin' somewhere else, lass.'

Kezzie knew that part of the reason that he advised her to leave was that he wanted her out of danger. She gripped Ricardo's hand.

'Be calm,' she said, 'and hope. My grandad was the best mining engineer in the west of Scotland. If they're alive under that then he'll get them out.'

CHAPTER 18

Evacuation

Kezzie called in at the nearest first aid post, which was operating out of the local primary school, to see if there was anything she could do. The warden noted her name and details.

'We need help with everything,' he said. 'You can make tea, dress wounds, take names and addresses, whatever.' He paused and licked the end of his pencil. 'Anything in particular you're good at?' he enquired.

'I worked as an assistant in a doctor's surgery in Canada,' she said, 'and I've driven an ambulance a few times.'

He thought for a moment. 'Unfortunately,' he said, 'we don't have an ambulance. Though there are folk here who certainly could do with being in hospital.'

Suddenly Kezzie remembered Casella's old van.

'I don't know whether it would be of any use,' she said, 'but . . .'

She thought the man was going to kiss her. Within half an hour Kezzie had returned to the café, told Ricardo's mother and aunt what was happening and checked that Lucy was all right.

'Of course I'm all right,' said Lucy scornfully.

She had on an apron which was several sizes too large for her and was standing in the kitchen making sandwiches. Her face turned pale when Kezzie told her that Peg and Alec were missing, but glancing quickly at Ricardo's mother she said confidently, 'If Grandad's there, then we shouldn't worry.'

When Kezzie returned to the first aid post the warden had two patients ready for her. He handed her some notes. 'We've no doctor here, so I've done my best. One of them's right poorly. I think he needs a blood transfusion. We can't give you an attendant, so you'll have to stop at least twice on the way and check his wound's not leaking too badly. Take him to the Glasgow Western, and pick up anything you can by way of medical supplies. Mind what I say now, *anything*. Steal it if you have to,' he called out after her as she set off.

As she drove the long hazardous road to Glasgow, Kezzie was glad that she had something on which to concentrate her mind to stop her thinking of Peg and baby Alec buried under tons of brick and stone. The roads out of town were still being cleared and she was diverted many times. The van jolted and juddered over ruts and around craters, but eventually she managed to get onto the Boulevard. There she was able to increase speed, and after checking her patients one last time she put her foot down on the accelerator pedal and didn't stop until she reached the hospital.

Casualties had been coming in all night, from

Hillhead and Hyndland in the west end of the city. Kezzie checked her patients in, managed to beg some supplies, and set out on the return journey to Clydebank.

And as she worked on through that day Kezzie knew that she would never forget the sight of the rows of covered bodies lying in lines by the side of the road. Those who had not survived, children, babies, rich and poor, wrapped in any available covering, blanket, table cover, curtain and carpet rug. Nor would she forget the rescue workers and relatives, as they dug in the rubble, many with their bare hands, their faces grey with dust, grey with fatigue and grey with grief.

In the early afternoon while queuing at a mobile canteen she found herself standing with Mr Sweeney and his son. They were part of a team working with the Royal Engineers trying to repair one of the burst water mains. Kezzie knew that Mrs Sweeney's body had been found, and she now lay in the emergency mortuary at the High School in Janetta Street.

'I'm sorry,' said Kezzie.

The son nodded quickly and looked away. Mr Sweeney said, 'She liked you, Kezzie. Not many folk got on with her. She had a sharp tongue,' he said, 'but it was just her way. She liked you though.' He studied her more closely. 'You look a bit peaky, hen. Take a rest sometime.' Then he picked up his tea and sandwiches.

It was so inadequate, thought Kezzie, as she watched the two men walk away. 'I'm sorry,' she had said. What good did that do? How did her 'being sorry' help them, or Mary Price, or the three little boys and their parents? Why was she alive and they weren't?

Around half past three, she parked her ambulance in the school yard and was taking stretchers from it and folding blankets, when the warden came to speak to her.

'There's someone here to see you,' he said. 'Take an hour's break,' he added, 'and that's an order.'

Kezzie walked around the side of her van into unexpected sunlight. Her grandfather was standing there. He had his cap pushed to the back of his head and he looked mighty pleased with himself.

'You found them?' Kezzie hardly dared breathe the words.

He nodded. 'They were a bit battered about, but we got to Peg and the baby. No sign of her brother and his wife, though.'

Kezzie leaned against the ambulance door, her senses swimming with relief. 'Are they safe?' she asked. 'The baby . . . how is he?'

'Yelling like a soldier,' said her grandad. 'It was his bawling that made us realise that we were digging in the right direction. It was a difficult one. There were a few times when I thought the whole lot was coming down on us.' He looked at his hands. 'I never thought I'd be doing anything like that again.'

Kezzie could imagine her grandad working away under the ground. The mining skills gained over half a century proving useful in circumstances no one could have foreseen. His ear sensitive to every sound, every little creak or groan above alerting him to secure a prop, or shore up some more earth before moving on.

'I'd say that, in some cases, it might be a better way of rescuing folk that are trapped. Safer than clearing the rubble from the top, I reckon. Anyway, the chief warden for the area came to take a look, and he wants to see me later.'

Kezzie and her grandad went to the café. Peg was not well at all. She'd tried to get her brother and his wife to go to the shelter but they had refused so she knew they were dead. Her clothes were torn and her face and arms were bleeding from a dozen different scratches and cuts. Sitting in the kitchen, dazed and covered in bruises, she was scarcely able to hold a spoon to her mouth.

'We need to get her out of here,' Ricardo whispered to Kezzie. 'But my mother and my aunt won't leave the café now. And, even if they did . . .' He paused, then pointed through the open door to where a weary line of people were waiting for a hot drink and some food. 'I couldn't go away knowing that I'm needed here. I don't know what to do.'

Kezzie touched his arm. 'I think I may know the best solution,' she said.

All day special buses had been taking refugees out of the town to emergency centres in the surrounding areas. Kezzie knew that they'd been going to places as far away as central Scotland. Relief had been offered by many towns, including the ones near her home village, Kirkintilloch and Shawcross.

She took Lucy by the hand and led her outside where they could speak without interruption. Kezzie sat her sister down beside the Anderson shelter and knelt beside her.

'There are things we need to talk about, Lucy,' she said. 'Serious, important things.'

319

The blue eyes looked at her steadily.

'Grandad says we will more than likely be bombed again tonight. He is going to remain here because the rescue teams will need help. I think that I also should stay to drive the ambulance.' She paused. 'But we have to get Peg and Alec far away before night-time. Peg isn't well enough to care for the baby by herself. She needs someone with her.' Kezzie met Lucy's gaze and did not look away. 'I want you to go with them,' she said.

Kezzie felt Lucy's hand tighten in her own. She leaned forward and stroked her sister's hair. 'I know that we decided that our family would never be separated, but . . . well, Peg and Alec are just like family. And Ricardo feels he has to keep the café open, so there is no one else.'

Lucy nodded slowly as Kezzie finished speaking. Then she said, 'I might never see you and Grandad again?'

Kezzie knew that she couldn't lie. 'Yes,' she said carefully, 'that is possible. In fact, that's another reason that I'd like you to go. If . . . the worst happens, then at least there would be one Munro left.' She felt her eyes fill up with tears as she spoke.

But strangely, Lucy's face was calm. She thought for a moment or two. 'I suppose that's being sensible. My teacher keeps telling us that we have to be sensible, especially during a war.' She put her arms around Kezzie's neck and hung on for a moment or two. Just like a little girl again, thought Kezzie. But as they came apart, and she looked at Lucy's face, Kezzie knew that her sister was a child no longer.

★ ★ ★

There were evacuee buses leaving from various places in the Burgh. After an hour's wait in Dumbarton Road Kezzie managed to get her little group on a bus which was going out to Shawcross.

'Try to get in touch with Aunt Bella,' she instructed Lucy. 'If she can't take you, then she'll find someone who will.' She hugged her sister tightly. 'Be brave,' she whispered. 'No matter how it turns out, remember I love you.'

'I love you too,' said Lucy.

Kezzie turned away quickly as the bus jerked forward and rattled down the street.

The tiny village of Stonevale had no need to listen to the news broadcasts or read the newspapers that Friday morning. On the Thursday night they saw the glow in the distant sky which told them Clydebank was burning. They'd heard the enemy planes, both on their inward and outward journeys.

When word came that homeless families were arriving in the town, Bella had walked into Shawcross and spent most of the day in or around the Town Hall. 'If they've managed to survive, then Kezzie will come here,' she told her husband.

It wasn't until early evening that Bella caught sight of Lucy. Still wearing her coat over her nightie and clutching a food parcel, she was dismounting from a ramshackle single-decker bus.

Bella struggled through the crowd in the reception area until she reached Peg and Lucy. She looked around. 'I thought the old man would stay on,' she said, 'but where's Kezzie?'

'She's driving an ambulance, she wouldn't leave,' said Peg.

Bella gave Lucy a big grin. 'So ye came to bide with yer Auntie Bella after all,' she said.

'Kezzie said it was my duty,' Lucy told her seriously. 'And apart from Peg, I'm the only one that baby Alec's really happy with. You know, there's a special way of feeding a baby, Aunty Bella. It's quite difficult, not everybody can do it.'

Bella winked at Peg. 'Well, ah've only had the six myself, hen,' she said, 'but I'll take your word for it.'

Bella looked around the hall until she found the officer dealing with the accommodation arrangements. 'These three are comin' wi' me,' she told her.

Peg grasped Bella's hand as though she would never let it go.

'A big plate o' broth is what you're needin',' said Bella. 'And then a good night's sleep.'

She took them to her own small house and fed them thick soup and potatoes. Then she chased out two of her own children to stay with their cousins, and tucked Lucy and Peg and the baby up in the room bed.

'There now,' she told them, as she turned down the lamp. 'Off to sleep wi' ye. The country air is healing air. I'll see ye and hear all your news in the morning.'

There was still some light in the night sky when the first heavy throb of aeroplane engines sounded overhead. Bella stopped stirring the pot on the fire. She lifted her head and listened. Then she looked at her husband.

'They're no' ours, are they?' she said.

He shook his head.

They both went and stood outside the front door. All along the miners' rows their neighbours were doing the same. And they watched without speaking as the Luftwaffe Third Air Fleet passed high over Stonevale. Formation after formation came across. From Holland initially and then Denmark, from Stavanger in Norway, and air bases in northern France, they flew steadily west towards Glasgow and the Clyde.

In the Clydebank Control Centre the telephone rang. The Civil Defence officer picked it up and listened to the voice on the other end of the line. After a few moments he replaced the receiver carefully on its cradle.

He turned to face his staff.

'They're coming back,' he said.

CHAPTER 19

The sirens sound again

The sirens went at 8.40 p.m.

Kezzie's grandad gripped her arm. 'Listen, lass,' he said. 'There's still time for you to go. No one would blame you.'

She smiled at him. 'And what about you?' she asked him. 'Are you going to leave?'

He began to speak. 'I . . .' Then he stopped. 'No,' he said.

Kezzie handed him his tin hat, and picked up her own. 'I honestly think that we don't have a choice,' she said. She pointed round the small hall in which they were sitting. It was situated on the outer edge of the town. Most of the rescue units had been sent out to the relative safety of the perimeter of the burgh to await the calls which would arrive as the raid progressed. 'Many of these people are volunteers who have chosen to remain,' she said. 'And Signoras Casella and Biagi are also staying so that they can open the café tomorrow to help out. We are needed here. You know that. It's a plain fact.'

Kezzie's grandad fiddled with the strap of his helmet. 'This might turn out very bad,' he said.

Kezzie nodded. 'I know,' she said. 'I spoke to Lucy before she left. I think she understands.'

Kezzie watched her grandad. He was ill at ease, buttoning and unbuttoning his tunic, fidgeting with his gas mask. Suddenly he turned to her.

'Kezzie, I would like you to know this, in case anything happens tonight.' He took her hand in his. 'You made my whole world,' he said simply. 'You and Lucy. If you hadn't come back from Canada, then I would have had only half a life. I want to tell you how much it meant to me.'

Kezzie felt her chin tremble. 'It was the same for us,' she said.

He drew her towards him and put her head on his chest. 'I know that eventually you'll spread your wings. I'm going to tell you this, you mustn't lose sight of your ideals. You've always wanted to be a doctor, so that's what you must do. Don't let anything stop you. Not even this war, no matter how long it lasts.'

He stroked her hair for a moment or two. Kezzie didn't trust herself to speak. Then he gently pushed her away from him, and raised his head. A sudden silence had crept over the little room. Voices hesitated, then spoke in lower tones. Conversations stopped. A steady drone, still some way off, was growing louder by the second. A ragged noise, penetrating the sandbagged walls and reinforced roof, vibrating in the night air. The special Blitzkrieg airborne units were approaching from the east. The Heinkels and Junkers which made up the Luftwaffe bomber squadrons, their engines a throbbing, pulsing underbelly of sound. Now everybody was sitting straight on their benches, alert and rigid.

'Let's have a cup of tea,' said the ARP officer loudly.

Kezzie and her grandad took theirs outside. It was a beautiful spring night, the moon pale and luminous in a clear sky. The drumming noise of the aeroplane engines closed around them.

'Those gas mains are blazing away like the fires of hell,' said Kezzie's grandad, 'and there's an oil tank still burning at Old Kilpatrick that they can't get doused. They won't need their pathfinders and incendiaries to mark their way tonight. We're supplying the bloody beacons for them.'

'Look, there,' said Kezzie.

A formation of planes had crossed the river to the south-west. She could see quite clearly the bomb doors opening and the grey IBs with their finned tails begin to fall, dozens and dozens and dozens of them.

'That's the Rolls-Royce works at Hillington they're after,' said her grandad.

All at once the whole world lit up. Thirty or forty huge searchlights started to sweep the skies, crossing and linking, fusing to form a cone shape. The ground crews swivelling and twisting their beams to hold a great dome of light above the stricken town. Finding the enemy for the gunners to shoot down, desperately trying to dazzle the pilots, keep them to a high altitude, and drive them as quickly as possible away from their target area.

The defence batteries at Duntiglennan roared out, soon joined by the bigger ack-ack guns at

Auchentoshan. Shell bursts exploded around and below the aeroplanes. They could hear the thump and crash, the echoes rolling around the Dumbarton hills and out to sea.

The rescue-party foreman came out. 'Message in,' he said. 'There's a wardens' post taken a direct hit. Civilians were sheltering in it.'

Kezzie's grandad slipped on his white armband with 'CASUALTY COLLECTION' stitched in black. He spoke to the sergeant. 'I'll be right there.'

He turned to Kezzie. ''Bye, darlin',' he said. He looked her full in the face and his eyes met hers. 'Thanks, lass,' he said. And for one brief moment he laid his hand upon her head.

Kezzie remained outside for several minutes after he had gone. The tea turned cold in the mug she held, and she neither heard nor saw anything around her.

She started as someone touched her arm. 'They need an ambulance at Parkhall.'

All through the night the people of Clydebank fought to save their burning town. The police and the rescue services, nurses, teachers, student doctors, bus conductresses, messenger boys as young as thirteen years old, veterans of the First World War, struggling desperately to survive and preserve their families and homes.

The beleaguered fire services, with little water, faced a hopeless task as oil tank after oil tank was set ablaze at Dalnottar and Old Kilpatrick, illuminating the targets and making the task easy for each following wave of bombers cruising in and unloading their cargo of death.

An immense and suffocating haze of flame and smoke drifted over the Clyde estuary. The blaze could be seen as far north as Aberdeen and as far east as Edinburgh.

Kezzie was helping with the stretcher cases, which had been laid out at the Janetta Street end of the High School, when a parachute mine dropped at the other end. There was a whistling crack, then a thunderous explosion and the walls on the west side caved in. Kezzie picked herself up and looked around. Plaster and glass were strewn everywhere. One of the messenger boys picked up her helmet and gave her a cheeky grin. He looked at the huge hole in the roof.

'Missed me again,' he shouted up at the sky.

Kezzie's hands shook as she replaced her helmet on her head. Earlier on she had seen a parachute mine which had been caught in a tree during last night's raid. It was a terrifyingly large black cylinder. At eight feet high, much taller than any man, they measured about three feet across. These and the high-explosive bombs usually followed on after the incendiaries were unloaded. She reckoned the main group of bombers must now be directly overhead. She suddenly thought of Michael. His experience in combat must be similar to this. Under bombardment, comrades falling, wounded and dying beside him, he would fight on. He was doing it, and so must she. This realisation gave her a small measure of comfort. She tightened the helmet strap under her chin. Then she got back into her van and drove off to answer the next call.

Men and equipment had come from John Brown's during the day to cut away the twisted tramway rails and clear roads and streets, but every road was difficult, and some impassable. She was driving along Livingstone Street when an explosion in a building beside her rocked the ambulance and she slewed to a halt. Kezzie noticed the white 'S' for shelter painted on the side of the wall. She climbed down from her cab.

'Need any help?' she shouted.

Two men ran out. One of them looked her up and down. 'Hell, it's a wee lassie,' he called to his mate. 'How old are you, that you're driving that thing?' he asked her.

'Old enough,' snapped Kezzie. 'This is the ninth run I've done tonight. Now do you need assistance or not?'

'You tell him, hen,' his friend laughed out loud.

Kezzie helped an elderly couple and a child who was very badly injured into the back of her van and drove on. The nurse who took the child from her at the first-aid post shook her head quickly, and then placed the little body to one side.

Kezzie turned away. 'Dear God, it must stop soon,' she whispered.

It was nearly dawn when the head warden of her group spoke to her. 'You need a change of clothing, miss.'

Kezzie glanced down at herself. She had spatters of mud and blood everywhere, and one of her sleeves was ripped. Her hands were bruised and scarred where she had helped drag people from rubble. She realised she was still wearing Ricardo's shirt and trousers which she had borrowed earlier.

'Is there somewhere you can get some clean clothes and maybe a rest for an hour or two?' he asked.

Kezzie nodded. She would go back to the café. She

had driven past it during the night and she knew that it at least had survived. She parked her van and walked the few streets to the Italians' shop. The murky pall of smoke which now hung everywhere was choking and stung her eyes. She practically bumped into Ricardo before she saw him.

'Kezzie,' he cried. 'I have been searching for you. Everyone I spoke to said you were with someone else.'

'I know.' She took her helmet off. 'I would be sent one place, and then diverted somewhere else. And I couldn't refuse to take injured people even if I hadn't been called out for them in particular.' She pulled her fingers through her tangled hair. 'Why did you come looking for me?' she asked him.

He didn't reply.

Kezzie looked at Ricardo more closely. He had leaned up against a nearby wall. His eyes were red-rimmed and he had an expression on his face that she had never seen before. Suddenly she knew why. He had been sent to tell her the most terrible news.

'What is it, Ricardo?' she said. 'What is it that you have to tell me?'

'Kezzie.' He drew her close to him. 'Your grandfather has been killed.'

She put her hand across her heart. 'Grandad?' she repeated.

'I'm sorry,' said Ricardo, 'so very sorry. Some people were trapped in the basement of a building. There was an unexploded bomb there. He volunteered to go in.' Ricardo held her tightly. 'It went off. No one could save him.'

'I think he knew,' said Kezzie unsteadily. She frowned. 'Earlier, he tried to tell me how much he cared about us.' She smiled sadly. 'It was difficult for him. He was so awkward about his feelings.'

'Why don't you cry?' Ricardo said very softly. 'I don't understand you British. Why do you not cry?' He shook his head. 'I don't understand,' he repeated.

And he was crying, Kezzie realised. Tears running down his cheeks as he stood helpless in front of her. She reached out her hands to comfort him, and suddenly there were great sobs tearing at her. From inside her heart and soul, a fierce violent grieving took hold of her, and she wept for her grandad. And not only for him, but for her father too, and the mother she had barely known. For the loss of their company and love. And for all the happy times, the Sunday School trips, the picnics, the outings and birthday parties and Christmases that had happened, and those that now would never happen.

She couldn't stop crying. Her exhaustion after the day's events came rushing in and she was no longer in control.

Ricardo picked her up and carried her to their Anderson shelter. Tucking her up in one of the little wooden-framed bunks, he made her drink some brandy. Then he wiped her face with his handkerchief and knelt down beside her. He held her hand as she lay there and, as Kezzie's breathing eventually deepened into sleep, the resonant note of the all-clear began to sound across the town.

CHAPTER 20

Greater love

'I knew there would be a big turnout to send him off,' said Bella.

She gathered up the teacups and carried them to the sink at the window. All day people had called at her house in Stonevale to pay their respects to old John Munro.

Many had already spoken to Kezzie that morning, in the kirk and by the graveside. Many more had dropped by later to offer condolences.

Kezzie picked up a tea towel and began to dry the dishes. 'He had a long life and many friends,' she said. 'But I didn't realise just what a high regard folk had of him.'

'Oh, aye,' said Bella. 'I could have told ye that. Straight, he was. Straight as a die.'

His grave was covered in flowers. Piled high with great bunches of spring blooms, from ornate bouquets to simple posies, as well as the traditional wreaths. It had been such a stately occasion. The old man brought home to his own town to rest.

A group of former pit workers, ex-miners, white-haired and silent, stood at the cemetery gates, their heads uncovered in the morning sunlight. His workmates from the shipyard, colleagues in the firewatching and rescue services, his cronies from the local welfare club. Colleagues, neighbours, family, friends, all were there. The man's own personal dignity reflected in the burial service.

The rescue-party co-ordinator for the West Side, Bob Black, spent a few minutes telling Kezzie that they were using her grandad's tunnel as an example of safe rescuing procedures.

'We knew there was an UXB in that tenement,' he told Kezzie, 'but he could hear folk calling for help. He volunteered to go in.' He shook Kezzie's hand as they parted. 'He was a brave man.'

She knew that they were having a memorial stone prepared for him, to mark the fact that Grandad had been killed while attempting to rescue his fellow countrymen. It would read: '*Greater love hath no man than this . . .*'

Peg had to go back to Clydebank to arrange the funeral of her brother and his wife. Kezzie went with her to help out. The appearance of the town stunned them both. Kezzie had hoped to moved back there with Lucy into some type of temporary accommodation. Bella would never say so, but Kezzie knew that her house was over-crowded. She needed the room for her own children. They couldn't expect her to put them up for too long. But now Kezzie saw that it would be months before any type of property was available in Clydebank. A sign of the relentless pounding the buildings had taken was that, out of the whole town, only eight houses were undamaged by bomb blasts.

To see it in daylight, in the hard glare of the cold spring sunlight made Kezzie feel quite weak. All along the main roads every window was shattered, the chimneys had fallen down, and the streets and pavements were piled with slates, splintered wood, brick and plaster. Raging fires which now burned out had left the charred and blackened gable ends of tenements poking up into the sky. The housing estates at Radnor and Kilbowie were devastated, the walls of the homes which were still standing, pitted and scarred. Kezzie found it strange that she'd managed to function during the actual raid, when hell was pouring out of the skies, yet now she felt confused and disorientated by it all.

It was the desolation, the sight of everyday things from ordinary households lying crushed in the street, which upset her most. A frying pan, a smashed framed photograph, a favourite chair, now broken and useless. Dozens of starving dogs and cats were running wild for days, until an animal clinic was opened in order to have them painlessly put to sleep. The sad remnants of little families could be seen searching through collections of furniture and personal possessions piled in the streets. What was left of them, brothers and sisters together with any close relative, tragically small groups of people, trudged to the Rest Centres carrying all they could salvage, sometimes with the youngest member trotting behind, clasping the birdcage.

Peg and Kezzie held on to each other as they made

their way through the streets. Clean water for drinking had been brought in barrels from Glasgow and there were long queues holding kettles, teapots or jugs. The YMCA tea cars parked their mobile canteens outside the church halls. In Casella's café a constant stream of refugees came through the door, where Ricardo, his mother and aunt handed out hot soup and slices of bread and margarine. Each night people slept on makeshift beds on their floor. They seemed incapable of turning anyone away.

She knew that they also had no space for her and Lucy. Signor Biagi's latest tribunal hearing had agreed that, in the special circumstances, he would be allowed to return to Clydebank. When things settled down, they wouldn't need Kezzie's assistance in the shop. Peg and the baby were now living there. With Ricardo, the three of them made such a compact and joyful unit among the surrounding chaos. Kezzie was deeply moved by their happiness. Each moment was now valued, each measure of time spent together precious.

Kezzie's heart ached for Michael. His company at this time would have lifted her spirits so much. Where was he now? she wondered. Under what foreign sky did he rise in the morning or lie down to sleep at night? Stationed in some far-away place in the hot desert, he would receive in time the letter she'd sent giving him her dreadful news. Why wasn't he here, so that she could tell him properly, and then he could comfort her? She was so tired that she felt like weeping for ever and never ceasing.

It wasn't openly discussed, but everyone thought that they would be attacked again, some time in the near future, especially as the yards had got off so lightly. Only hours after the all-clear had sounded, an enemy reconnaissance plane had come in at high altitude to assess the damage. Kezzie supposed that it was due partly to her country's spirit and determination that folk were trying to keep production going. In the week following the blitz thousands of workers walked miles from their billets and Rest Centres to return to work. John Brown's, the Royal Ordnance Factory, Singer's, Beardmore's, all struggled to get their output back up. And they were succeeding, they were producing the parts and supplying the forces.

Things were getting back to normal. So . . . she shouldn't feel so bad about thinking of leaving. It was the best thing to do, for both Lucy and herself. She knew that she would have to give up her studies for the present, but she needed time to recuperate anyway, and then to plan for the future. There was some small income due to them from her grandfather's dependency fund, but she'd soon have to make better provision for Lucy and herself. Kezzie took out the letter which she'd received yesterday and read it again.

Dear Kezzie,

I am sending this via the post office in Shawcross as I know it is the nearest town to your home village. I hope that it reaches you and that you and your family are in good health. It is very difficult to obtain clear news of what Clydebank has suffered in the recent blitz. Due to censorship the newspapers are frustratingly vague, but I have gleaned enough information to realise that you may

need some support. Please do come and stay with me,
Kezzie, I would welcome an opportunity to repay the debt
I owe you.
  With warmest wishes,
  Mary Elizabeth Fitzwilliam

  PS Travel arrangements may be complicated so I enclose
the name and address of a friend in Edinburgh. I shall wire
him to be ready to secure train tickets for you if need be.

Kezzie came to a decision. Tomorrow she would take
a bus to Edinburgh and find Lady Fitzwilliam's friend.
Then she and Lucy would make the journey to England.

PART TWO
England

CHAPTER 21

Travelling south

The train journey from Edinburgh south to England was long and tedious. Kezzie was glad that she'd managed to beg some books and comics for Lucy, so that she had something to read as they sat squashed together in the corner of one of the crowded compartments. They were lucky to have obtained a seat at all. At any moment Kezzie expected her sister to start to complain, and she was trying to think of some bright conversation and word games to divert her as soon as the inevitable boredom and petulance began. There was little room and the air soon became hot and stuffy, but Lucy said nothing. As the hours passed she squirmed around in her seat but still spoke no word of protest.

Kezzie thought about this. Something had altered in her sister since the Blitz, some subtle change which she couldn't quite describe. She recalled when they'd been making their farewells to Ricardo and his family, Lucy had been very composed, more so, in fact, than Kezzie. Saying goodbye to Peg had been particularly traumatic.

The two friends had become so much closer over the past eighteen months. Lucy had surprised them both by suddenly thrusting her rag doll into Peg's hand.

'I want you to keep her,' she said.

'Oh no!' said Peg, giving Lucy her doll back at once. 'I know how much she means to you. You can't possibly give her away.'

'Yes, I can,' said Lucy firmly. 'I don't need her any more.'

Peg looked at Kezzie. 'What do I do?' Peg mouthed the words silently across the top of Lucy's head.

Kezzie shook her own head. She bent down and she spoke to her sister. 'Are you sure about this, Lucy?' she asked. 'Kissy has been with us for a long time.'

'Yes,' said Lucy. 'But I'm grown-up now, and Alec will need something to cuddle if the bombers come back.' She tucked her rag doll under the little boy's arm.

This was an older and wiser child who now sat beside Kezzie on another part of their travels. And, although Kezzie knew that Lucy at some stage must leave her babyhood, she couldn't help a faint feeling of wistfulness for the little girl who had depended on her for so long.

The quiet countryside passed by on the other side of the glass. First the Lammermuir hills in the distance, a purply gold mantle which encircled the coastal towns, and then suddenly the train was running alongside the North Sea. Close by the beaches of Gullane and after Dunbar, the water was gentle, and the waves broke in long rolling lines among the sandy dunes. Further out the haar hung cold and damp, shrouding the lighthouses and marker buoys. Beyond them in the deep seas the U-boat wolf packs hunted the British merchant ships in an attempt to starve the island into submission.

Kezzie gazed out of the window. She was almost happy to be away. She needed to distance herself from the devastation and destruction. She had to have some rest, her mind and body were close to exhaustion. She was weary of this war, of the sacrifices and the constant doing without. The senseless loss of life she'd witnessed confused and bewildered her, and the death of her beloved grandfather had brought her down completely. Even the manner of his death, which should have been a source of pride, did not ease her grief. Her emotions were swamped and she felt unable to cope with any of the ordinary things of life. It was in fact Lucy who'd organised most of their arrangements. It was she who comforted Kezzie, had taken charge of her and made her eat when she was too listless to do so. And of them all, only her Aunt Bella had understood Kezzie's desire to leave Scotland and her friends.

'You go to England, hen. Let this lady friend of yours look after you. You're not running away. If you don't get a rest soon then ye'll have a breakdown, and be no use to anyone.'

The train crossed the border into Berwick-on-Tweed and headed further south. It was hard at times to know exactly where they were as the signposts had either been removed or painted out. They were frequently shunted backwards and forwards, or kept waiting in stations.

In a siding where they'd been left for nearly half an

hour Kezzie watched a gang of workmen laying some rail track a few yards distant. They had their caps pulled down over their faces as they worked. She put her head on one side. Their manner and appearance was strange, but she didn't know why. Was it the way their trouser legs were tucked into their boots, or how they held the heavy crowbars and pickaxes? What was it that was unfamiliar? One had shirt sleeves rolled up past the elbows, and it was those slim and pale arms that made Kezzie realise what was different. They were all female. Not such an unusual sight, now, in wartime, she thought, but worthy of comment all the same.

The whole aspect of a woman's life and dress was changing. Most of the trams and buses had female conductresses, and many of the older girls in the streets were in uniform. Women were now much less formally dressed in daytime. Headscarves were more usual, rather than a smart hat. Many women pinned their hair up and went hatless. A few were even wearing trousers in public. Kezzie smiled as she remembered her Aunt Bella telling her of one of her neighbours who had started to wear dungarees. This of course had caused great comment in the tiny village of Stonevale, as Bella related to Kezzie.

'Well,' the poor woman said defensively to Bella. 'They're very practical. And I'll be better off wearing them if I have to go into one of these air-raid shelters. You try crawling into an Anderson shelter with your skirt and suspenders on. At least *I* won't be showing off all of next week's washing for everyone to see.'

'Aw, hen,' replied Bella, 'if we do get attacked, an' Jerry starts droppin' bombs, ah'll tell ye one thing. See when we're all running' tae the shelters, they'll be naebody lookin' at your knickers.'

The rest of the passengers on the train also began to realise that the work squad outside was a group of women. There were lots of young men on the train: soldiers, sailors and airmen travelling to join their units. Very soon the whistling and catcalls started. The windows went up, carriage by carriage, and further down the train a door opened. Some soldiers jumped out and walked along the track to offer cigarettes. The girls chatted and joked with the young men before the guard eventually blew his whistle and waved them back aboard.

Kezzie studied the uniforms as they passed. She always felt that little bit closer to Michael if she saw the Argyll and Sutherland tartan or cap badge.

They changed at York to a branch line which skirted Sheffield, ran through Chesterfield and on down in the direction of Derby. The main station was very busy and they'd to wait some time for their connection, so it was late evening when the train finally arrived, wheezing and puffing, into the tiny station of West Fenton. Kezzie and Lucy stepped down onto the platform. They looked around them at the picket fencing and the brave display of daffodils and crocuses in one window-box beside the ticket office. Kezzie smiled. The other had carrots growing in it. There was no indication at all of where they were. It was fortunate that both the guard and the conductor had looked after them so well, and made sure that they knew when to get off. Kezzie gazed at the fields stretching far into the distance on all sides. She picked up the small cardboard suitcase which held all their belongings.

'There must be a post office nearby,' she told Lucy. 'We'll ring Close Manor House from there.'

She took out the letter from Lady Fitzwilliam which had the telephone number written on it, and went to speak to the man in the ticket office. He glared at her when she asked for directions to the village.

'Arr,' he said with a thick country burr. 'I don't understand a word of what you've said.' He came out from his little office and peered at Kezzie suspiciously. 'Are you a German spy?' he demanded.

Lucy giggled. 'No,' she said. 'Are you?'

The man narrowed his eyes and looked at her more closely. 'That's a very strange accent you have,' he declared. 'Very strange indeed.'

'Mr Penrose,' a voice called out loudly from behind them. 'This young lady is a friend of mine. Who do you think she is? Mata Hari?'

'A most peculiar way of talking,' muttered the man, as he reluctantly returned to his desk.

'My dear, I am so glad to see you once more.' Lady Fitzwilliam took Kezzie's hand and shook it formally. 'And this must be Lucy.'

As Lady Fitzwilliam bent down to say hello, Lucy, with a most natural gesture, kissed her.

Lady Fitzwilliam flushed with pleasure. She straightened up and touched her cheek with a gloved hand. 'Such a charming child. I don't wonder that you travelled so far to find her again.'

She led them outside to where a pony and trap stood in the country road. 'Here we are, my dear. I've managed to arrange transport for us. Unfortunately we must conserve petrol, so this will have to do. You don't mind, do you?' she asked.

Kezzie laughed. 'Not at all,' she said. 'I expected to walk.'

There was an elderly uniformed chauffeur standing respectfully beside the pony. He was holding its reins and regarding it nervously.

Lady Fitzwilliam introduced them. 'This is Samuel,' she said. 'He was my husband's driver. Now he is coping very well with this form of transport, aren't you, Samuel?' she asked him.

'A bit more unpredictable than motor cars, ma'am,' he said.

'Nonsense,' said Lady Fitzwilliam. 'I remember distinctly when my husband bought the first Daimler. You were very reluctant to try it out.'

'That was twenty years ago, ma'am,' murmured Samuel. 'I've got used to mechanical engines.'

'I don't think you should be so worried about driving a horse, even after a gap of twenty years, surely?'

Samuel eyed the pony again. 'It's not so much me being worried about the horse, ma'am,' he said. 'I think it's more a case of the horse being worried about me.'

Lucy had been hopping about, pulling grass from the banks of grass at the sides of the road and trying to feed the animal.

'Can I sit up at the front?' she begged.

Kezzie frowned at her, frightened that Lucy's natural exuberance would be taken for rudeness.

Lucy saw her sister's face. 'Please,' she added quickly.

Lady Fitzwilliam leaned over and pinched Lucy's cheek with her gloved fingers. 'You, my darling, can do exactly as you wish.'

CHAPTER 22

Close Manor

They made their way through the small village of West Fenton, over the level crossing, past some thatched cottages and out into the country. It was like no other part of the world, thought Kezzie.

'It's so . . .' She searched for the word. '. . . so picturesque.'

The evening sky was slatted with long low clouds, lit from behind with the rays of the sunset. The pleasant sound of birdsong, the steady trot of the horse and the wheels turning were all that could be heard.

Kezzie leaned back in her seat, and let the serenity of the English countryside surround her. 'It's quite beautiful,' she said.

Tucked away in an undisturbed part of a traditional British landscape, it appeared to her that nothing had altered here for many years. And I hope it never will, she thought, as they rode along past high hedgerows, fields and meadows.

She knew that the idyll before her was part illusion, of

course. Not many miles distant lay Derby, where there was a concentration of heavy and light industry. The Rolls-Royce works were working on the new Merlin engine and turned out the parts for Spitfires and Hurricanes. The town, despite its civilian population, had been a target for the Luftwaffe already, and would continue to be.

But for the moment she could pretend. She and Lucy could relax in this lush and fertile landscape. She did need some rest, some time to recuperate.

They entered a long drive through ornate stone pillars, gravel spitting out from under the horse's hooves as they made their way past the gatehouse.

'This is where I live.' Lady Fitzwilliam pointed to the red-brick building at the top of the drive. There were banks of thick rhododendrons, monkey-puzzles, tall gum trees, bushy yews and close-clipped box hedges. Croquet hoops were set out on the front lawn, with the mallets and balls lying carelessly to one side. Like a scene from *Alice in Wonderland*, thought Kezzie. She gripped the handle of her bag tightly. How were she and Lucy ever going to cope with all of this?

The horse clip-clopped its way sedately around the manor house to the stable yard at the side, where Samuel helped them dismount. Then, eyeing the animal suspiciously, he led it under cover to unharness it. Lady Fitzwilliam took them through the conservatory and into the house, pulling off hat, scarf, gloves and coat, and discarding them as she went. She waved a hand as Kezzie attempted to collect some of her clothes as she followed behind her.

'Samuel will see to them,' she said. 'He knows that I am far too busy to bother with things like that.'

Lucy and Kezzie exchanged glances. Lucy stuck her finger under her nose and pushed it up and to one side, wildly out of shape. Kezzie glared at her sister, but could not help but smile. Lady Fitzwilliam still had all the regal manners that Kezzie could vividly recall from her meeting with her on the boat to Canada.

'Tea,' declared Lady Fitzwilliam, 'we must have some tea.'

She led them into a large kitchen. 'It's Sally's night off,' she tutted in exasperation as she searched in cupboards and looked on shelves for the tea things. 'So inconvenient. I asked her to change, as you were arriving today, but she has an appointment with a young man, so she refused.'

Kezzie could tell that Lady Fitzwilliam considered Sally had seriously neglected her duty by taking the day off which was due to her.

'She did say that she would lay out some supper,' said Lady Fitzwilliam, looking around her vaguely.

Behind them Samuel coughed discreetly. 'Perhaps if you would care to go into the drawing-room,' he suggested, 'I've lit the fire there, and I will bring through a tray.'

Lucy peered around her as they followed Lady Fitzwilliam. The large paintings and ornate mirrors which hung on the walls were slightly overpowering. The drawing-room where they had tea appeared immense to them. Bella's whole house could have fitted easily into this one room.

'I suppose it is wartime, and one has to make do.' Lady Fitzwilliam sighed deeply as she handed Kezzie a plate of sandwiches. 'Everyone has the same story. The young girls now won't come into domestic service. They run off and join the munitions factory. I don't know why.'

'I expect it's because they are paid so much more,' said Kezzie. 'Also it might be more interesting to have lots of company your own age.'

'I have given these young women employment and their mothers before them,' protested Lady Fitzwilliam. 'They know that I will look after them.'

Kezzie thought about the girls she'd seen earlier laying the railway track. 'Perhaps they don't want to be "looked after",' she said. 'Maybe they want to do things for themselves . . . as equals,' she added.

'Equals?' said Lady Fitzwilliam.

'Yes,' said Kezzie. 'Equality of the sexes, for one example. It might actually happen after this war is over. We have made a start, at any rate.'

'Do you really think that this is progress?' asked Lady Fitzwilliam.

'I think that anything that makes people closer to each other is an improvement,' said Kezzie. 'And the war has done that. Men and women are working together, more truly equal than ever before. This is the beginning. And we're not going to let it go.'

'Well,' said Lady Fitzwilliam, as she bit daintily into a sandwich. 'There are things which I don't consider to be quite seemly. Modern manners are extremely . . . casual. And,' she hesitated before she spoke again, 'perhaps we aren't *meant* to be equal.'

'I'm sorry,' Kezzie apologised. She had hardly arrived in this lady's house and it looked now as though she was abusing her hospitality. 'I hope that what I've said hasn't upset you. It's just that we have to work this out. Equality must come. Men and women, rich and poor . . .'

Kezzie thought of the shrivelled and sometimes unrecognisable remains of humanity which she'd ferried in her van to the mortuary in the latter stages of the clearing-up operation in Clydebank. The mass burial on the Monday morning for the unclaimed victims, each person wrapped in a simple white sheet. She bent her head into her hands.

'We are all the same in death,' she whispered.

Lucy got up quickly and came and stood beside her. She took Kezzie by the hand.

'My sister is tired,' she told Lady Fitzwilliam. 'She needs to rest.'

'Yes, yes, of course.' Lady Fitzwilliam rose and led them upstairs to the bedrooms she'd set aside for them.

As Lucy helped her undress and slide between the sheets Kezzie began to worry about their position in this house. Perhaps she shouldn't have been so outspoken. She could sense that she had disturbed Lady Fitzwilliam and now she was not at all sure that she and Lucy should stay on. In the great feather bed she slipped into sleep and dreamed she was walking in bright green meadows where buttercups and daisies were growing. Yet each time she tried to pick a bunch the flowers withered as she touched them.

In the morning Lady Fitzwilliam brought her some tea.

'Lucy and I have had breakfast and I've sent her to play for a little while,' she said. 'It will give us a chance to talk. Kezzie, I look at your face and I see a young woman who is on the verge of complete exhaustion. Please allow me to take care of you. You must go for long walks, read and eat, and pass some time away from unpleasant things. So, perhaps we should agree not to discuss serious matters such as we did yesterday evening.' She smiled at Kezzie. 'You must understand it is very difficult for an old lady like me, who was born in the last century, to come to terms with all these new ideas. When I was your age I had a personal maid who laid out my clothes, ran my bath and dressed me in the mornings. Yet I read in the newspaper that the Princess Elizabeth has trained as a motor mechanic so that she can service her own jeep, and the Queen herself has a ration book. So I too must change my ways.'

Kezzie and Lucy found that it took them some time to adjust to the house itself. The rooms were huge, the furniture grand and imposing.

'It's staring at me,' Lucy told Kezzie one night, pointing at the wardrobe in her bedroom.

Kezzie laughed, but she could understand her sister's apprehension. The elaborate carvings and curved handles on the triple doors gave the appearance of some strange giant from folklore lurking in the corner. The few clothes which Lucy had been allocated by the relief agencies or given by friends were lost in its depth.

But the very size of the grounds around the manor house were a benefit to Kezzie. She could wander there the whole day, stroll along shady paths or walk in the walled garden at sunrise and never encounter anyone. She would choose an isolated spot under a tree to sit with her book or some knitting in the afternoon, and generally fall asleep. Very slowly her mind began to heal, and her dreams at night were less troubled. Lady Fitzwilliam didn't mind Kezzie's need to be on her own. She loved Lucy's company. They spent their time planting vegetables in the kitchen garden, or going for little drives to meet friends in the surrounding villages.

The lilac was blooming, when they heard that Clydesbank had been bombed on two more occasions. Samuel was away, so Lady Fitzwilliam herself drove into the nearest town to obtain news.

'Not nearly so severe,' she called as Kezzie came running to meet her on her return. 'Very little damage.'

Still Kezzie fretted, and she hurried to the post office each day until word arrived from Peg confirming this. Peg's letters were full of bright cheerful chatter about Ricardo and the baby. Alec was learning Italian words as fast as English.

He can say 'I want sweets' in two languages, Peg wrote, *and he is completely spoiled by everyone. His attempts to eat spaghetti are hilarious.*

'I worry about them,' said Kezzie as she read the latest letter at breakfast one morning.

'She would be very welcome here,' said Lady Fitzwilliam. 'Both she and the baby could have a holiday in the country.'

'She wouldn't leave Ricardo,' said Kezzie. She thought about it for a moment. About the whole situation. Herself and Lucy, the evacuated children and people risking death to stay together. 'And I'm not sure that she should,' she added.

'No, indeed,' said Lady Fitzwilliam. 'When I had the evacuee children billeted here, this village was so remote no parent was able to visit. The two that I did have went home after a few months. I tried very hard but they were terribly homesick. May I ask why you did not send Lucy away? You must have thought she would be safer.'

'I found it impossible after what had happened to her before,' said Kezzie. 'Then after Coventry was destroyed we tried to, and she ran away to come home to us. So finally the decision wasn't mine.' Kezzie looked at Lady Fitzwilliam. 'Do you think it was so awful not to have made her go? Perhaps I should have insisted. She could have very easily been killed.'

Lady Fitzwilliam leaned over and grasped Kezzie's hand. 'I don't blame you,' she said. 'I wouldn't have done it.' She wiped her mouth daintily with her cloth napkin, and then, folding it meticulously, she placed it alongside her plate. 'Very selfish of me, my dear, I suppose.' She smiled at Kezzie. 'However, one can only do as one sees fit at the time. History and,' she smiled wryly, 'and one's children will eventually be the judge.' She sighed. 'Let us hope that they will not be too harsh. As you say, with Peg and Ricardo, their love will survive.'

Yes, thought Kezzie, better to be together. Michael was now in Egypt and had seen action. The news was uncertain and patchy, his letters censored. Was he thinking of her as she did of him? How she longed for him, to hear his voice and see his face again, if even only for a short time.

The Blitzes of May continued. City after city was bombed relentlessly, the ports in particular were targeted. Liverpool, Belfast, Hull, Clydebank, Plymouth, Portsmouth. And then on the 11th May London suffered the most appalling raid. Over a thousand people were killed in one night, bringing London's total of civilian blitz casualties to twenty thousand. When the radio broadcast the sombre news, there was a grim, terse tone to the bulletins. It was several days before they managed to get newspapers which gave an account of the damage. The square tower of Westminster Abbey had fallen in, the chamber of the House of Commons had been reduced to rubble. The faces of the rescue workers and survivors seemed numbed and bewildered. It seemed as if the famous spirit of the Londoners might be cracking. People were weeping in the streets.

Lady Fitzwilliam read her newspaper and then she laid it to one side. Her face was white and her hands were shaking. She turned to Kezzie and whispered, 'We can't bear this much longer.'

CHAPTER 23

School lessons

That afternoon Kezzie and Lady Fitzwilliam took a long walk in the country. There was blossom on the trees and the smell of summer days to come and, as they strolled along the lanes, the idea of war and the reality of the Blitz seemed many miles away. Kezzie breathed deeply and tried to let the warmth in the sweet air act as a balm to her frayed nerves. But both of their minds carried the pictures of shattered cities all over Britain which were being relentlessly ground down into dust. Suddenly Lady Fitzwilliam stopped at a wooden gate. She turned to Kezzie.

'The reports say that the RAF fighter planes shot down twenty-nine of theirs.' Her eyes were tortured and she shredded her gloves with her fingers. 'Just twenty-nine destroyed out of over five hundred. It's not enough. Our boys cannot keep fighting night and day. There are too many of them, and too few of us.'

Kezzie put her hand on Lady Fitzwilliam's arm. She knew that William being in constant danger was causing his mother unceasing distress. She tried to find words to say which might comfort her.

'Last year, after Dunkirk,' she said, 'we were hours away from invasion. It was the flyers who fought them off. Day by day, keeping the Luftwaffe out of the skies. It will be the same this time. This is a last act of desperation to bring us down. It won't work. We won't let it.'

Lady Fitzwilliam leaned wearily on the gatepost. 'William says government intelligence sometimes exaggerate their scores to keep morale up. And that the press don't print all of our casualties. It is not always the whole truth that we read in the newspapers.'

'I know this,' said Kezzie. She remembered in the aftermath of Clydebank, the rescue workers and survivors, relatives of the victims, had been extremely upset at government statements which had minimised the damage and the number of people who'd lost their lives. It caused great resentment in the town which had suffered so much.

What a terrible responsibility the war leaders had. Making decisions which involved life or death for thousands of people. Trying to keep civilian hopes high and the spirits of the troops to fight on. Her grandad had often repeated the famous quote, '*The first casualty of war is truth.*'

She was aware that Lady Fitzwilliam was still gazing at her, as though in some way Kezzie might bring succour and inspiration. Kezzie searched in her mind for something to say. It was this lady, after all, who'd taken her in, offered her a home when she'd none. She must try to help her now when she was so anxiously seeking reassurance. Kezzie hesitated. Her next words might not be welcome, but she felt now she had to speak plainly.

'I think,' said Kezzie, 'that we should involve ourselves more. In the war effort, I mean.'

'My dear girl,' protested Lady Fitzwilliam. 'What I do already completely exhausts me. What more is there?'

'Yes,' said Kezzie. 'You do at times have rather a hectic round of engagements.'

There was the 'Save for a Spitfire' committee, the vicar's wife's weekly knitting bee, and various fêtes, fund raising events and social teas. Kezzie knew that Lady Fitzwilliam was actively involved in each of them, and she herself had taken to going along to help out. But there was a nagging thought in Kezzie's head that these didn't take much effort. They were on the fringes of the real war. Others were working harder, doing more. Perhaps driving her makeshift ambulance, and being involved in rescuing people first-hand, would make any-thing else seem tame. But now that she felt better in herself, she was more able to contribute, and she knew that she wasn't doing it. Her senses had recovered enough for her to be slightly restless at her own inactivity.

'I know that you don't have evacuated children living here any more,' she said, 'but there are some in houses round about. The village school has closed. Now, if you add on the remainder of the local children, then there are quite a few young people, Lucy included, who are receiving no education.'

'What do you suggest?' asked Lady Fitzwilliam.

'We could have lessons in the house in the morning. Samuel could use the trap to collect and return the children to the surrounding farms and houses. It would be good for them, and us,' Kezzie added. 'I think we need something more positive to do.'

'Yes, my dear. You are, as usual, quite correct. I'm sick to death of sitting around with the same old faces knitting comforters for soldiers.' Lady Fitzwilliam smiled. 'And I suppose I must find something more useful to do than embroider a cover for my ration book.'

They held the classes in the large dining room. At first it was complete chaos. They had to beg or borrow exercise books and pencils, and organising the children was extremely difficult. Some were overawed by being in the big house, others thought it a wonderful opportunity to run wild. Kezzie thought Lady Fitzwilliam was showing great patience in dealing with the more boisterous of them, and told her so.

'Well, they are the future, aren't they?' she told Kezzie. 'And it is, after all, their fathers who are fighting and being killed on our behalf.'

It was finally Samuel who found the best way of controlling them and keeping discipline. Those who behaved were allowed to drive the horse on the round trip, those who didn't were sent for an hour in the morning to collect the manure and spread it on the vegetable plots. Soon some of the mothers established a volunteer rota and the lessons and a baby and toddlers crèche were held each forenoon.

Meanwhile the war, and the restrictions, continued.

'Clothing coupons!' Lady Fitzwilliam announced one morning. 'Really, it is too much. Clothing coupons! Whatever next?'

She was reading from the newspaper in tones of great indignation. 'And we are to be allowed to utilise our margarine coupons while we await these new vouchers to be printed. What a choice to be faced with. Dry bread or a new skirt.'

Kezzie giggled. She imagined Lady Fitzwilliam calling at her hat shop in Nottingham to select something for autumn and being handed a quarter of a pound of Bluebell margarine.

Then the rationing of coal was announced. The weather was warm and the windows stood open for most of the day, but Lady Fitzwilliam was concerned. She spoke to Kezzie. 'The house is freezing in winter. We are exposed here, sitting as it does on the top of the hill. My husband's father planted trees to serve as windbreaks, but the gales come sweeping across at the end of the year. The children will be cold.' She frowned. 'If we are short of coal and there is no heating we might have to stop our school lessons.'

They began to stockpile wood in the stables. Bringing in broken and fallen branches from the trees around the house. During the holidays the children helped by making up bundle after bundle of twigs for kindling. One of their parents, a local farmer, offered to cut up logs for them.

'The only problem is transporting them,' he told Kezzie. 'I'm so short of manpower, half my machinery is lying idle.'

'I have driven,' said Kezzie. 'Is a tractor very difficult to learn?'

It was more unstable, she soon discovered, hanging on

to the wheel as it bounced along the rutted tracks. They worked hard during the summer, attaching chains to the tree trunks and dragging them back from the woods. The farmer was impressed with how she coped with it all. He spoke to her one day.

'I'll need help when the harvest comes,' he said. 'I don't have enough land girls working. Would you come over in the autumn and lend a hand?'

Kezzie didn't dare tell Lady Fitzwilliam, but she practically promised him her help. She thought she might enjoy it. There would be company of her own age which she found she missed, and it would make her feel that she was doing something to help the war effort. Lady Fitzwilliam would be quite capable of managing their little school with some help from the older children and mothers. Whether she would agree with that was another matter. She and Kezzie had found that they got on very well together. They had even managed to talk politics without disagreeing too violently.

Then, in an attempt to restore a mood of resistance and determination, the Government launched a new campaign, 'V for Victory'. It was to become a symbol of hope for those in occupied Europe where the BBC broadcast every night. There were soon posters every-where with the distinctive V sign surmounting the flag.

One late summer's evening when it was still warm enough to sit outside, they set out chairs in the garden, just below the terrace which ran the length of the back of the house. It was quiet and pleasant, and yes . . . peaceful, Kezzie decided. She fetched a cardigan for Lady Fitzwilliam from her bedroom and settled down to read. She could hear in the distance the cries of Lucy and some friends as they played in the long paddock on the other side of the house.

Kezzie was absorbed in her book, so that at first she did not notice the uniformed figure which stepped through the open French windows and walked quietly down the curved steps. Long shadows were grouping among the trees at the end of the path. Lady Fitzwilliam had fallen lightly asleep. Her lips apart, she was snoring gently. Kezzie carefully retrieved the journal which was slipping from her fingers. As she did so she glanced up, and saw the young man dressed in the blue of the RAF walking across the lawn towards them. Something about the way his left leg slurred as he approached caught her attention. She straightened her head and looked more closely.

'William?' she said quietly.

CHAPTER 24

William

Lady Fitzwilliam screamed in delight and scrambled very inelegantly to her feet.

'Darling boy!' she exclaimed. 'You should have warned us. I would have prepared properly for your return.' She smoothed out the skirt of her frock. 'I feel so shabby with this ancient woollen dress. It's several seasons behind in style.'

Kezzie was suddenly very much aware of her own short-sleeved blouse, with its decorated collar and capped sleeves, which was rather worn and very much out of date. William, however, wasn't concerned with any fashion garment, whether modern or not. He hugged his mother and kissed her several times and then turned his attention on Kezzie. He gazed at her for several moments then finally spoke.

'Kezzie,' he said. 'You look more handsome than ever.'

She smiled up at him. The thin sandy moustache which she remembered was now quite a respectable size and his face had matured into a strong firm profile. In his dark blue uniform, with the peaked hat and braid, he looked very attractive.

She grinned at him. 'So do you,' she said.

He gave a whoop of delight, and grabbing her round the waist, he spun her about the lawn.

'Behave yourself, child,' his mother laughed and smacked him with her magazine.

'I've got two days,' he declared, 'and the use of a jeep and some petrol. We're not going to waste a second of it.'

Lucy was at first terribly shy with William. He had no brothers or sisters and was unused to children, and he treated her with a formality which she couldn't understand. To complicate matters there were the two accents. His, a long slow drawl with many expressions which she found strange and incomprehensible. For his part, he was baffled by the speed at which she spoke and the variety of words she used which he had never heard before. He tried hard to be friends but they were awkward in each other's company. After dinner they played very politely with a jigsaw on the floor of the sitting room for nearly an hour until he suddenly sat up and snapped his fingers.

'Have you been through the attics yet?' he asked her.

When Lucy shook her head he pulled her to her feet.

'Oh, jolly good!' he cried. 'That means I can be the first to help you explore. I know! We'll find the hamper with the clothes for dressing up. Then we can have some super fun tonight.'

Lucy made a face at Kezzie as she followed him obediently out of the room. Kezzie gave her sister a warning look. After some time, when they didn't reappear, both she and Lady Fitzwilliam went to look for them. They found Lucy and William sitting upstairs surrounded by an enormous variety of exotic clothes, capes and wigs, long dresses, fans and parasols, pirate costumes and cowboy outfits.

Lady Fitzwilliam clapped her hands. 'I'd forgotten all about these clothes,' she exclaimed. 'It is so long since there've been young children in this house.'

'Let's play charades,' declared William.

It was a game Lucy had never played before, but she proved to have a great talent for acting. She and William had the most tremendous fun and, working together, managed to win most of the time. Kezzie and Lady Fitzwilliam eventually called a halt to the game, which would have gone on all night.

'Did you enjoy that?' Kezzie asked her sister as they prepared for bed.

'It was jolly good,' said Lucy.

Kezzie burst out laughing.

'I still don't know what he is saying half the time,' Lucy confided, 'but now I just say "yes" and nod a lot. He seems to like that.'

The next day they made a picnic and went to the seaside. It was many miles before they reached the flat fen country.

'Don't be too excited,' William warned them as they approached Kings Lynn. 'There are concrete blocks and barbed wire and anti tank devices all over the beaches, but we might find a place to get on to the sands.'

How beautiful England is, thought Kezzie, as they passed the little villages, the country pubs and steepled churches with weathercocks on top. It seemed such a desecration when they reached the coast and saw the defences against the expected invasion. The ugly rolls of jagged wire, and the danger signs with skull and cross-bones painted on. In some areas land mines had been planted to slow down or repel approaching enemy tanks. Kezzie shuddered. Thank God, it hadn't come to that. Churchill was right. The whole of Britain owed the RAF an unimaginable debt.

They found a place among the dunes to eat their sandwiches, and although they could not bathe they spread a rug on the tussocks of grass and sunbathed for an hour or two. Lucy and Lady Fitzwilliam made sand-castles. Kezzie watched them together as her eyes closed drowsily. Such friends they had become, crossing barriers of age and class with apparent ease. William joined them in their game, constructing a moat and a drawbridge and bossing them both like a spoiled child. Kezzie's eyes closed as she relaxed into sleep, head propped against some cushions.

It was dusk when they started for home. On the journey back Lucy cuddled in against Lady Fitzwilliam on the rear seat. At one stage Kezzie turned around to say something and then stopped. They were both asleep, their foreheads and cheeks pink where they had caught the sun.

William stretched across and grasped Kezzie's hand. 'It was so good of you to come all the way down here and spend some time with Ma,' he said. 'You and Lucy have been a tonic. She is much more cheerful than when I saw her last.'

Kezzie smiled at him. 'No,' she said, 'it is your mother who has helped us. When I came at first I could scarcely stand up. She looked after us both.'

'Tonight we will go to a dance,' William told Kezzie when they arrived at the house. 'There's a forces' base a few miles east of Nottingham. I know one or two chaps there. I don't know if I'll actually get you on the floor, but at least we can listen to the music.'

'I don't have anything to wear,' said Kezzie.

'Nonsense,' said Lady Fitzwilliam, who had just awoken. 'We will find something suitable.'

She searched through her own wardrobe until she came across a blue silk dress patterned with tiny rosebuds.

'We will have to shorten the skirt,' she told Kezzie. 'You have a bath, my dear, and I will see how rusty my sewing skills are.' She smiled. 'This length was very daring when I wore it. I was the first young lady in the county to reveal some leg – quite scandalous at the time.'

In fact, when she reached the army base and went into the room where the band was playing Kezzie realised that she needn't have worried about her dress at all. Many women were there in uniform, or wearing a plain skirt and cardigan. The idea was to relax and forget the war for a short time. She sat at a table and sipped lemonade while William went to the bar for a beer.

Shortly before it ended Kezzie persuaded William onto the floor. He was self-conscious about his leg, but she insisted that he should partner her for the last waltz.

On the way home William spoke to Kezzie quite

seriously. 'It is such a great comfort to me to know that Ma has you with her when I am away,' he said. 'Promise me that you'll stay on a little longer.'

He parked the jeep in front of the house and helped her out. Just as she stepped from the running board he lifted her into his arms and kissed her gently. She waited, quite still, as he put his fingers in her hair and stroked her face. Then he crushed her head tightly against his chest. She knew that they understood each other quite well. He was the brother she'd never had, and she was a sister. He kept her very close to him for many minutes, as if clinging on to some vibrant contact with life, knowing that when dawn came he would have to face death once more.

The next morning they got up early to wave William off on the long drive south to rejoin his fighter squadron. He kissed them all again many times, and shook hands warmly with Samuel, who stood on the bottom step holding his kitbag. His eyes were shining as he turned and waved one last time before switching on the engine and letting out the clutch. The jeep shot off at speed and soon disappeared between the stone pillars.

'You know,' said Lady Fitzwilliam to Kezzie. 'I do believe he is keen to get back to his base and into the air again.'

They waited in front of the house until the sound of the horn and the noise of the engine faded. Lady Fitzwilliam shivered slightly as they turned to go back to the house. She looked at the sky.

'Sun has gone in,' she said.

CHAPTER 25

Bad news

The first chestnuts were falling and the fields were the colour of baked biscuit when the local farmer called round at the house and reminded Kezzie of her promise.

'Working on a farm!' said Lady Fitzwilliam when Kezzie told her. She pressed her lips together. 'I thought you had intentions of becoming a doctor?'

'I have,' said Kezzie. 'And I will,' she added. 'But at the moment they need help to bring the harvest in. There are not many people who can drive the tractor and it will only be for a few weeks,' she reassured Lady Fitzwilliam.

On the first day she began work Kezzie dressed as she had seen the other land-girls do. The farmer's wife had given her some heavy-duty clothes to wear. Kezzie combed her hair and tucked it right up under a scarf, which she tied in a bandanna style around her head. Then she put on the rough checked shirt, thick brown dungarees, and dark green wellington boots. She went downstairs to the kitchen where Lucy and Lady Fitzwilliam were having breakfast together.

'Well,' said Kezzie, turning about to show off her outfit, 'what do you think?'

There was a silence. Then Lucy giggled and Lady Fitzwilliam breathed deeply, then cleared her throat. 'It's not really what one would call . . . em . . . *pretty*? Is it, my dear?' she enquired politely.

Kezzie laughed out loud. 'Dungarees aren't meant to be pretty,' she said. 'I think their designer had a more functional use in mind.'

Lady Fitzwilliam grimaced. 'Oh well,' she said. 'I read the other day that the Princess Margaret was wearing a boiler suit. So, one must adapt to the times, I suppose.'

Impulsively Kezzie went over and hugged her. 'Wish me luck,' she said. 'I am so nervous.'

'Gracious, child, what have you to be nervous about?'

Kezzie shrugged. 'I don't know,' she replied. 'I might not be able to keep up with the rest of the girls. I could have an accident with the tractor . . . all sorts of things.'

Lady Fitzwilliam stood up. 'You'll manage perfectly well,' she asserted. 'Just be careful that you don't develop . . . muscles.'

The work was hard and each minute of daylight precious. The girls rose before dawn and were in the fields as the first light of the sun was edging over the horizon. They worked together in a cheerful group of mixed personalities and backgrounds. And they knew how to entertain themselves. There wasn't a dance or singsong or get-together within a radius of twenty miles that they didn't hear of and wangle an invitation to. Despite an aching back Kezzie was enjoying herself. She loved being outdoors, driving in the fields and cycling home at night. Often she would stop for a few minutes before putting her bike away to watch the long drawn-out sunsets, the western sky painted in vertical lines of blues and reds.

Kezzie liked the colours of autumn, and the harmony of the land and nature that produced the harvest filtered into her spirit. The screeching, scavenging crows settled in a noisy cloud behind her as her tractor moved down the furrow, the clods tumbling behind as the blades sliced through the dun-coloured earth. Many of the farms had gone back to using horse-drawn ploughs, the grand shires making their stately way up and down the field.

She was sleeping well, and eating better than she'd done for months. There was something satisfying about the sight of the hay stooks and the smell of the apples in the brown wooden barrels. Honeysuckle grew around the barn door and blue and yellow gladioli stood on long green stalks in front of the white-painted farmhouse. And the land girls with their chat and laughter became part of the landscape itself. The farmer's wife was delighted with their company and her husband declared he'd never had better workers.

The other bonus for Kezzie was the fact that she was paid a wage. It wasn't very much, but Kezzie felt that at least she could contribute something to her and Lucy's upkeep. The farmer also gave her potatoes and turnips to bring home. She knew that Lady Fitzwilliam would not accept any of the money she earned. She'd tried tentatively to bring the subject up but it had been dismissed abruptly. 'My husband left me quite comfortably off. William and I are well provided for, and indeed, Samuel also. So there is no need to discuss the matter further.'

However, her income gave Kezzie some independence. She was able to buy some small things for herself and Lucy. She occasionally went to the clothing exchange in the nearest town. Lady Fitzwilliam had at first been very reluctant to accompany them, but eventually her curiosity proved too strong and she came along. To her astonishment there were several other titled ladies rummaging through the assorted bundles.

'I consider it my patriotic duty,' one declared loudly. 'We are being exhorted to "make do and mend" and that's what I intend to do.'

'They say it's saving our merchant fleet. They are in enough danger transporting essential foods,' said another.

Later, when Kezzie looked across the church hall, she saw Lady Fitzwilliam arguing with someone over possession of a hat. She finally came towards Kezzie clutching it firmly in one hand.

'Surely we can fight a war without rationing hats,' she said.

Kezzie obtained some shoes, a cardigan and an old army blanket from which she intended to make Lucy a winter coat. The weather was becoming severe and Kezzie was glad that they had the foresight to lay up supplies of wood. People were scavenging for coal in old bings, and along the seashore.

Kezzie knew from the newspaper reports that Michael had been in action again. As the Germans were moving so fast through Greece his unit had been sent quickly from Egypt to the southern coast of Crete. They took up a position on the Plain of Messara to defend the island from the expected invasion. Enemy paratroopers were dropped in great numbers and the British were forced to withdraw in confusion. Some were left behind, but Michael was with the detachment who reached Heraklion and were picked up by the Royal Navy. The ships were bombed heavily, and less than half of the battalion returned to Egypt.

We're having a wonderful holiday, he had written to Kezzie. *We try out all the beaches. Unfortunately some other people want the place to themselves. They're not so keen on our company, and don't like sharing. So most times one or other of us has to go. This time it was us . . .*

Kezzie kept the letter in the pocket of her shirt and took it out to read from time to time. He'd been in terrible danger and she hadn't known anything about it. She knew now the bond that she and Lady Fitzwilliam shared and why, every time she raised the subject of returning to Scotland, William's mother tried to persuade her to stay a little longer.

'Wait until the New Year,' she had begged Kezzie, 'until we are certain that there will be no more air raids, and things are more settled in Clydebank.'

Kezzie knew that they'd become close, and the older woman would miss her and Lucy dreadfully when they finally went home.

Towards the end of the year women between the ages of twenty and forty were called up. Lady Fitzwilliam's maid Sally went off and joined the WRNS. Kezzie was rising early, and working late, storing the last of the crop for the winter, so that it was Lucy who had to instruct Lady Fitzwilliam in the basic skills of cooking and keeping house. Kezzie marvelled at the development in her sister. She was becoming very competent in many practical things, and did not seem so troubled now by new and strange experiences. One day Samuel managed to shoot a rabbit. He came in and very proudly presented the carcass to Lucy and Lady Fitzwilliam in the kitchen.

'And what am I supposed to do with this?' Lady Fitzwilliam demanded, gazing with deep repugnance upon the dead animal.

'We need a sharp knife,' said Lucy. 'A very sharp knife.'

Lady Fitzwilliam shuddered. She stood up quickly. 'I shall be in the conservatory, if you require me,' she said.

It was left to Lucy to skin the rabbit, and joint and cook it. That night Kezzie could smell the savoury stew as she opened the back door. She sat down wearily on the steps and pulled her boots off.

'Something smells delicious,' she said.

'I did it all myself,' said Lucy proudly. 'Everything. Prepared the food, peeled the vegetables, cooked the stew. All of it.'

'So we're going to have a feast,' said Kezzie.

The doorbell rang as Lady Fitzwilliam was laying the table and setting out the dishes. Kezzie crossed to the small stone sink in the corner to wash up before dinner, and Samuel went to answer the front door. Kezzie was drying her hands on a towel when she noticed that

Samuel was standing just inside the doorway leading through to the hall. He stood very still, as though he'd been there some time, she thought. Almost at the same moment Lady Fitzwilliam looked up and saw him.

'Samuel, you startled me,' she said. 'I didn't see you there.'

'You have a visitor, ma'am,' Samuel announced slowly. 'The Wing Commander from Master William's squadron is in the drawing room.'

Kezzie realised that the old man was avoiding looking directly at either Lady Fitzwilliam or herself. He was staring stolidly at a point beyond their heads. 'The gentleman says he would like a word with you,' said Samuel. 'In private.'

Lady Fitzwilliam carefully put the plate she was holding onto the table. 'Kezzie,' she said, 'please accompany me.'

'Missing — believed killed.'

Lady Fitzwilliam repeated the words the Wing Commander had just said. He looked at her anxiously, and then at Kezzie.

'Some water?' he suggested.

Lady Fitzwilliam shook her head. 'No,' she said. 'No . . . thank you. Please tell me the details.'

'He was part of a flight arm escorting a group of RAF bombers on a sortie into France. They crossed the French coast south of Le Touquet and ran into an enemy patrol. There was a brief dogfight. He downed at least one Messerschmitt, before being struck himself. His plane exploded on impact. No one saw him bale out. I am sorry. He was a wonderful young man.'

Lady Fitzwilliam sat in her chair, her back straight, her head erect.

'Is there no hope?' she asked. 'Can you give me no hope? None at all?'

'It is very unlikely that he has survived,' said the Wing Commander.

'But not impossible,' persisted Lady Fitzwilliam. 'Not entirely impossible?'

The Wing Commander spread his hands. 'Not entirely, no,' he agreed.

'Then I will continue to wait for my son to come home,' said Lady Fitzwilliam. Her voice shook.

Kezzie accompanied the officer to the front door. The Wing Commander spoke to her before he left. 'I have reported that he is "missing in action: believed killed".'

He looks enormously weary, thought Kezzie. She placed her hand on his arm, touching for a moment the thick gold braid of his sleeve. His eyes met hers, faded grey, with lines of exhaustion etched around the sockets.

But, like William's mother, she too needed something to cling on to.

'No,' said Kezzie. 'File it only as "missing in action". Please,' she added.

He nodded and left. Kezzie gripped the door handle tightly. 'Women weep and young men die,' she said as she closed the door behind him.

When Kezzie returned to the drawing room Lady Fitzwilliam was not weeping.

'Am I a foolish old woman,' she asked Kezzie, 'to believe that there may be the merest chance of his surviving?'

Kezzie went and knelt by her chair. 'If you are, then I am foolish too,' she said.

Kezzie's work at the farm finished and the weather hardened into bleak winter. On the 8th of December 1941 the Japanese bombed Pearl Harbour and a week later America was in the war.

CHAPTER 26

1942: The Americans arrive

Kezzie had collected a parcel at the railway station one morning and was tying it onto the back of her bicycle when a tall tanned solider, with the captain's stripes of the United States Army on his sleeve, walked casually up to the ticket office. He leaned on the little wooden ledge and called through the glass partition to Mr Penrose.

'Say, buddy. D'you know anyplace hereabouts I'd get some gas?'

'Gas?' said Mr Penrose. He surveyed the young man suspiciously, taking in the strange uniform and the cropped hair, shorn all over so that the scalp gleamed through.

'Yeah, gas,' the soldier repeated.

Mr Penrose frowned at him. 'Are you a Germ—' he began.

'Excuse me,' said Kezzie quickly. 'I think he means petrol. Don't you?' She smiled at the American soldier. 'Gasoline for your motor car, sorry, automobile,' she said. 'We call it petrol over here.'

The officer grinned at her. 'Sounds fine by me, honey,' he said. 'Smile like that, and you can call it anything you please.'

Kezzie blushed as he stared at her boldly. She was suddenly conscious of the long trousers which she now wore on a regular basis. 'They're so convenient when cycling,' she'd told Lady Fitzwilliam. In actual fact she found them an easier way to dress for practically every occasion. However, in order not to upset Lady Fitzwilliam too much, she did still change into a skirt for dinner.

'I can show you where there's a garage which sells petrol,' Kezzie told the American soldier.

In the background Mr Penrose tutted loudly.

Captain Joe Petrowski introduced himself as a surgeon with the American Medical Division, and offered Kezzie a ride back to the manor house. He chatted away as he lifted her bicycle into the back of his jeep and they drove along the country lanes. His accent and easy informal manner reminded her of Ricardo, and she felt suddenly, and quite sharply, homesick. She had thought of returning to Scotland at the beginning of the year. When she had discussed it with Lucy, it had been her little sister who had told her earnestly that they should stay on for a bit.

Yes, Lucy agreed that she too missed Scotland and Aunt Bella. She would like to go back to the little café and see Peg and Ricardo, and the two signoras who had treated her so lovingly. And most especially she wanted to play with Alec, who would now no longer be a baby. 'But William's mother needs us so much, Kezzie,' said

Lucy. 'She is being very brave and not complaining, but she couldn't cope on her own. She can get through the days, but she wouldn't manage the nights.'

'The nights?' said Kezzie in surprise. 'What happens at night-time?'

'Her room is next to mine,' said Lucy. 'I hear her walking up and down for hours and hours. Sometimes I go in and pretend I'm frightened and can't sleep, and then she sings to me. She reads me William's letters, and shows me old photographs, and I tell her about Grandad and his stories. You know, Kezzie, they would have been great pals,' said Lucy.

Kezzie gazed at her sister in amazement. 'You and Lady Fitzwilliam?' she said. 'You help her when she is grieving for William?'

'Aunt Mary,' Lucy corrected her. 'She told me I had to stop calling her Lady Fitzwilliam. So you see, Kezzie, she needs to have someone with her.'

Kezzie marvelled at her sister, at her strength and resourcefulness, and at her perception in appreciating the similarity between the older woman and their own grandfather. Indeed, Kezzie realised, the two of them would have got on extremely well together. She could just imagine the terrific arguments and political discussions they would have had. And, Kezzie suspected, it wouldn't always have been her grandad who would have won the debate. She realised that she couldn't possibly return to Scotland just yet. It would be an act of cruelty to take Lucy away, and deprive William's mother of possibly the only person who was helping her to struggle through to each lonely dawn.

They created quite a stir when the jeep skidded to a halt below the front steps of the house. It was almost lunchtime and Lady Fitzwilliam and her helpers were ushering the children onto the trap to be driven home. One of the young mothers nudged Kezzie and whispered, 'Where did you find him? He's fabulous, absolutely gorgeous. Introduce us.'

Joe's American drawl and his charm had an immediate effect. The young woman giggled and, gazing up at him, said, 'Well, if you're around here, I, for one, am going to feel a lot safer at night.'

'That is an opinion not everyone might share,' Lady Fitzwilliam observed drily. 'In particular that young woman's husband,' she added under her breath to Kezzie.

They invited Joe to stay for lunch and as he came through the house he stared openly at everything. He was fascinated by it all. The wide corridors, the tapestries, the curved stairway and large rooms.

'Gee, would you look at this.' He looked around the kitchen, and touched the row of bells which had been used for calling the servants. 'It's for real! I thought you only saw these kinda things in the movies.'

Lucy watched him closely throughout the meal. He at once cut all his food up into small pieces. Then he put down his knife and, transferring his fork to his right hand, he began to eat.

Kezzie saw Lady Fitzwilliam raise her eyebrows. Not all the American ways were going to be welcome in Britain, she thought.

She was proved correct. The American soldier's weekly

pay equalled around seven pounds sterling, while the ordinary British private earned not much more than seven shillings. They called their uniforms Government Issue, so the British began calling the soldiers themselves GIs. All of them spoke, and a good many of them looked, like cinema stars. They brought their own supplies and were able to procure fruit, nylon stockings, and chocolate – things which hadn't been seen in Britain for years. They were hugely popular with lots of young women. Quite understandably, many British men loathed them.

Their presence struck the surrounding area like a multi-coloured firework. Lucy, to Lady Fitzwilliam's consternation, started using American slang. When she was cooking eggs she enquired if they preferred them 'overeasy' or 'sunny side up' and she would shout, 'Got any gum, chum?' when Joe appeared at the back door.

He became a frequent visitor to the house. He was establishing what he called a back-up base at an old aerodrome a few miles away. The United States Medical Corps was setting up a series of hospital units all over the country. They were located away from the major cities for fear of bomb damage, but near transport lines and railway stations. West Fenton was an ideal place to have one.

'We're going to have more and more casualties as the war goes on,' Joe told them. 'From bombing missions, from active service units in the major conflicts abroad, and when the big push comes next year or the year after. The first-aid posts in the field can only do so much, and the British hospitals at home won't be able to cope. We'll pick up on the more serious cases which will be flown back.'

He was very proud of having his operating theatre in working order so quickly. They'd done one emergency appendectomy on the small son of the owner of the village inn. The appendix had been on the point of bursting and the local doctor let it be known that, but for Joe and his team, the child might have died. After this incident the Americans found that the local people treated them in a more friendly manner.

Not long after, when Joe was having dinner at the house, and he was telling them about some new technical apparatus which had arrived, Kezzie recalled Dr McMath speaking of the same piece of equipment. She commented on this to Joe, and he began to ask her about her work at the pharmacy in Canada.

'We'll need more staff if things hot up,' he said, 'and I'd like someone who has had practical experience. I could train you just now as a theatre assistant.'

Kezzie's hands began to shake. She put her knife and fork down carefully. 'You don't mean it, do you?' she asked him. 'Would you actually take me on?'

'Sure,' he said. 'We could give it a try.'

CHAPTER 27

US hospital

Kezzie found that the hospital demanded all her energy. It was the most difficult work she had ever undertaken. Not only physically and mentally, but also emotionally.

When the first wounded began to arrive, isolated cases who were casualties from bombing sorties, she found the very youth of the patients distressing. The broken remnants of the young men would have caused the stoutest spirit to falter. It was a strain to be cheerful while nursing a boy, little older than herself, whose leg or arm, or both, had been amputated.

Joe was ruthlessly efficient and demanded the same standard from his staff that he gave himself.

'We're gonna be the best,' he said. 'That's the target. Nothing lower.'

He was training her in theatre skills and had bawled her out on several occasions for what he considered sloppy work. She found it hard to reconcile this Joe with the big easy-going guy who loved to clown around with Lucy and the rest of the children at the house. He was full of energy. No matter how hard the week had been at the hospital, the weekend always found him out dancing somewhere. Jitterbugging or waltzing round the floor crooning in her ear, *'Don't sit under the apple tree with any-one else but me . . .'*

When she wasn't on duty he plied her with textbooks and medical journals to read. She was learning fast under his direction. Lady Fitzwilliam was enthusiastic about the whole situation.

'You can apply to take a pre-university entrance exam course in the autumn,' she told Kezzie. 'We will write off now and find out what preparation you might have to do.'

And so it seemed to Kezzie that for the time being her life had been settled for her. Lucy was happy, more content than she'd been for a long time, in fact. Lady Fitzwilliam would be bereft if they moved away. And her own future . . . there was now a real possibility that her dream of becoming a doctor could come true.

While Kezzie worked in the base hospital, Lady Fitzwilliam and Joe were making plans together.

'This house is under-utilised,' she'd declared to Kezzie one day.

Kezzie guessed that this was Joe's influence. He found the enormous empty rooms at odds with his own cramped quarters in what was essentially Nissen hut accommodation.

'We could have patients to convalesce here,' said Lady Fitzwilliam.

She'd now almost completely handed over the daily lessons in the house to the children's parents. There was hope that the local school might reopen after Easter as someone knew of a former teacher who was to be invalided out of the RAF. Joe was keen for the rooms in the house to be freed up. He, more than any of them, realised how many more beds would be needed for the wounded as the war went on.

'Kezzie, Lucy, Samuel and myself can move up to the attic rooms,' Lady Fitzwilliam told him. 'We will store the furniture and then we could adapt the remaining space as an overflow from your unit.'

They discussed ideas, the possibility of converting the dining room into a general ward and making the conservatory into a day room.

Some of Lady Fitzwilliam's county friends were taken aback by the prospect of her actual involvement with the wounded convalescing in the house.

'We thought you would have a more supervisory role, Mary,' was the comment. 'You're not thinking of nursing the patients yourself, are you, dear? Do you realise that you may be asked to bathe or change some of these soldiers . . . *male* soldiers?'

'I think they imagined me walking about with a lamp at night and the men kissing my shadow on their pillow as I passed,' Lady Fitzwilliam said to Kezzie at dinner one evening. 'I just told them, "If you mean shit and smelly socks, then I'm perfectly capable of dealing with both. I can clean up dung as well as anyone else, don't you know".'

Kezzie choked on her food. 'You didn't actually say that, did you?'

'I certainly did,' declared Lady Fitzwilliam. 'I may not be invited to tea at the vicarage again.'

And she was doing it. There was no task that Lady Fitzwilliam considered too menial for her to perform. She had one particular boy who was quite clearly her favourite. He had developed gangrene in both his legs. She emerged from his room one night after cleaning his wound and changing his dressing. She caught Kezzie watching her as she rinsed out the foul bandages.

'You should take some time off,' Kezzie suggested. 'You could exhaust yourself. You do so much.'

Lady Fitzwilliam smiled at her wearily. 'My only hope is that someone somewhere is taking care of William,' she said.

Kezzie took the linen out of her hands. 'Come and have a cup of tea,' she said.

Kezzie felt quite humbled by the way this woman had coped with the many trials of her life and how well she adapted to the fantastic changes in her world and experience. From oil lamp, through gas, to electric power; from gramophone records to radio links which flashed around the world in seconds. She had stepped from one century to the next, watching an empire, which she and her kind had helped create, now slowly fragmenting and disintegrating. Things would never be the same again. Lady Fitzwilliam herself recognised this fact and had the wisdom to see that some changes were necessary and might perhaps be beneficial.

She talked to Kezzie about the role of women in society.

'I knew Emmeline Pankhurst slightly,' she said. 'I'd always thought . . .' Lady Fitzwilliam hesitated, 'that she made such a dreadful fuss about issues which most women were not the least concerned with. Now, I'm not so sure.'

'It will be different after this,' said Kezzie. 'There are nurseries for children and these will continue. It will give women more freedom.'

Lady Fitzwilliam smiled. 'I never imagined that I would hear myself say this,' she said. 'But, I do hope you're right, my dear.'

The civilian restrictions continued. In April the Government banned embroidery on women's underwear and nightwear. Joe thought this was very funny. 'How the heck are they gonna police this ordinance? I want to be the first guy to volunteer for duty as enforcement officer for that law.' He nodded and grinned at Lucy. 'I'll just have to approach ladies on the sidewalk and say, "Pardon me, ma'am, but I'm obliged to inspect your underwear. It's a government rule".'

Lady Fitzwilliam drew her brows together as Lucy giggled.

The war news, however, was not good. Joe read the newspapers and commented to Kezzie, 'We're gonna have lots of customers very soon.'

In Russia Sebastopol had fallen, and in the Western Desert Rommel's Afrika Korps struck. The Argyll and Sutherland troops, with armour and infantry from Australia, New Zealand, South Africa and India, were now part of Lieutenant-General Montgomery's Eighth Army in Egypt. At the end of May, in a great tank battle at Bir Hacheim, the Germans tried to turn the Allies' southern flank. In the middle of June Tobruk fell and twenty-five thousand Allied soldiers were captured. At the end of the month the Allied Army had to abandon Mersa Marruh in Egypt. Six thousand more prisoners were taken by the Germans. Rommel with his twelve divisions was within seventy miles of Alexandria and the Nile.

Kezzie felt ill. There had been no word from Michael for weeks and weeks. She'd received his last letter at the beginning of March and it had been written around Christmas-time.

He had told her of the beauty of the desert countries, the exotic dress of the natives, the strange languages, and the stillness and deepness of the dark blue nights. The sky and earth so close to each other. The feeling of history, of ancient and honoured traditions. He now felt that the Western powers were imposing on these people, demanding that they change to a lifestyle which they neither wanted nor needed. 'Theirs could be a future of exploitation,' he wrote to her.

Kezzie realised that Michael was thinking deeply, as she had, about the ultimate purpose of the war. He, like her, was aware of the significant changes which were taking place, of how society was altering, had altered already. And despite its being a frightening prospect, it was important that this time they tried to set the world right as best they could.

The German panzer divisions rolled on. Backed up by devastating aerial bombardment they advanced more than three hundred miles. By late summer the Allied troops were left defending a narrow front along the

Quattara depression. At a place called El Alamein the Eighth Army grimly held the line.

The more serious casualties were being flown home, the dead and the dying. The reputation of Joe's surgical unit spread. Generally they only received grievously wounded men, and as the summer progressed they became busier and busier.

At the beginning of autumn they were working and operating all round the clock. Late one night Kezzie was taking a patient out of theatre. As she stopped in the ante-room to connect the transfusion unit, another soldier was brought in. The junior doctor checked him over quickly. He shook his head and handed the clipboard with the case notes back to the stretcher-bearer.

'This one's a goner,' said the orderly to his friend, and began to turn the wheels around.

Kezzie pressed herself against the wall to make room for them to leave. As the trolley slid past her she glanced down at the wounded man. The bottle of blood she was holding slipped from her fingers and crashed to the floor.

'No!' she said. 'Oh God. No.'

Kezzie was looking on the wax-pale face of Michael Donohoe.

CHAPTER 28

Life or death

'What's up?' Joe Petrowski appeared at the door of his operating theatre.

'I think this one's too far gone to operate on, sir,' said the junior doctor.

Kezzie uttered a low cry. From behind her clenched teeth came a suppressed scream. She clutched at herself, wrapping her arms around her own body tightly. She was breaking apart, all of her, physically and mentally, her heart and her life, her very spirit, was disintegrating, and she could not control it.

'No,' she whispered. 'No.'

'Nurse, pull yourself together,' said the matron. 'We've got other patients here who would profit from your help.'

'No,' Kezzie said again.

The world was spinning . . . the whole great globe . . . never-ending, into eternity, and she herself was dying. She knew this. Before her eyes Michael's life force was ebbing away, and with it, so was hers.

If there ever had been any doubt at all that this man,

who now lay so cold and still before her, was part of her own being, then it was gone. They were inextricably linked. From the first moment, when his eyes had met hers in the autumn harvest in Stonevale, there had been no other path for her to take but the one that joined with his. No other course for either of them. She had kept the memory of it all in her heart. The gulls crying above them as they lifted the crop together from the ochre earth. The music and the tales around the fire. The smell and the sound of both their languages and cultures bonding together. Connected by fate, separated by circumstance and war, was death now to part them for ever?

'Kezzie!'

Her glazed eyes hardly registered what was happening. The name being called did not connect to her.

'Kezzie!' Captain Joe Petrowski cried again. 'Is this guy a friend of yours?'

She inclined her head.

Joe nodded at his staff. 'Bring him in.'

The stretcher attendants exchanged glances. 'Sir, it's not going to be worth the trouble.'

'Her face says it is,' the captain said curtly.

The junior doctor hesitated. 'Sir . . .'

'Wheel him in,' Joe snapped. Then he leaned over and spoke to Kezzie. 'I need an experienced assistant in there,' he said. 'So c'mon, clean up and help me.'

She stared at him.

'You hear me?' he shouted into her face. 'Pick up or get out!'

He turned and strode through the open doors.

She followed him more slowly.

'Get me plasma,' he ordered.

'I can't,' she whispered.

He changed his gloves in seconds. Then he looked at her before pulling his mask on. 'I'm not carrying passengers,' he said. 'Don't come in here if you can't handle it. There are no free rides on this trip.'

Inside the theatre they were cutting off Michael's uniform.

'Gee, what a mess,' said the junior doctor. 'What a bloody mess. It's all in his chest. One lung gone, definitely.' He looked questioningly at the surgeon.

Joe Petrowski nodded. If he was worried he didn't show it. 'I guess we're gonna have to work to hold him then,' he said. 'Let's do it.'

It was the hardest thing Kezzie had ever done. Fingers slippery with sweat, every part of her cringing as she saw the torn flesh. She could barely watch as the rubber bag began to rise gently as they tried to reinflate Michael's lung and get him breathing again. She knew she had to function, and fast, or Joe would throw her out.

'I'm needed,' she told herself. She held her hands rigid to prevent them shaking. 'Joe needs me.'

And Michael needed her too. She was the most experienced assistant on duty. She had to stay, do what she was trained to do. Be detached, professional. She'd wanted to be a doctor for as long as she could remember. Now was the time to prove she was capable. She had to do it.

And suddenly she was keeping up with Joe's instructions, watching his hands, listening to his voice.

She took her lead from him. The way he moved and how he handled the equipment. His actions not slow, but deliberate and sure. Cool, competent and efficient, even at the most difficult parts. He removed the shrapnel and cut out the dead and damaged tissue.

Only at one point, when Michael's heart stopped again, did he say in exasperation, 'Aw c'mon, buddy. You're gonna have to do a bit of this yourself.'

He grinned at Kezzie as the faltering pulse came back. It was the first time he had looked directly at her since he had begun to operate.

'What's his name?' he asked her.

'Michael.'

'OK, Michael,' he said. 'I'd sure appreciate for you not to do that again.' He glanced around. 'We'll close now,' he told his team. He looked at Kezzie again. 'Then it all depends on how much fighting spirit this guy's got.'

'How much fighting spirit have you got, Michael?' Kezzie whispered as she watched him being transferred to the recovery room. She followed the trolley down the corridor, and stood by his bed. How much? she wondered.

She wouldn't leave him. Not at all during the long days and longer nights which followed. She talked to him as she changed his drip. His hand was so cold when she reinserted the needle under the vein in his arm.

'Michael,' she said softly.

Lady Fitzwilliam understood Kezzie's terror. She knew Kezzie's fear was that Death stalked the corridors at night, and if she was not watchful then it would come for

Michael. If she allowed herself to slip into sleep for one moment then it would steal him away, and when she awoke he would be gone.

So Lady Fitzwilliam didn't tell her to come home and rest, or advise her to leave his side. She brought an easy chair into Michael's room and tucked a blanket around Kezzie. She made tea and sat and drank it with her or stayed out in the corridor within call, through the dark watches of those first few nights. Joe checked him every hour. Kezzie knew that he'd left word to be called at any moment, day or night, if Michael's condition changed.

And the friends she had made since arriving in England contacted the base hospital. The parents of the local children, the farm workers, and Lady Fitzwilliam's colleagues on her various committees sent words of comfort. Flowers and gifts, and offers of help came from all over the country. Kezzie was overwhelmed by their kindness.

'His colour is so poor,' she complained to Lady Fitzwilliam on the third day. 'His face has such a lifeless pallor.'

'We must not expect too much,' said Lady Fitzwilliam, 'and it would be so terribly cruel to give you hope when there might be none. But . . . that skin tone does not always mean the worst. A rosy glow on someone's face can be much more deceptive and sinister.' She sighed deeply. 'I lost three babies before I had William. Not one of them survived more than a year. That was their colour before they died. It was almost as though they were preparing to go. I often thought that it was some small kindness of the Almighty as they were about to be taken.'

As Kezzie looked at Michael, lying there so unmoving, she had an urge to pull all the tubes and tags aside and climb into bed with him. To lie down beside him and warm his body with her own.

Harvest-time was drawing to a close. The winter nights were closing in and the weather was chillier. About a week after his operation Kezzie noticed a very slight alteration in Michael's condition. During the day his body seemed less inert as she tended him, as if he were on a slightly higher level of consciousness. Kezzie was worried. Joe was operating and would be unavailable for at least another hour. She gazed at Michael and called his name softly, but there was no response. His breathing was different, not so shallow, but not as regular either. Did that indicate an improvement? Was he getting better? Or was she in fact deceiving herself? She remembered what Lady Fitzwilliam had told her. This change in Michael could be the last kind act of the Creator, easing him into the afterlife.

At five o'clock she switched on the small lamp by his bed and went to close the curtains. The sun was setting over the frosted fields. A red-golden ball of fire turning the whole sky crimson, the rays shafting into the room, reflecting on the walls and ceiling. Kezzie pulled down the blind and as she turned from the window she heard a voice speaking.

'Sure, I should have known that when I died and went to Heaven, the first angel's face I'd see would look like Kezzie Munro.'

CHAPTER 29

Recovery

Kezzie's heart turned over.

'Oh, Michael,' she said softly. She walked slowly from the window towards the bed and looked down at him. She smiled. 'Michael,' she said again.

His face was palest white with long shadows under his eyes, and his features were gaunt; the outline of cheekbones, nose and neck emphasising the hollows elsewhere. But his eyes were watching her. And it was those eyes, dark, dark blue with a slightly troubled expression, more than his voice, or his colour, or the change in his breathing, that gave Kezzie hope. He gazed at her, and she could see comprehension and life slowly returning in his look.

'I'm alive,' he said at last.

'Yes.' She could barely speak the word, her chin and face were trembling so much.

He tried to raise his hand on the coverlet of the bed but could not. He tried to lift his head a little but failed completely. He sank back down. 'And I'm not imagining you?' he asked.

She sat down on the edge of the bed and took one of his hands in both of her own. 'I'm real enough, Michael Donohoe,' said Kezzie.

'I dreamt I was dead,' he said at last.

'You almost were,' she said.

'Am I all of a piece?' he asked her.

'There's a bit of you inside which will never be the same, but the doctor says you'll be able to sing and dance nearly as well as ever you did.'

This time he managed a faint grin. 'Sure now, my prize-winning days are not over yet then,' he murmured.

He drifted into sleep.

Kezzie went to the door, opened it and slipped quietly out to the corridor. She walked sedately in the direction of the matron's office, but had gone no more than two hundred yards down the corridor before she began to skip with happiness.

Joe ordered her to take some days off, but she couldn't stay away from the hospital. She sat beside Michael and held his hand, whether he was conscious or not. And slowly, slowly, his condition improved.

She told him of Canada and Clydebank. Of her return to Scotland and her friends in the café. She described the destruction of the Blitz, and he wept with her when she spoke of her grandfather.

He spoke of being in combat, the vibration in the air and on the earth when they were under bombardment. The great gulping fear, inside your head and the taste in your mouth. And more than that, the terror that you might let your comrades down, that when the moment came you would not manage to fight. And the ultimate horror of seeing his friends fall beside him. She tried to comfort him, to reason away the distress he felt because he was safe at home. He knew that Montgomery was preparing his own offensive and he wouldn't be there, his Battalion would march forward without him.

At times the war in Africa and the Far East seemed far away and remote as Kezzie cycled home across this soft landscape, with the pretty farmhouses tucked in the folds of the hills. Then they would have a rush of wounded to the hospital, and hard reality would surface again. Kezzie was very aware of Lady Fitzwilliam's own position. With William gone it could have been awkward for her to rejoice in Michael's recovery, and very easy to resent someone else's happiness. But she didn't. She and Lucy were a solid unit behind Kezzie, helping and supporting her when she needed them the most. And as Kezzie watched the two of them together she realised that she had lost part of her sister to this woman. Lucy was the daughter Lady Fitzwilliam had never had.

They had news from Scotland. Peg and Ricardo were going to be married. They planned to have the wedding after Christmas and she and Lucy would be attendants. Peg was having trouble in obtaining any pretty clothes, and had been looking through the shops in Glasgow for lace and veil. Lady Fitzwilliam and Lucy searched the attics of the house for anything that might do.

'Peg is tall, almost an inch more than me,' said Kezzie, 'with lovely long slim legs, and a neat waist. Her hair is the colour of fresh honey.'

'My hair was blonde once upon a time,' said Lady

Fitzwilliam. 'When the regiment was in India people there used to ask my husband's permission to touch it.'

She looked out a beautiful sari folded away in tissue paper, a piece of Kashmiri cloth, and some chiffon scarves. In a decorated tin box they discovered a pair of cream buckram boots decorated with a bow which had tiny seed pearls sewn on. Joe turned up with a piece of parachute silk, but refused to divulge its source. Lady Fitzwilliam made all of their finds up into a parcel and sent Samuel off to the station to despatch them to Scotland. In her reply to thank them Peg said that she and Ricardo intended to emigrate to the United States as soon as they could.

'It's not that I don't love Scotland,' Peg wrote. 'It's just that Ricardo has told me so many wonderful things about America, and I have so many painful memories here.'

Kezzie knew how she felt. She too had a great longing to go back to Canada. She was sure she would do so one day.

Joe came in a few days later to give Michael a thorough checkover.

'I'm sending you up to the big house tomorrow,' he said. 'Lady F. can take care of you. We need this bed for guys who are really sick.'

'So I'm a lot better?' said Michael. He was sitting propped up in bed. 'How bad is this, only having one lung?' he asked.

'Well,' said Joe pulling his stethoscope from his ears, 'you ain't gonna jitterbug no more.'

'I didn't – what was it you said? – "jitterbug" in the first place,' said Michael.

'Then you're not going to miss it much, are you?' said Joe.

Michael glanced at Kezzie. 'Anything else . . . that I might miss?' he asked casually, keeping his eyes on Joe all the time.

'Well,' said Joe. 'You can't smoke. You can't drink.' He thought for a moment. 'You can go with women.' He grinned and looked at Kezzie. 'Have babies, if you want to.'

Kezzie blushed to the roots of her hair.

Michael leaned back on his pillows. 'That's OK then,' he said.

He too was looking at Kezzie.

CHAPTER 30

New beginning

Kezzie noticed a big improvement in Michael's health within a few days of his move to the manor house. Lady Fitzwilliam and Lucy completely spoiled him with their constant attention. There were fresh flowers in his room each day, his newspaper arrived first in the morning, and he had every little treat that was obtainable, on or off the ration.

'Bread with butter!' Kezzie exclaimed one evening, when she called in to see him on her way out to start a late shift at the hospital. She snatched the sandwich from his plate and ate a piece of it.

Michael reached over and grabbed her hand. He pulled her towards him and she was surprised at the strength in his arms.

'We're getting you up out of that bed tomorrow,' she declared as she struggled free. 'I think you are malingering.'

He watched her as she peered in his shaving mirror and tidied her hair. 'I love you,' he said.

She turned and looked into his eyes. 'I know,' she replied.

In the hospital the casualties kept coming. Meanwhile, in the Soviet Union the Russians were defending Stalingrad street by street, and house by house. In a dreadful war of attrition, they managed to regain at night what the Germans, with their superior fire-power, captured during the day. Driven right to the banks of the River Don the Soviet forces hung on determinedly, fighting hand to hand.

'If they can even delay Hitler a few more weeks,' said Lady Fitzwilliam, 'then he may find, as Napoleon did, that the Russian "General Winter" is an opponent that cannot be beaten.'

In the Western Desert the Eighth Army trained its newly arrived replacement troops in desert warfare. Exercises in breaching minefields and digging in; advancing under cover of their own artillery fire, and then rushing enemy positions, were practised intensively.

One morning when Michael had managed to get downstairs and they were sitting reading quietly and listening to the radio, it was time for the news bulletin. Lady Fitzwilliam rose to turn the sound up. She glanced out of the front window as she passed by.

'Dear God,' she said.

Kezzie hurried to her side and looked out. There was a helmeted policeman cycling slowly up the driveway.

Lady Fitzwilliam bowed her head and gripped the curtain. Kezzie thought she was going to fall down. They heard the bell at the front door jangling and Samuel crossing the hall to answer it.

'Please, Kezzie,' whispered Lady Fitzwilliam. 'Will you go and take the telegram? I cannot deal with it at present.'

Kezzie went out of the room. Samuel was standing by the open door, turning the flat yellow envelope over and over in his hand. He looked up as Kezzie approached him.

'This will kill her,' he said. And as he spoke, Kezzie saw that the old man was crying.

Kezzie closed the door and tore open the envelope. She unfolded the thick paper and read the typewritten message . . .

And read it again.

She grabbed Samuel's arm and dragging him with her she ran back to the sitting room. Lady Fitzwilliam was still holding on to the curtain, staring out beyond the lawn and the trees, her eyes wide and unseeing.

Kezzie held up the telegram. She could hardly read the words.

'It is a message from the International Red Cross,' she said. 'William is safe in the German Military hospital at St Omer in France. Injured but well. Do you hear me?' she cried out. 'William is alive! He is alive!'

She burst into tears and Samuel hurried forward as Lady Fitzwilliam slumped to the floor.

It was Lucy who organised them, making tea and spreading slices of bread with a thin smear of jam. Lady Fitzwilliam unlocked a small cupboard at the side of the fireplace. She brought out a bottle of brandy.

'I was keeping this to celebrate the end of the war

when it came,' she said. 'Michael, I would like you to open it just now.'

After everyone had retired for the night Lady Fitzwilliam sat down at her desk and taking a pen she began to write.

'*My dearest, dearest son . . .*'

That night, for the first time in many months, she slept through till the dawn.

'There is hope,' she told Kezzie the next day. 'You were right, my dear. One should never give up.'

Joe seemed to think so too. 'Hitler can't win now,' he said. 'It may take a coupla years, but he's beat. And this time we're really gonna fix it so that it doesn't happen again.'

And it appeared to Kezzie that there was hope in many other aspects of life for ordinary people. The Butler proposals and Beveridge Report, dealing with reforms in education and health care would lead the way to a complete change in society. A Welfare State would be created which would abolish want, with insurance against old age and unemployment. There would be family allowances and free medical treatment for all.

The war news was also full of promise for the spring. In Russia two relief columns reached the River Don and pushed the invaders back onto the steppes. Within days it became a rout. Two weeks later, in order to save his men from starvation and in direct disobedience of Hitler's orders, the German Commander surrendered to the Red Army.

And at El Alamein Field Marshal Montgomery made his move. Under a blanket of heavy artillery fire the

Eighth Army advanced and broke through Rommel's front line. The Germans retreated as the Allies recaptured Tobruk and pursued the Afrika Korps over a thousand miles of desert. Tripoli was taken and there was a 'Victory Parade', the very first of the war for Allied troops.

Michael and Kezzie were walking in the walled garden at the side of the house. He was very slow, and she became quite concerned at his leaning on her so much.

'You're tired,' she said.

'No.' He grinned at her. 'I like walking with my arm around you. And you have to take pity on a poor wounded soldier. Don't you now?'

She reached up and tugged his hair, then led him to a wooden bench where they sat down together.

'I'll report you to Joe, if you misbehave,' she said.

'Joe,' he repeated. He looked at her directly. 'He's very fond of you. Do you like him a lot?'

'Yes,' said Kezzie. 'And I like William too, and Ricardo, and lots of other people.'

'We haven't seen each other for such a long time,' said Michael. 'I often wondered if you'd forgotten me.' He waited a moment. 'Or perhaps, there would be someone else who was special.'

Kezzie turned and faced him. 'There was no one else,' she said. 'From the very beginning there was no one else. I loved you at that first moment, when I set eyes on you, at harvest-time at Stonevale. And I've never stopped.'

They held on to each other for a long moment.

'Can we work out some kind of future?' he asked her.

'I've had a letter from a teaching hospital, offering me a place,' said Kezzie, 'and a chance to take the university entrance exams for medicine next year.'

'I can get some kind of desk job,' said Michael. 'It's not great, but I could support you while you study.'

'You wouldn't mind that?' she asked.

'Why should I?' he said. 'I'd have my own private doctor to take care of me.' He gave her a sidelong glance. 'Your pay might not be so good, but there would be other compensations.'

Kezzie helped him to his feet. Churchill's latest speech seemed appropriate somehow. The two of them now would go together towards their 'new beginning'. The recent victory had been declared a day of national rejoicing. Now that there was no fear of invasion it meant that church bells could be rung to celebrate the news, to announce the surge towards the end of the war and peace.

She and Michael began to walk towards the house when she drew him to a halt.

'Listen,' said Kezzie. 'Listen.'

A sound echoed on the clear still air. It was the peal of bells. And they were ringing out from every church and steeple in the land.

REMEMBRANCE

Summer 1915, and the sound of the guns at the Western Front can be heard across the Channel in England.

Throughout Britain, local regiments are recruiting for Kitchener's Army. And in the village of Stratharden, the Great War is to alter irrevocably the course of five young lives . . .

'An immensely readable, passionately written epic'
Guardian

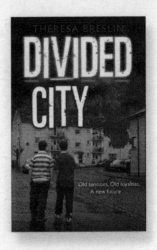

DIVIDED CITY

**A young man lies bleeding in the street.
It's Glasgow. And it's May – the marching
season. The Orange Walks have begun.**

Graham doesn't want to be involved. He just wants
to play football with his new mate, Joe. But then he
witnesses a shocking moment of violence . . .

A gripping tale about two boys who must find their
own answers – and their own way forward – in a
world divided by differences.

**WINNER OF THE CATALYST BOOK AWARD
AND THE RED BOOK AWARD**

'A cracking good read' *Guardian*

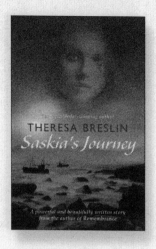

SASKIA'S JOURNEY

I know this place . . .

Why does Saskia feel so disturbed when she goes
to spend a few weeks with her reclusive great-aunt
Alessandra up on the Scottish coast? Why does she feel
such a sense of menace around Alessandra's house when
she has never been there before?

Just as the sea may give up its bounty, will Alessandra
reveal the secrets and tragedies of their family's past?

'Haunting . . . truly memorable' *The Bookseller*

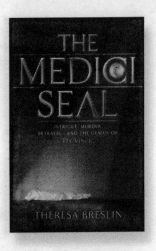

THE MEDICI SEAL

Italy, 1502

Fleeing from the murderous brigand Sandino, the boy
Matteo is rescued from drowning by the companions
of Leonardo da Vinci, and taken into his household.
And so Matteo is at the Maestro's side as he
carries out his work.

But, Leonardo da Vinci is employed by the cruel and
ruthless Cesare Borgia. And Matteo carries with
him a secret that both the Borgia and the
Medici families would kill to obtain.

'A superb historical thriller' *The Times*

THE NOSTRADAMUS PROPHECY

1564. Nostradamus predicts death in the royal court. But not everyone is prepared to take heed . . .

Melisande, daughter of the king's minstrel, pays little heed to the dire warnings of Nostradamus. But when misfortune befalls Melisande's family and she realises that it was predicted by Nostradamus, she turns to the soothsayer for help. Upon his death, he leaves Melisande with some papers which hold the secret of the royal line of France. It is up to her to help fulfil his final prophecy, but will she have the courage to do so?

'Terrific . . . enormously enjoyable' *Guardian*

PRISONER OF THE INQUISITION

The flames began to rise around her . . .

Zarita, only daughter of the town magistrate, lives a life of wealth and privilege. Saulo, son of a beggar, witnesses his father wrongfully arrested and brutally dealt with. Hauled off to be a slave at sea, he swears vengeance on the magistrate and his family.

When cruel agents of the Inquisition arrive in Zarita's town, they bring suspicion, terror and death. Then, amid the intrigues of the royal court, Zarita and Saulo meet once more, to face final acts of betrayal and revenge.

'Breslin's suspenseful story held me in its grip' *Guardian*

Hitler's Canary
by Sandi Toksvig

Bamse is used to drama: his mother is a famous actress,
and his best friend Anton is one of the most daring boys
in Denmark. When the German troops invade, Bamse
doesn't know how to act: should he stay out of trouble,
or follow his brother into the resistance and take
the most demanding role of his life?

A tale of daring rescue inspired by the experiences of
Sandi Toksvig's father during the Second World War.

'An extraordinary story . . . truly life-affirming'
Michael Morpurgo

Selina Penaluna
by Jan Page

Dropped as a baby into a deep pool on the Cornish
shore, Selina Penaluna emerges a different child – a
mermaid changeling – and is forever drawn to the sea.

Ellen and Jack are twins, evacuated to Cornwall at
the start of the war. Soon, Jack finds freedom in the
arms of the mysterious fisherman's daughter whose wild
beauty turns every man's head.

Selina's siren song has Jack captivated – but leaves Ellen
cold with jealousy. Can the young lovers find solace
and build a new life together?

A spellbinding novel full of passion and tragedy that
will enchant older readers.